EV

QUEEN OF BABBLE GETS HITCHED

Meg Cabot has lived in Indiana and California, USA, and in France. In addition to her adult novels *The Guy Next Door*, *Boy Meets Girl*, *Every Boy's Got One*, *Size 12 Is Not Fat*, *Size 14 Is Not Fat Either* and *Size Doesn't Matter*, she is the author of the highly successful series of young adult books, *The Princess Diaries*. Meg and her husband live in Key West, Florida.

Be sure to check out Meg's websites:

www.megcabot.com

www.megcabotbookclub.com

By the same author

The Guy Next Door
Boy Meets Girl
Queen of Babble series
The Heather Wells series

Books by Meg Cabot

The Princess Diaries series

The Mediator series

All American Girl
All American Girl: Ready or Not

Airhead
Airhead: Being Nikki
Avalon High
Avalon High manga: The Merlin Prophecy
Teen Idol
How to Be Popular
Jinx
Tommy Sullivan Is a Freak
Nicola and the Viscount
Victoria and the Rogue

Airhead: Runaway

For younger readers

The Allie Finkle series

Also available in audio

MEG CABOT

EVERY BOY'S GOT ONE

&

QUEEN OF BABBLE GETS HITCHED

PAN BOOKS

Every Boy's Got One first published 2005 by Avon Books,
an imprint of HarperCollins Publishers, USA
First published by Pan Books 2005
Queen of Babble Gets Hitched first published 2008 by William Morrow
an imprint of HarperCollins Publishers, New York
First published by Pan Books 2008

This omnibus first published 2011 by Pan Books
an imprint of Pan Macmillan, a division of Macmillan Publishers Limited
Pan Macmillan, 20 New Wharf Road, London N1 9RR
Basingstoke and Oxford
Associated companies throughout the world
www.panmacmillan.com

ISBN 978-0-330-54540-2

3 5 7 9 8 6 4 2

A CIP catalogue record for this book is available from
the British Library.

Printed and bound by CPI Group (UK) Ltd, Croydon, CR0 4YY

EVERY BOY'S GOT ONE

For Benjamin

Many thanks to Beth Adler,
Ingo Arndt, Jennifer Brown,
John Henry Dreyfuss,
Benjamin Egnatz, Carrie, Feron,
Michele Jaffe, Laura Langlie,
and Greg and Sophia Travis

Every Boy's Got One

1

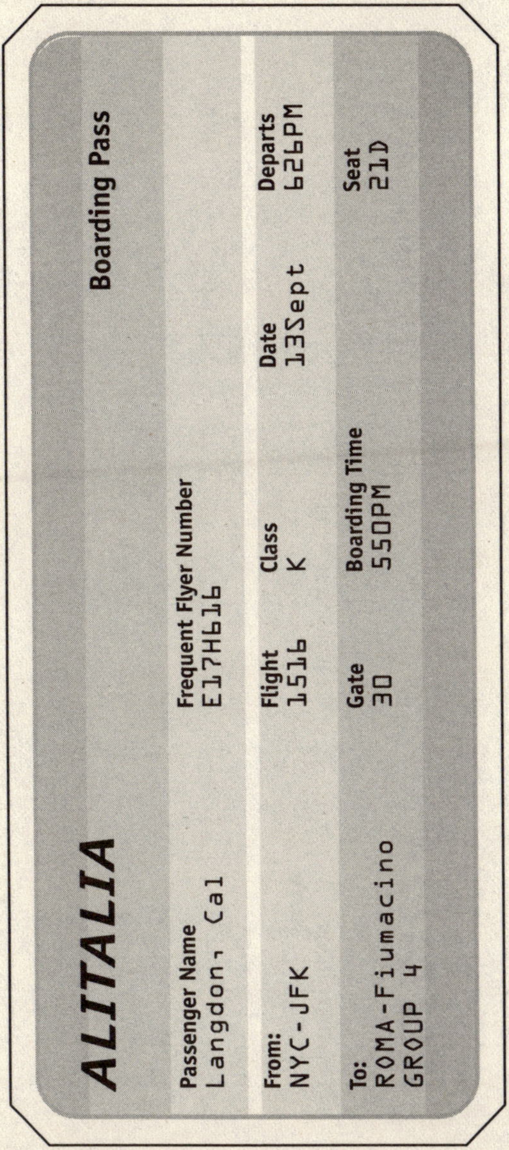

ALITALIA **Boarding Pass**

Passenger Name
Harris, Jane

Frequent Flyer Number

From:
NYC-JFK

Flight
1516

Class
K

Date
13Sept

Departs
626PM

To:
ROMA-Fiumacino
GROUP 4

Gate
30

Boarding Time
550PM

Seat
21C

John F. Kennedy
International Airport
-Duty Free-

Reg #06 Tran#8971
Cshr#0084 Str#2411

1 New Republic Mag $2.99
1 AA Batteries $1.59

Subtotal $4.58
Total $4.58

Payment Credit Card
C Langdon
**** **** *** ****
Exp 2/08
March 25 3:59PM

Thank you for shopping
JFK Duty Free
Enjoy your flight!

John F. Kennedy
International Airport
—Duty Free—

Reg #06	Tran#8972
Cshr#0084	Str#2411

1 Gift PK Toblerone	$9.99
1 Dramamine	$2.29
1 Earplugs	$0.79
1 Advil	$2.29
1 Us Weekly Mag	$1.99
1 Bottled Water	$1.29
1 Bottled Water	$1.29
1 Bottled Water	$1.29
1 Bottled Water	$1.29
1 Bottled Water	$1.29
1 Travel Diary	$12.95
Subtotal	$36.75
Total	$36.75

Payment Credit Card
W Harris
**** **** *** ****
Exp 3/08
March 25 4:02PM

Thank you for shopping
JFK Duty Free
Enjoy your flight!

Travel Diary of

Holly Caputo and Mark Levine

On Their Elopement

Composed by Jane Harris, Witness

aka Maid of Honor

aka Holly's best friend since first grade and roommate since freshman year at Parsons School of Design

Dear Holly and Mark,

Surprise!

I know neither one of you would bother to keep a record of your elopement, so I've decided to do it for you! This way, when you're approaching your twentieth anniversary and your oldest kid has just wrecked the Volvo and your youngest has just come home from her cushy Westchester private school with head lice and the dog's thrown up all over the living room rug and, Holly, you're asking yourself why you ever moved out of the righteous East Village pad we shared for so long, and, Mark, you're wishing you'd stayed in resident housing down at St. Vincents, you can open this diary and go, "Oh, so THAT's why we got married."

Because you two are the grooviest couple I know, and totally belong together, and I think eloping to Italy is a BRILLIANT idea, even if you did steal it from Kate Mackenzie in Human Resources.

The eloping part, I mean. Not the Italy part.

But she HAD to elope. I mean, with in-laws like hers? What CHOICE did she have?

But you two are doing it for the pure romance of the thing—not because you HAVE to, because both your families are perfectly respectable.

Well, I guess there is that teensy religion thing with your moms.

But whatever! They'll get over it.

Anyway, that's what makes your elopement so special.

And I plan to record every detail of that special-ness, starting now, before we even get on the plane. Before I even meet you guys at the gate. Which, by the way, where ARE you, anyway? I mean, we were supposed to get here three hours before our departure time. You know that, don't you? I mean, it says that right on the ticket. For international travel, please arrive no later than three hours prior to departure time.

So. Where are you guys?

I suppose I could email you on my new BLACKBERRY, but as you keep reminding me, Holly, it's for WORK PURPOSES ONLY, which is the only reason the IT guys let you have them (thanks for mine, by the way. I mean, it's nice of Tim and those guys to think of me, even though I don't exactly work there anymore).

God, I hope nothing happened to you. I mean, on the way. People drive like maniacs on the expressway.

Wait—you didn't change your minds, did you? About getting married? You can't. That would be awful! Just AWFUL! I mean, you two are so perfect for each other . . . not to mention, it would be totally unfair to cancel on me. My first trip to Europe, and my travel companions ditch me? As it is, I can't even believe I'm really doing it. Why did I wait so long? Who turns thirty without having been outside the continental United States at least once in her life? No Paris with French class in the 11th grade. No "Cabo" for Spring Break in college. What's wrong with me, anyway? Why am I such a non-transcontinental flying freak?

And okay, seriously, what is with the guy with the cell phone over there? I mean, he's cute and everything. But why is he yelling? We're going to Italy, dude. Italy! So chill.

Okay, ignore the guy on the cell phone. IGNORE THE GUY ON THE CELL PHONE. I can't believe I'm wasting the first pages of your travel diary on him. Who cares about him? I'M GOING TO EUROPE!

I mean, WE'RE going to Europe.

I think. If you two aren't lying in the twisted wreckage of your taxi to the airport on the Long Island Expressway.

Let's just assume you were running a little late this morning and that you aren't dead.

Thank God you two are making me do this. You and Mark, I mean, Holly. I'm finally crossing the Atlantic, and for what better REASON? God, it's so romantic—

(Oh, wait, that's the same guy who was in front of me at the duty free! The one who was rolling his eyes because I bought all those bottles of Aquafina. Obviously he hasn't read this month's Shape. They say air travel is very dehydrating, and that you should drink half your body weight in water during the course of your flight if you want to avoid jet lag.)

And okay, they have water on the plane and all, but is it good water? I mean, as good as Aquafina? Probably not. I saw this thing on Ask Asa on Channel 4 where they sent the water from a plane to a lab and it was filled with all these microbes! And okay, it was the water from the tap in the plane bathroom, and no one would really drink that, but still.

Not that MY mom and dad wouldn't kill me if I did what you're doing, Holly. Elope, I mean. And to ITALY, of all places.

But it's just so totally you, Holly. God, you're lucky. Mark is so . . . grounded. And Mark, I know I give you a hard time about being such a sci-fi geek and all, but seriously, if I could meet a guy as—

(Oh my God! Cell Phone Guy just practically threw his phone at one of those little carts with the old people in it! The one taking them to their gate! And just because the guy driving it made that backing-up-truck sound to warn him he was in the way. God, what's got his panties in such a bunch? Although he hardly looks like a panty-wearing type of guy. Jockeys, more likely. Or maybe boxers.

Oh, no. How can I give this diary to Holly and Mark if it's full of musings about some random guy's underwear????

NOW what am I going to give them? I can't give them candlesticks or something. This is HOLLY. It has to be something SPECIAL.

Okay, well, one mention of underwear. You guys don't mind, do you? I mean, it's just underwear.)

Where was I? Oh yeah. Mark. So cute, in spite of the Star Trek Next Generation marathons he makes you watch, Holl. So responsible, with the whole doctor-and-health-column thing. Which reminds me, I need to ask him about this mole on my elbow. God, Holly's so lucky, she can get her moles checked for free anytime she wants. Why can't I find a boyfriend with a useful skill like that? All Malcolm can do is beat me at Vice City. And what good is that? Can a high score on Vice City save you from a life-threatening carcinoma? No.

Okay, now I totally can't give this to Holly and Mark. What is wrong with me?

Cell Phone Guy just hung up on whoever it was he was talking to. I just heard him go, "That is inexcusable," but that was all I could get because they've got CNN turned up so loud in here. Now he's got out his Blackberry. He's typing into it furiously. I will never be able to type that fast into mine.

But maybe that's a good thing. Cell Phone Guy is a classic example of a Type A personality, as illustrated in last month's Shape. I can practically SEE his blood pressure going up. I hope he doesn't stroke out on the plane.

Although I wouldn't mind giving him CPR.

Oh my God, I can't believe I just wrote that.

But he is kind of cute. I mean, if you like the tall, rugged, sandy-haired, razor-stubbled-with-piercing-blue-eyes-who-knows-how-to-use-a-Blackberry type.

Okay. Now I definitely won't be able to give this to Holly and Mark as a wedding present.

Oh, wait, I can just rip out the pages with Cell Phone Guy comments. Or black them out with a Sharpie.

Or maybe I should just get Holly and Mark a nice silver frame from Tiffany's instead. But that seems like kind of a lame present to get for someone who has held your hair back while you were throwing up tequila shooters as many times as Holly has for me.

Although of course I've done it for her often enough, most recently Friday night when the entire art department took her out for a bachelorette party. For two people who are supposed to be eloping, Mark and Holly told an AWFUL lot of people beforehand.

!!!! On CNN it says a plane is being held at the San Francisco airport under suspicion that a passenger aboard it has a highly contagious virus that they're worried will spread worldwide!!!!

You know what this means:

I need more snacks for the plane.

Seriously, those people have been on board that plane for TWO HOURS with no food service. If I go two hours without eating, I get that weird thing where I can't see out of one eye. And Toblerone won't do it. I need something with protein. Like smoked almonds. And maybe some cheese popcorn. Which I bet they don't even have in Italy. I better go back to the duty free and stock up, just in case. . . .

To: Tara Samuels <tara.samuels@thenyjournal.com>
Fr: Cal Langdon <cal.langdon@thenyjournal.com>
Re: Travel Services

Where is everybody? I've been calling for the past half hour, and nobody there is picking up. Does Travel get half days on Fridays through September, or something, while the rest of us slobs have to give them up on Labor Day?

I asked you guys to book this ticket a month ago, but I'm at the airport now and they claim I'm in coach, not business class.

In a *middle seat*. For a *seven-hour flight*.

Freaking Frodo wouldn't last for six hours in a seat that small. How is a six-foot-four, two-hundred-pound man supposed to do it?

Someone had better pull some strings or you're going to have one very unhappy journalist on your hands.

C. Langdon

To: Dolly Vargas<dolly.vargas@thenyjournal.com>
Fr: Cal Langdon <cal.langdon@thenyjournal.com>
Re: Last night

Thanks for last night. However, I think moving in together might be a little precipitous. And I don't think your husband would really appreciate it.

Let's just keep things casual for now, and see how things go. Okay? I'm off to some podunk part of Italy no one's ever heard of because Levine has some idiot idea he's going to get married there, but I'll be in touch when I get back in a week.

C.

✉

To: Cal Langdon <cal.langdon@thenyjournal.com>
Fr: Tara Samuels <tara.samuels@thenyjournal.com>
Re: Travel Services

I'm SO sorry, Mr. Langdon, we were in a budget meeting, which is why no one picked up. I've been calling the airline ever since I got back, and they're booked solid. I could get you in business class on another flight . . . but not until tomorrow. Would that be all right?

Again, I'm so sorry about the misunderstanding. I can't imagine how you ended up in coach. We ALWAYS book you in business class, as you know. Except of course when the plane you're taking is so small, there isn't a business class. Which isn't the case here. I can't apologize enough, really. Could we upgrade you to a suite when you get to your hotel?

Tara

✉

To: Cal Langdon <cal.langdon@thenyjournal.com>
Fr: Dolly Vargas <dolly.vargas@thenyjournal.com>
Re: Last night

There you are! I've only left ten messages on your cell phone. How COULD you have snuck out like that this morning, without even leaving a note?

And Peter and I aren't *married*, sweetie. We have an understanding—the same one you and I have.

And of *course* I wasn't asking you to move in permanently. Just offering you the spare guest room until you find a place of your own. I know how brutal the New York real-estate market can be.

Not that you'll have any problems, the way sales are going for *Sweeping Sands*. In fact, the penthouse across from mine just went up for sale, a steal at two million. Interested? I could speak to the co-op board on your behalf. . . .

In any case, darling, call me when you get back from Mark's little elopement.

XXXOOO
Dolly

Travel Diary of

~~Holly Caputo and Mark Levine~~

Jane Harris

OK, I asked Cell Phone Guy to watch my stuff for a minute while I ran to buy snacks, and he was TOTALLY rude about it. He said, in this very snarky way, "I highly doubt anyone is going to steal your water, miss."

!!!!!

Which wasn't even what I was asking him to watch. My water, I mean. Clearly, I meant my BAG. I mean, the last thing I need is for the airport to blow up my stuff because I left it unattended.

Whatever. It's just like Malcolm says. Some people just suck, and there's nothing you can do about it. I should have known Cell Phone Guy was one of them. Especially the way he keeps banging at the keyboard of that Blackberry. He's still at it. How can someone so anal retentive look so good in a pair of jeans? I don't get it. I mean, evolutionarily speaking, his kind should have been wiped out a long time ago. Because who'd want to mate with someone with THAT kind of attitude?

OOOOOOH, I see Holly!!!! Holly and Mark are here, at last! YAY!

I wonder where Mark's friend Cal is. The best man, I mean. We were all supposed to meet at the gate. . . .

To: Mark Levine <mark.levine@thenyjournal.com>
Fr: Cal Langdon <cal.langdon@thenyjournal.com>
Re: Where are you?

I'm at the gate. I don't see you. You didn't take my advice and cancel the thing at the last minute, did you?

Forget it, you're not the leave-em-at-the-altar type.

So. Nervous yet? I've got the flask, don't worry. We're going to need it, too, there's a real nut job on this flight. Apparently she thinks there's a possibility we might crash land in the Sahara.

Hurry up and get here, I want to kiss the bride—

Oh, there you are.

Cal

Travel Diary of

~~Holly Caputo and Mark Levine~~

Jane Harris

Oh my God.

Cell Phone Guy is Cal. Cal Langdon, Mark's best buddy since elementary school, the one who's been traveling all around the world for the Journal, writing about social unrest and economic instability for the past ten years. The one with the new book that's just out—the one he supposedly got this huge advance for.

I wish I were on that plane that's stuck in the San Francisco airport instead of on this one. I would rather have a deadly virus than have to spend a minute more in the company of Cal Langdon, aka Cell Phone Guy, aka Mark Levine's Best Friend.

Oh, but guess what? HE'S SITTING RIGHT NEXT TO ME. That's what he was so mad about before. He was calling Travel Services at the Journal, trying to get them to change his seat so he could sit in business class, or at least on the aisle, and not in the middle, like he is now.

Ha ha. Ha ha, Cal In the Middle. Hope you like bumping your elbow into mine every five seconds, Mr. I-Highly-Doubt-Anyone-Is-Going-To-Steal-Your-Water,-Miss. Because I am SO not giving up my aisle seat. No way.

And don't expect me to share my water with you, either. OR my Toblerone. Or my cheese popcorn. I don't care how long we're stuck on this runway, or what kind of virus might get into the ventilation system. You're getting nada from me, mister.

I'm not telling Holly how much I hate her husband's best man, though. I don't want to spoil this special time for her.

I am so not going to be able to give them this travel diary as a wedding gift. Oh well. It's probably just as well, since my handwriting is barely legible, thanks to the Armrest Nazi next to me. Excuse me, Mr. I'm-So-Big-I-Need-To-Take-Up-Your-Space-Too. Could you please move your stupid hairy arm with the stupid waterproof watch that tells the altitude and the exact time on all seven continents which I know you so need, being such a fancy world traveler who knows so much about foreign policy and things a poor little cartoonist like me couldn't even begin to understand?

I'll tell you one thing: if this is a setup, Holly is dead. I mean, I know she doesn't like Malcolm, but could she seriously, even for one second, entertain the idea that I might like Mister Nothing-Comes-Between-Me-And-My-Blackberry here? Please! He asked me what I do for a living (he was so just making conversation because Holly and Mark are seated right behind us, and he didn't want to look like the Uptight Anal Retentive Control Freak he really is in front of them), and when I said I was a cartoonist, he was like, "You're kidding."

Totally deadpan. You're kidding.

And get this: he's never heard of Wondercat.

Never. Heard. Of. Wonder. Cat.

He has to be lying. He <u>writes</u> for the paper in which Wondercat was born.

And ok, he's abroad all the time, and you can't get the <u>Journal</u> everywhere. But doesn't he watch <u>television</u>? He may have been gallivanting all around the world for the past decade, but excuse me, he's back now, promoting his stupid book. Hasn't he seen Wondercat's commercial for energy-saving products on New York One? Everyone watches New York One, if only to check the temperature.

My God. Who is this guy? And why does Mark even <u>like</u> him????

I think I'm going to have to have a word with Holly. Does she know what she's getting herself into, marrying a man who'd be best friends with a guy who doesn't watch TV????

✉

To: Mark Levine <mark.levine@thenyjournal.com>
Fr: Cal Langdon <cal.langdon@thenyjournal.com>
Re: I'm going to kill you

What in hell is a Wondercat?

Cal

✉

To: Cal Langdon <cal.langdon@thenyjournal.com>
Fr: Mark Levine <mark.levine@thenyjournal.com>
Re: I'm going to kill you

Excuse me. I don't believe you are allowed to use these things on planes.

Mark

PS You didn't *tell* her you didn't know who Wondercat is, did you?

✉

To: Mark Levine <mark.levine@thenyjournal.com>
Fr: Cal Langdon <cal.langdon@thenyjournal.com>
Re: I'm going to kill you

You can't use them while you're in the air, according to the FAA—although I doubt the veracity of this, as I've left mine on plenty of times and none of my flights have ever plummeted into the sea because of it.

You can, however, still legally use them when you're sitting uselessly on the tarmac while the air control tower guys are having a limbo contest, as they are apparently doing right now because I can see no other conceivable reason why we're not being allowed to take off.

And yes, I did ask her what a Wondercat was. Is that why she is busy scribbling into the travel diary she bought at the duty free? Because I offended her so deeply with my lack of knowledge about her cat?

Cal

✉

To: Cal Langdon <cal.langdon@thenyjournal.com>
Fr: Mark Levine <mark.levine@thenyjournal.com>
Re: I'm going to kill you

Yes. And stop emailing me, Holly keeps asking who I'm writing to. I told her it was the hospital, and now she's mad that the hospital is emailing me when I'm supposed to be eloping.

Mark

✉

To: Mark Levine <mark.levine@thenyjournal.com>
Fr: Cal Langdon <cal.langdon@thenyjournal.com>
Re: I'm going to kill you

How would the hospital even know that, anyway? The word elope means to run away with a lover with the intention of wedding in secret. How secret is your wedding going to be if the hospital knows about it?

C

✉

To: Cal Langdon <cal.langdon@thenyjournal.com>
Fr: Mark Levine <mark.levine@thenyjournal.com>
Re: I'm going to kill you

I had to tell the hospital I was getting married. *And* the paper. They weren't going to give the time off, or let me out of my column, otherwise. DON'T TELL Holly. She still thinks the only people who know what we're really doing are the four of us.

And of course the entire art department at the *New York Journal*. But she doesn't know that I know that.

Mark

PS Quit writing to me. I'm turning this thing off.

✉

To: Mark Levine <mark.levine@thenyjournal.com>
Fr: Cal Langdon <cal.langdon@thenyjournal.com>
Re: You Dog

Your secret's safe with me.

But seriously. Is this girl one of those cat people? For the love of God please tell me I'm not going to be stuck in a middle seat in coach next to one of those cat people. She doesn't carry around pictures of it in her wallet, does she? Her cat? Because I will suffer an aneurysm midair if that's the case—

AT THIS TIME THE CAPTAIN HAS REQUESTED THAT ALL ELECTRONIC DEVICES BE TURNED OFF AND STOWED AWAY UNTIL WE HAVE REACHED CRUISING ALTITUDE

What do you think of him?

Oh my God, Holly. What is this, the ninth grade? You're passing me *notes*? On the *PLANE????*

Well, how else am I supposed to talk to you with the stupid food cart in the way? And they won't let us turn on our Blackberries. Come on, hurry up, while he's asleep. What do you think of him?

He's not really asleep. He's just faking it so he won't have to talk to me. I know because he's still playing armrest war with me. Every time I put my elbow on the armrest, he puts his there, too, to block mine.

You don't like him?

Holly, he's never heard of Wondercat!!!!

Janie, he's been doing foreign correspondence for the past ten years. They don't get family papers like the ones that run Wondercat in places like Kabul.

But you said he moved back to the US a couple of weeks ago—

And you think he should have spent those weeks catching up on YOUR comic, as opposed to, I don't know, FINDING A PLACE TO LIVE???

Well. He also made fun of me for bringing so many bottles of water onboard.

You do have kind of a lot.

Excuse me. Nine out of ten people found dead after getting lost in the desert actually have water left in their canteens, they were just so concerned about conserving it, they didn't drink enough of it to survive. It's true. I saw it on the Discovery Channel.

Okay, okay. But what do you think of him???? Do you like him? He's cute, right? I told you he was cute.

He seems very . . . smart.

The Blackberry thing. I knew it. I *told* Mark to tell him to put that thing away. I know nothing freaks you out more than guys who are smarter than you.

I can't believe you just wrote that. First of all, it's not even true, and second of all, in no way is Cal smarter than me. I mean, yes, he has traveled all over the world covering news stories about grisly wars and Ebola outbreaks and has written a book and stuff, but that does not mean he is smarter than I am. I mean, can he draw a cat?

Besides which, I happen to like smart men.

Right. Like Malcolm.

Oh, that's low, even for you. I will have you know that Malcolm can do a 360-degree spin in midair and not lose his board.

You have got to stop dating snowboarders and musicians, Jane. You're 30 years old now. You've got to start thinking about the future, and date people who will actually stick around for a change, instead of going off to their next X-Game or gig.

Maybe I don't WANT a boyfriend who sticks around. Have you ever thought about that?

Then why did you cry so much those first couple weeks after Malcolm moved out?

I just felt bad for The Dude. You know they'd bonded.

Yeah, well, there's that, too. The Dude needs some stability in his life. He might not bite people as much if he had a positive male role model in his life. The same could be said of you. Plus, financially, you'd be much better off with a partner who actually has steady employment. As a freelancer, you are paying a premium for health insurance. If you married a guy who had his own insurance—through, say, the paper—that'd be a big chunk of change saved. Plus you'd have security. And a 401K.

This is pretty funny coming from a woman who once spent an entire month's rent money on a pair of purple leather pants.

Hello. Can we talk about things that happened in this millennium, please?

Fine. You know what? It's very unfair of you to throw all that stuff about 401Ks and all of that into my face, when you know perfectly well that I HAD all that when I was dating DAVE, and you saw how THAT turned out.

OK, well, I'll admit walking in on your boyfriend in bed with your HR rep can be psychologically scarring. Especially considering it was Amy Jenkins. But you'll recall that I ALWAYS told you it was never a good idea to date a foreigner. You can never tell when they're lying.

Hello. Dave was BRITISH.

Yes, but that accent had us fooled. If he'd been from this country, we'd have known right away he was an HR rep–whoremonger. But really, Janie, just because things didn't work out with Dave is no reason to start dating unemployed losers half his age–

Need I remind you that Malcolm is not unemployed? You know he got that big Winter Cal Games contract. That's the only reason he left. I mean, he had to move up to Canada. For the snow.

And the fact that he was a chronic wake and baker had nothing to do with you ENCOURAGING him to move.

Well, at least he isn't an anal-retentive control freak like SOME people who happen to be sitting next to me, HOGGING THE ARMREST.

Jane, your bedroom still smells like the inside of a bong.

It is so typical of you to bring this up at a sensitive time like this. After all, YOU'RE the bride. I'm only the bridesmaid. Or witness. Or whatever.

Well, other than the "smart" thing, what do you think of Cal? Do you like him?

I get fan mail from Wondercat readers in SRI LANKA, Holly. SRI LANKANS have heard of Wondercat. But not Mark's friend Cal.

So? Have you ever read any of his articles on landmines?

At least I know what a land mine is!!!!!!!!!

Just try to get along with him, will you? Because otherwise it's going to be a really long trip.

No problem. Now stop writing to me, please, my food is here.

Benvenuti in
(Welcome to)

Alitalia Inflight Menu

Durante il volo da New York a Roma verra servita la cena e, prima dell' arrivo, la colazione. I piatta che gusterete sono stati preparati per voi. Buon appetito.

(During the flight from New York to Rome we will be serving dinner and then, prior to arrival, breakfast. The dishes on today's menu have been specially prepared for you. Enjoy your meal.)

Cena
(Dinner)

Farfalle al pomodoro pachino e foglie di basilico
Rolle di tacchinella e broccoletti accompagnata da caponata de melanzane e patate
(Farfalle pasta shapes in a fresh pachino tomato and basil sauce Turkey roll with broccoli stuffing served with aubergine stew and potatoes)

Oppure
(Or)

Filetti de pescatrice con potage de zucchine e insalata Catalana
(Monk fish fillet with green zucchini potage and Catalan style salad)

Assortimento dei fromaggi, accompagnali da composte di frutta e cruditees
Caffe "Espresso" e cioccolatini
*(Cheese assortment accompanied by crudites and fresh fruit compote
Italian "Espresso" coffee and chocolates)*

Travel Diary of

~~Holly Caputo and Mark Levine~~

Jane Harris

Oh my God. The Italian food on the plane is better than the Italian takeout around the corner from my apartment. And I thought their insalata caprese was to die for.

The movie is starting. It's the new Hugh Jackman! OH MY GOD, I HAVE DIED AND GONE TO HEAVEN! I AM GOING TO EUROPE WITH MY BEST FRIEND AND THEY ARE SHOWING A HUGH JACKMAN MOVIE ON THE PLANE.

If only the Armrest Nazi would MOVE HIS ELBOW.

PDA of Cal Langdon

As usual, the food on this flight is barely edible. And what passes for entertainment in this country these days is truly depressing. The in-flight movie appears to be yet another romantic comedy about a harried young career woman who finds love in a completely unexpected place. My traveling companion is watching it with rapt attention, as she swills from her many, many bottles of water. She is clearly envisioning herself in the role of the harried young career woman.

I think I can say with a certain amount of confidence that she is NOT picturing me in the role of the handsome young leading man. In fact, her marked lack of enthusiasm for me borders almost on the comical. She is taking great pains never to allow her elbow to touch mine on our mutual armrest, as if she fears she might contract some sort of deadly virus from doing so.

And all this, because I happened to remark on her rather remarkable penchant for bottled water.

Oh, and the Crazy Cat thing. Or Wondercat. How was I to know *Wondercat* is a comic strip, and that she is its creator? I haven't read a comic since Mark and I were kids, and used to shell out 35 cents a week for the latest edition of *Spider-Man* at the Big Red Food Mart. I certainly have never made a habit of reading comic strips in the newspaper—not since I turned ten. The newspapers I choose to read don't *have* comic strips in them.

Although I don't suppose it would be politic to admit that, seeing as how the tome we all work for features two pages of comics daily—not to mention horoscopes and *Dear Abby*. In fact, now that I'll be living in one place for an extended period of time, I suppose I'll have to start subscribing. So I have that to look forward to. In addition to so many other joys I've missed while I've been living out of a bag, such as apartment hunting, buying various electronic devices like a toaster and stereo equipment, and waiting all day for the cable guy who promised to come between ten and two, and then didn't show.

Ah! Domesticity! How I haven't missed you!

But I suppose domesticity can have its benefits. Mark is happier than I've ever seen him. He seems almost to *welcome* the noose that awaits his neck at the end of this journey. Although I suppose when the noose looks like Holly . . .

And she does, I'll admit, seem to think about topics outside of her nails and yoga and Must See TV, unlike most of the American women I've encountered lately. I even had an intelligent conversation with her last week about Gore Vidal.

But I had intelligent conversations with Valerie in the early days, as well.

And as for this friend of Holly's . . . I don't know. I suppose allowances must be made because she's an artist.

But is cartooning really art? My mother would surely think so.

But Mom thinks the lint she picks from the dryer and hot-glues to clothespins is art. And sadly, she is supported in this belief by the art community of Tucson, where she's lately set up a studio.

Still, though she may be an artist, Ms. Harris does have very shiny hair. It's brown, like her eyes.

The tattoo of a cat head—Wondercat, I'm supposing—she wears just above her right ankle is somewhat off-putting, however. And her mouth never seems to stop moving. Now she's telling the flight attendant how much she enjoyed the male lead's last film, in which he played some kind of mutant.

This seat is so uncomfortable. I can just fit into it, if I don't inhale.

Oh, well. I've slept in worse places. At least there aren't any guerrillas hiding in nearby undergrowth, waiting for the opportunity to slit my throat. Or snakes.

God, I hate snakes.

So that's something, anyway.

Benvenuti in
(Welcome to)

Alitalia Inflight Menu

✢ Colazione ✢
(Breakfast)

Spremuta fresca di arancia

Omelette alle erbe fini con funghi, pomodori e bacon ala griglia

Assortimento di tieviti e pano tostate caldi

Caffe, te, latte

Freshly squeezed orange juice

Herb omelette accompanied with mushrooms,
grilled cherry tomatoes, and bacon

Assortment of pastries and croissants

Coffee, tea, milk

Travel Diary of

~~Holly Caputo and Mark Levine~~

Jane Harris

Cell Phone Guy was right. There is plenty of water onboard this flight. There's also a lot of wine. Being drunk by the very loud group of people behind us. Who keep yelling to the flight attendant in Italian so I don't know what they're saying. But it doesn't sound very nice.

I also don't think it's necessarily appropriate to drink wine with breakfast, which is what they just woke us all up to have. I would have preferred to sleep for the rest of the flight, since it seems like we just had dinner after all.

But they came around with the cart and asked us all if we wanted breakfast and that woke everybody up, and now we're all cranky. But especially me because I fell asleep with my mascara still on and I guess it got kind of gunked up underneath the sleeping mask they gave us, and when the flight attendant woke me up to ask me if I wanted breakfast and I took off my sleeping mask, I still couldn't see him because my eyelashes were all stuck together. And then he said, "Oh, no, I think not," about me wanting breakfast in a kind of horrified voice.

So then I had to hurry to the bathroom to try to pick the chunks of mascara from my eyes before Cal could see it. Which he didn't, thank God, because he was still asleep.

But that's not the worst part. The worst part is that Cal woke up while I was gone, and I guess went to the other bathroom, where I suppose he brushed his teeth with the little kit they gave us just like I did, because his breath was minty fresh when he replied to the question I asked him, which I only asked him to be polite and make conversation, something I'll be sure not to do again where he's concerned.

Anyway, I asked him if he was excited about the wedding, he said, "Not exactly."

Which is not especially something you want to hear from the best man of your best friend's husband-to-be, in my opinion.

I have to admit I was so shocked I just sat there and stared at the thing on the wall that counts down the kms until we get to Roma (425). I couldn't think what he meant by it.

It seemed to me that the only thing he could mean by it was that maybe he doesn't like Holly or something, which is ridiculous because of course who doesn't like Holly? She's very kind and pretty and is the art director for a huge urban newspaper, which is a thankless job that doesn't pay nearly as well as it should, considering the fact that she has to work with crazy cartoonists like me, not to mention all the other psychos at the Journal, like that Dolly Vargas from the Style section who is always on Holly's back for not making the reds in the Valentine's Day issue red enough.

Plus she completely adores Mark. So why wouldn't Cal like her?

So I asked him—maybe a little defensively, I'll admit, but hello, I've known Holly for years, and if it weren't for her, Wondercat would never have seen the light of day, but would still be just a silly sketch in my notepad, and I still wouldn't be able to pay my American Express bill every month—what he had against her, and he said, totally politely, "Oh, I haven't got anything against Holly. I think Holly's great and Mark's lucky to have her. It's just marriage I have a problem with."

So then I realized he's one of those monogamy-phobes.

So I told him about how lobsters mate for life, and if they can do it, why can't we, and he looked at me sort of funny and said, "Yes, but they're crustaceans."

To which I replied that I knew that, but that lots of mammals mate for life as well, such as wolves and hawks (at least that's what Rutger Hauer said in LadyHawke, so I assume it's true), and how I think it's romantic and the way things should be.

And then Cal said, "If it's so romantic, how come over fifty percent of marriages end in divorce? How come the leading cause of death for pregnant women in the US isn't complications from childbirth but murder by their spouses?"

What can you *even* say to something like that?

I swear, if this guy starts spewing those little factoids of his about divorce and murder rates while Holly's within hearing distance, I'll kill him. KILL HIM. She's got enough on her mind right now without hearing THAT kind of stuff . . . I mean, what with her mother and all.

Ack! We're landing! In a few minutes, I'll be on foreign soil, for the first time in my life! I'm sure the Armrest Nazi, being a seasoned world traveler, would think it's stupid, but . . . I'm so excited!

PASSPORT

The Secretary of State
of the United States of America
hereby requests all whom it may concern
to permit the citizen/national of the
United States named herein to pass
without delay or hindrance
and in case of need to give all lawful
aid and protections.

Jane Harris

Signature of bearer
Not valid until signed

Entries / Entrée / Entradas
FIUMACINO
14SE

Travel Diary of

~~Holly Caputo and Mark Levine~~

Jane Harris

I got it! My first stamp in my passport! It's kind of smudgy and you can't really read the date. But it's THERE!

Though it TOOK long enough to get it. What is with the LINES in this place? I mean, seriously, do you think they could have opened more than one customs booth? There must have been three hundred people in line ahead of us. This NEVER would have happened in the US. I mean, Americans just would not have put up with it.

Still, it gave me a chance to look around and realize right away that my shoes are all wrong for this country. NO ONE here wears Steve Madden slides. NO ONE. The Italian women have slides, all right, but they have these wicked pointed toes and tiny little heels. Plus they are all wearing long pants, not jeans like Holly and I, and they have these cashmere scarves thrown casually over one shoulder even though according to the Weather Channel it's going to be 24 degrees Celsius every day while we're here, which is in the 80s. I think.

So what's up with that?

Also, it was just SLIGHTLY disturbing when the Customs guy was all, "And where in Italy are you staying," and I said, "Le Marche," hoping I'd pronounced it right, and he made a face and went, "Why would you go THERE?"

Frankly, I do not believe that by offering me his opinion on my final destination that he was allowing me to pass without delay or hindrance into his country, as my passport says he has to.

Besides which, he's wrong. Holly always said her uncle's house was in the most beautiful section of Italy there is. And okay, according to my guidebook, Le Marche (also known as the Le Marche in English) isn't that well known to foreigners. But her uncle seems to have liked it well enough to spend a million bucks on a sixteenth-century villa there.

Besides, what's not to like? Le Marche "forms the eastern seaboard of central Italy—with the Apennine Mountains, noted for their bare peaks and dramatic gorges, forming a natural boundary between it and Umbria and Tuscany. The areas nearer the coast are celebrated for their fertile rounded hills topped by ancient fortified towns."

Um, at least according to my guidebook.

And OK, maybe it's not super popular with anyone but Italians (except for my customs agent). But my guidebook also goes on and on about its unspoiled beauty. . . .

Whatever. Why is my bag always the last one to get through the fricking carousel? And why is Cal laughing so hard at it? My bag is not funny. OK, I painted a Wondercat head on it. But that's only because it's a black rolly bag, and there are only five billion other black rolly bags that look exactly like it. At least I can tell mine apart from all the others at a distance of a hundred yards.

Plus, my bag's not as big as HOLLY's. I mean, I didn't cram a wedding gown into MINE. Just because HE has this dinky little backpack, Mr. Jet-Set-Travel-Guy—

Oh, here's the taxi stand, at LAST. I can't WAIT to get to the hotel and take a nap. Even if it IS only ten in the morning here. I'm so TIRED. . . .

What is that incessant BEEPING coming out of my bag? Not just MY bag either . . . EVERYBODY is beeping!

✉

To: Jane Harris <jane@wondercat.com>
Fr: Claire Harris <charris2004@freemail.com>
Re: You

I hope this thing works! You said you'd be able to get emails in Italy, so I hope you get this. Everything here is fine, don't worry. Well, Dad stuck his hand in the wood chipper again, but he was wearing his chain-mail gloves, so he just broke a blade, didn't lose a finger. He is so forgetful sometimes!

Anyway, I know I'm not supposed to say anything to Holly's mom about how she and Mark are eloping, and you don't need to worry, I haven't said a word, even though I saw her at book group last night and she was practically in tears when we were discussing the scene in which the couple in the book—another one by that nice man who wrote *A Walk to Remember* . . . he's just *so* talented. But why do all his characters have to die at the end?—got married.

When we asked what was wrong, poor Marie said all she's ever wanted is to see Holly settled. You know how Holly was always dying her hair purple and getting things pierced and dating the most inappropriate people all through those years you two were in school together. (Thank goodness you were never like that! You've always been so sensible. I thought your new friend Malcolm was so sweet when I met him last July. How is his investment banking job, anyway? I'm so happy you've finally found someone so responsible! And he looks so *young*! You'd hardly know he was your age. Must be good genes!)

I *really* wanted to say something to Marie like, "Well, you aren't going to have to worry much longer about Holly staying single," but of course I didn't.

Although I sort of wish I had said something now, since Marie went on to say, "I don't care who she marries, as long as he's a nice *Catholic* boy! I have nothing against this *Mark* of hers, but he's, you know. Not one of *us*."

Oh, dear. I don't think Marie is going to be very happy when she gets Holly and Mark's telegram telling her they've gotten married.

And Mark is such a *nice* boy, too. It's such a shame.

Well, I hope you arrived safely. Be careful of pickpockets in Rome. I hear they like to careen past tourists on Vespas through those little narrow streets and snatch handbags and cameras right off by the shoulder strap! So be sure not to wear your shoulder strap slung across your body or you could be dragged to your death.

Love,
Mom

PS Love to The Dude!
PPS What is Mark's friend like? Is he nice? I'm sure he must be, if he's a friend of Mark's!

✉

To: Mark Levine <mark.levine@thenyjournal.com>
Fr: Ruth Levine <r.levine@levinedentalgroup.com >
Re: Hello!

Hi, sweetie! I know you're off to Europe today with your little friends, but I just wanted you to know that last night we had dinner with the Schramms—you remember, you learned to swim in Susie Schramm's backyard pool when you were four—and Lottie Schramm told me that Susie is a corporate lawyer in—get this—NEW YORK CITY! Yes! She works at a firm called Hertzog, Webber, and Doyle on Madison Avenue (so fancy!), and lives on the Upper East Side, not three blocks from your own place! Isn't that incredible? I'm surprised the two of you have never run into one another at H & H Bagels!

In any case, Lottie gave me Susie's email to pass along to you. It's sschramm@hwd.com. You really ought to drop her a line, Mark. Dottie showed me a picture. Susie's grown into a real beauty, and lost every bit of her baby fat (Dottie says because she does Pilates three times a week and hasn't touched a carb in three years).

Hope you're having fun! Don't forget to wear a sweater in the evenings. I understand it can get chilly there at night.

Love,
Mom

✉

To: Ruth Levine <r.levine@levinedentalgroup.com >
Fr: Mark Levine <mark.levine@thenyjournal.com>
Re: Hello!

Ma. Stop trying to fix me up with other women. I am in love with Holly. Got it? HOLLY.

Mark

✉

To: Holly Caputo <holly.caputo@thenyjournal.com>
Fr: Inge Schumacher <i.schumacher@freemail.co.it>
Re: Greetings!

I am understand you will have arrived today! This is perfect. I am making your uncle's house, Villa Beccacia, a home for you. All is ready except the towels which dry on line. I am understand three rooms beds to be made. You arrive by car tomorrow afternoon? You will call me at Villa Beccacia and I will greet you on the autobahn to show you way to villa.

I am hoping you do not mind, my great-grandson Peter visits me on school holiday during your stay. He is good boy, and drives each morning on his motorino to fetch the brotchen for you. Tschuss!

Inge Schumacher
Villa Beccacia
Castelfidardo, Marche

✉

To: Cal Langdon <cal.langdon@thenyjournal.com>
Fr: Tara Samuels <tara.samuels@thenyjournal.com>
Re: Travel Services

Success! I've booked you a seat to Rome on the 6 P.M. flight today. I'm SO sorry about the confusion, and to make up for it, we managed to upgrade you to first class. Enjoy your flight!

Tara

✉

To: Claire Harris <charris2004@freemail.com>
Fr: Jane Harris <jane@wondercat.com>
Re: You

Hi, Mom! I'm writing this to you from an Italian taxi cab! We're on the way from the airport to the hotel where we're staying for the night before going on to Holly's uncle's villa in the morning. Holly made the paper give us Blackberries for emergency use. I can see why they gave one to Holly, because she's the art director, so her job is actually important. But ME??? I'm a freelancer,

I don't even really work there anymore. But Holly talked them into it. Isn't that cool? Of course we have to give them back when we get home. But whatever.

It is so . . . different here. I mean, I'm only in the cab, but already, it looks way different from home. All of the billboards are in Italian! Well, I mean, I know you'd expect that, but I mean, REALLY in Italian. Like there are no recognizably English words AT ALL.

And all of the buildings have these roll-down metal shutters, painted in all these bright colors, to keep out the sun, because I guess it can get really hot, and no one has air-conditioning.

And there are window boxes EVERYWHERE, with CASCADES of red and pink and blue flowers frothing down them. It's so pretty!

And everywhere you look are these funny little half-cars, like Volkswagen bugs that got cut in half, called Smart Cars. In fact the biggest car I've seen here is the minivan we're in. I guess Italians aren't really having big families anymore. Either that, or they don't go anywhere with the kids.

I really don't think you have to worry about my bag getting snatched, Mom. The only people I see on Vespas here are fashionably dressed, skinny women, with long flowing hair, driving around in long, pointy shoes with tiny little heels!

I'm so tired, I can't type anymore. I can't WAIT to get to the hotel so I can crash. I need a shower in the WORST way.

Love to Dad. Tell him to keep wearing those gloves.

Janie

PS The Dude was fine when I left him. Julio, the super's son, is going to look in on him every day after school. I bought him some special tuna Pounce for a treat. For The Dude. Not Julio.

J

PPS Mark's friend is NOT a nice guy. He's totally awful! His name is Cal Langdon and he's some hotshot reporter who thinks he's all that. He doesn't believe in marriage and thinks Mark is making a huge mistake. I don't know how I'm going to survive a whole week in his company. HE'S NEVER HEARD OF WONDERCAT.

J

✉

To: Julio Chasez <julio@streetsmart.com>
Fr: Jane Harris <jane@wondercat.com>
Re: The Dude

Hi, Julio! It's me, Jane! I realize I've only been gone a day, but I just wanted to make sure everything is all right. You know, with The Dude. I know how he can get. Just make sure he gets two cans of fresh food a day (one before you leave for school, and one before you go to bed) PLUS dry food and fresh water, and he should be fine.

Be sure to wear the oven mitts if you have to touch him! And whatever you do, DON'T give him any catnip!

Thank you SO MUCH for taking care of him for me. You are the BEST!

Love,
Jane

To: Jane Harris <jane@wondercat.com>
Fr: Holly Caputo <holly.caputo@thenyjournal.com>
Re: His Mother

Can you believe it? He got an email from his freaking mother about some girl from his hometown who lives in NY now. I'm going to lose it.

Holly

To: Holly Caputo <holly.caputo@thenyjournal.com>
Fr: Jane Harris <jane@wondercat.com>
Re: His Mother

Um . . . why are you emailing me from inside the same car we are both sitting in? Also, I thought we were only supposed to use these things for work purposes.

J

To: Jane Harris <jane@wondercat.com>
Fr: Holly Caputo <holly.caputo@thenyjournal.com>
Re: His Mother

I can't exactly talk to you about the email he got from his mother IN FRONT OF HIM, now can I? Except this way.

And how are they ever going to know what we use these dumb things for, anyway? How are you holding up?

Holly

To: Holly Caputo <holly.caputo@thenyjournal.com>
Fr: Jane Harris <jane@wondercat.com>
Re: His Mother

Good. It's pretty here.

How do you know that his mom emailed him, anyway?

J

To: Jane Harris <jane@wondercat.com>
Fr: Holly Caputo <holly.caputo@thenyjournal.com>
Re: His Mother

Duh. I read it over his shoulder just now. I saw you and Cal talking at the baggage carousel. What did he say?

Holly

To: Holly Caputo <holly.caputo@thenyjournal.com>
Fr: Jane Harris <jane@wondercat.com>
Re: His Mother

Oh. Nothing.

J

To: Jane Harris <jane@wondercat.com>
Fr: Holly Caputo <holly.caputo@thenyjournal.com>
Re: His Mother

Come on! SPILL!

Holly

To: Holly Caputo <holly.caputo@thenyjournal.com>
Fr: Jane Harris <jane@wondercat.com>
Re: His Mother

Is this a setup? Are you and Mark playing Fix Up the Best Friends? Because I told you before, I'm TAKEN. Besides. He's not my type.

J

To: Jane Harris <jane@wondercat.com>
Fr: Holly Caputo <holly.caputo@thenyjournal.com>
Re: His Mother

You have a *type*? What is it? The only thing the guys you've dated have in common is that they've all been unemployed. Or, if they HAD jobs, they were also screwing Amy Jenkins, like Dave.

Holly

✉

To: Holly Caputo <holly.caputo@thenyjournal.com>
Fr: Jane Harris <jane@wondercat.com>
Re: His Mother

Whatever happened to her, anyway?

J

✉

To: Jane Harris <jane@wondercat.com>
Fr: Holly Caputo <holly.caputo@thenyjournal.com>
Re: His Mother

Who? Amy Jenkins?

She married a rich lawyer, moved to Pound Ridge, and squeezed out two kids.

Holly

✉

To: Holly Caputo <holly.caputo@thenyjournal.com>
Fr: Jane Harris <jane@wondercat.com>
Re: His Mother

No! No, she didn't! Why did you tell me that? THAT'S NOT FAIR!!! She tried to ruin my life!!! Why should SHE have a happy ending?

J

✉

To: Jane Harris <jane@wondercat.com>
Fr: Holly Caputo <holly.caputo@thenyjournal.com>
Re: His Mother

You call living in Pound Ridge with a lawyer and two kids a happy ending? You so know she spends her days working out and helping the nanny make wheat-free snacks.

Don't worry. In a couple of years she'll pudge out and he'll trade her in for a younger model and she won't be able to get a job to support herself anywhere because she doesn't have any references, and one day you and Cal will pull into an outlet Benetton to pick up a pair of socks and she'll be working the cash register.

Holly

✉

To: Holly Caputo <holly.caputo@thenyjournal.com>
Fr: Jane Harris <jane@wondercat.com>
Re: His Mother

I don't want to talk about this anymore.

J

✉

To: Jane Harris <jane@wondercat.com>
Fr: Holly Caputo <holly.caputo@thenyjournal.com>
Re: His Mother

Why not?

Holly

✉

To: Holly Caputo <holly.caputo@thenyjournal.com>
Fr: Jane Harris <jane@wondercat.com>
Re: His Mother

Well, for one thing, he's sitting right next to me! He might see! Cut it out!

J

✉

To: Jane Harris <jane@wondercat.com>
Fr: Holly Caputo <holly.caputo@thenyjournal.com>
Re: His Mother

He's not paying attention. He has his own emails to catch up on. Come on. What did he say? He must have said SOMETHING. You guys just sat next to each other for seven hours. Are you telling me he didn't say ANYTHING that entire time?

Holly

✉

To: Holly Caputo <holly.caputo@thenyjournal.com>
Fr: Jane Harris <jane@wondercat.com>
Re: His Mother

Nothing. Really. Oh, at the baggage carousel, he said he was sorry for stepping on my foot.

J

✉

To: Jane Harris <jane@wondercat.com>
Fr: Holly Caputo <holly.caputo@thenyjournal.com>
Re: His Mother

That's IT? Wow. That's weird. Did he talk about his marriage at all?

Holly

✉

To: Holly Caputo <holly.caputo@thenyjournal.com>
Fr: Jane Harris <jane@wondercat.com>
Re: His Mother

HIS WHAT??????????????????????

J

✉

To: Jane Harris <jane@wondercat.com>
Fr: Holly Caputo <holly.caputo@thenyjournal.com>
Re: His Mother

God, use question marks much?

His MARRIAGE. He was married once, you know. He's divorced. I just wondered if he'd mentioned it.

Holly

✉

To: Holly Caputo <holly.caputo@thenyjournal.com>
Fr: Jane Harris <jane@wondercat.com>
Re: His Mother

He didn't say a word about this. But it explains an awful lot. Who was the NOT SO lucky girl?

J

✉

To: Jane Harris <jane@wondercat.com>
Fr: Holly Caputo <holly.caputo@thenyjournal.com>
Re: His Mother

Her name was Valerie Something. I don't know, really, it was ten years ago, back when he and Mark just graduated from college. They met in a bar. He was the newest cub reporter, and she was a model. They went out for about a month before he decided she was the best thing that ever happened to him and married her. They only lasted about a year. Apparently, as soon as the divorce was final, she married an investment banker, and Cal asked for an overseas post. According to Mark, she broke Cal's heart.

And what did you mean by that explains an awful lot?

Holly

To: Holly Caputo <holly.caputo@thenyjournal.com>
Fr: Jane Harris <jane@wondercat.com>
Re: His Mother

Nothing.

Oh, so you're saying he has a heart after all?

J

To: Jane Harris <jane@wondercat.com>
Fr: Holly Caputo <holly.caputo@thenyjournal.com>
Re: His Mother

Come on. He's a nice guy. He's had a crappy time with women—I guess his mother left to "find herself" when he was still in high school, and lately, his little sister's followed suit. He was just put through the wringer by another model, and spent the past decade recovering in places where they don't have cell phone service. Or working toilets. Can you blame him for being a little rough around the edges?

Besides, he can't be THAT bad. Mark says Cal's always been a real ladies' man—that he's got a girl in every port, if you know what I mean. In fact, Mark was sure you two would hit it off right away. He said you're just Cal's type. Apparently, he's partial to brunettes.

He really must not like you.

Holly

To: Holly Caputo <holly.caputo@thenyjournal.com>
Fr: Jane Harris <jane@wondercat.com>
Re: His Mother

Wow. That's really nice to know. Thanks so very much for that.

J

PS Oh, and thanks for trying to fix me up with him, but even if I COULD stand him, which I can't, he's a modelizer. You KNOW once a guy's had a model, he can never go back. So, nice try.

To: Cal Langdon <cal.langdon@thenyjournal.com>
Fr: Mark Levine <mark.levine@thenyjournal.com>
Re: Benvenuto

The girls are emailing back and forth about us.

Mark

To: Mark Levine <mark.levine@thenyjournal.com>
Fr: Cal Langdon <cal.langdon@thenyjournal.com>
Re: Benvenuto

That is blatantly obvious.

Cal

To: Cal Langdon <cal.langdon@thenyjournal.com>
Fr: Mark Levine <mark.levine@thenyjournal.com>
Re: Benvenuto

What do you think they're saying?

Mark

To: Mark Levine <mark.levine@thenyjournal.com>
Fr: Cal Langdon <cal.langdon@thenyjournal.com>
Re: Benvenuto

I honestly could not care less.

Cal

To: Cal Langdon <cal.langdon@thenyjournal.com>
Fr: Mark Levine <mark.levine@thenyjournal.com>
Re: Benvenuto

Don't you like her? Jane, I mean? Holly was sure you'd like her.

Mark

✉

To: Mark Levine <mark.levine@thenyjournal.com>
Fr: Cal Langdon <cal.langdon@thenyjournal.com>
Re: Benvenuto

She seems harmless enough.

Cal

✉

To: Cal Langdon <cal.langdon@thenyjournal.com>
Fr: Mark Levine <mark.levine@thenyjournal.com>
Re: Benvenuto

You don't like her.

Mark

✉

To: Mark Levine <mark.levine@thenyjournal.com>
Fr: Cal Langdon <cal.langdon@thenyjournal.com>
Re: Benvenuto

I didn't say that. All I said was that she seemed harmless. Much in the way an anaconda seems harmless, when it's wrapped around a tree branch ten feet above your head.

Cal

✉

To: Cal Langdon <cal.langdon@thenyjournal.com>
Fr: Mark Levine <mark.levine@thenyjournal.com>
Re: Benvenuto

She's not like that.

And she already has a boyfriend, anyway.

So get over yourself, fathead.

Mark

✉

To: Mark Levine <mark.levine@thenyjournal.com>
Fr: Cal Langdon <cal.langdon@thenyjournal.com>
Re: Benvenuto

Fathead. Harsh.

Cal

✉

To: Cal Langdon <cal.langdon@thenyjournal.com>
Fr: Mark Levine <mark.levine@thenyjournal.com>
Re: Benvenuto

Seriously. ARE you seeing anyone—anyone SPECIAL—these days?

Mark

✉

To: Mark Levine <mark.levine@thenyjournal.com>
Fr: Cal Langdon <cal.langdon@thenyjournal.com>
Re: Benvenuto

They're all special, my friend.

But special enough to shackle myself to her for the rest of eternity, the way you're doing?

No.

But your concern for my romantic well-being is, as always, greatly appreciated.

Cal

✉

To: Cal Langdon <cal.langdon@thenyjournal.com>
Fr: Mark Levine <mark.levine@thenyjournal.com>
Re: Benvenuto

Look, it's just that I know how tough things were for you after—

✉

To: Mark Levine <mark.levine@thenyjournal.com>
Fr: Cal Langdon <cal.langdon@thenyjournal.com>
Re: Benvenuto

Oh, look. The hotel. Stop e-ing me, please.

Cal

RICEVUTA TAXI-ROMA
Percoso:
Da . . . Fiumacino A . . . Hotel Alexander
Firma [redacted]
Importo Corsa 80.00 Euro

Benvenuto al nostro albergo!
(Welcome to our Hotel!)

Gentile Ospite,
Nel porgerLe il nostro cordiale benevuto, abbiamo pensato fe FarLe cosa gradita offrendoLe, al suo arrivo, un assaggio di acqua dalle proprietaria salutari.

Dear Guest,
We wish to express our warmest welcome to our hotel. Given our genuine care for our Guests, we invite you to enjoy the healthy qualities of this bottled water.

Travel Diary of
~~Holly Caputo and Mark Levine~~
Jane Harris

We're HERE!!!!!!!! At the hotel, I mean.

It's the sweetest little place, tucked into a side street that isn't wide enough to let a car coming from the other way pass by. And packed with people! I thought it was a pedestrian walkway and that the taxi driver was going the wrong way. But it turned out it was the Via di Buffalo, which is the street our hotel is on.

Still, it was kind of scary when those Italian school kids kept knocking on the car windows. I wonder what the driver yelled at them to make them run away like that. This is what comes of not having enough social programs for young people. Those kids should have had something better to do on a Saturday than stand around the Via di Buffalo, knocking on tourists' car door windows.

Not that I want to tell another country how it ought to be bringing up its children, or anything. But still.

All I wanted to do was get to my room and take a nap, but Cal had to start arguing with the taxi driver when he saw the receipt. He said over his dead body was he paying 80 euros for a ride from the airport and that the taxi driver might think he could bilk the tourists that way, but that he, Cal, had been to Rome before, and he knew the fare from the airport wasn't a cent over 40 euros. In English. Which it turned out the driver perfectly understood. And after a lot of grousing, he finally agreed that 40 euros would do.

So it's good Mark invited Cal along with us. I guess.

Anyway, my room is so adorable, a tiny little blue-and-white thing with gold curtains that, when I opened them, turned out to be for a window that looks out over the most beautiful courtyard, with white doves flying around it, and bougainvillea spilling from window boxes all over the place, and a sky stretched over it that, I swear, looks bluer than the sky over Manhattan, somehow. It is EXACTLY like Helena Bonham Carter's room in the pensione in Room with a View. Only there's no view. Well, except for the courtyard and the sky.

And there are big bottles of water right here in my room, for later, and I turned on the TV, and everything was In Italian!

I mean, I knew it would be. It's just SO WEIRD!

I thought I would be way too tired to want to go out and sightsee, but now that I'm finally here, I'm really stoked! I want to get out there and see EVERYTHING. After all, we only have about 24 hours in Rome before we leave for Le Marche.

On second thought, I didn't sleep very well on the plane, thanks to The Armrest Nazi. I suppose I shouldn't call him that anymore on account of him having been so tragically jilted all those years ago by that model.

But seriously, what did he expect, marrying a model? Modelizers get exactly what they deserve.

Maybe I'll just rest my eyes for a minute or two. . . .

Funny. I miss The Dude. I'm so used to his big gray body curled up to mine in bed, I don't know if I'll be able to get to slee—

—

—

—

—

—

—

To: Cal Langdon <cal.langdon@thenyjournal.com>
Fr: Arthur Pendergast <a.pendergast@rawlingspress.com>
Re: The Book

Where are you this week? Nigeria? Well, wherever it is, just thought I'd give you the good news: *Sweeping Sands* made the *Times* extended list. Number 18. If you'd agreed to tour, we'd have probably debuted even higher. But I know, I know. You've got this wedding to go to. Oh, it's also number 48 on the *USA Today* list. Which isn't bad for a hardback.

Check out this cover sketch for the UK edition and let me know what you think.

Have you given any thought lately to what #2 is going to be about? The second book on your contract, I mean. No hurry, just that it's due in a couple months, and you still haven't submitted a proposal. Have you given any thought to dirty diamonds? That's a pretty hot topic these days. And I hear Angola is nice this time of year.

Arthur Pendergast
Senior Editor
Rawlings Press
1418 Avenue of the Americas
New York, NY 10019
212-555-8764

To: Cal Langdon <cal.langdon@thenyjournal.com>
Fr: Aaron Spender <a.spender@cnn.com>
Re: Things

What's this I hear about you throwing in the foreign-correspondence towel and taking a post stateside? What are you, going soft on me in your old age? It can't be because of this multimillion-dollar book deal I hear you landed a while back, because the Cal Langdon I knew never cared about money. I distinctly recall you saying, that night we were trapped in that bomb shelter in Baghdad, that you never wanted to own any material goods because they might "weigh" you down.

All I can say is, you can buy a heck of a lot of pot holders with the kind of green you're raking in, buddy.

Anyway, if you're serious about staying home for a while, why work for that rag? Believe me, I've been there, and it is not where you want to be. Come on over to where the REAL news is being made. Print media is dead. It's all about television these days. I can set you up with a really sweet deal, if you're interested. Let me know.

Barbara says hello.

Aaron Spender
Senior Correspondent
CNN—New York

✉

To: Cal Langdon <cal.langdon@thenyjournal.com>
Fr: Mary Langdon <m.langdon@freemail.com>
Re: Mom

So I heard from Dad you're back in the States for a while—well, except for some jaunt to Italy to be a witness to some guy named Mark's wedding (it's not Mark from next door, is it? Didn't he end up becoming a doctor or something else really boring? Typical).

I also heard you got a cool mil for some book you wrote, and that they want a second one. What are you going to do with all that scratch? Try to lure the ex back from Mr. Investment Guy?

Why don't you send some of it my way? I'll keep it safe for you. This whole weaving thing isn't really working out, anyway, and I was thinking of heading up north with this guy who's got a tie-dye biz going out of his van.

Anyway, keep in touch. And welcome back to the good old US of A. It sucks just as much now as it did when you left.

Mare

PS Have you heard the latest about Mom? She actually has a SHOW. An ART show. Of her stupid lint/clothespin people. I don't know how SHE can get a show and I can't. My weavings are way more artistic than her lint people.

To: Cal Langdon <cal.langdon@thenyjournal.com>
Fr: Graziella Fratiani <graziella@galleriefratiani.co.it>
Re: You

What is this I hear about you coming to Roma and not calling to me? I would not have known a thing about it if Dolly Vargas hadn't happened to mention it during our interview. You are a naughty, naughty boy. Where are you staying? Call me. You know the number. I will come by your hotel and give you a true Italian welcome.

Ciao, amore XXXX
Grazi

PDA of Cal Langdon

Art sent the UK cover design for *Sands* today. It's got a very romantic feel to it that I'm not sure is entirely appropriate, considering the book's subject matter. Well, I suppose if it tricks unsuspecting readers into buying it, expecting it to be a work of fiction about a mummy's curse instead of a nonfiction treatise on Saudi Arabia's tiring oil fields, all the better.

I can't believe Aaron Spender is still among the living. I'd have assumed Barbara Bellerieve bit his head off and ate it on their wedding night. I still marvel at my own lucky escape from her clutches. If it hadn't been for that Daisy Cutter . . .

And Mary. I guess that grand I sent her last month didn't last very long. What the hell does she do with it all? It's not like she ever has anything to show for it. She can't smoke it ALL away, can she? I wish Mom and Dad had taken some control over her earlier in her adolescence. She probably wouldn't still be living out of some guy's van at the age of twenty-five.

But I guess they weren't necessarily the best role models, as parents go, considering Dad's obsession with the track and Mom's conviction that she's the next Grandma Moses. It's surprising, actually, that Mary isn't a bigger flake than she is. . . .

Much like some people I could mention. It was amusing, coming from the airport, to hear Holly's friend squeal at the sight of every monument—and every passing billboard. It's been a long time since I've seen anyone get so excited about a sign for mouthwash. I thought she was going to have a coronary when we drove by the Colosseum. I'm not entirely sure which impressed her more . . . the fact that it's stood for over two thousand years, or the fact that Britney Spears was recently there, filming a television commercial (at least, that's what Holly's friend announced to all of us).

There is something refreshing about American enthusiasm for antiquity. I guess I forget, having been away so long, that there is still a place on this earth where there are no structures older than half a millennium. It must be impressive to see something that existed fifteen hundred years before the *Mayflower*. . . .

Of course, if we hadn't slaughtered all the Indians and destroyed their native lands, it would be different.

Good Lord. It just occurred to me. What if that wasn't what she was impressed by? What if it was the Britney Spears thing?

But no. No, that couldn't be. Not even an artist could be that shallow.

I'll have to remember to change money later, if I can find a place with a decent exchange rate. I blew my last euro on that cab ride—

That was the concierge. Grazi is here. That didn't take her long. I called her less than half an hour ago. Still, I thought she'd be coming over later tonight, not NOW.

I guess it would be ungentlemanly of me not to see her, though. . . .

✉

To: Julio Chasez <julio@streetsmart.com>
Fr: Jane Harris <jane@wondercat.com>
Re: The Dude

Hi, Julio! Me, again! Just checking in, since I haven't heard from you. How's The Dude doing? Does he like that salmon paté I got him? I figured he'd appreciate a few treats, with me being gone. I hope you found the Pounce. I left it on the counter, with the oven mitts. Really, you should only need the Pounce if he tries to attack. Which he really shouldn't, I mean, he KNOWS you. You two are buds. Right?

Well, let me know how he's doing as soon as you get a chance. No biggie. You can just email, if you want. Or call. From my phone in the apartment. That way it won't cost you anything. Don't worry about the time difference, you can call at any time. I don't mind being woken up, if it's for The Dude.

J

Travel Diary of

~~Holly Caputo and Mark Levine~~

Jane Harris

Oh my God, this place is FABULOUS! When I woke up from my nap, it was two, and I called Holly to see if she was hungry, and she was, but Mark was still asleep, and Modelizer/Armrest Nazi didn't pick up his phone (much to my relief) when Holly tried him . . . you know, to be polite, and not exclude him.

So Holly and I met in the hall and the two of us just strolled right out onto tiny Via di Buffalo, which I suppose is named after the mozzarella, which is made from buffalo milk, at least in Italy, and we started walking, and in half an hour, not five blocks from our hotel, we'd seen the Trevi Fountain, the Pantheon, the Piazza Navone, and a bunch of other sights I can't even remember, as they all involved monolisks with bumpy writing on them.

But that's not all! We saw portrait artists, right on the street—good ones, not like the cheesy ones in New York—and people eating gelati, and groups of senior citizens following around tour guides holding a flag, and I threw money in the Fontana di Trevi—I don't know how much, because it was Italian—which apparently guarantees you'll be back there someday. Which I hope is true, because it's a kick-ass fountain, almost as cool as Ozzy's pool on The Osbournes.

And we were solicited by a humpbacked dwarf with no shirt on and a tattoo that said Antonio on his shoulder, and I gave him some money, and then I bought a bottle of Diet Coke that cost five euros, which is more than a six-pack back home, and I realized I gave the humpbacked dwarf enough money to buy FIVE Italian Diet Cokes.

I really need to get a grip on this money thing. Although I'm sure Antonio (if that's his name) needs the money more than I need Diet Coke.

And then Holly wanted her picture taken with a hot guy dressed as a gladiator in front of the Pantheon, so I started to take one, but then this very blowsy older woman dressed in a toga came over and demanded ANOTHER five euros, just for letting me take the picture with her hot gladiator boyfriend! The guy just stood there looking all sheepish while this went on, but Holly was all, "I want it, it'll be funny," so I forked over five more euros and took the picture.

Holly said later that right before I took the picture, the gladiator handed her his plastic sword, and when she asked him, "What should I do with this?" he went, in a long-suffering voice, "Keel me. Please."

Which in and of itself was totally worth five euros.

And everywhere we went, lots of Italian vendors came up to us, another one every five seconds, it seemed, going "Bag, California?" I guess because we look like we're from California, even though of course we're not, though we are sort of tan thanks to Holly and Mark's share in East Hampton.

Only how they knew we were American I can't tell, though we were talking a lot, I suppose. And I am apparently the only girl in all of Rome who wears Steve Madden slides.

But then Mark called on Holly's cell and said he was hungry and Cal wasn't answering the phone in his room, so we agreed to meet Mark for a snack.

Except that on the way back to the hotel, we passed a church where a wedding was going on—or about to go on, anyway. I saw the crowd and assumed it was another sight we should see, but then it turned out to be a lot of tourists like us waiting outside a church with some flower girls and maids of honor, and we realized it was a wedding!

So then Holly said she had to stay to see the bride for luck, since she was getting married too.

So we edged into the church and stood there and waited and it wasn't long until a sleek beige Mercedes sedan pulled up and the bride, looking incredibly chic in an ivory sheath with a tiny veil got out, beaming and speaking in Italian to the little flower girls who started jumping up and down.

I got some very good photos of the whole thing and wanted to ask her if she wanted me to send her copies (the bride I mean), but I didn't know the right words in Italian, and besides, by that point her father had come out of the church and lent her his arm, and that's when Holly and I realized we were standing right in the aisle, with the groom at the front of the church with the priest, trying to see past us to catch a glimpse of his wife-to-be in her gorgeous ivory sheath.

So we scampered out of the way and I looked at Holly and saw tears in her eyes!!!!

I thought she'd been stung by a bee or something so I was like, "Let's go find some ice!" but it turned out that wasn't it at all. Holly looked at me all tearfully and went, "I want my father to lead me down the aisle! Only he doesn't know I'm doing this. And I'm not even going to have an aisle. Because we're going to get married by some clerk in some office."

Then she burst into tears right there on some street I can't remember the name of.

Of course I had no choice but to hustle her as fast as I could to the café where we'd said we'd meet Mark for snacks. Only I knew it was my duty as witness/bridesmaid to get her cleaned up before her future husband saw what a psycho he was marrying. Not that he didn't already know, since Holly cries at the end of every episode of Seventh Heaven she sees, even the reruns, and won't pick up the phone on Monday nights as a consequence.

But still.

We got a seat right away at the café across from the Pantheon—an outdoor table, even. In New York, you practically have to chew off your own foot to get an outdoor table anywhere. Maybe the waiter saw how dire our need was, considering Holly's tears. Anyway, he sat us under the shade of his restaurant's big fluttery awning, and I said, "Un verre de vin blanc pour moi et pour mon amie," forgetting I wasn't in 11th-grade French, but in Italy.

The waiter totally took it in stride though. "Frizzante?" he asked me.

I had no idea what he was talking about, but remembering I was in Italy and not France, I managed to say Si and not Oui.

My first foreign language exchange! I'd spoken English with the Diet Coke guy and Mr. Gladiator's pimp. And OK, the exchange hadn't been in the actual language spoken in this country. But it had still been foreign.

Then the bread basket came, with a little pot of silky white butter, and we dug in, because even when she's crying, Holly can still eat, which is one of the many reasons I love her.

And I told her how lucky she is her father ISN'T here, since, like her mom, he doesn't exactly approve of Mark. Which is ridiculous, because Mark is totally perfect husband material, being completely sweet and thoughtful and funny and self-deprecating and totally the opposite of his horrible friend Cal the Modelizer in every way. Plus Mark's even reasonably good-looking. Oh, and a doctor. With a weekly health column in a New York paper that's read by millions. What more could the Caputos ask?

A Catholic, apparently.

Sometimes I get so mad at Holly's parents for what they're doing to her, I just want to *spit*.

But then, Mark's parents are just as bad, in their own way.

"L–like it even matters to us," Holly sobbed, as the waiter reappeared with two glasses of white wine on a tray. "I mean, I haven't been to church since I was eighteen! Church was their thing, not mine. And Mark hasn't set foot in temple since his bar mitzvah. We have no intention of raising our children any particular religion. We're going to bring up the kids a-religious. And then when they're old enough, they can decide which religion—if any—they want to belong to."

I nodded because I had heard this many times before. The wine in the glasses the waiter was putting down in front of us seemed to catch the sun and dance around before my eyes like fool's gold in the bottom of that stream Laura found on that one episode of Little House on the Prairie.

"Why can't they just respect that this is the man I love?" Holly asked, picking up her glass and taking a gulp. "And, yes, he's Jewish. *Get over it*."

I sipped my wine too—

And nearly spat it out! Because it wasn't wine at all! It was champagne!

Only better than champagne! Because the bubbles in champagne usually give me an instant headache.

But these bubbles were tiny and light—barely there at all.

"What is this?" I asked, in wonder, holding my glass up to the light and looking at all the lovely bubbles.

"Frizzante," Holly said. "Remember? He asked, and you said Si. It's like . . .fizzy wine. Don't you like it?"

"I love it."

I loved it so much, I had another glass of it. By the time Mark joined us, I was in a VERY good mood.

Fortunately, so was Holly. There was so much people-watching to do in our corner of the piazza that she soon forgot all about the wedding we'd seen, and her yearning for her dad to give her away at her own. Soon we were able to pick out the American tourists as quickly as the Italians obviously could. I don't mean to say anything negative about my countrymen and women, but hello, the Fab Five have their work cut out for them.

Holly was instantly cheered, as always, by the sight of Mark. He asked for a menu and got one—in English!—and ordered mussels and an antipasto platter, and we sat and ate chunky crumbles of parmesan and fresh tangy olives and buttery slivers of salami and garlicky mussels and had fun watching other suckers get fleeced by the handsome, morose gladiator and his pimp.

Then the shadows started getting longer and Mark checked his Blackberry and said we should be getting back to the hotel to change for dinner. So we got the bill—which Mark insisted on paying—and started back, Mark with arm around Holly's waist, and her head leaning on his shoulder, her unhappiness from a few hours earlier blissfully forgotten.

And I wished SO HARD that awful Modelizer Cal was with us, so he could see how cute Holly and Mark are together, and how great a couple they are, and what sweet parents they'll make, and what a crime it would be if they didn't get married. I mean, how could anyone look at Holly and Mark and think, for even one minute, that marriage is an antiquated institution that ought to be abolished? They are living proof that it works. Just because Modelizer's wife turned out to be a money-grubbing beeyotch doesn't mean—

Ooooh! I got an email! On my Blackberry! PLEASE let it be Julio!!!!

✉

To: Jane Harris <jane@wondercat.com>
Fr: Malcolm Weatherly <malcolmw@snowstyle.com>
Re: Ciao!

Hey, babe! How's it hangin? So ya there yet? Whaddaya think? Pretty rad, huh? Yeah, I-ty blew my mind when I was there last year for the European Open. Even the freaking *coffee* tastes better there.

But I don't get the whole "everything closing from noon to four and lunch and everybody serving nothing but pasta after ten" thing. Bummer if you wake up at one and want a freaking waffle.

But make sure you try one of those bidets. It'll change your life!

Stay away from those I-ty Latin Lover types. I know how those guys operate. They only want a green card, anyway. Not that you're not, you know, totally hot.

Aw, gotta go, I'm up next on the halfpipe. Luv ya.

Mal

PS Know what? I kinda miss The Dude. Give him a big kiss for me, willya? Oh, you can't, cause you're in I–ty. Sorry.

Isn't that sweet? I miss The Dude, too. If he were here right now, he'd be curled up around my feet.

And my toes would be losing all circulation because he weighs so much. But still.

I don't understand why Julio hasn't written, though. What if he forgot? To feed The Dude, I mean?

But how could he forget? I stuck a giant sign on his dad's door, to remind him. . . .

Where was I? Oh, yeah. Walking through the piazza behind Mark and Holly.

Well . . . while I was looking at them, and thinking how cute they are, and what a shame it was that Modelizer Cal wasn't there with us to see them and all, I got a pang.

A PANG.

I'll admit it. I mean, I am totally happy for Holly and in full support of this elopement scheme. Really, given the situation, I don't see how she and Mark have any choice BUT to elope.

But seeing them together like that, her head on his shoulder, his arm around her—I felt a pang.

Because where is MY Mark? Really? Where IS he?

Because I know he's not in Canada right now, hitting the halfpipe—or the full pipe. Or even both, as in Malcolm's case. I mean, I like Malcolm and all, and we have a blast together. But I can't really picture him strolling through the piazza with his arm around my waist. Skateboarding through it, certainly. But having a nice glass of bianco frizzante as the sun sets? Not so much.

I'm sure he's out there, somewhere. My Mark, I mean. He has to be, right?

But what if I never find him? Or what if I already met him, and I messed it up somehow? This would not be unusual, since I mess up everything. I mean, what if My Mark was DAVE who cheated on me with Amy Jenkins (that whore)?

Oh, God, no. Fate would never be so unkind.

Or what if My Mark was Curt Shipley, who took me to the prom in 11th grade, and we made out in his Chevette afterwards, and then that summer, I found out he'd been making out, in that same Chevette, with Mike Morris after the fireworks on the Fourth of July?

Which means I must have turned Curt gay, because he certainly wasn't gay BEFORE we made out.

Oh, my God. What if Curt Shipley was the man of my dreams, and I TURNED HIM GAY?????

Killing self now.

To: Mark Levine <mark.levine@thenyjournal.com>
Fr: Cal Langdon <cal.langdon@thenyjournal.com>
Re: Sorry

Sorry I missed it when you called earlier. I was dead to the world. We still on for dinner tonight?

Cal

To: Cal Langdon <cal.langdon@thenyjournal.com>
Fr: Mark Levine <mark.levine@thenyjournal.com>
Re: Sorry

Yes, I happened to hear how "dead to the world" you were as I passed by your room on my way to meet the girls. I wasn't aware that corpses were sexually active . . . at least, if I'm to assume the heavily accented female voice calling your name with ever-increasing volume as she climaxed was, indeed, coming from Room 204.

Mark

To: Mark Levine <mark.levine@thenyjournal.com>
Fr: Cal Langdon <cal.langdon@thenyjournal.com>
Re: Sorry

Oh. That was Graziella. She won't be joining us tonight.

Cal

✉

To: Cal Langdon <cal.langdon@thenyjournal.com>
Fr: Mark Levine <mark.levine@thenyjournal.com>
Re: Sorry

I am sorrier to hear that than words can adequately express. See you at eight.

Mark

PDA of Cal Langdon

It was a mistake to invite Grazi in. I should have insisted on going to her place. I'd forgotten how . . . *loud* she can be.

ANTIPASTI

Insalatina mista all'aceto balsamico
Carpaccio tiepido di manzo con parmigiano e rucola
Medaglioni d'astice con insalata di stagione

PASTA

Fusilli con pomodori e basilico
Garganelli con pesto, patate e fagiolini
Tagliolini con zafferano, gamberoni e zucchine

SECONDI PIATTI

Medaglioni di vitello in crosta di basilico con purea de melanzane e parmigiano
Filetto di manzo alle erbe aromatiche
Tagliata di manzo con timballo de patate e cardamomo
Filetto di rombo al forno con limone e capperi

INSALATE DI STAGIONE

SELEZIONE DI FORMAGGI ITALIANI

DOLCI

Bavarese al cioccolato bianco con crema cocoa alla liquirizia e latte di madorle
Mousse al cioccolato fondente con sedano candito
Crema al limone
Budino al cocco con frutto della passione

PDA of Cal Langdon

Insisted on paying for dinner, as spent majority of it pontificating on *Sweeping Sands,* and felt I had to make amends. Also, it was the least I could do after Mark's revelation regarding Grazi. Eight hundred euro, but worth it—especially the wine.

Don't think I made a friend of Ms. Harris, however. Which is a shame, because she looks rather fetching in heels—a point that was driven home rather hard when she stumbled outside the restaurant, and I was forced to pry her heel from where it was wedged between two cobblestones.

The tattoo IS of Wondercat. It's the same cat's head that she's got on her luggage. I've never been one for tattoos, but hers is rather fetching.

I can't believe I wrote the word *fetching*. This country goes to my head like prosecco.

Travel Diary of

~~Holly Caputo and Mark Levine~~

Jane Harris

Oh, my God, that restaurant was so fancy that they even had tiny little chairs for ladies' purses! Seriously! Like the waiter held my chair for me, then he pulled out this matching stool for my bag! The bag I bought off an outdoor table on Canal Street in Chinatown, then bedazzled with Wondercat's face! In a seat of honor!

It was almost too much. There was silverware on the table I had never seen before.

Plus, in the ladies' room, there were actual folded hand towels for every visitor. Not paper towels. But a huge stack of tiny hand towels, so when you dried your hands, you reached for one, then threw it into a laundry basket underneath the sink.

I have no idea what I ate for dinner. It was delicious, though. The waiter said a bunch of stuff, and Holly, who speaks a little Italian, and Modelizer Cal, who I guess speaks a little more than that, just nodded and went, "Si, si." And then plates began to appear, of squash blossoms stuffed with goat cheese, and perfect little circles of foie gras, and curls of endive dripping in butter and cheese. . . .

That meal had to have been three thousand calories, at least.

But I didn't care. Because it was all so delicious. THIS IS SO FUN!!!!!!!

Well, except for Cal. It's no WONDER he's never heard of Wondercat. I doubt he's ever read anything for fun in his entire life. Holly made the mistake—BIG one—of asking him what the book he wrote is about.

Of course a modelizer like him can't be writing something

cool like a spy thriller or dick lit, like Nick Hornsby or anything. Oh, no. HE has to have written a book about—get this—how Saudi Arabia's oil fields are on the decline, and soon won't be able to meet the world's demands. This, of course, is going to crush Saudi Arabia's economy, and have serious repercussions throughout the rest of the globe, as well.

Yeah. Who cares? Guess what, Cal? In Saudi Arabia, women aren't allowed to vote or drive cars. Why should I care if that nation's economy goes down the tubes? Maybe if they'd let women have some say in their country's governance, they wouldn't be in this sorry position in the first place.

Sadly, he SAW me yawning. Cal, I mean.

And instead of just politely accepting my apology—"Sorry, jet lag"—he was all, "This could have a profound impact on you, too, Jane. What do you think those water bottles you're so fond of are made from? Petroleum."

Geez! I love Mark to death, but why is he even friends with this guy? Oh, sure, maybe the ex left him a bitter shell of a man. But does he have to take it out on me?

Also, he may think he's slick, but when I was leaving my room to meet Holly and Mark for cocktails down in the lobby, I got a major eyeful of what he spent the afternoon doing, as she slunk out of his room and down the stairs. I don't care what Holly says about me being his type, it's a total lie. Cal Langdon's "type" is STILL clearly five-foot-eleven blonde models, NOT five-foot-four brunette cartoonists into whose jeans TWO of said models could easily fit.

As if that's not bad enough, when we were waiting for a taxi to take us home, I looked over and saw Mark take off his jacket and wrap it around Holly, who was shivering a little in her sleeveless pink dress. Then he put his arm around her, and the two of them nuzzled each other.

NUZZLED. They were NUZZLING.

And I looked over to see if Cal had noticed, and he totally had, he was looking right at them.

And I will admit that it was impossible to tell what was going on behind those steely baby blues of his.

But I imagined—my second BIG MISTAKE—that he was feeling the way I was . . . that Mark and Holly are the cutest couple EVER and totally belong together and it's a CRIME what their families are doing to them, being so unreasonable about the differing faiths thing.

So I went, in a soft voice so Mark and Holly wouldn't overhear, "Do you STILL think those two shouldn't get married?"

And the Modelizer went, "I give it a year. Two, tops."

!!!!!!!!!!!!!!!!!!!!!!!!!!!!!!!!!!!!!

I couldn't believe it! I mean, where could he POSSIBLY be getting that?

So I went, "Are you crazy? They're totally in love. Look at them."

Cal: "You know love is just a chemical reaction in the brain caused by surges of phenylethylamine, don't you?"

Me: (confused) "You're saying Holly and Mark don't really love each other? That it's all in their heads?"

Cal: "I'm saying no one loves anyone. People are attracted to one another and pair up to breed due to our natural mating instinct. But that attraction doesn't last. As with all drugs, the body develops a tolerance for the phenylethylamine, and eventually, the attraction you once felt for your partner fades. It's all perfectly natural. You can get the same amount of phenylethylamine, a stimulant the mind craves, by ingesting vast amounts of chocolate as you can by, quote, falling in love, endquote."

Me: "So . . . you don't believe in romantic love?"

Cal: "I believe I just said that."

Me: "Because of the vast amount of time you've spent studying the subject?"

Cal: "From my own personal experience, yes. And from the relationships I've observed around me."

Me: "So Holly and Mark are going to break up because there's no such thing as love?"

Cal: "Oh, no. Well, yes, eventually. But well before that happens, they're going to break up because their backgrounds are too different."

I really don't think I can be blamed for saying, "At least they're both human, unlike the skank I saw leaving your hotel room earlier."

I had the satisfaction of seeing him, for the first time since we've met, completely speechless.

Sadly the effect was ruined when one of my stiletto heels got caught between the cobblestones outside the restaurant. It gouged away all the silver lamé. I don't think it can be fixed, either.

I'll admit the cobblestones are charming, but have these people never heard of asphalt? It was totally humiliating too, the Modelizer had to help me pry it loose. My heel, I mean.

His hand fit all the way around my ankle. You know, his fingers met his thumb on the other side.

Thank God I remembered to shave my legs in the shower before dinner.

God, I'm so jazzed from all that good food, I don't think I'll ever fall asleep. Plus, I keep thinking about The Dude. He has to be all right, doesn't he? I mean, Julio would have called if there was anything wrong. I left my cell number by the phone, so Julio could call from my phone, and not wrack up a bill on his parents' line.

And I just checked it, and he hasn't called. So The Dude is good. No news is good news, right? The Dude HAS to be good.

It's just that we've spent maybe only five nights, total, away from each other since he was a kitten. Who is going to get up during The Dude's 4-AM windowsill yowl at the moon and comfort him if I'm not there? That yowl used to drive me insane. But now I sort of miss it. I'd give anything to hear that yowl right now. In fact, I don't think I'll be able to go to sleep without it—

—

—

—

—

—

—

—

—

—

—

—

To: Customer Service New York Journal Travel Privileges
<TravelPrivcustser@thenyjournal.com >
Fr: Mark Levine <mark.levine@thenyjournal.com >
Re: Car Rental

I realize it's Sunday, and that your offices are closed. However, when I made the reservation for a rental car in Rome, I specified that I needed a four-door sedan with trunk room for four VERY LARGE bags. I asked for a Jaguar or Mercedes, NOT a Toyota. Now I have to cram one of the bags in the backseat with two passengers, and we're going to be driving through MOUNTAINS. Do you really think it's safe to drive through a mountain range with a large, overstuffed suitcase between passengers in the backseat?

I didn't think so. I'll expect to hear from you on Monday.

Mark Levine, MD

To: Julio Chasez <julio@streetsmart.com>
Fr: Jane Harris <jane@wondercat.com>
Re: The Dude

Hi, Julio! I have to admit, I'm getting kind of worried. Is everything OK? I mean, you haven't written back to me, and I just want to know if everything is going all right. I know you're busy with school and hockey and all, but if you could just send me a tiny message, letting me know The Dude's all right, I'd really appreciate it.

I think I'll try your pager.

J

✉

To: Jane Harris <jane@wondercat.com>
Fr: Holly Caputo <holly.caputo@thenyjournal.com>
Re: Where are you?

????????????????????

✉

To: Holly Caputo <holly.caputo@thenyjournal.com>
Fr: Jane Harris <jane@wondercat.com>
Re: Where are you?

I'm still in the dining room, finishing breakfast. Where are YOU?

J

✉

To: Jane Harris <jane@wondercat.com>
Fr: Holly Caputo <holly.caputo@thenyjournal.com>
Re: Where are you?

Outside. Hurry up and finish and get out here. You've got to see this. Mark and Cal are trying to cram all of our bags into the trunk, only they won't fit. So they're doing physics. All serious, like it's a puzzle or something. Something actually IMPORTANT. Get out here, or you'll miss it.

Holly

To: Holly Caputo <holly.caputo@thenyjournal.com>
Fr: Jane Harris <jane@wondercat.com>
Re: Where are you?

I'm not done with my yogurt yet.

J

To: Jane Harris <jane@wondercat.com>
Fr: Holly Caputo <holly.caputo@thenyjournal.com>
Re: Where are you?

Oh my God, it's just YOGURT. Get out here. You can have yogurt anytime.

Holly

To: Holly Caputo <holly.caputo@thenyjournal.com>
Fr: Jane Harris <jane@wondercat.com>
Re: Where are you?

Not like this. This is the best yogurt I've ever had.

What does Fett-Grassi 3.7g mean anyway?

J

To: Jane Harris <jane@wondercat.com>
Fr: Holly Caputo <holly.caputo@thenyjournal.com>
Re: Where are you?

Fat grams.

Holly

To: Holly Caputo <holly.caputo@thenyjournal.com>
Fr: Jane Harris <jane@wondercat.com>
Re: Where are you?

SERIOUSLY??? SATURATED OR UNSATURATED??? OH MY GOD, I'VE EATEN FOUR CONTAINERS!!!!!!!!!!!!!!!!!

To: Jane Harris <jane@wondercat.com>
Fr: Claire Harris <charris2004@freemail.com>
Re: How are you?

Hi, honey! Thank you for emailing me back so promptly. I hope you made it to your hotel all right. Things here are good. Well, except for Dad nearly broke his tailbone from a fall off the roof as he was cleaning the gutters. But he bounced off the hydrangea bush, so all is well.

I don't want you to worry, but after I wrote you yesterday I ran into Holly's mother again, this time at the Kroger Sav-On, and I mentioned how lovely I thought it was that you all were going to Italy to stay in her uncle's villa, and Marie didn't seem to know a thing about it. I know I wasn't supposed to mention the elopement, but Holly did tell her mother she was going to her uncle's, didn't she? I hope I haven't spoiled anything.

Love,
Mom

PS Cal Langdon, the reporter with the *New York Journal*? Why, I just saw him on *Charlie Rose* the other night! He was being interviewed about some big book he's just written. Apparently, it's selling very well. He's very handsome, Janie.

Still, imagine not thinking Mark should marry Holly. Those two were made for each other! And who's never heard of Wondercat? What has he been doing, living under a rock???? Well, I guess so, actually, since his book is about Saudi Arabia. . . .

Mom

✉

To: Claire Harris <charris2004@freemail.com>
Fr: Jane Harris <jane@wondercat.com>
Re: How are you?

Hi, Mom! Things here are fine. Well, except that Holly and I are waiting for the guys to go check out of the hotel so that we can rearrange the way they've packed the rental car. It's too small for all of us, plus our luggage, so Holly and I have to sit in the back with Holly's giant suitcase. Which we don't mind, especially, except that they packed our bag of Toblerone in the trunk. What good will it do anyone there?

We leave for Holly's uncle's villa today. It's about a four-hour drive from Rome to where the house is, on the Adriatic coast. I can't wait to see it! Everything here is just so different and fun. Even the yogurt is better.

But then I found out that's because I was eating full fat yogurt for the first time in my life. Oh well.

I wouldn't worry about Holly's mom. People in their family borrow their uncle's place all the time, since he's away so much.

Tell Dad there are people he can hire to clean the gutters.

Love,
Janie

PS You saw Cal Langdon on *Charlie Rose*? It figures. He is so full of himself. And as for his not thinking Holly and Mark are perfect for each other . . . Please! I don't even like to remember what Holly was like before she started dating Mark. I mean, remember the whole green hair phase?

And you'd have to have lived under a rock not to have seen Wondercat's recycling campaign at D'Agostino. There are circulars for it everywhere.

J

✉

To: Holly Caputo <holly.caputo@thenyjournal.com>
Fr: Jane Harris <jane@wondercat.com>
Re: What is up with this?

Why did you let Mark drive?

J

To: Jane Harris <jane@wondercat.com>
Fr: Holly Caputo <holly.caputo@thenyjournal.com>
Re: What is up with this?

Hello? You were there. How was I supposed to stop him?

Holly

To: Holly Caputo <holly.caputo@thenyjournal.com>
Fr: Jane Harris <jane@wondercat.com>
Re: What is up with this?

Yeah, but he sucks at it. I mean, really, really sucks at it.

J

To: Jane Harris <jane@wondercat.com>
Fr: Holly Caputo <holly.caputo@thenyjournal.com>
Re: What is up with this?

Hello. It's Italy. Everyone sucks at driving. He blends.

Besides, I had to let him drive, after that whole thing with Cal re-arranging all the suitcases.

Holly

To: Holly Caputo <holly.caputo@thenyjournal.com>
Fr: Jane Harris <jane@wondercat.com>
Re: What is up with this?

Yeah. What was UP with that, anyway? Why is Cal so . . . bossy?

J

To: Jane Harris <jane@wondercat.com>
Fr: Holly Caputo <holly.caputo@thenyjournal.com>
Re: What is up with this?

Mark says it's because Cal has an enormous you know what.

Holly

To: Holly Caputo <holly.caputo@thenyjournal.com>
Fr: Jane Harris <jane@wondercat.com>
Re: What is up with this?

Head?

J

✉

To: Jane Harris <jane@wondercat.com>
Fr: Holly Caputo <holly.caputo@thenyjournal.com>
Re: What is up with this?

No, you idiot. You KNOW what I mean.

Holly

✉

To: Holly Caputo <holly.caputo@thenyjournal.com>
Fr: Jane Harris <jane@wondercat.com>
Re: What is up with this?

Wait. WHAT??? SHUT UP!!!!!!!!!!!

J

✉

To: Jane Harris <jane@wondercat.com>
Fr: Holly Caputo <holly.caputo@thenyjournal.com>
Re: What is up with this?

Mark swears it's true. He says Cal has always been supremely self-confident because of the enormity of his you know what. Well, at least up until that model broke his heart and all.

Holly

✉

To: Holly Caputo <holly.caputo@thenyjournal.com>
Fr: Jane Harris <jane@wondercat.com>
Re: What is up with this?

You are making that up. About his you know what, I mean.

J

✉

To: Jane Harris <jane@wondercat.com>
Fr: Holly Caputo <holly.caputo@thenyjournal.com>
Re: What is up with this?

Um. Have YOU seen him sit with his legs crossed?

Holly

✉

To: Holly Caputo <holly.caputo@thenyjournal.com>
Fr: Jane Harris <jane@wondercat.com>
Re: What is up with this?

That doesn't mean—Oh, my God, you ARE serious.

J

✉

To: Jane Harris <jane@wondercat.com>
Fr: Holly Caputo <holly.caputo@thenyjournal.com>
Re: What is up with this?

Apparently, despite his ex-wife's desertion on what was to be their first wedding anniversary, he has every reason in the world to feel quite pleased with himself.

Does THAT make you think a little more fondly of him?

Holly

✉

To: Holly Caputo <holly.caputo@thenyjournal.com>
Fr: Jane Harris <jane@wondercat.com>
Re: What is up with this?

NO!!! Size doesn't matter, and you know it.

Well, not that much.

She really left him on their first anniversary?

J

✉

To: Jane Harris <jane@wondercat.com>
Fr: Holly Caputo <holly.caputo@thenyjournal.com>
Re: What is up with this?

He came home from work, preparing to change clothes and take her out for an evening of celebration, and found a note.

She'd had movers in while he was at the office. They took everything. Except the cat.

Holly

✉

To: Holly Caputo <holly.caputo@thenyjournal.com>
Fr: Jane Harris <jane@wondercat.com>
Re: What is up with this?

They had a CAT????

J

✉

To: Jane Harris <jane@wondercat.com>
Fr: Holly Caputo <holly.caputo@thenyjournal.com>
Re: What is up with this?

It was her cat. She left it with Cal because her new boyfriend was allergic. Cal took care of it for almost a year, hoping Valerie would change her mind and come back. But she didn't. So Cal got himself assigned to Iraq.

Holly

✉

To: Holly Caputo <holly.caputo@thenyjournal.com>
Fr: Jane Harris <jane@wondercat.com>
Re: What is up with this?

What happened to the CAT?????

J

✉

To: Jane Harris <jane@wondercat.com>
Fr: Holly Caputo <holly.caputo@thenyjournal.com>
Re: What is up with this?

Oh. The cat died right before he decided to leave. Of cancer. Mark says he isn't sure which left Cal more brokenhearted—his wife leaving him, or the cat dying.

Holly

✉

To: Holly Caputo <holly.caputo@thenyjournal.com>
Fr: Jane Harris <jane@wondercat.com>
Re: What is up with this?

You are such a liar. You made that whole thing up about the cat dying. What really happened to it?

J

✉

To: Jane Harris <jane@wondercat.com>
Fr: Holly Caputo <holly.caputo@thenyjournal.com>
Re: What is up with this?

He gave it to Tim Grabowski in IT.

Still. The cat COULD be dead now, for all I know. Poor, poor Cal.

Holly

To: Holly Caputo <holly.caputo@thenyjournal.com>
Fr: Jane Harris <jane@wondercat.com>
Re: What is up with this?

You are so pathetic.

And I wouldn't feel too sorry for Cal Langdon if I were you. He's doing just fine for himself.

Promise you won't let Mark drive through the mountains. He will plunge us to our deaths.

J

To: Jane Harris <jane@wondercat.com>
Fr: Holly Caputo <holly.caputo@thenyjournal.com>
Re: What is up with this?

Um. Yeah. Maybe I'll drive after lunch. Or we can get Cal "Large Appendage" Langdon to do it.

Holly

To: Holly Caputo <holly.caputo@thenyjournal.com>
Fr: Jane Harris <jane@wondercat.com>
Re: What is up with this?

SHUT UP!!!!!!!!!!!!!!! You trust him to drive????

J

To: Jane Harris <jane@wondercat.com>
Fr: Holly Caputo <holly.caputo@thenyjournal.com>
Re: What is up with this?

Yes, of course! Unlike some people, he's actually used to driving in a foreign country.

What is your problem with him, anyway? He was perfectly nice during dinner last night, didn't you think? And he's been nothing but charming all morning. So what gives?

Holly

To: Holly Caputo <holly.caputo@thenyjournal.com>
Fr: Jane Harris <jane@wondercat.com>
Re: What is up with this?

Nothing. Stop e-ing me, they totally know we're talking about them.

Thank God they don't know WHAT we're talking about, though.

Ew.

J

✉

To: Mark Levine <mark.levine@thenyjournal.com>
Fr: Ruth Levine <r.levine@levinedentalgroup.com >
Re: Hello!

Is that any way to speak to your mother, I would like to know? I KNOW you think you're in love with Holly.

And I will admit she is a very nice girl.

But I don't think she's the RIGHT girl for you, Mark. You two come from two different worlds. Don't get me wrong, I completely appreciate the Italian heritage. They brought so many important things to the world, such as pasta and that nice Mario Batali from the Food Channel.

But what kind of future do you and Holly have together? What religion would you raise your children? Are you going to have a Christmas tree? You know the DiMarcos down the street have an entire holy manger scene in their front yard every year, made from cut-out pieces of plywood. Is that what you want, Mark? The baby Jesus in your front yard? Are you trying to kill me?

I'm just saying, I'm sure Susie Schramm has grown into a very interesting, vibrant girl. Why don't you see her, just for lunch? What could one lunch hurt? You have a little lunch, catch up on old times . . . who knows where it could lead?

Call me, Markie. I'm worried about you. Really.

Mom

To: Holly Caputo <holly.caputo@thenyjournal.com>
Fr: Darrin Caputo <darrin.caputo@caputographics.com>
Re: Hello, it is your mother

I am using your brother's email to write this to you. Your father says I should not, that you are an adult and I should let you lead your own life, like your brothers.

But all of your brothers found nice Italian girls—except for Frankie with that stripper. But even she is a good Christian, when she is not taking her clothes off for money.

Even Darrin, even HE found a nice Italian boy. Bobby came over for dinner last night and finished up ALL my chicken parmigiani. Such a good appetite.

I don't understand why you cannot do the same as your brothers. What is so wrong with finding a nice Italian boy to settle down with? Even a Polish boy would be all right, if he were Catholic. Why do you have to be with this Mark? He is a very nice boy, but he is not Catholic. What does he know about anything?

I am asking you to think about what you are doing with your life. People are starting to think things about you and this Mark. I saw Jane Harris's mother in the grocery store, and she was talking like you and Mark are getting married. If you are not careful, other people will begin to think the same, and eventually word will spread to Father Roberto, and then how will I be able to hold my head up at Mass on Sunday?

Think about your life, Holly. Do the right thing.

Mom

✉

To: Cal Langdon <cal.langdon@thenyjournal.com>
Fr: Graziella Fratiani <grazielle@galleriefratiani.co.it>
Re: Yesterday

It was so lovely to be seeing you yesterday afternoon. You are a twenty-first-century man, not like these Italian boys I constantly meet. You know, still living with Mama, and expect all women to cook and clean for them. It's nice to be with a man who washes his own socks.

Did I tell you, I'm between shows at the moment, so I can take a little time off from the gallery. Might I to be joining you at your little villa later in the week? I think I can—"rough it"? Let me know.

Grazi

✉

To: Jane Harris <jane@wondercat.com>
Fr: Julio Chasez <julio@streetsmart.com>
Re: The Dude

Hey, Ms. Harris. I got your messages. Just wanted to let you know your cat is fine. Really.

And no, I haven't had to use the oven mitts yet. And yeah, he ate all his salmon pate. And the Tender Vittles. And the Science Diet. And the Fancy Feast. And the Sheba. And he tried to gnaw through a box of Girl Scout cookies you left on the counter, but I took it away before he could.

Also, he chewed a hole through your sofa. But I guess you knew that. And he took a pretty big chunk out of my thumb when I caught him eating a tube of your toothpaste and tried to take it away. But the doctor says I'll be fine. I guess cats have cleaner spit than humans or dogs or something.

Hope you're having a nice trip.

Julio

✉

To: Julio Chasez <julio@streetsmart.com>
Fr: Jane Harris <jane@wondercat.com>
Re: The Dude

Oh, my God, I'm so sorry about your thumb! PLEASE save your doctor's bills so I can reimburse you when I get back!

You are the BEST!!! I cannot thank you enough for taking such good care of him!

Yes, I know about the sofa. It's okay, really.

THANK YOU!!!! I'll see you in a week!

Love,
Jane

Travel Diary of

~~Holly Caputo and Mark Levine~~

Jane Harris

It's actually kind of hard to write this with the suitcase wedged onto the seat between me and Holly, but it's better than trying to make conversation, because everyone seems to be in a bad mood since we all checked our Blackberries after lunch. Well, *except* for me. Since Julio says The Dude is fine!

I'll have to make sure I reimburse Julio for his medical expenses, of course. But just knowing that Dude was in a good-enough mood to bite him must mean he's not missing me too much.

I don't know what's eating everybody else in this car. . . .

Well, I sort of do. It turns out Mark, who was supposed to be the one in charge of bringing CDs to listen to in the car, forgot. So the only thing we have to listen to is Italian radio (Hello. You do not know what disturbing is until you've heard Italian rap) or the Queen CD Cal happened to have in his backpack.

Yes. Queen.

I have now heard "Fat-Bottomed Girls" twelve times. Holly joked that it's going to be her and Mark's wedding theme song.

Thank God Mark pulled over when we got to the foot of the mountains and let Cal take over. You never saw such narrow, twisty roads in your life. I thought I was going to heave. Thank God I had Dramamine with me.

Plus, every time we made a turn, Holly's suitcase fell on me. Well, not really fell, since Holly was holding onto it, but it LEANED HEAVILY on me. By the time we pulled over for lunch, I was chafed from the stupid thing rubbing against my shoulder, and in a pretty bad mood myself . . . especially when I saw the restaurant Cal had pulled up in front of.

I mean, God forbid he should choose a place in an actual TOWN. Oh, no, not Mr. I've Backpacked Around the World With Nothing But a Razor and My Queen CD (and some condoms, I hope, if he makes a habit of porking supermodels at every stop with his ABNORMALLY LARGE APPENDAGE—if what Holly says is really true, which I doubt. She's probably only saying it to make me like him. Well, it's NOT going to work).

Anyway, Modelizer has to pick this ridiculous looking Ho-Jo type place with these plate-glass windows in the middle of nowhere, perched on a CLIFF, practically.

Only when we walked in—me trying to rub some life back into my shoulder—we saw that there were like a million people there, looking out the plate glass windows at this beautiful waterfall rushing right past the dining room.

And the waiter was totally nice even though we didn't have a reservation, and sat us at a really lovely table right by the waterfall window. And instead of giving us menus, he just told us (in Italian, of course) what they were serving, which Holly and Cal said Si to, even though I didn't understand a word.

And then the next thing I knew, a carafe of bianco frizzante appeared as if from nowhere!

And then the waiter brought a giant bowl of deliciously cheesy pasta, which he spooned out onto each of our plates, and which seemed to melt as soon as it reached my tongue.

And then he brought a HUGE fish, swimming in butter, for the table to share, and a giant bowl of crisp, fresh, vinegary salad, and all this bread, and the whole thing only cost—get this: twenty-eight euros.

That is five Roman Diet Cokes right there.

The real question is, of course:

Why aren't more women in Italy fat? That's what I want to know. Because the women in that restaurant looked totally normal weight.

Mark said it's because they aren't loading up on empty calories the way Americans do. You know, soda and fries and stuff like that.

And maybe so.

But a few more meals like that one, and I guarantee I won't be fitting into my one-piece. Which would suck, because Holly says the villa's got a kick-ass pool.

So then after lunch we walked around the parking lot a little to get our circulation back and take in the view, which was stunning. And I was standing there enjoying the sun on my face and listening to the rushing water when Cal—I mean, Large Appendage—came up to me, and was all, "About what you said last night . . ."

I assumed he meant what I'd said about Holly and Mark being so perfect for each other, and that he was going to apologize for saying otherwise—especially since they were over by the car bickering about how it was Holly's turn to drive and Mark was saying how he was more comfortable with stick than she was and it was a totally cute argument that was making me long for my own soul mate with whom to bicker.

Only instead, he went, "Graziella Fratiani happens to own one of the most popular art galleries in Rome, and is both an enterprising businesswoman and a good friend. She is hardly a—what did you call her? Oh, yes. A skank."

CAN YOU BELIEVE THAT???? I was totally shocked. I just stood there looking up at him (why does he have to be so tall, anyway? And why are tall men always so . . . hot?) totally unable to think of anything pithy or witty to say. As usual.

And in a way he DID have a right to be mad. I mean, I don't know Graziwhosits Fratiwhatever. Maybe she's not a skank at all. Maybe she's this totally kindhearted and generous woman who gives huge amounts of money to cancer research and volunteers at the local orphanage. . . .

Yeah, right. No one in her thirties has thighs that thin without the help of the medical community.

And no one who's had that much work done is hanging out with orphans.

Plus, no one who stops by guys' hotel rooms for an afternoon quickie isn't a skank.

And even though Holly had asked me to try to get along with Large Appendage, just for the trip, and is making him out to be this big tragic hero, on account of his ex leaving him for someone richer (I bet she regrets it now, if she saw that episode of Charlie Rose my mom was talking about), I looked up at him and before I could stop myself, was all, "Wow, really, one of the most popular art galleries in Rome?"

Cal: "Yes."

Me: "And she didn't, like, inherit it from her dad or get it in a divorce settlement from an ex-husband?"

Cal: (looking kind of chagrined) "Well. Yes. I mean, her grandfather started the business, but—"

Me: "I see. Well, it might interest you to know that there are women who've actually started their own businesses from scratch without any help from their fathers, and who've managed to land seven-figure development deals with the Cartoon Network due to their own hard work and perseverance."

Which is all true. I mean, I don't actually GET the seven figures unless the Cartoon Network picks up Wondercat as an animated series.

But he doesn't have to know that.

Besides, even without those seven figures, I'm doing fine. Just as well as Graziwhosits. Probably.

And even if I'm not, the money is MINE. I earned it from

MY hard work, not my grandpa's. And so what if I live in a studio apartment? He doesn't have to know that. What do I need a lot of space for anyway? It's just me and The Dude, after all.

He didn't even have the grace to look embarrassed, though. He was just all, "Regardless. You don't have the right to call her a skank."

So then I looked him dead in the eye—well, as close as I could, anyway, from my twelve-inch height disadvantage—and said, "Well, you don't have the right to say Mark and Holly shouldn't get married."

"Actually," he said. "I do."

AND THEN HE STALKED AWAY!!! Before I could get another word in! Before I could stalk away!

Which actually is probably a good thing because when I tried to stalk away in the other direction, my Steve Madden heel slipped in the gravel and I nearly fell down and I would have fallen if I hadn't grabbed hold of the fender of a Smart Car parked nearby.

He didn't see, though.

Anyway, this pretty much settles it:

Cal Langdon = Spawn of Satan.

But at least now I know where we stand. And I will be able to begin taking evasive action. Obviously, from this moment on, I can never

a) Leave Cal and Mark alone in a room together
b) Leave Cal and Holly alone in a room together
c) Leave Cal alone anywhere

I will have to watch him like a hawk. It would be SO like him to drop unsubtle little hints about phenylethylamine and the dissolution of his marriage here and there in order to shake Mark's conviction to go through with his.

And Holly, as I know only too well, is already wondering if she's doing the right thing. I CANNOT let that man destroy the one actual solid romantic relationship left in the universe . . . well, except for my mom and dad's, but ew, don't want to think about that right now.

The only thing is, he obviously thinks he knows what's best . . . not just for Mark, but for everybody. I mean, that bossy way he chose where we were going to have lunch, and then, once we were there, what we were going to have.

And yeah, it was delicious.

But still.

I have to find a way to let him know he is NOT in charge here—WITHOUT letting Holly suspect anything's wrong. Because Holly's worried enough about everything. If she finds out the best man doesn't even think this wedding is a good idea, it's all over.

I've got to prove to this guy that I am not at ALL impressed with the size of his member. His having a huge you know what does absolutely NOTHING to intimidate ME.

And you know, I don't think his thing can really be all that big because it's not like he walks all bow-legged or whatever. Curt Shipley's was HUGE and you could see the sun shine between his inner thighs when he was coming toward you. . . .

Oooooh, I have an idea. If his email is the same as everyone else's who works at the Journal. . . .

✉

To: Cal Langdon <cal.langdon@thenyjournal.com>
Fr: Jane Harris <jane@wondercat.com>
Re: Holly and Mark

It's me. What you said back there in the parking lot—about how you're going to do whatever it takes to make sure Mark doesn't make the biggest mistake of his life—that's pretty presumptuous of you, don't you think?

J

✉

To: Jane Harris <jane@wondercat.com>
Fr: Cal Langdon <cal.langdon@thenyjournal.com>
Re: Holly and Mark

Ms. Harris. What a surprise. You're emailing me.

From the backseat.

✉

To: Cal Langdon <cal.langdon@thenyjournal.com>
Fr: Jane Harris <jane@wondercat.com>
Re: Holly and Mark

Oh, please. Like you and Mark weren't doing the same in the cab yesterday.

I realize you and Mark are friends—good friends, since childhood, just like Holly and I are.

But you haven't seen him in a long time. How do you even know what's good for him anymore? And you certainly don't know

Holly well enough to make any kind of judgment about her. How can you presume that you know what's best for either of them when the truth is, you hardly know them at all?

J

✉

To: Jane Harris <jane@wondercat.com>
Fr: Cal Langdon <cal.langdon@thenyjournal.com>
Re: Holly and Mark

You are certainly entitled to your opinion. Just as I am entitled to mine.

Cal

✉

To: Cal Langdon <cal.langdon@thenyjournal.com>
Fr: Jane Harris <jane@wondercat.com>
Re: Holly and Mark

You're not entitled to your opinion at ALL. Because it's WRONG. You have absolutely no factual basis for it. You can't know Mark is making "the biggest mistake of his life" by marrying Holly because you hardly know Holly. You're basing your opinion on your own personal biases against love and marriage. And that has nothing to do with Mark OR Holly. That was just your own stupidity.

J

To: Jane Harris <jane@wondercat.com>
Fr: Cal Langdon <cal.langdon@thenyjournal.com>
Re: Holly and Mark

Now who's stating an opinion for which she has no factual basis?

Cal

To: Cal Langdon <cal.langdon@thenyjournal.com>
Fr: Jane Harris <jane@wondercat.com>
Re: Holly and Mark

Um, hello, any MORON can tell you that marrying a model you've known for a month is stupid. I'm sorry, but it's true.

J

To: Jane Harris <jane@wondercat.com>
Fr: Cal Langdon <cal.langdon@thenyjournal.com>
Re: Holly and Mark

Has anyone ever told you, Ms. Harris, that your tactlessness is astounding?

Cal

✉

To: Cal Langdon <cal.langdon@thenyjournal.com>
Fr: Jane Harris <jane@wondercat.com>
Re: Holly and Mark

ME??? I'm not the tactless one, Mr. There's No Such Thing as Romantic Love. Holly and Mark are in their thirties, not their twenties, and they've lived together for over two years. They are NOT making the same mistake you did. They are consenting adults—neither working in the modeling industry—who are in love. End of story.

J

✉

To: Jane Harris <jane@wondercat.com>
Fr: Cal Langdon <cal.langdon@thenyjournal.com>
Re: Holly and Mark

Perhaps we should discuss this face-to-face. My persuasive powers are at a disadvantage on handheld portable devices.

Cal

✉

To: Cal Langdon <cal.langdon@thenyjournal.com>
Fr: Jane Harris <jane@wondercat.com>
Re: Holly and Mark

No way! I don't want Holly getting wind of the fact that you aren't one hundred percent behind this wedding thing. She's freaking out enough about her family not being behind the idea. If she finds out the best man's against it too, she'll die.

J

To: Jane Harris <jane@wondercat.com>
Fr: Cal Langdon <cal.langdon@thenyjournal.com>
Re: Holly and Mark

I meant sometime when Holly and Mark were not with us.

Cal

To: Cal Langdon <cal.langdon@thenyjournal.com>
Fr: Jane Harris <jane@wondercat.com>
Re: Holly and Mark

Well, I don't see when that's going to happen.

J

To: Jane Harris <jane@wondercat.com>
Fr: Cal Langdon <cal.langdon@thenyjournal.com>
Re: Holly and Mark

You don't anticipate that, during the next seven days we will be spending together, there will be a time when we will be alone together?

Cal

✉

To: Cal Langdon <cal.langdon@thenyjournal.com>
Fr: Jane Harris <jane@wondercat.com>
Re: Holly and Mark

God, I hope not. I mean, no, I don't. Let's just keep this conversation on paper. Or email. Or whatever. I don't want Holly getting wind of it. I—

AAAAAAAAAAAAAAH!

Travel Diary of

~~Holly Caputo and Mark Levine~~

Jane Harris

Well, THAT was totally humiliating. Holly's cell phone went off right when I was about to rewrite that last message to Cal, and I accidentally pushed Send.

Then Holly asked me to answer her cell phone, since she was concentrating on driving, and her purse was in the backseat anyway with me and Mark (Cal, of course, got the front seat, since he's so TALL) and the phone was ringing.

And so I answered it, and this weird old lady was all, "Hellooo? Hellooo-ooo?" and I was all, "Holly Caputo's line," and the old lady was like, "Vat? Vat?" with this German accent, and I was like, "Holly, there's a German lady on the line."

And Holly went, "Oh, that's Frau Schumacher, my uncle's housekeeper. She's meeting us at the exit to take us to the house since I haven't been there since I was little and I don't remember the way, and she says it's too hard to explain. Tell her we're on our way."

So I went, "Oh. OK. Hello, Frau Schumacher?"

And Frau Schumacher was all, "Helloooo, Holly?"

"No, this is Holly's friend, Jane," I said. "Holly can't talk now because she's driving. But she said to tell you we're on our way."

"Vere are you?" Frau Schumacher wanted to know.

So, to be helpful, I looked out the car window, and saw one of those green-and-white signs that let you know the name of the next city that's coming up.

"We're just outside Carabinieri," I said.

Which made Cal start laughing VERY VERY hard. Even though to my knowledge, I hadn't said anything funny.

"Vat?" Frau Schumacher sounded confused. But it was hard to tell with all the LAUGHING in the car. "Vere are you?"

"We just passed Carabinieri," I said into the phone. Now Holly was laughing, too. I leaned forward and swatted her, while Mark asked, confusedly, "What's so funny?"

"Jane," Holly choked, between chortles. "Carabinieri isn't the name of a town. It means police. We drove by a police station just then."

Really, I don't see what's so funny about that. I mean, how am I supposed to know what carabinieri means? I've only just gotten down si—yes—and grazie—thank you. I'm still trying to keep buon giorno—good day—and buona sera—good night—straight . . . not to mention Non ho votato per lui (I didn't vote for him) in the event of any rampant anti-Americanism that might rear its ugly head.

"Vere are the carabinieri?" Frau Shumacher wanted to know, sounding panicky. "Zey are following you?"

"No, no," I said, into the phone. "Sorry. No, I made a mistake."

"Zey zink zey own the roads, the carabinieri!" Frau Schumacher shouted. "In Germany, the polizia, zey know zeir place!"

"No, no carabinieri," I said. "There isn't any carabinieri . . . I made a mistake . . ."

"Give me that." Suddenly, the Modelizer was leaning over, trying to snatch the phone from me.

"I've GOT it," I said, outraged, and yanking the phone out of his reach.

"You guys," Holly yelled, jerking the wheel.

"I told you you don't know how to drive a stick," Mark said, as Holly's suitcase landed on him.

Then, because of the knowing look Cal threw me—as if, just because Mark was criticizing Holly's driving, they weren't destined for each other—I tossed the phone at him.

"Here, you big baby," I said—probably sounding like a baby myself. But I don't care.

Cal picked up the phone and began talking to Holly's uncle's housekeeper in smooth, fluent German. While the two of them were yakking away, I poked Holly in the shoulder and asked, "Why does your uncle have a German housekeeper in Italy, anyway?"

"How should I know?" We were almost out of the mountains now, but Holly was still paying rapt attention to the road. "She's just lived in the cottage next door forever, so Uncle Matteo made her his housekeeper."

This was a very unsatisfactory explanation.

About as unsatisfying as that email conversation with Cal. Just who does he think he is, anyway, presuming to tell me MY friend isn't worthy of his? And what did he mean by wanting to talk about this face-to-face? Is he high? I am never letting myself be alone in the same room with him. He might try to work his Large Appendage magic on me! Just like Curt Shipley used to! Girls—and, I know now, boys too—were powerless when Curt Shipley had them in his sights. It could be the same with Cal Langdon! Men who are supremely confident in the size of their own you know what do seem to exude a certain something. . . .

Although, really, he's so pompous, I can't actually see myself falling for him, Large Appendage magic or not.

He is kind of hot, though, the way his hair sometimes falls over his eye . . .

If only he'd shut up about stupid Saudi Arabia once in a while.

AAAAAAAAAOOOOOOOOOOEEEEEEEEEEOOOOOOOOO

Sorry. Suddenly we went over this peak, and my eyes were DAZZLED by what I was seeing below us:

Deep green valleys, over which tiny little cities are perched (the ancient fortified cities from the guidebook) clustered together within stone walls on brightly sunlit hillsides. . . .

Crumbling castles presiding over a patchwork of farmyards below them . . .

Sun-baked houses with orange tiled rooftops, with chickens in the yard pecking beneath brightly colored laundry hanging from lines outside shuttered windows. . . .

Oh, my God. I think we're <u>here</u>! Le Marche!

And that Customs guy was wrong. It's BEAUTIFUL.

✉

To: Graziella Fratiani <grazielle@galleriefratiani.co.it>
Fr: Cal Langdon <cal.langdon@thenyjournal.com>
Re: Yesterday

If you really meant it when you said you'd come, you'd be entirely welcome . . . by me, at least. I can use an ally. My ego has taken about enough bruising as it can during this trip. The maid of honor is, to coin a phrase, a bitch.

Looking forward to seeing you.

Cal

✉

To: Cal Langdon <cal.langdon@thenyjournal.com>
Fr: Ruth Levine <r.levine@levinedentalgroup.com>
Re: Hello!

Cal, it's me, Mark's mom! How are you? I understand you're with Mark right now on his little European jaunt. I hear it's very nice in Italy this time of year. I hope you're getting plenty of rest and relaxation—you certainly deserve it after all that hard work you put in on your book. I saw it the other day at the Barnes and Noble. It was in the number-six spot for the bestsellers. Congratulations! That is fantastic.

Of course, Mark's father and I always knew you were destined for great things. It was pretty obvious from the day we met you, when you and little Markie took apart our vacuum cleaner's motor on the kitchen floor to see how it worked. It still ran perfectly well after you put it back together, despite those leftover pieces.

Well, I'm sure you're wondering why I'm writing to you after all these years, so I'll get to the point:

I'm worried about Mark. I'm sure this Holly is a very nice girl.

But I'm not so sure she's right for our Mark. She's the ARTISTIC type, for one thing. I know she has a very good job with the paper Mark sometimes writes that little column for. But let's face it: she doesn't exactly earn the kind of money I know some of Mark's past girlfriends are making now—Susie Schramm, for instance. You remember Susie, don't you, Cal? She's a lawyer now, with a very high-powered firm. I think Susie's SO MUCH more of Mark's type than this Holly girl.

And I DON'T mean because Holly's not Jewish. You know I NEVER judge people by their religion. After all, your family was—what was it again? Protestant?—and it never bothered me a bit! We quite enjoyed your mother's Christmas Eve cocktail party every year.

It's just that Mark has always been such a romantic. I'm sure deep down he thinks things like religious background don't matter. But you were always much more practical, Cal—not to mention, you've been around the world, and seen much more than Mark has—so I know you understand.

Plus, having been through a divorce yourself, I'm sure you wish someone had taken you aside in a brotherly manner and warned you not to rush into anything with that Valerie person. She was no good for you, anyone could see that. I knew it the minute I met her. What was she thinking, wearing that off-the-shoulder thing at your wedding? I realize it was couture and that Oscar de la Renta designed it just for her. Still, it hardly fit in at the country club here, now, did it?

And what about the children? Mark and Holly's, I mean, if, God forbid, they should have them? How are they going to raise the children? I don't want my grandchildren having no sense of identity because they've been raised in TWO religions. That's worse than being raised with none!

Anyway, I'm just hoping that since you're with Mark right now, you could try to talk some sense into him. He's always respected you, and I just know if you told him not to rush into anything—to give Susie Schramm a call when he gets home—he'd listen. She has completely outgrown that underbite, you know. It's a miracle what orthodontia can do.

Thank you, Cal. And please give my love to your parents. Except for an annual Christmas newsletter from your mom, I haven't heard much from them since they split up. But Joan's hacienda in Tucson looks lovely—at least, judging from her newsletter. And I hope Hank is enjoying himself in Mexico City, and that that little misunderstanding at the track back in Dayton got cleared up.

Affectionately,
Ruth Levine

PDA of Cal Langdon

Well . . . this is definitely going to be an interesting trip.

The bride-to-be's uncle appears to employ a German half-wit as a housekeeper, who went on ad nauseum about how things are so different now in Le Marche than they were right after the war (no need to ask which one . . . around here, there was only one war) and that Americans are welcome now with open arms, in spite of what they did to Ancona. No mention, of course, about her own country of origin's having started that war.

The groom's mother has another girl in mind for her daughter-in-law.

And the maid of honor appears to hate my guts.

This should be a lot of fun.

Sarcasm aside, Le Marche is an extraordinarily beautiful area of the world, filled with Renaissance towns still virtually untouched by American influence . . . no McDonalds, no twenty-four-hour convenience marts, no superstores. No wonder so many Italians flock here every summer. The waterfront resorts are reportedly packed from July though August. And there are even supposed to be some beaches down by Portoforno and Osimo that rival the Cote d'Azur for natural beauty.

Still, stunning vistas and Renaissance churches aside, Le Marche is not exactly where I'd choose to get married. If I were to make the mistake of getting married again. Which, of course, I never will.

And I feel a sense of responsibility toward Mark to keep him from making the same mistake as well. Not because, despite what Jane Harris might think, that I believe Holly is another Valerie. And not even because his mother asked me to. But because the guy has never lived! He's been in school for what, twenty years? And then he went straight from that to practicing full time. . . . the guy's done NOTHING. Never backpacked in Nepal. Never trekked the Amazon. Never swallowed the worm at the bottom of a tequila bottle in Belize. Adventure, to Mark, is a *Star Trek* convention.

And he thinks he's ready to get *married*? He's ready for a therapist's couch, is what he's ready for.

Holly's a great girl—I have no doubts about that. But marriage? No. Not now. The guy needs to have a life first. Then, if he and Holly were meant to be, they can attach the old ball and chain.

Obviously, I'm going to have to be subtle about this. Ms. Harris will undoubtedly be watching for any signs of mutiny. Which isn't necessarily a bad thing. She looks kind of cute with her chin thrust out in righteous indignation.

I can't believe I just wrote that. First fetching. Now cute. I think I need out of this car. And a drink.

She does have the worst problems with her footwear of any woman I have ever met. First the stiletto between the cobblestones last night, and today, the heel twisting in the gravel. I don't know how she manages to remain upright.

And she has this unnerving habit of staring at my crotch. Yes, she's short, but certainly not so much that this is where her eye level might naturally rest.

Ah, we've reached the exit where Frau Schumacher is going to meet us. She says she drives a silver Mercedes. Her grasp of English seems to have been derived from watching too many subtitled episodes of *Murder She Wrote.*

This should be an exceedingly entertaining week.

Travel Diary of

~~Holly Caputo and Mark Levine~~

Jane Harris

Oh my God, we're HERE. Villa Beccacia!

And it's GORGEOUS.

I will admit, at first I had my doubts. That Frau Schumacher—I think she might actually be as old as some of those castles we zoomed by. And, um, she's just SLIGHTLY in love with Large Appendage. It's sickening! Just because he speaks German! We got out of the car to meet her on the shoulder of the exit, and she was all, "Vich vun is Cal?" and when he raised his hand, you could practically see her melt onto the asphalt.

And she's got to be a hundred if she's a day! Who knew Large Appendage's magic works on centenarians?

The next thing I knew, the two of them were totally chattering away in German, leaving the rest of us out of the conversation.

Fortunately she had her great-grandson with her, Peter, who's fourteen and speaks English . . . well, pretty well anyway. Don't ask me why Peter is living with great-granny in Italy and not attending school, either here or his native Germany. Possibly she's home-schooling him? He does look a bit like he'd get the you know what knocked out of him in an American high school. I mean, he's a little on the chubby side and very soft-spoken, with an X-Men T-shirt under his jean jacket.

In any case, I didn't think it would be polite to ask. About why he wasn't in school, I mean.

Anyway, Peter asked us non-German speakers how the drive was, and if we were hungry, and said he and "Grand-muzzer" had stocked the fridge at the villa, so we should be all right until the "shops" opened again tomorrow, they're all being closed today on account of it's Sunday.

Mark asked him about liquor—you can tell sitting shotgun while Holly drove had worn away his last good nerve—and Peter said, looking confused, "Vell, I zink zere are many bottles in the house now."

Mark looked visibly relieved.

Then Frau Schumacher said for us all to get back in the car and follow her. So we did. And we were driving along, me not being able to help notice that there was a big wall of clouds climbing over the nearby, castle-crested hill, and realizing I probably wasn't going to be able to squeeze in an evening swim, when all of a sudden Holly went, "Look! The Adriatic!"

And there it was, this beautiful slice of sapphire blue, right there! There was no one on the beach, because being the middle of September, it's off season, of course . . . even though it's still in the 80s, temperature-wise (or the twenties, if you're going Celsius, like the Italians).

But somebody had still put out all of these white-and-yellow-striped lounge chairs, just in case.

And we drove through this adorable little seaside town, Porto Recanati, filled with the sweetest shops—a gelateria, and an Italian Benetton—and something called the Crazy Bar and Sexy Tattoo Shop, which I'm not sure really qualifies as sweet—and then hung a left onto a road I'm not even sure, technically, really IS a road. I mean, it's DIRT, and all of this dust was flying as we went down it, so that we had to close the windows.

Still, it was tree-lined, and through the spaces between the trees, we caught glimpses of the Centro Ippico—a horse-riding center down the road from Villa Beccacia . . . although not far ENOUGH down the road, if you ask me, since even as I write this I can hear neighing.

And there's a slightly horsy odor in the air when the wind shifts.

But whatever. We followed Frau Schumacher to this electric wooden gate, and waited while she hit a button and it slid slowly open. . . .

And then we saw it. Villa Beccacia, Holly's uncle's house, which has been around for a really long time . . . hundreds of years, since it was built in the 1600s!

Of course, it's been remodeled since then.

But not so you'd notice from the outside. As we drove down the long driveway, past fruit trees around which bees were humming and butterflies were flitting, past a deep green pond, its surface covered with lily pads, past rolling, grassy hills, the stone house, with vines creeping up all over it, came into view.

And it was just the way I'd pictured it!

Well, okay, there weren't any turrets. But really, it's LIKE a castle. I mean, it's really old, and inside, there are these darkly beamed and vaulted ceilings. And there are tapestries hanging on the walls, and in the old-fashioned kitchen, there's a brick oven.

You can't USE it . . . they put in a modern stove to cook on. But the brick oven is still THERE.

The casement windows are sunk into these deep walls with sills you can sit on, and open out like shutters. There are no screens, because if there were, you wouldn't be able to open the windows.

And out back, the pool is just steps away from the covered stone patio—the terrazza, according to Peter—with the ancient built-in grill/fireplace. This is apparently where Zio Matteo spends most of his time when he's home, since there was wax all over the wrought-iron table from the many candles that had dripped onto it while he was enjoying what Frau Schumacher intimated was one of his many enormous meals (from the photos I've seen scattered around the house, Zio

Matteo definitely enjoys his food). There was lots of firewood in the pile for the future, and a few sad-looking fly-strips hanging from the rafters.

The pool is gorgeous, 50 by 20 feet at least, with blue-and-white-striped lounge chairs all around, and palm trees at each end, the fronds swaying gently in the breeze (which is picking up, thanks to the approaching rain clouds). I am going to be so glued to the side of that pool as soon as the weather clears up.

Oh, and the whole wedding thing is taken care of.

Holly broke the news to Frau Schumacher as we were following the old lady around the house, listening to her rattle on in broken English about how there were plenty of clean towels but she'd just finished washing them and they were still drying on the line over at her cottage farther down the driveway.

"You vill need lots of tovels," Frau Schumacher was saying, "for the svimming and the beach."

"Well," Holly said, glancing sweetly at Mark. "We aren't really here for the watersports, Frau Schumacher. Mark and I plan on getting married this week, over in Castelfidardo."

Frau Schumacher reacted the way a NORMAL—read, not Cal Langdon—person would react upon finding out a young and attractive couple like Mark and Holly were getting married: She clapped her hands for glee and wanted to know all the details, like what Holly would be wearing and did her uncle know and when were her parents coming.

To which Holly replied, her face getting red, "Well, I didn't tell Zio Matteo or my parents. We're eloping, actually—"

Which threw Frau Schumacher into a tizzy of excitement—once Cal translated, since neither Peter nor she was familiar with the word elope. She exclaimed, in her broken English, that she knew the mayor of Castelfidardo very well, and that if any problems developed, she was to be consulted immediately.

Where was the wedding breakfast going to be? What? We hadn't planned for a wedding breakfast? Well, there had to be a wedding breakfast. She would supply it—

Then Frau Schumacher's gaze fell on Cal (it never actually strays away from him long, I've noticed) and she glanced from him to me quickly and asked, no longer smiling, "And you two? You are having vedding, too?"

Both Cal and I hastened to assure the housekeeper that we were not—Cal a little more hastily than I think was actually polite, to tell you the truth. I mean, he may not know it, but he'd be LUCKY to be married to a girl like me. At least I can support myself without Daddy's—or some investment banker's—money, unlike SOME women he might know.

And I am at a completely normal body weight, and don't have to stick my finger down my throat to maintain it.

Plus, I have two television sets. How many does Cal have? Oh, that'd be none. I asked. Yeah, Cal doesn't "believe" in TV.

Right. You know what I don't believe in? People who don't believe in TV.

And then there's The Dude. Any man would be lucky to get to share a domicile with The Dude.

But whatever. His loss.

Not like I WANT to marry him. Or anybody. I mean, I have a development deal. What do I need a husband for?

Anyway, Frau Schumacher insisted on making us some snacks while Peter helped us take our bags upstairs. Mark picked up Holly's bag plus his own and Cal had his stupid backpack (Queen. That's the only CD he travels with. QUEEN. Although come to think of it, I sort of like Queen. But I'll never let HIM know that) so the only bag left was mine and when Peter went to pick it up he stiffened suddenly and said, "Vundercat?" in this astonished voice, staring at me.

Then Holly, halfway up the stairs, called down, laughingly,

"Yeah, Peter, didn't you know? Janie's the creator of Wondercat."

And Peter—to my everlasting gratification—cried, "You are Jane Harris, the artist of Vundercat? Vundercat is my favorite comic of all time! I have all of the Vundercat collection! I have Veb site dewoted to all things Vundercat!"

"Oh, do you?" I couldn't help stealing a look at Cal as he was following Holly and Mark up the stairs. Was it my imagination, or was he smiling a little ruefully? Yes, you BETTER feel full of rue, Mr. I Never Heard of Wondercat. Wondercat is INTERNATIONALLY RECOGNIZED. Oh, yes. Even strange, apparently home-schooled German boys in Italy have heard of Wondercat! I may not know what carabinieri means, buddy, but at least I can draw something that has INTERNATIONAL appeal.

"Well, while I'm here," I said, mostly to get Cal's goat, "I'll be happy to draw you some original Wondercats, Peter, for your Web site or whatever."

A look of total joy suffused Peter's round-cheeked face, and he raced up the stairs with my bag, chattering a mile a minute about his favorite Wondercat cartoons. I made sure to keep him talking too, so that Cal Langdon heard every word.

Villa Beccacia has seven bedrooms. Holly told Cal and I to pick whichever ones we liked best. Six of the bedrooms are huge, with ancient canopied beds with curtains around the sides, just like Scrooge's bed in A Christmas Carol, and walls lined with dark panels and bookshelves, on which sit copies of everything from books on bird-watching to Valley of the Dolls in Italian.

The seventh bedroom is tucked away beneath a sloping roof, its single dormer window facing the pool. It's clearly a boy's room, with dark blue bedspreads on its twin beds, and matching dark blue tiles in the adjoining bathroom. All of the paintings on the walls are of ships. The oldest one has the words A sua eccellenza il sig Cav Francesco Seratti engraved beneath it. Whatever that means.

I knew at once this was the room for me.

Peter was horrified. He said, "No, you don't vant this room. You vant the pretty pink room."

But I said, "Cal can have that one." (I know he heard me, too, because I heard a snort from the hallway.)

So Peter grudgingly put my bag down and went downstairs to see what his grandmother wanted, since she was bellowing for him (she has quite a set of lungs for such a tiny old lady).

And now I'm lying on one of the twin beds writing this, while everyone else is doing who knows what. All her life, Holly's talked about Villa Beccacia, the money pit her eccentric uncle bought with his first million doing . . . well, whatever it is Holly's uncle does. And now I'm finally IN it! And it feels as much like home as if Zio Matteo were MY uncle!

Oooh, Frau Schumacher is calling us. Authentic Italian (if German-made) snacks must be ready. Yum!

✉

To: Jane Harris <jane@wondercat.com>
Fr: Malcolm Weatherly <malcolmw@snowstyle.com>
Re: Ciao

Hey! Where are you? I haven't heard from you. Hope things are going good.

Listen, do you remember if I left my green ESPN hat at your place? Because I can't find it anywhere. I know I could just go buy a new one, but that was my lucky one. If you remember, could you let me know? And when you get back, send it to me, if you still have it?

Cool.

Rock out.

M

✉

To: Listserv <Wundercat@wundercatlives.com>
Fr: Peter Schumacher <webmaster@wundercatlives.com>
Re: JANE HARRIS

Listen up, kids! You are not believing what is happening! JANE HARRIS, creator of our beloved Wundercat, is here in Italy! Yes! IN THE HOUSE THAT IS NEXT DOOR TO THE ONE OF MY GRANDMOTHER!!! She is helping her friend to get the elopement in Castelfidardo!

And I have conversed with her! She says she will be drawing me some original sketches of our most favorite cat for this site! YES!!!!!

And JANE HARRIS is looking to be HOT! She has the dark brown hair (long, like we like it, boys!) and big brown eyes, and the very cute figure (sorry, girls!). She is looking very much like the beautiful vampire warrior Selene (played by the ravishing Kate Beckinsdale) in the finest film ever made of all time, *Underworld*!

And she has slain this mortal's heart!

I will be reporting more of the news of JANE HARRIS as it is happening!

Until then,

WUNDERCAT LIVES FOREVER!!!!

P. Schumacher
Webmaster, www.wundercatlives.com

Travel Diary of

~~Holly Caputo and Mark Levine~~

Jane Harris

Okay, I know the Italians have contributed a lot to our society, what with da Vinci and Mike Piazza, not to mention cannoli.

But seriously, why couldn't Holly and Mark have eloped to some country where they actually have electricity?

All right, all right, I KNOW Italy has electricity. In theory. In most areas. It just doesn't, apparently, extend to her uncle's house. When the stove is on, anyway.

Because the minute Mark turned the stove on to start boiling water for the pasta Frau Schumacher left us, all of the lights went out.

And when we called Frau Schumacher to ask her if her power was out, too, she was all, "No," and then when we explained what we'd been doing when the light went off, she cackled, "Oh, you cannot turn the owen on vile the lights are on as vell!"

Seriously. She was laughing like a crazy person at the idea of the stupid Americans trying to use a stove AND have lights on at the same time.

So then we asked her where the fuse box was, so we could turn the power back on (and I guess just eat antipasto for dinner) and she went, "Oh, yes. Vell, you go down the road to the gate—"

And Holly was all, "The ELECTRONIC gate? To the driveway?"

And Frau Schumacher was like, "Yes," as in, "What other gate would I be talking about, dorkus?" and then went on to say, "Go through the gate to the Wirgin Mary statue under the big tree—"

Seriously. THROUGH the gate. MILES from the house.

Well, okay, but like two hundred yards. TO THE VIRGIN MARY STATUE. Under the big tree.

"—zen open her back and you will find the fuses."

Yeah. That's how they turn the power back on when it goes out in Italy. They go DOWN the road, THROUGH the gate, UP TO the VIRGIN MARY statue, OPEN her back, and flick the switch.

Oh yeah. In the dark. And the pouring rain.

Since Holly thought she hadn't understood Frau Schumacher correctly, she handed the phone to Cal and made him ask again, in German.

Same answer.

So Cal said he'd go do it.

Which I have to say is the first sign of generosity—well, except for paying for dinner last night—from him so far. Especially since Frau Schumacher said she could send Peter.

But Cal insisted. He ran outside, and Holly and Mark and I sat in the dark making jokes about all the escaped Italian convicts that might be lurking outside, just waiting for someone to turn their stove on so that their lights would go out and they could rob them.

After a little while we heard the front door slam and Cal came back, dripping wet and cursing like a sailor.

But the lights weren't on.

"What happened?" Mark wanted to know.

Only Cal wouldn't say. He stumbled around in the semidarkness, found the bottle of Jack Daniel's Holly's uncle had in his liquor cabinet, poured himself a stiff one, and downed the whole thing in one gulp. Then he sat down—getting Zio Matteo's white couch all wet—and buried his head in his hands.

"Oh," Mark said suddenly, like he knew what was wrong. "Was it—?"

Cal just nodded, not looking up.

So Mark went, "Okay. Never mind. I'll go." And grabbed the crummy flashlight we'd found in Zio Matteo's pantry.

Of course I couldn't let him go after that. I mean, I totally had to see whatever it was that had so destroyed the Modelizer.

And all it turned out to be was a little snake! A tiny one, curled up at the bottom of the fuse box, which someone had cleverly bolted to the Virgin Mary's back. Mark said Cal has been terrified of snakes his whole life.

Which is kind of sweet, in a way. You know, that he actually has a weakness? I mean, I can almost forgive him for the phenylethylamine thing.

Almost.

Except that now I'm soaking wet and one of my Steve Maddens got stuck in the mud in the road and came off and I had to pry it out with my fingers while Mark laughed his head off at me and now we can't make any hot food unless we do it by candlelight (even though Cal, recovering from the snake sighting, is out on the terrazza or whatever it is, trying to stoke up a fire in the stone barbecue thingie, saying we could grill up the fish Frau Schumacher left us. As if somehow if he accomplishes this it's going to make us forget the whole part about how he was scared of that tiny snake. Yeah, so not going to happen, Mr. Million Dollar Advance for My Big Boring Book But I'm Scared of Snakes).

And I miss The Dude—even waking me up at 4 A.M. for a moonlit serenade.

And I can't seem to stop thinking about how I missed this week's ER because I was too busy packing to come here, and how it really is a shame that Holly asked me and not her brother Darrin to be her maid of honor. I'm sure DARRIN wouldn't be sitting in his room trying to dry his hair with a damp towel (what is up with these tiny Italian towels? They are the size of those hot cloths they handed out on the airplane on our way here—not to me, of course, but in first class. I just happened to see them because the line to the bathroom was too long in coach, so I snuck in to use the facilities in the forward cabin) thinking about Dr. Kovac.

No, at a time like this, Darrin—and his boyfriend Bobby—would probably be brainstorming about what to get for Holly and Mark. You know, as a wedding present. Like Egyptian cotton sheets, or a hand-tinted Audubon print, or a George Foreman grill, or something really meaningful like that.

Not a stupid travel diary that, guess what, I can't even give to them now because I've mentioned the best man's alleged Large Appendage a few too many times—

Holly just tapped on the door to say that Cal got a fire started and that he and Mark are trying to grill the fish and that it's hilarious and I should come down and by the way, do I like Cal better now that I know he has a phobia of snakes?

Trust Holly, at a time like this, when the elopement she's been planning for a whole year is finally just days away, to be wondering if Cal might be The One for me.

I can so totally tell she's hoping that Cal and I will fall in love and get married and buy a house next to the one you so know she and Mark are going to buy someday in Westchester (aka the Hellmouth) and send our kids to the same school and get together for barbecues on Saturday nights and sit around drinking Amstel Lights while spraying our progeny with Off to keep them from getting West Nile.

Yeah. Don't think that's going to be happening, Holl. The

best man doesn't BELIEVE in love. But don't worry, I'm sure his toast will be VERY heartfelt. . . .

Oh, wait, no, it won't. Because he doesn't HAVE a heart.

So now I'm wet and cold and sitting in my room with a too-small towel around my head, trying to scrape the mud off my Steve Madden, wondering what's wrong with me. I should be having fun. This is my first trip abroad, after all. And I haven't had a proper vacation in months, possibly years. I just spend all my time cooped up in my tiny studio apartment drawing stupid cats.

And I know that despite what the Customs guy said, Le Marche is supposed to be this magical place, even though since we've gotten here it's been pouring rain and the drops make this weird hollow sound as they hit the red terra-cotta roof tiles above my window and I swear to God if Cal Langdon and I end up cooped up in this house together for a week because of rain, only one of us is going to emerge alive, and it will be me because I know his weakness now.

But oh my God! What's with the mud and the everything being closed on Sunday and the power going out when you turn on the oven and the whole not-speaking-English thing? Not to mention, what is up with all the fish? I mean, I like fish, I guess, sort of, in small doses, and of course I am concerned about my Omega 3 fatty acid intake. Who isn't?

But I can certainly rectify that by having H & H throw a little nova on my bagel three times a week. I do not need to eat fish morning, noon, and night, like these Italians apparently do.

Wait. Could this explain why they're all so fit?

Oh, God, what is wrong with me? I am in an exotic foreign country, staying in a lovely house (except for the no-TV thing. And the Virgin Mary paintings everywhere—Holly's uncle seems to collect them, the ones whose eyes watch you wherever you go, so creepily that I had to take the one in my room down and put it in the wardrobe; oh, and the fact that there are no bathtubs, only showers, in any of the bathrooms. Oh, and my best friend's husband's best man keeps using words like vicissitudes and apparently wants to find some time to be alone with me so we can "talk." But other than that, the place is lovely) with my best friend, who is getting married, MARRIED, to the man she has loved forever. I should be happy for her.

It's just that really, with this storm overhead, pouring down buckets, we are stuck in this house together, with nothing but the Virgin Mary statues and the fish Frau Schumacher left us, and all I can think about is how crappy the weather is and how mean Mark's best man is and how much work I am going to have when I get back and how probably Julio is going to be resentful of The Dude's biting him and consequently forget to tape all my shows and then I won't know what's happening on any of them and I'll have to ask Dolly Vargas who will tell me all pityingly that a single woman who cares as much about television as I do has no life and why don't I let her introduce me to someone.

Holly is calling me. She says dinner is ready.

I swear to God, if any of them finds the playing cards some previously rain-swamped guests left behind and suggests we play bridge or something equally chummy, I am definitely going out to the pool, rain or no rain, and drowning myself.

✉

To: Holly Caputo <holly.caputo@thenyjournal.com>
Fr: Jane Harris <jane@wondercat.com>
Re: Where is he?

Holly, is Mark with you?

J

✉

To: Jane Harris <jane@wondercat.com>
Fr: Holly Caputo <holly.caputo@thenyjournal.com>
Re: Where is he?

Oh my God, Jane. Where are you? Why are you e-ing me? I'm still awake. Why don't you come talk to me in person? I'm in our room. It's OK, Mark's still downstairs.

Holly

✉

To: Holly Caputo <holly.caputo@thenyjournal.com>
Fr: Jane Harris <jane@wondercat.com>
Re: Where is he?

Is Cal with him? Mark, I mean?

J

To: Jane Harris <jane@wondercat.com>
Fr: Holly Caputo <holly.caputo@thenyjournal.com>
Re: Where is he?

How should I know? I told you, I'm in my room. I came up to bed because I'm exhausted. What is WRONG with you? Where ARE you? Why are you acting so weird all of a sudden?

Holly

To: Holly Caputo <holly.caputo@thenyjournal.com>
Fr: Jane Harris <jane@wondercat.com>
Re: Where is he?

Nothing's wrong. I'm on my way to bed too. I'm in a downstairs closet. I just don't want to run into Cal. Go back to sleep. Sorry if I woke you up.

J

To: Jane Harris <jane@wondercat.com>
Fr: Holly Caputo <holly.caputo@thenyjournal.com>
Re: Where is he?

Right. Like I'll be able to go back to sleep NOW. Janie, WHY are you in a downstairs closet? And WHY don't you want to run into Cal? Tell me now, or I'm coming down there and ripping that closet door open.

Holly

✉

To: Holly Caputo <holly.caputo@thenyjournal.com>
Fr: Jane Harris <jane@wondercat.com>
Re: Where is he?

It's NOTHING, okay? After you went up to bed, and Mark went to see if he could find another bottle of scotch after we polished off the last one, Cal said he wanted to have a word with me alone before bed. That's all. Now I am hiding in the closet because I don't want to have a word with him. OK? Are you satisfied?

J

PS If you figure out where he is, let me know, and if he's far from the stairs, I'll make a run for my room. Then I can turn out all the lights and pretend to be asleep if he knocks.

✉

To: Jane Harris <jane@wondercat.com>
Fr: Holly Caputo <holly.caputo@thenyjournal.com>
Re: Where is he?

Janie, don't be such a freak! He LIKES you. He MUST. Why else would he want to see you alone? He probably wants to . . . you know.

And why not? You're both on vacation, you're both attractive, you're both single . . . why WOULDN'T you hook up?

Holly

✉

To: Holly Caputo <holly.caputo@thenyjournal.com>
Fr: Jane Harris <jane@wondercat.com>
Re: Where is he?

Um, why WOULD we? He is a modelizer, lest you forget.

And believe me, sex is NOT what he wants from me.

J

✉

To: Jane Harris <jane@wondercat.com>
Fr: Holly Caputo <holly.caputo@thenyjournal.com>
Re: Where is he?

Then what is it? What on earth do you think he wants to talk to you about?

Holly

✉

To: Holly Caputo <holly.caputo@thenyjournal.com>
Fr: Jane Harris <jane@wondercat.com>
Re: What on earth I think he wants to talk to me about

Oh, you might be surprised.

J

✉

To: Jane Harris <jane@wondercat.com>
Fr: Holly Caputo <holly.caputo@thenyjournal.com>
Re: What on earth I think he wants to talk to me about

Janie, you really have to get over this absurd prejudice you have about Cal. Mark and I were talking about it earlier, when you were doing the dishes, and Cal was cleaning the grill. You two actually have a lot in common. I mean, you both come from small towns. You both are extremely successful, and you both built up your careers from basically nothing. You're both attractive and creative. And you're both friends with us! You two would make an AWESOME couple. Just give him a chance. I know he's not up to your usual standards—seeing as how he has a job and is over twenty-five—but he might surprise you.

Holly

✉

To: Holly Caputo <holly.caputo@thenyjournal.com>
Fr: Jane Harris <jane@wondercat.com>
Re: What on earth I think he wants to talk to me about

Excuse me, but did you just use the word AWESOME?

J

✉

To: Jane Harris <jane@wondercat.com>
Fr: Holly Caputo <holly.caputo@thenyjournal.com>
Re: What on earth I think he wants to talk to me about

Stop being so silly. Come out of the closet. See what he wants!

Holly

✉

To: Holly Caputo <holly.caputo@thenyjournal.com>
Fr: Jane Harris <jane@wondercat.com>
Re: What he wants

Believe me, I know. And it is so not going to happen. Trust me on this, H. It's in your own best interest.

J

✉

To: Jane Harris <jane@wondercat.com>
Fr: Holly Caputo <holly.caputo@thenyjournal.com>
Re: What he wants

Well, I think you're being completely ridiculous. And I'm not having this conversation anymore. I'm going to get some sleep. We have a big day ahead of us tomorrow—you promised you'd go into Castelfidardo with us to petition for the marriage license and pick the day for the ceremony. I don't know about you, but I want to look good for the mayor's office. Good night.

Holly

✉

To: Holly Caputo <holly.caputo@thenyjournal.com>
Fr: Jane Harris <jane@wondercat.com>
Re: What he wants

Fine, go to sleep. Traitor. I'm doing this for your own good, you know.

Well, no, I guess you don't.

And believe me, I intend to keep it that way!

Buona sera.

J

PDA of Cal Langdon

God bless Zio Matteo. The man may not care much about his home's electrical wiring, but at least he keeps a well-stocked liquor cabinet. Mark and I finished off the better part of a bottle of twelve-year-old scotch, and though it's a bit hard to type this, with my fingers feeling so numb, at least I got the picture of that snake out of my head at last.

The rain's finally stopped, too. The stars have come out, and there's a lovely warm breeze—slightly scented with horse manure—coming from the east. The pool and the wet stone surface around it are glistening in the moonlight, and somewhere in the distance—over the snoring of Mark, passed out facedown at the table beside me—I hear the braying of a donkey. It reminds me of those nights in Baghdad with Barbara Bellerieve, before she finally gave up on getting a ring out of me and hooked up with Aaron Spender—poor bastard.

Something which I realize has begun to happen with alarming regularity. Women I've slept with settling down with someone else, I mean.

I guess I shouldn't complain. God knows I'm not looking to register at Williams-Sonoma with any of them.

But it is a bit strange that all of my friends are pairing off. Mark, for instance. Well, not that I wouldn't have expected it of Mark, seeing as how he never exactly blazed any trails for rugged individuality in his lifetime. He does grill a mean turbot though.

But even people I'd pegged as lifelong bachelors—John Trent, for instance, over at the *Chronicle*—and Spender are taking the plunge.

Will it be long before I am the only single male my age left in the world? And if so . . . why? Don't these guys realize what they're getting themselves into?

I will admit, in Mark's case, the situation doesn't seem as dire as I once thought, despite what Ruth Levine might claim. Holly appears to be a cheerful, caring companion, who doesn't fall short in the looks department, either. She put together a wicked antipasto to go with the fish, an artfully arranged platter of marinated artichokes, mushroom, olives, fresh mozzarella, roasted red peppers, sundried tomatoes, and parmesan, all drizzled with olive oil and balsamic.

And when Mark mentioned something self-deprecating about his column, she chastised him, and proudly told me that his pieces are the Health section's most popular.

And when we sat down at the table her friend Jane had set—somewhat whimsically, with, I believe, every candle from the house on it, since we were dining al fresco on the logia, as the rain beat down just beyond the stone arches around us—Holly insisted on taking a picture, to mark our first meal at Villa Beccacia.

Then Ms. Harris—rather pointedly—insisted on taking a picture of Mark and Holly together—"To remember one of your last meals as an unmarried couple"—and the two of them wrapped their arms around each other. . . .

Well, I could see Jane's point about the two of them being perfect for each other. They are a lovely couple. Holly doesn't strike me—so far—as the type who'll, as soon as she gets a ring on her finger, quit her job and divide her days between Neiman-Marcus and her Pilates classes at the gym—

Must remember to stop judging all women by Valerie.

If Valerie had been at our evening meal, for instance, instead of Holly, she'd have consumed two of Zio Matteo's excellent bottles of montepolciano all on her own. And if Valerie had been here, she'd have made sure that the conversation, instead of flowing humorously from the troubles with the oven to the possible sex life of Frau Schumacher, would have revolved solely around her.

And afterward, of course, she'd have staggered to the toilet and heaved everything she'd just consumed into it.

Somehow, I can't picture Holly Caputo doing any of these things.

Still, that doesn't mean Mark is completely out of danger. A man can enter into a marriage thinking he's getting one thing, when the reality is, he's getting something very, very different. Mark's Holly may seem like a perfect helpmate at this point in their relationship, but who's to say once the blush is off the rose, so to speak, and they're declared man and wife—or *uomo* and *moglie,* as the case may be—she isn't going to turn into a stark raving bitch, demand that he make more money in order to buy her more expensive jewelry and spend all of her time obsessively weighing herself and recording every morsel that passes through her lips in a food journal?

I think Mark needs be made aware of this possibility.

And if he were conscious right now, I would make sure he knew.

As it is, however, I will have to wait until morning, and hope that we have another chance to talk privately before we make the trip to the marriage license office.

Speaking of hoping for a chance to talk, I mentioned to Ms. Harris that I was desirous of a private audience with her this evening, and she promptly disappeared into the house, never to return. I looked for her not long ago, and saw that she had retired to her room, the door of which was firmly closed. I have no doubt that, if there is a lock, she'd turned it.

For a woman who's capable of sending such blatantly hostile emails, she is remarkably reticent about face-to-face confrontations. It's always been my experience that women enjoy telling men what to do. Jane Harris, on the other hand, seems only willing to do this when it is her fingers, not her lips, doing the telling.

She strikes me as a very odd girl, overall.

But then, she is an artist . . . and a popular one, at least if the drooling half-wit boy from next door, who can't seem to take his eyes off her whenever they happen to be in the same room together, is to be believed.

How well I recognize his pain. I believe I had the same sort of all-consuming crush on my tenth-grade science teacher, Miss Huff.

Although Miss Huff did not exactly share Jane Harris's most impressive attributes . . . those slim ankles—the slenderness of the right one emphasized by that grinning cat's head—and that insouciant smile.

Insouciant. God. How in hell did I get a book contract, anyway?

Speaking of which . . . what in hell am I going to write about for my next book?

Oh, well. Much too tired—and too late—to think about it now. Will put this away and get to bed. It must be past midnight, and I'm still on New York time. Thoughts on the follow-up to *Sweeping Sands*—and further speculation about Ms. Harris—will have to wait until tomorrow.

PDA of Cal Langdon

One last thing before I go, though:

She still seems bizarrely fixated with the fly of my jeans. I am starting to wonder if Mark didn't resuscitate that ridiculous rumor from our days at Ohio State, about my having a super-sized wang, and share it with Holly, who in turn shared it with Ms. Harris. How else to explain why I keep catching her staring in that general vicinity?

If this is true, I will be forced, simply, to kill Mark. You would think that, at his age, he'd be over such childish pranks.

But he does work in the sciences, and those gifted in that arena do occasionally seem not to have quite as evolved a sense of humor as the rest of us.

Remember to ask him tomorrow.

✉

To: Listserv <Wundercat@wundercatlives.com>
Fr: Peter Schumacher <webmaster@wundercatlives.com>
Re: JANE HARRIS

Good morning all of you fans of Wundercat! I go now to take my motorino into town to get the brotchen for JANE HARRIS! She is not yet awake. I can see that she has not yet opened the curtains of her bedroom window.

But when she does, she will find that there is fresh brotchen to enjoy with her coffee! Courtesy of me, #1 Wundercat Fan Of All Time!

Wundercat Lives—4eva!
Peter

✉

To: Mark Levine <mark.levine@thenyjournal.com >
Fr: Customer Service New York Journal Travel Privileges <TravelPrivcustser@thenyjournal.com>
Re: Car Rental

Dear Sir,

Our great apologies for the misunderstanding concerning your vehicle. Our offices, as you discovered, are not open on Sundays. However, if you return the automobile you were assigned to the car rental agency in Ancona on Monday, we will happily allow you to exchange it for the four-door sedan you mentioned.

Sally Marx
New York Journal Travel Specialist

Travel Diary of

~~Holly Caputo and Mark Levine~~

Jane Harris

OK, everything I wrote in here last night about hating Italy and wishing I were home watching ER? Strike that.

I LOVE Italy. I LOVE it here.

Just now when I woke up, I pushed back the heavy curtains from my window, expecting to see more of the hard cold rain from yesterday. . . .

Gone. No more rain.

Instead, there was a cloudless blue sky. And a distant, green, castle-topped hillside straight out of a fairy tale. And a crystal pool sparkling below me. And the scent of freshly cut hay. And the sun-washed stone walls of the terrazza dripping with the thick green leaves and fire pink blossoms of bougainvillea, and birds singing in the treetops—

Well, what else could I do but slap on my swimsuit and hit the water?

And it was so very, very . . .

COLD!!!!

OK? The water is REALLY cold. Like ice-cube-tray cold. I'm writing this half-shivering to death on one of the lounge chairs, completely draped in towels.

But even though it's only like nine in the morning, or something, the sun is already beating down. Steam is coming up from the damp towels on my legs. Soon I should be toasty. . . .

YES. Now THIS is how I've always pictured a European vacation. Just me, the water, clear blue sky, bright hot sun, and a bottle of acqua con gas (sparkling water, which I found in the fridge). It's SO quiet here. No car alarms. No sirens. No neighbors squabbling over possession of the remote control next door. Just birds tweeting, and horses neighing, and the wind rustling through palm fronds and the leaves of the olive tree beside me, its branches heavy with little round balls deepening from a pretty pale green to a deep brown color . . . totally bitter and indigestible (yes, I tasted one. Who knew they had to be marinated or whatever? The pomegranates from the tree at the other end of the pool are MUCH better).

In the air is the crisp, clean smell of chlorine from the pool, the scent of freshly cut hay from the field beyond the hedge, and . . . OK, well, the smell of horse manure drifting over from the Centro Ippico, but it's very faint.

And off in the distance, atop a deep green rise that seems to come from the middle of the hay field, sits another fortified city, topped by a castle . . . Castelfidardo, where we're going to go today to apply for Mark and Holly's marriage license. If they can pry me from this spot. Which I sincerely doubt. Because the only way I'm moving is if—

AAAAAAAAAHHHHHHHHHHHHHHHHHHH!!!!!!!!!

✉

To: Listserv <Wundercat@wundercatlives.com>
Fr: Peter Schumacher <webmaster@wundercatlives.com>
Re: JANE HARRIS

Greetings! I have served breakfast to JANE HARRIS! I surprise her very much with the brotchen and hot coffee! She had just had her morning swimming when I come into yard with tray prepared by my grandmother! She scream very big!

But then she sees it is only me, and I put down tray beside her pool couch, and we have the coffee and brotchen. I bring also the Nutella, and JANE HARRIS likes this very much! We have nice chat, and I find out IMPORTANT NEWS FLASH:

JANE HARRIS HAS DEVELOPMENT DEAL WITH CARTOON NETWORK FOR WUNDERCAT ANIMATED SERIES!!!!!!!!!!

Yes!!! Perhaps we will be seeing Wundercat on television soon!

I am very interested as JANE HARRIS is telling this to me, but then one of the mans she is traveling with (don't worry, boys, he is NOT her boyfriend. In the words of JANE HARRIS: "HIM? MY BOYFRIEND? NO WAY!") Cal Longdon comes out of the house and says he wants to speak alone with JANE HARRIS.

So I start to go, but JANE HARRIS says "No, Peter, you stay." And so I give Cal Longdon some brotchen and coffee too and we three sit and talk about politics for very long time before daughter of the sister of the man who owns the villa where JANE HARRIS is staying comes out and says they must go to Castelfidardo.

I am thinking I will ride on my motorino to Castelfidardo also today to see if JANE HARRIS needs anything more.

That is the report from WUNDERCAT CENTRAL! More news as it is received!

Over and out,

Peter, #1 Wundercat Fan Of All Time

✉

To: Peter Schumacher <webmaster@wundercatlives.com>
Fr: Martin Schneck < m.schneck@comixunderground.com>
Re: JANE HARRIS

How is JANE HARRIS looking in a bathing suit? You did not tell!

Martin Schneck

✉

To: Claire Harris <charris2004@freemail.com>
Fr: Jane Harris <jane@wondercat.com>
Re: Hi!

Right now we're in the car on the way to Castelfidardo to apply for Mark and Holly's marriage license! It's so exciting!

It's also soooooooooo beautiful here. Even the BILLBOARDS seem more attractive than they do back home. They're definitely more interesting . . . even though I can't read them.

And the food! I just had the best breakfast of my LIFE . . . something called Nutella on this freshly baked—still warm from the oven—bread. Oh my God, I thought I had died and gone to heaven.

Anyway, hope you and Dad are well!

Ciao for now!

J

✉

To: Jane Harris <jane@wondercat.com>
Fr: Cal Langdon <cal.langdon@thenyjournal.com>
Re: Time to talk

Since you seem so reticent to discuss this face-to-face, I see no alternative other than to continue our e-versation. I believe you were saying something to the effect that I ought to mind my own business where matters of Mark's heart were concerned, and I was busy maintaining that I felt it my duty as a loyal friend to warn him of the emotional and financial jeopardy in which he is placing himself. Have you given the matter more thought, or are you still blinded by the romance of the thing?

Cal

✉

To: Cal Langdon <cal.langdon@thenyjournal.com>
Fr: Jane Harris <jane@wondercat.com>
Re: Time to talk

Oh my God, I can't believe you're e-ing me from the front seat AGAIN. CUT IT OUT!

J

✉

To: Jane Harris <jane@wondercat.com>
Fr: Cal Langdon <cal.langdon@thenyjournal.com>
Re: Time to talk

What other choice do you leave me when you won't speak to me in person? I haven't budged from my position that these two are making an enormous mistake. Have you, perhaps, come around to my way of thinking? I notice you seemed reluctant to leave the pool today when your friend Holly was urging us to get ready for the trip to Castelfidardo. . . .

Cal

✉

To: Cal Langdon <cal.langdon@thenyjournal.com>
Fr: Jane Harris <jane@wondercat.com>
Re: Time to talk

Because I was having a nice time at the pool! At least until YOU showed up there.

And no, I haven't changed my mind. Holly and Mark belong together, and I don't understand why anyone would think otherwise.

And I'm not "blinded by the romance of the thing," as you put it. It's sweet, that's all. And if you do anything to try to ruin it, you're a creep!

J

✉

To: Jane Harris <jane@wondercat.com>
Fr: Cal Langdon <cal.langdon@thenyjournal.com>
Re: Time to talk

A creep?

Cal

✉

To: Cal Langdon <cal.langdon@thenyjournal.com>
Fr: Jane Harris <jane@wondercat.com>
Re: Time to talk

You heard me. Or read me. A CREEP. Only a creep would try to talk his best friend out of marrying the girl of his dreams. Don't even tell me that isn't what you were up all night doing down there on the terrazza.

J

✉

To: Jane Harris <jane@wondercat.com>
Fr: Cal Langdon <cal.langdon@thenyjournal.com>
Re: Time to talk

How do you know what I was up all night doing? You went to bed at ten.

Cal

✉

To: Cal Langdon <cal.langdon@thenyjournal.com>
Fr: Jane Harris <jane@wondercat.com>
Re: Time to talk

I just happened to get up to get a drink of water, and I saw you out there. You and Mark.

But it didn't work, obviously. Or we wouldn't be making this trip to Castelfidardo, now, would we?

J

To: Cal Langdon <cal.langdon@thenyjournal.com>
Fr: Jane Harris <jane@wondercat.com>
Re: Time to talk

I didn't get a chance to speak to Mark, due to the fact that the excessive amount of alcohol he put away at dinner rendered him comatose. Not, I would like to add, a good sign that he is looking forward to his impending nuptials with joy.

Cal

To: Cal Langdon <cal.langdon@thenyjournal.com>
Fr: Jane Harris <jane@wondercat.com>
Re: Time to talk

Oh, please. *I* could drink Mark under the table. He's always been a lightweight. He was probably just trying to keep up with you. That doesn't mean ANYTHING.

Besides, every guy has the right to let off a little steam before he gets married.

J

To: Jane Harris <jane@wondercat.com>
Fr: Cal Langdon <cal.langdon@thenyjournal.com>
Re: Time to talk

> every guy has the right to let off a little steam before he gets married.<

Proving my point that marriage is an unnatural and antiquated institution that ought to be abolished. The fact that it is traditional for men to get blind stinking drunk the night before their wedding just shows that it is a state into which they are entering against their better judgment.

WOMEN want marriage. Men do not. Mark's behavior last evening proves deep down, he doesn't want this. And you know it.

Cal

✉

To: Cal Langdon <cal.langdon@thenyjournal.com>
Fr: Jane Harris <jane@wondercat.com>
Re: Time to talk

You're so weird. Seriously. Are you this way about EVERYTHING? I mean, do you have to overthink every little thing? Don't you ever just DO stuff, without thinking about it first?

Or is it BECAUSE you did something once, without weighing the consequences, and got burned, that you are so anti-marriage?

J

✉

To: Jane Harris <jane@wondercat.com>
Fr: Cal Langdon <cal.langdon@thenyjournal.com>
Re: Time to talk

And I suppose you're going to claim you haven't been dreaming about your wedding day since you were seven? Dressing your Barbies up in bridal veils and walking them down the aisle with poor hapless Ken since you were nine? Sketching designs of your dream wedding gown since your teens, and viewing every male you met after the age of twenty as potential husband/father-of-your-children material, weighing his earning potential against his looks and assessing the chances of his remaining faithful to you?

Cal

To: Cal Langdon <cal.langdon@thenyjournal.com>
Fr: Jane Harris <jane@wondercat.com>
Re: Time to talk

You didn't answer my question.

J

To: Jane Harris <jane@wondercat.com>
Fr: Cal Langdon <cal.langdon@thenyjournal.com>
Re: Time to talk

You didn't answer mine.

Cal

To: Cal Langdon <cal.langdon@thenyjournal.com>
Fr: Jane Harris <jane@wondercat.com>
Re: Time to talk

Fine. Yes, I had Barbie weddings. Yes, I've sketched bridal gowns.

And, yes, I've sized up potential boyfriends, wondering whether or not they were going to be faithful to me.

But I've never cared about their EARNING potential. Truly. You can ask Holly.

And as for being good father material, how can I worry about who's going to be the father of my children when I'm not even sure I WANT children? My career is just starting out. I want to see how that goes before I attempt to bring another life form into this world.

Besides which, I already have a cat. That is quite enough responsibility right now.

J

✉

To: Jane Harris <jane@wondercat.com>
Fr: Cal Langdon <cal.langdon@thenyjournal.com>
Re: Time to talk

Are you seriously comparing owning a cat to raising a child?

Cal

✉

To: Cal Langdon <cal.langdon@thenyjournal.com>
Fr: Jane Harris <jane@wondercat.com>
Re: Time to talk

Um, you haven't met The Dude.

J

To: Jane Harris <jane@wondercat.com>
Fr: Cal Langdon <cal.langdon@thenyjournal.com>
Re: Time to talk

Who is The Dude?

Cal

To: Cal Langdon <cal.langdon@thenyjournal.com>
Fr: Jane Harris <jane@wondercat.com>
Re: Time to talk

My cat. And you still haven't answered MY question.

J

To: Jane Harris <jane@wondercat.com>
Fr: Cal Langdon <cal.langdon@thenyjournal.com>
Re: Time to talk

I can't remember what it was.

Cal

To: Cal Langdon <cal.langdon@thenyjournal.com>
Fr: Jane Harris <jane@wondercat.com>
Re: Time to talk

Isn't it true that the only reason you're so anti-love-and-marriage is because your own didn't work out?

J

To: Jane Harris <jane@wondercat.com>
Fr: Cal Langdon <cal.langdon@thenyjournal.com>
Re: Time to talk

Absolutely not. The failure of my own marriage plays absolutely no part in my conviction that human beings are genetically incapable of monogamy. I believe we were meant to have seven or eight partners in a lifetime, not one. The idea that as a community we applaud those couples who manage to stay together forty or fifty years or longer is simply ridiculous. There's something inherently wrong with celebrating couples like that. It simply isn't natural to want to spend that much time with another human being.

Cal

To: Cal Langdon <cal.langdon@thenyjournal.com>
Fr: Jane Harris <jane@wondercat.com>
Re: Time to talk

My parents will be celebrating their fortieth wedding anniversary next year. Are you saying there's something inherently wrong with them?

J

✉

To: Jane Harris <jane@wondercat.com>
Fr: Cal Langdon <cal.langdon@thenyjournal.com>
Re: Time to talk

No offense to your parents, but basically, yes. Are you going to tell me that in all of those forty years, they've never fought or cheated on each other?

Cal

✉

To: Cal Langdon <cal.langdon@thenyjournal.com>
Fr: Jane Harris <jane@wondercat.com>
Re: Time to talk

Sure they've fought. They're HUMAN. But cheated on each other? No way.

J

PS You're an ass.

✉

To: Jane Harris <jane@wondercat.com>
Fr: Cal Langdon <cal.langdon@thenyjournal.com>
Re: Time to talk

I never said my theory was a very popular one. But it happens to be true.

Cal

PS Has anyone ever told you that you're kind of cute when you're mad?

✉

To: Cal Langdon <cal.langdon@thenyjournal.com>
Fr: Jane Harris <jane@wondercat.com>
Re: Time to talk

Are you FLIRTING with me?

It won't work. I'm a little brighter than the women you're so obviously used to.

Stop e-ing me, we're here.

J

PS You're still an ass.

Marriage of an American Citizen in Italy

An American citizen planning to marry in Italy must obtain a declaration (called STATO LIBERO) sworn by four (4) witnesses before the Italian consulate, stating that according to the laws in which the citizen is subject in the United States there is no obstacle to his/her marriage. Therefore he/she must appear at this Consulate General with four unrelated friends not related to him/her nor to each other. Each of them has to bring a valid identification (Passport or Drivers License).

The citizen's passport must also be presented and, if applicable, evidence of the termination of any previous marriage (final divorce decree or death certificate) translated into Italian and legalized by the competent Department of State with an "Apostille" (see page 2). The sworn statement has three months' validity.

Travel Diary of

~~Holly Caputo and Mark Levine~~

Jane Harris

Cal Langdon is a stupid jerk.

He's the KING of all jerks. He's the undisputed CHAMPION of all-time jerks. How can Mark even be friends with him? Really? How?

I mean, I GUESS he can be interesting, and even witty, when he's talking about some arcane topic such as the accordion-making industry. Which, considering that Castelfidardo is apparently the accordion-making capital of the known universe, is at least kind of useful. Who knew Zio Matteo is a world-renowned accordionist, and that's why he bought a villa so close to the town that makes his chosen instrument?

There is even an accordion MUSEUM here, featuring—what else?—the world's largest playable accordion. It's as tall as Cal Langdon.

There's also a statue on the village green of a large man playing the accordion. He is, oddly, in the buff. I'm not sure this would fly in America. I mean, a statue of a naked accordionist in the town square.

Still, topics unrelated to human relationships, such as Saudi Arabia's declining oil reserves and the history of accordion-making? Those are the only subjects about which Cal Langdon ought to be allowed by law to converse. Because when it comes to people, he's totally and completely in the dark.

No wonder his wife left him.

I honestly don't even see how he lasted as long as he did on the foreign correspondence trail. I mean, Cal Langdon has been flying around the world—when he wasn't apparently bouncing around it in the back of a jeep—interviewing dignitaries and world leaders and guerrillas alike.

And yet he seems to know less about people than ME, and I've barely left my apartment these past five years, I've been so busy drawing. How can someone who knows so many people know so little about them? That's what I'd like to know.

Whatever. I'm not going to let him spoil this beautiful moment for me. We're sitting outside the Office of the Secretary of Castelfidardo, which is where they give out the marriage license applications and schedule the town weddings. Mark and Holly are up at the desk, trying to make the clerk understand what they want. They already have all these forms they filled out back at the Italian consulate in New York. It turns out that if an American citizen wants to elope in a foreign country, they can't just do it all willy-nilly. You have to fill out a bunch of paperwork first, back in the States. For one of the forms, Mark and Holly even had to drag four separate witnesses—unrelated to them, or to each other—to the Italian embassy to swear that they weren't already married to anyone else (Holly and Mark, I mean).

I don't know why this is taking so long. Or why Cal Langdon felt compelled to go up there too, and listen in. I'm keeping an eye on him to make sure he isn't trying to sabotage the proceedings. Now the secretario himself has come out to join in the conversation.

Still, the secretario keeps going, "Non."

This doesn't sound good. Shouldn't he be saying, "Si"?

Holly keeps gesturing to the paperwork from the Italian consulate and going, "But in New York they said—"

And the secretario keeps going, in his broken English, "Yessa, but, in New Yorka, thees is not how we do theengs here in Italia."

Hmmm. Holly looks stressed. I sense trouble brewing.

Now the secretario is starting to look annoyed.

"I donna understand," he's saying. "Why you have to get married here in Castelfidardo? Why not Las Vegas, like normal Americans?"

Uh-oh. Holly's mad now.

"Because we're NOT normal Americans," she says. "We want to get married here in Castelfidardo. We have the right forms. What's the problem? Just open your calendar and tell us when the mayor has a time available to perform the ceremony, and we'll be on our—"

Oh, my. Peter Schumacher just walked in. He must have followed us on his little motorino.

Poor boy. He must really not have anything else to do. . . .

Oh, the secretario is handing something to Holly—

HAGUE CONVENTION ABOLISHING THE REQUIREMENT OF CONSULAR LEGALISATION FOR FOREIGN PUBLIC DOCUMENTS

The United States of America and Italy and some other countries have signed a convention abolishing the requirements of diplomatic and consular acknowledgements or legalizations of public documents originating in one convention country and intended for use in another convention country signatory of the convention.

This consulate general, therefore, will not henceforth acknowledge or legalize public documents: notarial documents, deeds, certificates of vital statistics, wills, court decrees, etc.

To be valid in any other of the countries signatories of the convention, all documents must carry an APOSTILLE.

To obtain the "APOSTILLE" in any of the United States, a document is first notarized by a Notary Public in that state and then authenticated by the Country Clerk in the country in which the notary is qualified.

✉

To: Listserv <Wundercat@wundercatlives.com>
Fr: Peter Schumacher <webmaster@wundercatlives.com>
Re: JANE HARRIS

NEWS FLASH! JANE HARRIS is here in Italy to be the witness for the wedding of her friends. Today they go to the Ufficio di Secretario of Castelfidardo for the license to marry, and the secretario said NON! He would not allow it, as the friends of Jane Harris did not get APOSTILLE from the US consulate in Roma!

I have driven my motorino straight from the Ufficio di Secretario myself to let you in on the news, and also to tell my grandmother, who says she will speak to the secretario herself after lunch, because she knows his mother! And she says his mother will be very angry when she learns her son would not let the American lovers marry! Grandmother says she will take this to Mayor Torelli himself, if she must!

At the Ufficio di Secretario, JANE HARRIS was wearing pink short-sleeved shirt, trousers in black cotton, and pink sandals! Her toenails are painted pink to match! JANE HARRIS is still looking very cute!

More later from #1 fan of Wundercat!

Wundercat Lives—4eva!
Peter

✉

To: Claire Harris <charris2004@freemail.com>
Fr: Jane Harris <jane@wondercat.com>
Re: You

Disaster! The city of Castelfidardo won't allow Holly and Mark to get married here! Not without some stamp from the US consulate in Rome!

Which means we have to drive all the way there and back to get it. That's another eight hours there and back in the car! And we only have the house until Friday, when Holly's uncle comes back from his latest accordion tour. And the Secretario says the mayor's calendar is totally booked, and only the mayor can perform wedding ceremonies!

Everybody is pretty bummed. Well, except for Cal, of course. He is totally against marriage on principle. He thinks there must be something inherently wrong with you and Dad for having been together for so long. He has absolutely no idea how normal human beings function. It's possible he's a robot.

Anyway, we're going to grab lunch in town and reconnoiter back at the secretario's office later. Holly's uncle's housekeeper might be able to do something, according to her great-grandson. Apparently, she knows everybody's mother, and can shame them into doing whatever she wants.

Hope Dad's back is feeling better! Good thing, those gloves.

Love,
Janie

PDA of Cal Langdon

Insisted on buying lunch, as everyone in our party was completely dejected (excepting myself, of course).

It seems that Italian bureaucracy is doing my job for me, insofar as keeping Mark and Holly from wedded bliss (or bust). It appears the young couple cannot be wed unless they get a specific stamp on a form that can only be secured at the American embassy back in Rome. Their choices are to skip the whole thing or pile back into the car and drive back to Rome tomorrow.

At this point, Mark seems to be leaning toward making the trip. Surprisingly, it's his lady love whose resolve seems to be flagging. I wonder if Holly is quite as enthusiastic about the idea of marrying Mark as I—and her friend Jane—once presumed.

This, at least, explains why Ms. Harris insists upon carrying on our conversations via text. She must have known that her friend's enthusiasm was not all it should be.

And I must say, if a small detail like a stamp on a form and an eight-hour drive are enough to drive Ms. Caputo into such dudgeon, perhaps Mark really is better off single.

The girls are in the ladies' room, doing whatever it is women do when they enter such facilities together. Mark is on his cell with the car rental agency in Ancona. Apparently, the replacement vehicle *New York Journal* promised him earlier this morning is no longer available. Good thing he called before we made the trip.

Lunch was delicious, by the way. We found a small family-run establishment popular with the many accordion-factory workers in town. For twenty euros total we enjoyed an exquisitely prepared lemon pasta, grilled scallops, insalata caprese, and a carafe of bianco frizzante. We received a number of odd looks, to be sure, from the natives. This is clearly a restaurant that doesn't see many Americans.

And clearly has never heard of a non-smoking section.

Still, a pleasant meal, in all.

Now, I presume, we shall be trekking back to town hall to argue some more with the presiding officials. With any luck, we'll be joined by Inga Schumacher—taking this tragi-comedy to a whole new level of hilarity—and her great-grandson, who seems to have glued himself to our sides . . . not that his near-constant presence seems to bother Ms. Harris. In fact, I'm starting to believe she actually likes having the kid around. Peter's presence makes it very difficult for me to say all the things I'd like to say to the object of his devotion. . . .

Perhaps this is just as well. I always seem to be thinking—and saying—the oddest things around that woman. Telling her I think she's cute when she's angry? What was I doing? I NEVER say that kind of thing, much less write it.

That's right. She has it in *writing*, permanent proof of my idiocy.

I ought to be shot.

Especially since it's more than clear that she thinks I'm—what was it? Oh, yes. An ass. That's very nice. Being called an ass by a woman who makes her living drawing a cartoon of a cat. Excuse me, did *I* create something that people have forever since been forcing me to look at, dangling from suction cups on the back windshield of their car? No, I did not.

It's all this damned fizzy wine. That's what it is. I just need a beer. Maybe this afternoon, since it doesn't look as if we'll be changing cars in Ancona, I'll talk Mark into going to a bar with me—there's that Crazy Bar and Sexy Tattoo Shop in Porto Recanati—and we'll talk this whole marriage thing out over a couple of cold ones. . . .

Though I think I'll keep my thoughts about Ms. Harris to myself. And the fact that today she's got on a pair of shoes I haven't seen before. Open-toe, of course, with these pink straps that criss-cross over the cat tattoo—

I need some air.

Travel Diary of

~~Holly Caputo and Mark Levine~~

Jane Harris

Poor Holly. She's crushed.

Stupid secretario. And stupid Italy. I hate it here again! How can they be so mean? Can't they see they're destroying one of the sweetest, gentlest girls in the world with their ridiculous bureaucratic red tape?

At least Frau Schumacher understands. She's really letting that secretario have it. He looks kind of scared. He keeps saying something about the mayor. Apparently, he doesn't have the authority to do . . . something.

But the mayor does.

I think Frau Schumacher told him to let us in to see the mayor, then.

Wow! For an old lady, Frau Schumacher sure can be intimidating!

Thank God for Peter running home to get her. Well, really, thank God for Wondercat. Because without Wondercat, Peter wouldn't have even known about our problem and gone to get his great-grandmother.

And of course, there'd be no Wondercat if it weren't for The Dude. So really, none of this would be happening if it weren't for my cat.

As usual. Just further proof that The Dude, as I've always suspected, really is God.

Now the secretario's left his own office. Frau Schumacher looks very pleased with herself. I asked Peter what's going on, and he said, "The secretario is going to see if ze mayor vill change his schedule to let your friends get married on Vednesday. There is maybe an opening in ze calendar on zis day."

When I commented that this seemed like a positive development, Peter nodded and said, "Yes. Zey are all very frightened of my grandmuzzer. She will go to the mayor's muzzer, and zat zey do not want."

Yes! Joy!

You would think Holly would be happier to hear that. But she's just sitting next to me, holding her stomach and looking kind of queasy.

Well, I guess I can't really blame her. She's been looking forward to getting married for so long, and all of these delays have to be—

The secretario is back. Oh my gosh! We're being summoned to the mayor's office!

✉

To: Jane Harris <jane@wondercat.com>
Fr: Claire Harris <charris2004@freemail.com>
Re: You

Oh, sweetie, that's horrible news about poor Holly! Sorry it took me so long to get back to you, but Daddy dropped a picture frame on his big toe so we were just at Promptcare getting it X-rayed. Not broken, thank God, but a bad bruise. I sent him to bed with a bowl of Breyers.

I do hope you're able to work something out for Holly. It would be such a shame for she and Mark—well, all of you, really—to have gone all that way and then not be able to have your little elopement. I feel just terrible.

But, even if they can't get married, you can still have a nice vacation, can't you? What is Holly's uncle's house like? Is it pretty? Do the windows lock? Because you know I just saw on the news that in a lot of those oceanside communities, people leave the windows open at night to let in the sea breezes, and it's like an invitation to thieves and rapists! They just slip in on through the windows and take whatever they want! I hope you're making sure all the windows are locked at night.

And I hope you're not being too mean to that handsome Cal Langdon. You're a very vibrant and pretty girl, Janie, and you know men can't help falling in love with you. Remember how many of them asked you to the senior prom? Well, it's true a lot of them were freshman boys who couldn't have taken you anyway. . . .

But the way they mooned around the house, asking Daddy if they could mow the lawn, when we knew perfectly well they just wanted a glimpse of you. Keep in mind that some of those boys you wouldn't give the time of day to went on to have very good jobs at Pfizer.

And Helen Shipley told me her son Curt makes six figures in the cruise ship industry!

Why you keep insisting Curt is one of those bisexuals, I can't imagine. Helen says it simply isn't true. Curt's not married yet because he just hasn't met the right girl, according to Helen. Probably YOU were the right girl, and he's just waiting for you to get in touch.

Also, according to Charlie Rose, Mr. Langdon got a VERY nice advance for that little book he wrote. That's not something you ought to turn up your nose at, you know. Wondercat is darling, but it won't always be as popular as it is now. You need to think about your future, you know, Janie.

Love,
Mom

PS Daddy says to tell you it looks as if that cartoon about the flying serving utensils has been canceled. That might open up a slot for the Wondercat animated series, don't you think?

✉

To: Listserv <Wundercat@wundercatlives.com>
Fr: Peter Schumacher <webmaster@wundercatlives.com>
Re: JANE HARRIS

SUCCESS!!! My grandmother has arranged it all! The friends of JANE HARRIS will be married Wednesday morning at nine o'clock, before the mayor had to go and coach the American football game at the primary school, where he is also the athletic director when he is not being mayor.

But they must get the stamp from the consulate of the US before they can be married. So tomorrow they will go to Rome to receive it.

All is done, and by my grandmother! Everyone was much excited! Except for the secretario and the mayor.

But best of all—

JANE HARRIS KISSED ME!!!! YES!!!! To say thank you for making it so that her friends can have their marriage!!!

Never will I wash this face again.

That is all for now. I am Peter Schumacher, #1 fan of Wundercat, saying

TSCHUSS!

Wundercat Lives—4eva!
Peter

GE. SP. AL. S.N.C
Viale Europa 44
Porto Recanati (MC)
GROCERY

	EURO
PelliCola Co	0,50
6 Minibiscot	2,50
Olive Bella	2,50
Kinder Sorpr	1,80
Birra Peroni, 24	12,76
Insalata Rom	0,66
Tomato Ketch	2,23
Uva Italia P	1,95
The Twinings	1,90
Insalata Tro	0,41
Puro Succo	1,33
Naionese Cal	1,22
Latte Fr.A.Q.	1,37
Insalata Gen	0,38
Latte Fr. Int	1,30
Oro Duepic'c	2,34
637 Pom.Ross	1,90
Banco Taglio	1,01
Oro Piu'caca	1,53
Olive verdi	0,78
Bisc. Conad G	0,89
Pane Dolci I	0,55
Pomodori Pel	0,55
Doricream	0,65
Mais Pop Cor	0,60
Banco Taglio	27,21
Caffe Classi	2,09
Caffe Classi	2,09
Arance Taroc	2,55
TOTALE	77,55
Contanti	100,00
Resto	22,45

N.Pezzi 50
Oper: 10
Cassa 1 1
Regalo Bollini: 15
Codice: Bollini

Arrivederci e Grazie!

La Cantinetta
Enoteca
Ricrea di Morresi G. & C.
SNC Viale Europa 36
Porto Recanati

		EURO
Vino	1	8,66
Vino	1	7,80
Vino	1	7,40
Vino	1	5,40
Vino	1	7,00
Vino	1	9,00
Vino	1	9,00
Vino	1	6,50
Vino	1	6,50
Vino	1	5,00
Vino	1	5,00
Vino	1	10,20
Vino	1	9,00
Vino	1	14,00
TOTALE		110,46

Grazie!

Travel Diary of

~~Holly Caputo and Mark Levine~~

Jane Harris

The mayor said yes!!!!

It seemed touch and go there to me for a while, but Frau Schumacher totally came through for us! I couldn't tell what she was saying to the big man behind the desk—a very intimidating desk, too, with lots of important looking documents all over it, for a very intimidating man, wearing a big green shiny sash over his track suit—but Cal later translated that basically, she said, "Marry these two delightful young people or I will make you sorry."

Cal says he doesn't know HOW Frau Schumacher was going to make him sorry, but the mayor apparently believed her enough to make a time in his schedule for Holly and Mark.

And OK, it's super-early in the morning for a wedding—9 A.M.—but it's better than nothing! Frau Schumacher was right about wedding breakfasts, I guess. That's what they do here, instead of receptions.

Now all we have to do is drive to Rome tomorrow, get the form Holly and Mark need, and drive back.

At last, we can relax a little. We went grocery shopping for food for the rest of the week (and Cal and Mark hit the liquor store, this cute little shop called La Cantinetta in Porto Recanati. Frankly, I think 14 bottles of wine, champagne, J & B, and something called limoncello might be a bit much, but it IS a wedding, after all, even if it's just four of us attending) and then came home and hit the pool right away. At least, Holly and Mark and Peter and I did. Cal got a call from his editor or somebody, so he's sitting in the terrazza, yakking into his cell, saying things like, "But I said you'd have it next month. No, I never said that."

Sounds like somebody's a little late on a project. Ha ha.

I got the skinny on Peter while we were in the mayor's office, too. When we walked in, I was surprised to see a girl about Peter's age sitting on the mayor's desk, going "Papa" in the unmistakable wheedle of a teenaged daughter. She was a pretty little thing named Annika—all big blue eyes and blonde ringlets and knobby knees—and when she saw Peter, she completely forgot about whatever favor she was begging her father for. Her eyes narrowed in that mean way only teenaged girls' eyes can, and she went, "What are you doing here?"

And Peter was all, "I am here on official business with the mayor."

And the girl started laughing and said, "What business can *you* have with my fazzer?"

And everything was suddenly SO clear to me, just from those—let me see—OK, eight little words. You know, that Peter adores Annika with a passion that cannot be denied, and that she wants him, too, but Peter isn't considered cool enough to date in their social set, and so she has to act scornful towards him.

It was all so obvious and sad.

Then the mayor hung up the phone and went, "Annika. Shush."

Then he and Frau Schumacher started going at it in Italian, so I used the opportunity to ask Peter who the girl was, sotto voce (Italian for "in a soft voice." I am really getting this language down, if I do say so myself).

And he was like, his voice dripping with (obviously feigned) scorn, "Zat's Annika. She is the mayor's daughter. She zinks she is queen of all of Castelfidardo even zo she is not."

And I asked Peter if he and Annika went to school together, and he told me he goes to "Internet school" because the schools in Castelfidardo aren't "adwanced" enough for him, and that he can't go to school back in Germany because there's no one there for him to live with, his "fazzer" currently being "in the jail."

In the jail! Peter's dad—Frau Schumacher's grandson—is in the jail!

For what, I don't know. But now I understand why it is that Peter is able to hang around us all day. Annika, presumably, was on her (three-hour) lunch break from school. Can you imagine all the trouble American teens could get up to if we gave them a three-hour lunch break? And all of the malls were CLOSED during it? My *God*, civilization as we know it would break down completely.

Anyway, after the mayor and Frau S. negotiated their little compromise, there was a lot of cheering and relieved sighs (and, from Cal Langdon, a frown), so I took the opportunity to lean down and give Peter a peck on the cheek—to thank him, you know, since if he hadn't gone and got his great-grandmother, none of this would have happened.

And, while Peter turned bright red, I had the pleasure of seeing Annika, who'd witnessed the kiss, scowl prettily.

Score one for Peter.

Poor Annika. One of these days she's going to wake up and realize Peter was the one for her. Only by the time that happens, Peter will have his own software company and be making millions and be dating a starlet from some Fox sitcom . . . or whatever the Italian equivalent of Fox might be.

Cal Langdon just barked, "You'll get it when you get it, Art," into his phone.

God. He is so Type A. He really needs to learn to chill, like me, or he's going to have a coronary before he's forty.

And how dare he suggest that there's something wrong with MY parents for staying together so long? I asked him while we were in the hallway outside the mayor's office, out of earshot of Holly, how long HIS parents stayed together, and he said, "They were married twenty years, and are much happier people now that they've gone their separate ways."

Which is all very well and good for them, but if Cal Langdon were MY kid, I'd want to get away from him, too. No wonder they split up. The North Pole and Antarctica aren't far enough to get away from that voice: "I told you, Arthur, I will have the proposal for you when I get back. No, not the DAY I get back. But a few weeks later—yes, well, I still haven't figured out exactly what I'm going to write about. No, not dirty diamonds. No, I'm not going to Angola—"

Some women, I suppose, might find Cal Langdon's voice sexy. And IT is kind of deep and gravelly, in a Robert Redford kind of way.

But the stuff he SAYS with it! EW!

And OK, he's hot. I mean, I'm not going to lie and say he's not. All I have to do to KNOW that isn't true is flip back to the beginning of this journal and read the part where I first saw him—God, was that really only four days ago? It seems like months—to know that initially, I thought Cal Langdon was hot.

And it's true that even now, knowing what I do about him, he still has his moments. Like when he pried my foot out of that crevasse between the cobblestones, and his whole hand fit around my ankle.

And sometimes when he looks at me with those too-blue eyes, it seems like there's a light shining from out of his head, like a jack-o'-lantern—a light only I can see, and which makes it very hard to maintain eye contact.

But still. In the car on the way back from Castelfidardo, I made a comment about how ludicrous it is that everything in this country closes from noon until four, sometimes five, every single day, and that really, it isn't any wonder that America is a superpower and Italy isn't, given that we only take half-hour lunches, for the most part.

And Mr. I Know Everything There Is To Know in the Entire Universe has the nerve to go, "Believe me, if the average temperature in America during the summer months was forty degrees Celsius, we'd be shutting down everything between noon and four as well."

Whoa! I am sorry, but that is nothing but showing off. CELSIUS? What American knows how to tell the temperature in Celsius?

OK, enough ranting against Cal Langdon. Not while I've got all this delicious sun to bask in. It's actually kind of hard to get worked up about anything, you know, with this sun beating down and the palm fronds overhead swaying gently in the breeze from the sea—carrying with it, as always, that slight hint of horse manure—and the only sounds those of bees buzzing and the crystal blue water in the pool gently rippling and Cal pecking at his Blackberry.

The sun is so hot, in fact, it seems to seep into your skin like thick heavy lotion. Really, it's hard to tell whether it's the bianco frizzante (SOOOOO good mixed with a little Orangina) or the sun, but I really feel, I don't know, like nothing matters right now . . . not even what happens to Dr. Kovac on ER. I feel like I could just lie here forever. . . .

✉

To: Cal Langdon <cal.langdon@thenyjournal.com>
Fr: Arthur Pendergast <a.pendergast@rawlingspress.com>
Re: The Book

Would you cool it? I'm not trying to bust your chops. I know you've got a lot going on right now. Hell, if I'd moved back to the States after a ten-year absence, and had to find a place to live, furniture to put in it, buy a car, etc., I'd be going stark raving mad.

Well, not really, since I'd just leave all that to my wife. But you don't have a wife. So don't worry about it.

Just, you know. If you could give me a rough idea of what you're thinking about doing for your second book. That would be nice.

Arthur Pendergast
Senior Editor
Rawlings Press
1418 Avenue of the Americas
New York, NY 10019
212-555-8764

✉

To: Jane Harris <jane@wondercat.com>
Fr: Holly Caputo <holly.caputo@thenyjournal.com>
Re: Did you see that?

????????????????

Holly

✉

To: Holly Caputo <holly.caputo@thenyjournal.com>
Fr: Jane Harris <jane@wondercat.com>
Re: Did you see that?

Hello. Aren't you getting married the day after tomorrow? What are you doing ogling other men's naked chests?

J

✉

To: Jane Harris <jane@wondercat.com>
Fr: Holly Caputo <holly.caputo@thenyjournal.com>
Re: Did you see that?

I'm getting married, but I'm not DEAD. My God, who knew that under that mild-mannered Oxford lurked a chest of such exquisite proportions? Did you notice the abs?

Holly

✉

To: Holly Caputo <holly.caputo@thenyjournal.com>
Fr: Jane Harris <jane@wondercat.com>
Re: Did you see that?

They were slightly hard to miss. Don't you think he was showing them off just SLIGHTLY by ripping off his shirt and diving in like that? I mean, DIVING?

J

✉

To: Jane Harris <jane@wondercat.com>
Fr: Holly Caputo <holly.caputo@thenyjournal.com>
Re: Did you see that?

Well, he's been working, while the rest of us were just out here lounging around. I think he just got frustrated and gave up, turned off the Blackberry, and went for it. I didn't catch anything "stagey" about it.

Wow, look at him go. That's a lot of laps. He must really be annoyed about something—or somebody—to be swimming that fast.

Holly

✉

To: Holly Caputo <holly.caputo@thenyjournal.com>
Fr: Jane Harris <jane@wondercat.com>
Re: Did you see that?

He's ruining my afternoon of total relaxation. How can I relax when someone is exercising that hard in front of me? He's making me feel guilty about all that pasta I had at lunch.

J

✉

To: Jane Harris <jane@wondercat.com>
Fr: Holly Caputo <holly.caputo@thenyjournal.com>
Re: Did you see that?

He'll stop soon. Oh, see. There you go. Oh, look, how sweet. He's coming to sit by YOU, Janie! I *told* you he likes you. Maybe even as much as PETER does.

Holly

✉

To: Holly Caputo <holly.caputo@thenyjournal.com>
Fr: Jane Harris <jane@wondercat.com>
Re: Did you see that?

I hate you.

J

Travel Diary of

~~Holly Caputo and Mark Levine~~

Jane Harris

Why are men—and boys—so weird?

I mean, they certainly LOOK nice enough, for the most part. Cal Langdon, in particular, though it GALLS me to admit it. I mean, look at him, sitting there in that lounge chair, with the sunlight winking off the drops of water still clinging to his golden body hair.

Oh my God, I can't believe I wrote the words golden body hair.

Still, not like he's got so much of it. Just enough, really.

Just enough to make me wonder how much more he's got, you know, below the waistband of his shorts.

I can't believe I wrote that EITHER!!!

Still. It doesn't matter how good they look—and just how, I'd like to know, does a guy whose job entails sitting behind a desk, typing stuff, get such defined biceps?—men are still weird.

Seriously. Just look at what they're doing now. The Modelizer, Mark, and Peter are having this totally in-depth—and boring—conversation about the Hubble space telescope and dark energy—whatever that is—and they are WAY into it. I mean, as much into it as Holly and I get when we're talking about ER.

They're going on about how dark energy—whatever it is—fills up most of the universe, along with dark matter, and how no one knows what either of those things is (which is a bit of a relief, since, um, I was thinking I'd missed something), but they seem to think it's responsible for the anti-gravitational force that is causing the universe to expand, rather than contract, the way everything else does, when gravity pulls on it.

Hello. Don't they realize they're in ITALY? Can't they shut up for FIVE MINUTES and enjoy the way the light is trickling through the green leaves as the sun sinks down, dappling the pool and veranda in golden half-light? Or the way the setting sun seems almost to create a mist across the patchworked hills, making them seem blurry to the eye—except for where the outbuildings on them are silhouetted against those great big purple clouds built up behind them, the aftereffects of a fleeing storm?

THAT's what they should be talking about. The miracles of nature right in front of them. Not some stupid dark energy, billions of miles away.

Oh, great. Those clouds, that I thought were fleeing? They're headed this way. It's going to rain in a second.

Aw, screw it. It's time for dinner anyway.

✉

To: Cal Langdon <cal.langdon@thenyjournal.com>
Fr: Joan Langdon < joan.langdon@artintucson.com>
Re: Mary

Hi, Calvin! It's me, Mom. I don't know where you are right now—are you still in Riyadh? I know you were on *Charlie Rose*—one of my neighbors told me. But of course I missed it, because you know I don't own a television—so you must have been back in the US for that.

I did buy your new book. It was very long.

But they have it in the window at Books-A-Million, so I'm sure you'll sell lots of copies.

Anyway, I hope you're well, and not working too hard . . . but knowing you, I'm sure that's the case. You were always such a workaholic. Remember in high school, when you were so determined to get into Yale? Your dad and I couldn't understand it. What's so wrong with a state school? We went to one, and didn't turn out so badly.

But you got your way, in the end. As always. Well, I mean, you got in. Too bad they wouldn't give us enough financial aid to let you go. But hey, you turned out all right! Looks like Ohio State didn't hurt you too much!

I myself am doing extremely nicely—I have a show at the Tucson Senior Center next month, featuring my latest series of "lint people." I really think these latest pieces are going to put me on the map in the art world. I see myself as a sort of middle-aged, female Matthew Barnye. You know, the artist who made a name for himself with Vaseline sculptures?

I can't tell you how good it feels, Cal, to finally be expressing my creative side. I felt so STIFLED all those years I ignored the artistic part of me. I really hope you're finding a way to let your own creativity flow, Cal. I know some people call writing art, but what you write . . . well, I don't think nonfiction counts. You've always looked down on your sister and me, I know, calling us "flakes."

But there's nothing "flakey" about creative expression, Cal. Nothing at all.

Speaking of your sister, I was wondering if you'd heard from her. I only ask because I had the oddest dream last night, in which you, your dad, and Mary and I were trapped on a frozen pond, and the ice had begun to crack. Oddly, you were the only one who managed to pull yourself to safety.

So I was just wondering if you knew if Mary was all right.

That's all.

Mom

To: Cal Langdon <cal.langdon@thenyjournal.com>
Fr: Hank Langdon < hank.langdon@expat.net>
Re: Hey

Hey! Whaddaya think? I got myself online! Yeah! I know! It's a miracle!

So when are you coming for a visit? I got an extra set of clubs. The courses here ain't bad at all. Well, you know, except for the spics. But you can't escape the spics in Mexico City, let me tell you!

Hey, I heard you landed some big book deal, or something. Think you can loan your old man ten grand or so? I got myself in a little deep with this guy over a horse—

Well, let me know. And if you talk to your mother or sister, tell 'em to lay off me. They've bled me dry. I don't have two pesos left to rub together.

Mañana.
Dad

To: Cal Langdon <cal.langdon@thenyjournal.com>
Fr: Mary Langdon <m.langdon@internetcafenetwork.com>
Re: You

So I take it from your not emailing me back that you have no interest in me or my life. I guess the word FAMILY doesn't mean anything to you.

Whatever. I can get along fine without you—which is why the judge granted me Emancipated Minor status in the first place.

I'm in Canada, now, in case you're interested. Not that MY travels could be of any interest to such a jet-setter like yourself. Where are YOU now, anyway? Gstaad? Ougoudagou? Some place more fabulous than where I am, I'm sure.

Don't worry (like you *would*), I'm sure I'll be fine. It's not that cold here yet. Well, except at night. But I've been sleeping in the van. Too bad Jeff can't leave the heat on overnight, but it wears out the battery.

See you in the next life.

Mare

✉

To: Mary Langdon <m.langdon@internetcafenetwork.com>
Fr: Cal Langdon <cal.langdon@thenyjournal.com>
Re: You

What is wrong with you? Why are you sleeping in some guy's van? I thought you'd have learned a lesson about that, given what happened last time.

And I DID reply to your last email. If you'd quit changing your email address every two days, you might actually hear from some of the people you've written to once in a while.

I can give you another thousand bucks if you let me know where I can wire it. But what happened to the grand I sent you last month? What are you doing with all of my money, anyway? If I find out you're blowing all of my money on drugs, Mary, I'm cutting you off. Do you understand me? Because I don't think you're quite getting the Emancipated part of being an emancipated minor. Which, by the way, at 25, you're not anymore.

Cal

✉

To: Cal Langdon <cal.langdon@thenyjournal.com>
Fr: Mary Langdon <m.langdon@internetcafenetwork.com>
Re: You

Oh my God, you are the best big brother any girl's ever had EVER! Send the money to the Western Union here in Whistler, BC.

And we have to live in the van because all the cheap apartments and hotel rooms are taken by Winter X boarders right now, gearing up for the games. But it's cool, because we're selling TONS of tie-dyed shit. We can't dye it fast enough, it seems.

And I need the cash for necessities, tampons, and food and stuff, until we start showing a profit. Jesus, Cal. I would never do drugs. I need my brain cells for my ART.

Thanks—U R the BEST!!

Much love,
Your little sis

✉

To: Mark Levine <mark.levine@thenyjournal.com>
Fr: Ruth Levine <r.levine@levinedentalgroup.com >
Re: Hello!

Sweetie, I'm sorry to bother you, I know you're having fun on your little European jaunt, but I need to know ASAP: What size sweater are you wearing lately? I know usually you like a Large, but you joined that gym, didn't you? So maybe you've bulked up a little, and need an Extra Large?

I only ask because it turns out Susie Schramm—you remember, I told you about her in my last email—she knits! Yes! On top of being a high-powered legal eagle AND a size four, she knits in her spare time (I mean, the time she spares from her work and volunteering for B'Nai Brith, of course).

And I've commissioned a sweater for you from her. Apparently, she isn't afraid to use bold colors, either. I know how much you love yellow, so that's what you're getting. . . .

Ooops, it was supposed to be a Hannukah surprise! Oh, well!

Write soon and let me know.

Love,
Mom

✉

To: Holly Caputo <holly.caputo@thenyjournal.com >
Fr: Darrin Caputo <darrin.caputo@caputographics.com >
Re: Hello, it is your mother

Holly, it is your mother again. Darrin says I'm not to use his email anymore to write to you, but you do not pick up your cell phone when I call. Either your cell phone doesn't work in Europe, or you are using that Caller ID, and not picking up when you see it is me.

Which is fine. I understand that you do not want to speak to your mother. Even though I am the one who gave birth to you, and wept with joy when I heard the doctor say you were a girl, the little daughter I had almost given up hope of having after four boys in a row.

I am writing now because I saw Jane Harris's mother at the Kroger Sav-On yesterday, and what she said to me there disturbs me very much. Your father says it is nothing, but I do not agree. I was telling Mrs. Harris how lucky she is to have a daughter like Jane, who sees only nice Christian boys, like that very pleasant British boy, Dave, and the investment banker, Malcolm.

And Mrs. Harris says to me, "But Mark Levine is very nice, too. Listen, Maria, you must stop thinking of it as losing a daughter, but instead, of gaining a son."

What does Claire Harris mean by this? Why would she think I am gaining a son? I do not need any more sons, I already have four . . . five if you count Darrin's Roberto. Holly, you are not thinking of doing something foolish when you are in Italy, are you?

I hope you know that if you marry this boy Mark, he will NOT be a son to me. Just as you will no longer be my daughter. Think on this, I beg you.

I will pray for you.

Your mother

Travel Diary of

~~Holly Caputo and Mark Levine~~

Jane Harris

Somebody needs to take Cal Langdon aside and tell him that that shirt he is wearing, which I am sure he thinks is very cutting edge and SoHo, actually makes him look gay. How can a straight man not know this?

And I know Cal is straight. Not just because he was married before, or the skank I saw slinking from his hotel room, because you know, those don't really prove anything anymore, in today's day and age (just look at Curt). I know because of what happened just now at the restaurant we're having dinner at since it was raining again (what is WRONG with this country?) and nobody felt like cooking outside, much less risking all the electricity going off again by turning the oven on inside.

Plus everybody seems to be in a really bad mood, although no one will tell me why.

It must be the rain.

Anyway, they only let us into this restaurant after we stood at the door for like ten minutes tapping at the glass, then begging the proprietors in broken Italian to please please serve us, as they, like every restaurant owner we have encountered in Porto Recanati (except of course the Crazy Bar and Sexy Tattoo Shop), are actually very reluctant to prepare food and sell it to people, though they haven't bothered to put a closed sign in their window. Apparently in the off-season what Le Marche restauranteurs do is invite all of their aged friends to sit in their restaurant at night and watch Magnum PI—in Italian of course—and ignore any actual paying customer who might wander in.

Thank God Mark is incapable of taking no for an answer, or we would never get fed. He carries this Guide to Le Marche handbook around with him and insists we have to eat at all the places Holly's uncle marked for us. He even showed the restaurant proprietors their ranking, and insisted they feed us. Maybe it's something to do with him being around sick patients all day, but Mark just exudes this "Be nice to me" vibe, which people totally seem to respond to.

I mean, except for Holly's mom.

And it's not really as sickening as it sounds. On him, it works, and doesn't leave you feeling like you want to hit him over the head with a pool cue or anything.

Anyway, the way I know Cal is not gay, in spite of the shirt and the model ex-wife—and Holly's assurances to the contrary, of course, but hey, the future wife of the best friend is not always the first to know—is that after *Magnum*, the movie *Babe* came on, the one about the little pig who can herd sheep, and all of the Marquesians or whatever they are sat there, enrapt, in their traditional Le Marche-wear of jeans and Bon Jovi T-shirts, but Cal never blinked an eye. He just went right on drinking his grappa like it was actually good and not something that should only be sold as a facial astringent.

No gay guy can resist the lure of *Babe*. Not that I think the restauranteur and all of his aged friends are gay. They're just foreigners. They probably cried at the end of *Magnum*, only I missed it because I was in the men's room, trying to smuggle out a roll of toilet paper, because of course there wasn't one in the ladies' room. Ditto a toilet seat.

Which, by the way, I have to say *What's up with that?* about. Clearly, Italian women never go to the bathroom outside of their own homes. That is the only thing I can think of to explain the state of some of the ladies' washrooms in Le Marche. What do all the Italian ladies do, anyway, when they have to go? Just squat? I can barely make it into a squat during Pilates, and that's in drawstring pants. What are the chances of me squatting in control-top panties and a pair of tight capris around my knees? Seriously? Think about it. The restaurant owners obviously haven't.

And yes, I know, it's a summer community and we're here on the off-season, but I highly doubt the owner of this place has all the toilet seats stored somewhere in the back until the beach starts getting crowded again. I mean, clearly this is a culture where toilet seats just aren't that important.

To which I say, Um, again, this is why America is a superpower and you, Italy, are not. Because we care about our comfort in the john.

Anyway, now everyone is arguing about tomorrow. You know, who's going back to Rome to visit the US consulate. At first I just figured Holly and Mark would go by themselves, and I could lounge by the pool drinking bianco frizzante and reading the latest Nora Roberts. Um, hello, this is my vacation, right?

But no. Cal had to be all, "I'll come with you," to Holly and Mark.

Hello? Go with them? Why? Don't you have a book you're supposed to be writing, or something? They don't need you, Cal Langdon. A translator, maybe. But not a modelizer.

I know what he's up to. He might think I don't, because I am just a lowly cartoonist and he is the big Saudi Arabian oil crisis guru journalist. But I am ONTO his devious plan. He thinks he's going to go with Holly and Mark and make subtle anti-marriage remarks that will feed into Holly's insecurities and make her so freaked out about marrying against her parents' wishes that she's going to call the whole thing off!

Well, I am not going to let it happen. I just declared that if Cal's going, I'm going, too!

Now he's staring at me all squinty-eyed-Robert-Redfordy across the table, like I'm going to be so intimidated, I'm going to back down.

But it won't work. I am staring squinty-eyed right back at him, while Holly and Mark argue over whether they should let either of us come with them. Mark says it will give us a chance to try one of the Roman restaurants Holly's uncle recommended in the Guide to Roma book Mark found back at the villa.

But Holly says it's our vacation too, and we shouldn't have to spend it shuttling back and forth between Rome and Le Marche in a Toyota. Even though this time there won't be a suitcase in the backseat, since it's just a day trip.

I could see Cal wasn't going to back down, so I said, "I happen to be extremely fond of Toyotas," causing Holly to look at me and go, "Oh, God, what's WRONG with you? And what are you writing in that book?"

I've been outed. More later.

Travel Diary of
~~Holly Caputo and Mark Levine~~
Jane Harris

The horror continues.

As soon as Cal got up to go use the facilities himself just now, I told Mark if he was any kind of friend he'd tell Cal to stay home at the villa with me (even though I don't want him there, as it will mean spending the day alone with him while Holly and Mark are off US consulating tomorrow, but whatever). Also, that he should tell Cal his shirt looks gay. Mark pointed out that he had already encouraged Cal to stay home to no avail, and that the shirt is from Bangladesh and it's the only clean thing left in Cal's backpack. Apparently, he's sweet-talked Frau Schumacher into doing his laundry while we eat.

I can't believe he'd take advantage of that sweet old lady's crush on him in such an obvious manner, even if he DID give her ten euros for her trouble, according to Mark.

Still.

At least the food is good. REALLY good. Even when it's prepared by someone who won't take their eyes off Babe. Although Cal and I both eschewed the raw oysters, Cal because he doesn't like them, and me because I may be a travel neophyte, but I am not eating raw fish in a foreign country. Holly and Mark were both like, "Oh, well, more for us," and slurped down like twenty each.

Whatever. It's their funeral.

After this, since it's stopped raining, we're going to get gelati from the Gelateria and take a moonlit walk along the beach. Romantic! Well, for Holly and Mark.

Uh-oh, back to the Who's Going To Rome Tomorrow argument. . . .

Who buys their shirts in BANGLADESH??? What is wrong with the Gap, for God's sake?

✉

To: Jane Harris <jane@wondercat.com>
Fr: Claire Harris <charris2004@freemail.com>
Re: Holly

Hi, honey! Don't worry, everything's fine. Well, I mean, your dad burst a blood vessel in his eye just now trying to move the stereo, but he says it doesn't even hurt.

Anyway, I hope I didn't mess anything up, but I saw Marie Caputo in the grocery store just now, and she was down in the mouth as usual about Holly (and telling me how lucky I was that you only date boys like Dave—whatever happened to him, anyway? He was so sweet) and I might have mentioned something about how she shouldn't think of Holly's marrying Mark as losing a daughter, but as gaining a son.

Then I remembered she's not supposed to know anything about Holly marrying Mark this week.

I hope I didn't let the cat out of the bag, or anything!

And as for that Cal, well, I agree, Saudi Arabia is a very boring subject for a book.

But still, he looked quite nice in that turtleneck he was wearing on *Charlie Rose*. I think it might have been cashmere. I'm just saying it wouldn't hurt to give the boy a chance.

And what do you mean, I shouldn't worry about him falling in love with you? I don't want to hear that kind of negative talk from you, young lady. You know you're irresistible. At least when you don't have PMS and you wear your hair out of your eyes.

Love,
Mom

✉

To: Claire Harris <charris2004@freemail.com>
Fr: Jane Harris <jane@wondercat.com>
Re: Holly

MOM! THIS IS REALLY REALLY BAD!!!! I TOLD YOU NOT TO SAY ANYTHING!!!

DO NOT SAY ANYTHING ELSE TO ANYONE UNTIL I TELL YOU IT'S OK!

AND DON'T GO TO THE KROGER SAV-ON OR ANYWHERE ELSE WHERE YOU MIGHT MEET HOLLY'S MOM!!!!!!!!!!!!!!!!!!

J

✉

To: Darrin Caputo <darrin.caputo@caputographics.com>
Fr: Jane Harris <jane@wondercat.com>
Re: Your mother

Oh my God, Darrin, does your mother know? About Holly and Mark, I mean? Because I think my mother might have spilled something. YOU know, right? I mean about them—

Oh my God, what if you're not supposed to know either? Holly will KILL me if she finds out I told. She really wanted to surprise you, on account of all those times you kidded her that she would settle on one guy.

But whatever, this is an emergency. Holly's been acting all weird since this afternoon, kind of down, and I think it might be because she heard from your mother. Darrin, Holly and Mark are eloping this week! But everything is going wrong! The marriage license people here in Le Marche aren't cooperating and your uncle's oven doesn't work and there's this friend of Mark's who keeps saying the meanest things and—

Well, never mind all that. Anyway, you have GOT to keep your mom from figuring out what's going on, because I don't think Holly can take much more. Can you do something to throw her off the scent? Pretend you and Bobby are adopting or something?

Oh, I know! Tell her you're going to have a sex change operation!!! YES!!! Transgenderism will TOTALLY distract her!

Thanks, Darrin, you're the best! I'll write when I know more. . . .

AND DON'T TELL HOLLY I TOLD!!!! WHEN YOU HEAR SHE'S MARRIED, ACT SURPRISED!!!!!!!!!!!

J

Travel Diary of

~~Holly Caputo and Mark Levine~~

Jane Harris

AAAARRRGH. MOTHERS. I mean, I love her and everything—how great is it to have someone in your life who, every time you complain about a guy, is all, "He must be secretly in love with you, that's why he's acting that way"?—but she has the BIGGEST MOUTH.

I mean, this is a CRISIS, her spilling the beans—well, sort of, anyway—to Mrs. Caputo.

And really, it's my own fault, because I never should have said anything to her in the first place . . . to Mom, I mean. She hasn't been able to hold a secret since . . . well, ever.

I just don't know how to fix it. This new crisis, I mean. This is something Frau Schumacher's not going to be able to shout at anybody about until it's, you know, done.

As soon as I got that email I went to Holly and Mark's room—Holly went to bed as soon as we got home from the restaurant, saying she had a headache . . . and no wonder, if she'd heard from her mother the way I suspected she had—and tapped on the door, since I knew Mark was down on the terrazza having a nightcap with Cal.

Anyway, Holly called "Come in" all weakly—she looked awful! Just AWFUL! I asked her if she'd heard from her mom and she said she had, and I said I was sorry and that it was all my fault.

Holly was just sweet as could be, and told me not to worry, that she didn't blame me a bit. . . .

But it's all my fault. I just know it.

"I'm starting to think this wedding's just not to be, anyway," Holly said.

!!!!!!!!!!!!!!!!

I told her that she HAS to marry Mark. That if she doesn't, it will shake my faith in romantic love to its very core. That the two of them were made for each other. I mean, look at the way he has those really big feet, and hers are so little and dainty! And look how she hates tomatoes and he loves them, and he hates sauerkraut and she loves it. . . . They routinely finish each other's plates.

And they BOTH love Seventh Heaven, not just Holly. Mark won't admit it, but HE doesn't answer the phone when I call on Monday nights, either. And Holly says HE always cries at the end, too.

I told all this to Holly and she just nodded weakly and said she guessed she was just tired. So I told her to go to sleep and that she'd feel better in the morning.

But of course this was not the most reassuring of conversations. So I went downstairs to find Mark—and ran smack into him coming up the stairs, since he said he wasn't feeling so hot either, and had decided to go to bed early as well.

So I grabbed him by the arm and dragged him into one of the empty bedrooms—I guess Cal didn't end up taking the pink one after all—and told him what happened with my mom and Holly's mom.

All he said was, "Aw, Jane. I wouldn't worry about that."

"But Holly's devastated!" I cried. I can't believe he couldn't see that! I mean, it's true I've known Holly since the first grade when her family moved onto my street and I went over and rang the bell and asked if they had any little girls for me to play with.

But Mark's been living with her for the past two years! You would think he'd know her at least as well as I do! I mean, they sleep in the same bed!

"Holly's just tired," Mark said. "She's beat, same as me. It's been kind of a long day."

"Then . . ." I have to admit, I had tears in my own eyes, as if I had just watched the end of Babe or an episode of Seventh Heaven, "you're not thinking of calling it off?"

"The wedding?" Mark looked down at me like I was crazy. "No way. Why would I do that?"

"Well, because—"

And then, before I could stop myself, it all came tumbling out. The truth. About his friend Cal.

I know it wasn't very nice of me. To tattle, I mean. Especially to a groom about his best man. Especially just thirty-six hours before the wedding.

But still. Cal totally deserves it. Who does he think he is, anyway, with his phenylethylamine and his thinking he can sabotage my best friend's wedding by planting doubts in her—or worse, her husband-to-be's—head?

Mark listened to everything I had to say (I talked really sotto voce, so Cal, still down on the terrazza, wouldn't overhear) and, when I was done, he did the weirdest thing.

He threw back his head, and laughed.

Yes! Actually laughed! Like it was the most hilarious thing he'd ever heard!

Frankly, I don't see what was so funny. I mean, if I had been about to get married, and I found out one of my friends was planning on using whatever influence she had over me to talk me out of it—

Well, that's just ridiculous, because if I were set on marrying someone, no one would be able to talk me out of it.

Which is exactly what Mark said to me.

Mark: "Janie, Cal's one of the best friends I've ever had. But no one is going to talk me out of marrying Holly. Particularly not someone whose own marriage was such a spectacular disaster."

This information dried my tears right up.

And I know it was really wrong of me, but I totally couldn't help going, "You knew Valerie, Cal's ex?"

Mark: "Knew her? Yeah, I knew her. About as well as he did, anyway. And for about as long. I was there the night they met."

Me: (extremely interested in this) "Really? And was she really beautiful? She was a model, right?"

Mark just shrugged. I have to admit, he didn't look so hot. But maybe it was the light from the harsh Italian bulb inside a pinky shade.

Mark: "She was all right. Not my type. Tall and blonde and skinny. You know. Typical model."

Me: (nodding sympathetically) "And very, very dumb, right?"

Mark: "Well, not so dumb that she didn't know she'd latched onto a guy flush with his first-ever paycheck. And the whole modeling thing wasn't going as well as she'd have liked. Contrary to what she was apparently led to believe by the Barbizon School or wherever she trained, modeling is quite hard. You have to get up early. And she didn't like that."

Wow! Mark really hated Cal's wife! He hardly EVER says anything bad about anyone, seeing as how he's, you know, nice and all.

"So . . ." I still wasn't sure it was safe to leave Mark alone with his friend. "If Cal DOES try to talk you out of marrying Holly . . ."

"He's not going to try any such thing," Mark said. But at my skeptically raised eyebrows, he added, "Fine, well, he can try, but it won't work. I can't believe you, of all people, would even think such a thing is possible, Janie. I love Holly, and no one's going to talk me out of marrying her. Not Cal. Not my mother. Not even Holly's mother. Nothing is going to stand in the way of our doing it. NOTHING."

Sadly, the conclusion of this very inspiring speech was somewhat anti-climactic, since about the time he uttered the words 'Holly's mother,' Mark got kind of green around the gills, and went, "Um. Excuse me. I don't feel so hot all of a sudden" and ducked into the bathroom, from which some explosive sounds soon emanated.

So I wished him well and left him for my own room, happy in the knowledge that, should Cal try anything, Mark, at least, would stay strong.

As for Holly . . . well, we'll have to see. I THINK she knows she's doing the right thing.

I'll work on her some more in the car tomorrow.

Now to let Cal Langdon know he won't be able to talk Mark out of it. . . .

Travel Diary of
~~Holly Caputo and Mark Levine~~
Jane Harris

Oh my God, you'll never guess what I just caught Cal Langdon doing!!!! Mr. Hardened News Journalist was down on the terrazza, holding out a plate of Zio Matteo's tuna to all of these scrawny stray cats that had come slinking over to the villa from the stables.

He jumped like I'd shot him when I said his name, and the cats all ran, but I saw them.

Oh, I saw them, all right.

Between the being-afraid-of-snakes thing, and now a soft spot for cats, I guess Mr. No Heart might just have one after all.

Still, I didn't let on that I knew. About his heart, I mean. Instead, I told him—because I couldn't help myself—that I'd spoken to Mark, and that he (Cal) was living in a fantasy world if he thought he could talk him (Mark) out of marrying Holly on Wednesday.

To my surprise, Cal just totally ignored that. Instead—while staring at my Christian Louboutins, as usual—he asked me instead if I knew Indian women sometimes decorate their feet with henna.

????????????

There is something seriously wrong with this guy.

Me: "Um, no. But I do know if they show their ankles in public, they can be punished by having their feet cut off. Why don't you write a book about how unfair that is, instead of what's going to happen to the Saudis when the oil runs out?"

Cal: (finally looking away from my feet) "Do you think women's lives there are going to get easier when their country is essentially shut off from contact with the outside world, due to their no longer having a product we want to exploit? Or do you think they'll get harder?"

Me: "Harder, obviously. But what can I do about it? Use fewer water bottles?"

Cal: "Yes, overconsumption of petroleum-based products is a leading cause of global warming."

Seriously, I can't believe he ever got any woman to marry him. I mean, with a line like that. Even a model.

Hey, maybe that's why he only dates foreigners now. Because they can't tell what's coming out of his mouth.

Me: "Well, then maybe we'd better just use it all up and get it over with so we run out already and can go back to how things were before."
Cal: "You mean before they started bottling spring water and selling it for a buck fifty a pop and pretending it's better for you than tap?"

!!!!!!!!!!!!!

Me: "I don't know. You're the one who wrote a book about it. Why do you keep looking at my feet, anyway?"
Cal: "Why do you keep looking at my crotch?"

I SWEAR TO GOD!!! THAT IS WHAT HE ASKED ME!!!!

Then THANK GOD Peter showed up from out of nowhere and went, "Jane Harris, I am hearing your woice and knew you vere avake. Now will you be drawing me the sketches of Vundercat you promised for my Veb site?" and handed me a sketch pad and some markers.

So I said, "Of course, Peter," in my most gracious voice—even though I was FREAKING OUT about the crotch thing—and drew him about fifty Wondercat sketches, while Cal sat there scowling in the candlelight and going, "Peter, shouldn't you be in bed by now? Don't you have school in the morning?"

But of course Peter explained that he goes to Internet school and doesn't have to log on by any particular time.

And all I could think was, what if Peter hadn't shown up right then? I mean, Cal and I had basically been in each other's face over that whole petroleum thing. Close enough that, you know, it occurred to me—just kind of randomly—that if we didn't hate each other so much, we might have started, I don't know.

Kissing or something.

I KNOW! I don't even LIKE him. He's a totally pompous know-it-all—a modelizer!

But still, he does kind of . . . <u>exude</u> something. I don't know what it is. I mean, I was having a pretty good time hating his guts right up until I saw him with those cats. CATS!!!! HE LIKES CATS!!!!

And he so clearly didn't WANT to be caught feeding them. He looked so GUILTY when he saw me.

And then, when we got close there, during our little argument . . .

BAM. There it was. I couldn't stop noticing how handsome he looked in the candlelight, with those too-blue eyes and his messy Brad Pitt-y hair and his shirt open a little at the neck so I saw a tiny bit of that chest he'd had out on display earlier by the pool and—

WHAT'S WRONG WITH ME??? I ALREADY HAVE A BOYFRIEND!!!!!!!!

Well, okay, not really.

But I have one if I want one. All I have to do is go to British Columbia, and WHAM, there he is, the boyfriend. A boyfriend who BELIEVES in love. A boyfriend who would NEVER say love is a mere chemical reaction in the brain caused by surges of phenylethylamine (um, especially since Malcolm doesn't know any words that big).

SO WHY AM I EVEN THINKING ABOUT CAL LANGDON IN THAT WAY????

It can't just be the cat thing. It must be all this fresh air. It DOES things to a girl. As soon as I get back to the city and breathe in good old New York exhaust fumes, I'll be all right again.

I hope.

In the meantime, I've just got to STAY AWAY from him and his pheromones or whatever it is that makes me keep thinking about what it would be like to sleep with Cal Langdon.

Tomorrow I'll make sure to wear my Adidas, too. No guy looks at your feet when you're in your Adidas.

God, how am I supposed to get to sleep NOW?

PDA of Cal Langdon

I have GOT to stay away from prosecco. It makes me do the most damnable things, things I'd never do were I in my right mind . . . feed perfectly fine tuna to a lot of stray cats, for example. Or admire the way the moonlight brings out the highlights in a certain cartoonist's hair . . .

Who drank all the scotch?

✉

To: Jane Harris <jane@wondercat.com>
Fr: Darrin Caputo <darrin.caputo@caputographics.com>
Re: Your mother

ARE YOU SERIOUS???? HOLLY AND MARK ARE ELOPING???? In Castelfidardo?

Well, that's kind of a weird place to do it (have you seen the whang on that naked accordionist statue in the town square? That dude is HUNG), but I couldn't be happier for them. OF COURSE we'll do something to throw Mom off the scent. I don't know what, exactly. . . . Bobby's going to think something up, he's better at this kind of thing than I am.

Oh my God, that is just the BEST NEWS. NO ONE deserves a romantic wedding in Italy more than my sister Holly. Give her a big kiss from me, and don't worry, I won't tell a SOUL!!!!

Love,
D

✉

To: Jane Harris <jane@wondercat.com>
Fr: Claire Harris <charris2004@freemail.com>
Re: Holly's mother

Really, Jane, you don't have to SHOUT at me. That's what they call it when you write an email in capital letters, you know. SHOUTING. And it's very rude.

I didn't mean to say anything to Marie. Obviously. It just slipped out. You should be a little more understanding, you know. I'm under a lot of stress these days over at the Salvation Army, where I've been volunteering. The past three Saturdays in the row I've signed up to work in the thrift shop, and each and every time they've put me in the back, ironing the donated baby clothes! I know I'm very good with an iron, but can't they at least once let me work the cash register? Or help the poor people find the right clothes for their body type?

But no. "Oh, look, here comes Claire. Get out the ironing board."

I am seriously considering quitting and going over to Good Will. Marcy Clark told me they don't make anybody iron ANYTHING over there.

Plus your dad touched a mango yesterday, and you know how allergic he is. I WARNED him there was a mango in the fruit bowl. I was going to use it in the fruit salad I'm bringing to the gourmet potluck at Helen Fogarty's this weekend.

But Dad had to go and cut it up, thinking it was a papaya, and now he's got hives all over his hands and arms. I've been putting calamine lotion on them, but I think we're going to have to take another trip over to the Promptcare for some prednisone. . . .

So don't be so snappy with me, young lady. I have a lot going on.

I don't know what Marie's problem is, anyway. At least *her* daughter's got a man who wants to marry her. All MY daughter has is a development deal with the Cartoon Network. And while Daddy and I are very proud of you, sweetie, you can't exactly honeymoon with a development deal, now, can you? Or gaze into a development deal's sweet angelic eyes while you're changing its diaper.

So cut your mother some slack.

Love,
Mom

Travel Diary of

~~Holly Caputo and Mark Levine~~

Jane Harris

Okay. Okay. Everything is going to be all right. I can figure this out. I can totally figure this out—

No, I can't. This is a disaster. A total and complete disaster. What am I going to do????

✉

To: Listserv <Wundercat@wundercatlives.com>
Fr: Peter Schumacher <webmaster@wundercatlives.com>
Re: JANE HARRIS

Good morning fellow lovers of Wundercat! There is BIG NEWS today about JANE HARRIS! Her friends who will be getting the marriage both eat the bad oysters last night, and this morning are sick as dogs! YES! They cannot get up out of the beds!

And this is bad because they are supposed to get the form from the Consulate of the US today, so they can have the marriage tomorrow!

But when I drove by the villa this morning on my motorino, to bring JANE HARRIS fresh brotchen, she is very upset, and says, "Ask your grandmother what can be done." So I get my grandmother, and she comes to the villa and says that nothing can be done from eating the bad oyster, they will have to wait until it has passed through.

Which, if it does not do soon, there will be no marriage tomorrow!

So this is BAD NEWS for JANE HARRIS.

I will keep you informed as news continues! This is Peter Schumacher, #1 Fan Of Wundercat!

Wundercat Lives—4eva!
Peter

Travel Diary of

~~Holly Caputo and Mark Levine~~

Jane Harris

Oysters. They just HAD to have the oysters.

I warned them. They can't say I didn't warn them. Who eats raw shellfish in a foreign country, I ask you? Who? This isn't Japan. Italy is not known for its raw seafood. What were they THINKING?

Poor Mark. I guess that's what I heard him throwing up last night. And he's STILL throwing it up. He can barely move from the bed.

And Holly . . . my God, when I knocked on their bedroom door to see why they weren't up yet for our drive to Rome, and Holly answered, she looked like . . . well, the undead. She hasn't looked this bad since that Fourth of July we invented the drink with the watermelon balls and vodka (Rockets' Red Glare).

"I don't think there's going to be any wedding," she said. And then had to run to the bathroom.

What could I do but follow her? It's not like I haven't held her hair for her while she barfed plenty of times before—Rockets' Red Glare in particular.

"Holly," I said, as gently as I could, when she'd sunk back down onto the bathroom tiles in exhaustion. "You guys HAVE to make it to Rome today. You know tomorrow's the only day the mayor said he could fit your wedding into the schedule."

Which turned out not to be the right thing to say, since Holly promptly started to cry.

"I know!" she wailed. "But what can we do? We wouldn't last five minutes in the car. We'd have to pull over every thirty seconds to throw up. Oh, God, Janie. It's over. We're not getting married. Not now, anyway. Not in Italy. And the way everything seems to be going against us . . . maybe not ever. Maybe my mother is right. Maybe HIS mother is right. Maybe we should just forget it. Maybe it's just not meant to be."

I know! I couldn't believe what I was hearing.

"Not meant to be? Holly, I know you don't feel well, but are you NUTS? You can't just forget it. You guys HAVE to get married. And you have to get married here, in Italy."

She just looked at me through miserable, swollen eyes. "Why?"

"Because I already told Darrin!" was what I ALMOST said. I remembered that I wasn't supposed to have told anyone, though, and at the last possible second changed it to, "Because it's what you've always wanted to do. You've been planning this forever. And Mark wants it, too, I know it. More than anything. You can't just give up because of a little food poisoning!"

To which she responded by barfing some more.

I got her back to bed, somehow. Then I found Peter outside with more of those breakfast rolls, and asked him to get his grandmother. Frau Schumacher came over, looking very concerned, and went in to see the stricken couple. Her expression, when she came out of the room again, was grave.

"No good," she said to me. "Zey vill not make the drive to Roma and back today. Tomorrow, yes. But not today."

"But it HAS to be today," I cried. "There's no other time! The mayor said Wednesday was the only day . . .and we leave Friday anyway."

But I know Frau Schumacher is right. She's downstairs making some hot broth for Mark and Holly to choke down—it doesn't matter if the lights go out right now, since it's daytime. A beautiful day, as a matter of fact. The sun is beaming down, and the pool is sparkling, and the breeze is causing the palm fronds to sway gently. . . .

Damn it! Why did they eat those oysters?

And why does this country have to be so BACKWARD??? If a person wants to get married here, and has all the right forms from back in the US, why CAN'T she??? Why do they have to send her all over creation for MORE forms??? Is it some kind of test to see how dedicated they are to the idea of being married? I mean, it's just a FORM, anybody can get a form—

Holy crap.

Anybody can get a form.

PDA of Cal Langdon

Honest to God, I don't know how this happened. Last thing I knew, I was sleeping blissfully.

Then, not five minutes ago, a small but very determined missile hit my bed, tearing off my very comfortably arranged sheets and shouting in my ear that it was time to get up and get in the car.

I vaguely recall that this missile seemed feminine in form—not an unpleasant way to be roused. Until I realized just which, precisely, female the form belonged to.

Then a cup of coffee was shoved in my hand, and I was urged to dress. Which I did. And then, when I wandered downstairs, wondering what was happening and why Frau Schumacher was at the stove, making what appeared to be soup of some kind, I was very rudely snatched, shoved outside, pushed into the passenger seat of the car, and driven off at considerable speed down the driveway by someone who is apparently not exactly familiar with a stick shift.

A someone who looks remarkably like Jane Harris.

On crystal meth.

Oh, that's right. It's all coming back to me now. We're supposed to be escorting Mark and Holly to Rome so that they can apply for some sort of form at the US embassy.

Except that for some reason, Mark and Holly do not appear to be in the car with us.

"Um, Jane," I ask, in what I hope is a soothing tone that won't startle the young woman beside me, looking so wild-eyed behind the wheel. "Aren't we forgetting something? Or should I say, someone? A *pair* of someones?"

She seems barely to register my presence in the car, she's checking so frantically in the rearview mirror for a hole in the oncoming traffic so she can make the turn onto the strada principale.

"Mark and Holly have food poisoning," is her surprising response. "They won't be able to make it. We have to go without them."

"I see." I'm trying to sound as reasonable as I can, seeing as how she is clearly unaccustomed to driving and conversing at the same time. "And am I to understand that we'll be applying for whatever form it is they're lacking?"

"Yeah." She tosses something into my lap. Looking down, I see that it's a pair of passports. "Don't worry, I got their passports. Their birth certificates, too."

This strikes me as highly amusing.

"And do you really think that the US embassy is going to issue this form to us just because we're holding our friends' passports and birth certificates," I ask, playing along, "simply because we ask them to, as a favor?"

"No," comes Jane Harris's somewhat startling reply. "They're going to issue the form because we're going to tell them we're Mark Levine and Holly Caputo."

This is definitely the funniest thing I've heard all morning.

"Isn't that going to be a little difficult?" I ask. "Seeing as how Mark is dark-haired and wears glasses, and I'm fair-haired, and have twenty/twenty vision?"

Next thing I knew, Mark's glasses were hurled into my lap.

"I filched them off his bedside table," my kidnapper explained. "And you can't tell his hair is that dark in the picture. It's black and white. You could say it got bleached in the sun, or whatever, if anybody asks. Which they won't."

Sadly, I'm starting to wake up now. Even more sadly, this is all starting to seem less and less like a dream, and more and more like a real-life nightmare.

"Wait a minute. Are you serious?" Because she LOOKS totally serious. And we are hurtling down the strada principale—past signs that say ROMA—at a very serious speed. "We're going to POSE as Mark and Holly?"

"Why not?" She is passing a large truck carrying—predictably—numerous live chickens, stacked high. They squawk at us hysterically. "All we have to do is show our IDs and sign some forms. What's the big?"

"The BIG," I say (since when did people start leaving off the word 'deal' when asking what the big deal is, anyway? Is this an artist thing? Mary does this, as well), "is that that is what I believe is called forgery. And probably perjury. And maybe a whole bunch of other things, as well."

Jane Harris has not once turned her head in my direction. She is wearing sunglasses, which makes it extremely difficult to see her eyes, and thus whether or not she has gone absolutely and completely bonkers.

"Oh, please," she's saying. "Like we'll get caught. Mark's a doctor, remember? No one can read his signature anyway. And I'm an artist. I've been forging Holly's mom's name on report cards and tardy slips for ages. I think I can easily manage to do Holly's. You can just scribble something for Mark's."

This has progressed from a pleasant game to an entirely unpleasant situation.

"Jane," I try again. "Are you kidnapping me and forcing me to go to Rome with you to commit fraud against the US government?"

She refuses to see the gravity of the situation, replying merely, "Oh, shut up and drink your coffee and keep writing in your little machine there, if it makes you feel better. There's some of Peter's brotchen in the back if you want it. And I'm not kidnapping you. I'm not demanding a ransom from anybody for you. As if anybody'd pay it if I did."

There must be some sort of Italian law that forbids this sort of thing . . . taking advantage of a man in a less than wakeful state, and forcing him to drive hundreds of kilometers to a city he only just came from a day or two before, where he will be forced to impersonate another man. . . .

She's wearing Adidas, but I can see still see the cat tattoo. Is it because it's so early, or can it really be . . . well . . . winking at me?

Travel Diary of

~~Holly Caputo and Mark Levine~~

Jane Harris

This is going to work. This HAS to work.

I know Cal doesn't think it's going to (big surprise).

But what does HE know? He's been against those two getting together since before any of this even started. Look at him now, asking for the key to the men's room. He STILL looks as if he doesn't know quite what hit him. His hair is sticking up in the back in the most peculiar—but strangely erotic—fashion.

EROTIC???? What am I THINKING???? I am on a MISSION here. I can't be thinking about sex at a time like this!!!

This HAS to work. We're halfway to Rome now, and it's only a little after ten. We should get there before lunch . . . well, probably just as they're closing for lunch.

But that's okay. It's the US embassy. They can't POSSIBLY take a four-hour lunch at the US embassy. They're AMERICAN, for God's sake. They probably take an hour lunch, like all normal people. So we can fill out the form, get the APOSTILLE, and get back on the road by two or three o'clock, and be home before dark.

PLEASE let them only take an hour for lunch. . . .

To: Jane Harris <jane@wondercat.com>
Fr: Holly Caputo <holly.caputo@thenyjournal.com>
Re: Where are you?

Sorry if there's typos in this, I can't really see very well, my head is pounding so much. But where are you guys? Frau Schumacher—who is being so sweet to us—says she doesn't know, that you just took off without a word to anyone. . . .

Well, I'm glad, anyway. I mean, that you're not here to see this. I hope you're off having fun somewhere. I'm so sorry for spoiling your vacation. And the wedding. I know how much you were looking forward to it. Almost as much as me—02q9375)(*&@

Sorry, I couldn't stop crying there for a minute, and lost sight of the keyboard.

Anyway, I'm glad you and Cal seem to be getting along now, and hope you've gone to Loredo or somewhere. There really is some lovely sightseeing in the area. The Madonna's house, for instance. Apparently angels lifted it and brought it from the Holy Land and dropped it here in Le Marche. . . .

I was just wondering, though, have you seen Mark's glasses? He swears he left them on the nightstand, but now they're gone.

Not that it matters, since the only place he's going is the bathroom. Still, it's strange.

Well, write when you get a chance. Oh, God, not again—I have to go—

Holly

Travel Diary of

~~Holly Caputo and Mark Levine~~

Jane Harris

We're here!!!! The US embassy!!! We made it with minutes to spare!!!! Cal took over the driving after the Mobil station, and we practically FLEW the next few hundred kilometers.

Plus, he insisted on taking this different route, which didn't go through the mountains. Which was good, since I forgot my Dramamine. We reached Rome at five minutes to twelve.

And now we're here!!!!

I must say, this place isn't at all like what I would have thought. I mean, inside, it's kind of like my dentist's office. There are all these chairs and people waiting and a glassed-in reception desk and you have to take a number (well, that's more like at my butcher's than at my dentist's, but whatever). Our number is 92.

I have to say, the Modelizer is being much better about this than I'd thought he'd be, judging by his initial reaction in the car, when he finally woke up. I admit I kind of shanghaied him. I knew he wasn't really awake when I made him get in the car.

Still, he's taking it like a total sport. He hasn't uttered a peep of anti-marriage propaganda all morning. Maybe the guy's finally coming around after all.

<u>Fat-bottomed girls/They make the rockin' world go round</u>—

Oh my God, I can't BELIEVE that's all we had to listen to the whole drive! We are heading STRAIGHT to a music store the minute we get out of here and buying another CD. I don't care what. ANYTHING but Queen.

Although I have to admit, Freddy Mercury is totally growing on me. <u>We are the champions, my friends</u>—

Ooooooh, they're calling a number. 92, 92, let it be 92!!!!!!

28?

28????

Cal just looked at me and went, "Looks like we're going to be here awhile."

Understatement of the year.

And all they've got to read is International Time magazine! International Time is like watered down real Time, which is already so watered down it's like watching the local news, without the grisly power mower accidental decapitations.

I'm going to DIE.

But it's worth it. It's worth it for Holly. This is for her. And Mark. This is—

OH MY GOD, THIS IS MY WEDDING PRESENT TO THEM!!!!

YES!!! Why didn't I think of it before??? Since I can't give them this journal—um, especially not now that I've mentioned Cal's pheromones—I'll give them this . . . the form that will allow them to be married tomorrow.

Genius. Total genius. This is MUCH better than candlesticks or something dopey like that.

Oooooh, they're calling another number . . . 92. COME ON!!! Maybe 29 through 91 left already.

Wait. That's not a number. The guy's putting a sign up on the glass. What's it say?

Office Closed
for Lunch
12:30 P.M.—
3:30 P.M.

Chiuso
12.30 a 15.30

PDA of Cal Langdon

I can't believe this is happening. I can't believe this is what I've been reduced to. I'm in Rome, possibly one of the most gastronomically diverse cities in the world, renowned for its cuisine, the long and languid lunch hour . . .

And I'm having warmed over eggplant pizza at Amici Amore, a ubiquitous Italian fast-food joint.

There's a VIDEO ARCADE in the back.

I should have put my foot down. I should have explained that when a Roman hangs a sign that says the office will be closed until a certain hour, he absolutely means it.

But no. She kept insisting. She's convinced if we scarf down a quick meal and get back to the embassy, we will somehow move up further in the line. Even though there is no line, and she is, in fact, holding a number that will doubtlessly not be called until tomorrow, or possibly next week.

Why didn't I insist? This trip didn't have to be an entire waste. We could be having a leisurely, romantic lunch in some restaurant's cozy back garden right now—listening to doves coo rather than the sound of asteroids being blasted by a computer-generated laser gun—enjoying the sunshine instead of the obscene purple neon of this place.

Why did I let her have her way? Especially when her way is so often so very, very wrong?

I don't even *like* eggplant.

I have to take a stand. When she gets back from the ladies' room, I *will* take a stand. I'll tell her this whole scheme is destined for failure. I'm going to tell her that this is a ridiculous waste of time, and that we're heading back to the villa to salvage what's left of our vacation time. I'm going to tell her—

Here she comes.

Oh. She says we're leaving.

Travel Diary of

~~Holly Caputo and Mark Levine~~

Jane Harris

Stupid restaurant! Stupid Rome! Stupid Italy!

What is the DEAL with the bathrooms here???? Seriously. I had to go at that stupid Amici Amore, so I head on off to the ladies', and first off, the whole place is lit by black light—why? Oh, because (Cal just told me) it's to make it impossible for junkies to find a vein if they take it into their heads to shoot up in there.

But that's not the worst of it. Oh, no!

THERE WAS NO TOILET. No. None. Where a toilet ought to be was a hole. A HOLE IN THE FLOOR. With two cut-out footprints on either side of it, and two bars to hold onto.

Okay, maybe ITALIAN WOMEN know what this is. But I've never seen anything like it, and I have NO IDEA what you're supposed to do there. Obviously you put your feet on the cutouts. And clearly you're supposed to hold onto the bars.

And then do what? Squat?

I DO NOT SQUAT.

Oh my God, what is WRONG with this country?

Cal says he knows of another restaurant we can go that isn't far from here, and that he swears will actually have a toilet in the ladies' room. I'm so traumatized, I'm actually letting him drive me there. A HOLE. A HOLE. What does Amici Amore even MEAN, anyway? BIG HOLE HERE?

Oh. Cal says it means Love Friends (amici = friends, amore = love).

Love Your Friends. Ha! Fuck Your Friends is more like it. By telling them to go there. TO SEE THE HOLE.

Where is he TAKING me, anyway? I told Cal we better not go too far from the consulate, since I'm SURE they won't actually be taking a three-hour lunch. I mean, they're AMERICAN, for crying out loud. That sign was probably just a scam to throw off the people with dumb, petty problems like lost passports or whatever. It won't daunt ME. I'm in this for the long haul. I don't care how long it takes. I'm going to sit there until I get—

Oooooh, what a beautiful building!

Hotel Eden

Sesto piano, la nostra terrazza ristorante da dove si può ammirare uno dei più bei panorami sulla Città Eterna.

Gli altri ce la invidiano, noi ve la offriamo.
Oltre all'incantevole panorama, "La Terrazza dell'Eden" è da segnalare per i prestigiosi riconoscimenti tra cui uno Stella Michelin.

Hotel Eden

The Sixth Floor of Rome:

Our Restaurant which will delight you with the best Mediterranean cuisine accompanied by the unrivalled view over the Seven Hills of Rome.

"La Terrazza dell'Eden" is one of the most prestigious gourmet Restaurant in Rome and is proud to be awarded with one Michelin Star.

Degustazione

Carpaccio scottato di branzino e capesante
con olio extra vergine al basilico

Mezzi rigatoni grezzi all'aragosta con crema di zucca

Ravioli di barbabietola con polenta e taleggio

Coda di rospo al forno con speck e lenticchie

Medaglioni di vitello in crosta di pecorino senese
con zucchine croccanti

Crostata aromatizzata con mele e mandorle,
semifreddo alle nocciole e Ferrari Maximum Demi-sec

Caffe
Delizie friabili

Gourmet Menu

Warm sea-bass and scallops carpaccio,
extra virgin olive oil flavoured with basil

Rigatoni with lobster and pumpkin cream

Beetroot Ravioli filled with polenta and taleggio cheese

Oven-baked monkfish with smoked ham and lentils

Veal medallions in a Pecorino cheese crust,
crispy courgettes and marjoram

Apples and almonds on pastry, hazelnuts semifreddo
and Ferrari Maximum Demi-sec sauce

Coffee
Petits fours

PDA of Cal Langdon

Now *this* is more like it. Sunshine. A nice prosecco. Panoramic views of the entire city. La Terrazza Dell-Eden at the Hotel Eden never fails in a pinch. Since 1889, it's been pampering guests, battle-worn from Roman sightseeing and psychically scarred by the traffic. This is where we ought to have come from the start.

Let that be a lesson to us all: Never let an artist choose the restaurant.

Travel Diary of
~~Holly Caputo and Mark Levine~~
Jane Harris

Oh my God, I totally know this place! This is where Britney Spears and Pink stayed when they were filming that Pepsi commercial in the Colosseum, the one they showed at the Superbowl! And the photographers got all these shots of Britney up on this very sundeck, hanging out with that married dancer.

Cool.

It's just GORGEOUS here, all yellow and green, with this view to DIE for. You can see all the way to the Vatican. You can wave to the Pope. Hi, Pope! Holly's mom sends her love! I'm sure Dan Brown didn't mean it!

And prosecco . . . yum. The food is delicious, too.

But we better hurry up. The office opens again in 45 minutes. Cal wants to go to the Spanish Steps, which are down the street from here. Like we've got time for sightseeing.

Still, I don't want to say no. He's being so NICE, all of a sudden. I mean, taking me here, and showing me this place, and buying lunch, and just being . . . well, like a nice guy, for a change.

And he looks so . . . well, hot too, sitting there in his jeans and chambray shirt. He finally got his hair under control, I see—which is good, if he ever hopes to pass for Mark, who doesn't have as much of it as he does—hair, I mean. The sun is really bringing out his golden highlights.

And he's telling such funny stories, about things he and Mark did in school. You can hardly tell he's the same person who just the other day was insisting that marriage is an outdated institution, and that love is nothing but a chemical reaction in the brain.

You know, between this and the cat thing last night, I'm almost starting to LIKE him.

Maybe that's just the prosecco. *God*, this is so romantic, sitting up here on top of the city, looking down on all the treetops and ancient ruins, drinking sparkly wine and eating these luscious olives. I can't believe Holly and Mark are missing it—

Holly and Mark! We've got to go!!!!

To: Jane Harris < jane@wondercat.com>
Fr: Claire Harris < charris2004@freemail.com >
Re: You

I don't know if you're just ignoring me now, or if something's happened to you. I hope it's the former, of course. I was flipping through the channels last night and I happened to see that on the Travel Channel they were doing a show on the lesser-traveled regions of Italy, so I watched it, and sure enough, they did a story on Le Marche, and they said there are WOLVES there.

Yes. WOLVES. In the hills.

I hope there are no hills near Holly's uncle's villa, and that if so, there are no wolves in them. And that you're keeping your window closed at night. Because wolves can jump very high. At least according to this documentary.

I suppose you aren't writing back because you're angry about my telling Holly's mother that she is gaining a son, not losing a daughter. I still don't see how Marie is going to extrapolate from this that Mark and Holly are eloping in Italy.

But I just thought I'd let you know that it looks like Marie is going to have a lot more important things to worry about soon: Daddy and I were just at the Promptcare for a splinter he got in his foot (I TOLD him the dining room floor needs sanding) and ran into Holly's sister-in-law Brandy, who was there with little Heather because she'd stuck a Red Hot up her nose.

Heather, not Brandy.

Anyway, according to Brandy, the Caputos are fit to be tied because Darrin just announced that he's getting married. To his boyfriend, Bobby. Apparently, they are having some sort of commitment ceremony on the steps of City Hall to rub the mayor's nose in it.

And I already phoned her—I HAD to, to let her know Angela di Blasi has the flu and book club is going to have to be at my house this week—and she was STILL in hysterics over the fact that Darrin is inviting the paper to cover the event and Father Roberto will know Darrin is gay.

I hope you're happy now.

Nancy Jansen wants to know if you'll autograph a copy of *Wondercat: The Early Years* for her nephew Jeff. I told her you would. She's sending it to you in New York with a self-addressed stamped envelope so you can just pop it in the mail back to her when you're done.

Love,
Mom

Travel Diary of

~~Holly Caputo and Mark Levine~~

Jane Harris

Those Spanish Steps weren't anything so big. I mean, they were all smooth from being walked on so much, since they're like three hundred years old. They are definitely a safety hazard. I nearly twisted my ankle a couple of times going down them.

And yeah, okay, so Shelley's house was right next door. Shelley. Wasn't he the one whose wife wrote Frankenstein?

I don't know why Cal got so tight-lipped when I asked him this. How am I supposed to know stuff about literature? I was an art major. I bet he doesn't know that Michelangelo got so sick of people complimenting him on his David statue's hands that he cut them off.

So I asked him if he knew this, and he said he didn't. Also that he didn't understand why, if so many people liked the hands, Michelangelo would cut them off.

So I explained about how artists want people to view their work as a whole, not parts. If people were too busy concentrating on the hands, they wouldn't see the rest of the statue. And that's not what Michelangelo wanted . . . to make a great pair of hands. He wanted to make a great statue.

I could tell he was impressed by this. I think it made up for when I told him about the Britney thing back at the Hotel Eden. He'd looked kind of scared then.

Whatever! I can't help it if he's the Wall Street Journal and I'm Us Weekly. I obviously have to know SOMETHING or I wouldn't have had to switch over to quarterly income tax returns this year, would I?

There were all these hippies sitting on the steps, playing guitars and singing about peace and stuff. Seeing them obviously reminded Cal of something, since he was like, "I have to go to Western Union." I was all, "Why?" and he was like, "I've got to wire some money to my sister."

So we went to Western Union—fortunately the Spanish Steps are in this totally high-tourist area, so we found one right away—and Cal wired a thousand dollars to someone named Mary Langdon. I know I shouldn't have looked, but what else was I supposed to do?

Besides, I was curious.

Even though he didn't seem to want to talk about it, I asked him how old his sister was, and he said she was 25. So he's her big brother. It's hard to imagine Cal having a little sister.

It's hard to imagine Cal ever having been a kid. But I know he was one, once, because that's how he and Mark came to be friends.

I wonder if Mary's afraid of snakes too.

Also, what she needs a thousand bucks for. Who hits their brother up for a loan that big? That is just bound to get the two of them on the People's Court, you just know it.

But when I asked, Cal was just like, "Mary's an artist," in this tone that suggested he didn't think much of the profession. Um, MY profession.

But whatever. It's sweet of Cal to help out his little sister. I really wouldn't have pegged him as a soft touch for money, but you can tell that girl's got him wrapped around her gold-digging finger. . . .

Generous with his sister. Nice to cats. Scared of snakes.

Still. Modelizer. And anti-marriage. Hmmm.

We're back at the consulate. Cal wanted to give up, but I wouldn't let him.

And I'm glad I didn't, because things are totally speeding up around here. They're on number 67 now. Don't even ask me how.

One annoying thing . . . there's this woman here, about my age, who I guess is trying to get the same form we are. She's marrying this Italian guy named Paolo. I know because she is telling anyone who will listen about it. Paolo is sitting there beside her, this hulk of a man, who doesn't look very happy. She says he doesn't speak any English. Also, that she can barely speak Italian. She says their relationship is based entirely on physical attraction.

Which, if it's true, is kind of sad. For her. I mean, Paolo's hot, don't get me wrong. But she's nothing to write home about. I wonder if Paolo even knows where they are, and that they're getting married.

I just elbowed Cal, who was busy typing into his Blackberry (as usual) and asked him (sotto voce) if he thinks Paolo knows what he's getting himself into. Before he had a chance to reply, the future Mrs. Paolo was all, "He's a mechanic. My parents don't approve. They think I can do better than marry an Italian mechanic who doesn't even speak English. But the sexual energy between us is so strong, how can I deny it?"

This last question was directed solely at me. Unfortunately, I've made eye contact. Now she won't go away.

"I'm Rhonda," she says. "What are you writing in that book there?"

Me: "Nothing."

Rhonda: "Oh, it's a travel journal. I just love journaling. You know, I can't sleep at night if I don't journal about my day. Sometimes I'll go for twenty, thirty pages."

Me: "Wow."

Rhonda: (batting her mouse brown eyelashes at Cal) "So is this your honey?"

Me: "Um. Yes. Yes, I guess it is. This is Mark. I'm Holly."

Rhonda: "Hi, Holly. Hi, Mark. Aren't you handsome! What are

you two doing here? Lose your passport? I'm here to pick up a form I need to get married."

Me: "So I heard. We're here to pick up a form we need to get married too."

Rhonda: "Oh, you two are getting married? Here in Italy? Why, if you don't mind my asking? I mean, what's wrong with Vegas?"

Cal: "We just can't wait, Rhonda. My love for this woman is so strong, I want to marry her right away, and not wait a minute more. I want to make her Mrs. Mark Levine as soon as is humanly possible."

!!!!!!!!!!!!!!!!!!!!!!!!!!!!!!!

He's funny!!!!!

Who knew?????

Rhonda: "Oh, boy, do I ever understand that! It's just like me and Paolo. Have you met my future husband, Paolo? He doesn't speak any English. And I don't speak any Italian. We met three days ago. My cruise ship stopped here, and I went to rent one of those little scooters, and there he was, and . . . well, I wouldn't get back on the cruise ship. My parents are furious with me—it was a cruise to celebrate their thirty-fifth wedding anniversary—but what can I do? Our physical attraction is overwhelming. Paolo's like an animal in bed."

Me: (patting Cal on the knee) "So's this guy."

Cal: (putting his arm around my shoulders) "Now, honey, don't be modest. You're no slouch in the sack, either."

Me: (looking modest) "Well, we did make love—how many times was it yesterday, sweetie?"

Cal: "Seven, I believe."

Me: (trying hard not to notice that Cal Langdon smells really,

really good) "Well, yes, but that's just because you had that sports-related injury."

Cal: "Of course. Yesterday was kind of a slow day, actually."

Rhonda: (looking excited) "Paolo went nine once! In one day!"

We all looked at Paolo with respect. He blinked back at us, without the slightest glimmer of recognition of what we were talking about—or of intelligence.

Me: (Cal's arm is still around me. It's warm. And distracting.) "That is very impressive. No wonder you're marrying him."

Rhonda: "I know. If only my parents would try to understand! They called from Greece last night, and were furious with me when I told them what Paolo and I were doing today. I thought they'd be happy for me—happy that I've finally found the happiness they've been enjoying for thirty-five years! But no. They think I'm crazy, and that in a week we'll be divorced. But of course Paolo's Catholic, and doesn't believe in divorce. I think. It's hard to tell what he's saying, exactly, but I think that's the deal. Anyway, too many people get divorced these days. They don't understand that a marriage takes work and that you can't just move out because your husband's cheating on you or whatever. You've got to stay and try to MAKE it work. You would think Mom and Dad would understand that."

Cal: "Families can be so difficult sometimes."

Rhonda: "Tell me about it. I was journaling about mine just the other night, when it occurred to me that—"

Consulate guy: "Ninety-two! Number 92!"

THAT'S US!!!!!!!!!!

MARRIAGE OF U.S. CITIZENS IN ROME'S CONSULAR DISTRICT

U.S. citizens planning to marry in Italy must present certain documents and comply with specific requirements of Italian law in order to obtain a marriage license. Marriages cannot be performed by American Consuls, nor on the premises of the American Consulate. The documents required and the procedure to follow are described below.

1. Valid U.S. passport.

2. Birth certificate (original or certified copy).

3. Evidence of the termination of any previous marriage, if applicable (e.g., final divorce decree, annulment decree or death certificate of former spouse).

4. Affidavit, sworn to by the U.S. citizen before a U.S. Consul commissioned in Italy, stating that there is no legal impediment to the marriage, according to the laws of the State of which the citizen is a resident.

NOTE: Once issued, this affidavit must be stamped by the Legalization Office of any *Prefettura* in our Consular District (there is one in every province capital).

5. Atto Notorio: This is a declaration, in addition to the sworn statement described under point 4, stating that according to the laws to which the citizen is subject in the United States there is no obstacle to his/her marriage. This declaration is to be sworn to by two witnesses (a witness may be of any nationality, but must be over 18, with current photo ID), before an Italian Consul outside Italy or, in Italy, before an official at the *Pretura* (Lower Court) in the city where the marriage is to take place. U.S. citizens coming to Italy to be married must obtain this declaration from a Consul of Italy, before leaving the United States.

6. Declaration of Intention: Bride and groom should present all the above documents to the *Ufficio Matrimoni* (Marriage Office) of the *Municipio* (Town Hall) in the city where the marriage will

be performed, and make a "Declaration of Intention to Marry" before an *Ufficiale di Stato Civile* (Civil Registrar).

NOTE: All documents originating out of Italy (birth certificate, divorce decree, etc.) MUST be translated into Italian. Both the original documents and the translations MUST be legalized for use in Italy, with the so-called "APOSTILLE" stamp, in accordance with The Hague Convention on the legalization of foreign public documents. In the U.S., the "APOSTILLE" stamp is placed by the Secretary of State in the state where the document was issued.

I swear the information contained in the documents submitted herewith is both true and valid.

Signature: *Holly Ann Caputo* Holly Ann Caputo

Signature: Mark Levine

Stato Civile

✉

To: Cal Langdon <cal.langdon@thenyjournal.com>
Fr: Mark Levine <mark.levine@thenyjournal.com>
Re: Wheere adre you?

Hgey. Il cvan;t find mt glasdes. Whiohe are yyi????

MKal

PDA of Cal Langdon

I am an international fugitive from justice. At any moment I expect our car to be overtaken by Interpol, and for Jane and me to be yanked out, slammed to the asphalt, and slapped into cuffs. I suspect Black Hawk helicopters are hovering over us at this very moment. Undoubtedly, we'll be thrown into an Italian prison, and no one will ever hear from us again.

And Rhonda, ultimately, will have the last laugh.

We did it. We perjured ourselves. Committed fraud. Forged our friends' names on government documents.

And they never suspected a thing.

Jane was right. It was a cinch. The guy behind the bulletproof glass barely even glanced at us or our passports. He just asked us where we were staying, made a laconic comment when he found out it was Le Marche, slid the form through the slot for us to sign, then gave us back our documents with the form stamped appropriately. All that waiting—we didn't get back on the road until almost five-thirty—and we were done in five minutes.

I thought Jane was going to have an embolism, she was so delirious with joy. She kept clutching my shirt—not an unpleasant sensation, by the way—and hissing, "It worked! We did it! It worked!" as we rode down the elevator.

Then she seemed to sober up and asked, "What did that man say about Le Marche?"

So I told her he'd said, with a grunt, when he heard where we—I mean, Mark and Holly—were planning on being wed: "Better a corpse in the house than a man from Le Marche."

This filled Jane with righteous anger—"What did he mean by that? What's wrong with Le Marche? I think it's beautiful. Just because it's not overrun with American tourists like Rhonda, that means there's something wrong with it? That pig," etc.

This struck me as highly amusing, considering her sentiments on Le Marche after coming out of the bathroom at the restaurant where we dined just last evening.

Still, it's true that Le Marche is beginning to have a certain charm. I'm actually eager to get back there.

I haven't been eager to get anywhere since . . . well, ever. I wonder what that's about. It seems as if places have always been just that to me . . . places. I can't imagine what's happened to make Le Marche seem less like a place and more like . . . well. Home.

✉

To: Jane Harris <jane@wondercat.com>
Fr: Malcolm Weatherly <malcolmw@snowstyle.com>
Re: Ciao!

Hey, babe! How's it going? Haven't heard from you in a while. What happened? You run off with some Italian stallion or what?

Drop me a line, will ya? I miss your face.

And I really need to know if you've seen my lucky hat.

M.

Travel Diary of

~~Holly Caputo and Mark Levine~~

Jane Harris

Talk about weird.

I mean, that I'm stuck in a car with Cal Langdon, and I'm actually having a not-bad time.

What's HAPPENING to me?

Why did he have to put his arm around me back at the consulate? Not that I didn't like it—far from it, of course—but ever since then, I've been wishing it would happen again. Why do I even want to touch him, anyway? He's a modelizer!

But he did come through for Mark and Holly. And against his will, even. I mean, he never wanted them to get married in the first place.

But I haven't heard a peep of protest out of him all day. In fact, thanks to him, those two are going to have their dream wedding after all.

That's gotta come as a blow to someone who is violently opposed to the institution of marriage. I wonder if he even realizes this.

Me: "Hey, so what happened to being all anti-marriage?"

Cal: "What?"

Me: (turning down Queen) "I thought you were totally against Holly and Mark getting married. So why'd you go along with this whole thing?"

Cal: "Are you recording this conversation in that book?"

Me: "Um. Sort of."

Cal: "Great. What else did you say about me?"

Me: "That you drool in your sleep."

Cal: "I do not."

Me: "You do too. I saw it for myself this morning when I woke you up."

Cal: (making a grab for this book) "Let me see that."

Me: "Hey! Eyes on the road, mister. Seriously, what changed your mind?"

Cal: "About what?"

Me: "MARRIAGE!!! Why are you pro now, when you were anti before?"

Cal: "I'm still anti. Just not in the case of Mark and Holly. I changed my mind."

Me: "Obviously. But why?"

Cal: "They just seem very . . . together. Like a couple should be. I guess."

Me: "I told you."

Cal: "That doesn't make me pro-marriage, you know. It just makes me pro-Mark and Holly."

Me: "That's all I wanted. You remember. Back on the plane?"

Cal: "Well, I barely knew Holly then. I still think Mark would be better off seeing the world before he settles down. Don't snort. It's a big place, there's a lot to see. A man shouldn't let himself get tied down too young."

Me: "Excuse me. Mark is thirty-five. That is middle-aged in many countries. And he TRIED exploring the world, remember? He got food poisoning for his efforts."

Cal: "I realize all of that. That's why I amended my opinion. About Mark and Holly."

Me: "But not love and marriage in general."

Cal: "I still believe marriage is an outdated institution. I also believe it robs people of their individual sense of self. I mean, just look at how women take their husbands' names—"

Me: "Not ALL women."

Cal: "The majority of them. Would you?"

Me: "Um. I'm the creator of Wondercat. YOU may never have heard of me, but lots of people have. If I changed my name, it would confuse my fans. And besides. I like my name the way it is. Even though, of course, it was handed down to me by a patriarchal society that subjugates women by robbing them of their birth identity upon marriage."

Cal: "See? That's what I'm talking about!"

Me: (snorting again) "Hello. I was kidding."

Cal: "Oh. Well, that's still what I'm talking about."

Me: "No, it isn't. That isn't what you said before. You said you don't believe in marriage because mammals are genetically incapable of monogamy, and I cited wolves and hawks as examples. Also that chemicals in the brain cause us to believe ourselves in love, when actually, we're merely in lust. It's right here in this book if you don't believe me, I can look it up."

Cal: "You put that conversation in there, too? Holly and Mark are going to read that!"

Me: "Er. Yeah. Maybe. Stop trying to change the subject. Do you really believe that? That human beings are incapable of monogamy? Because I can cite a lot of examples of marriages in which neither partner strayed—"

Cal: "How do you know?"

Me: "I think I'd know if my own parents were cheating on each other."

Cal: "How? Unless they told you. You wouldn't know. You'd have no idea."

Me: "Well, what about Rhonda's parents?"

Cal: "Who the hell is Rhonda?"

Me: "Rhonda. Of Rhonda and Paolo. Her parents were celebrating their thirty-fifth wedding anniversary."

Cal: "You have no possible way of knowing whether or not

Rhonda's parents have been monogamous for those thirty-five years."

Me: "True. Still. I'll bet you twenty bucks they have been. Nobody goes on a cruise with a cheating spouse."

Cal: "You are unbelievable."

Me: "No, you are. Just because your ex-wife cheated on you, you think all women are incapable of being faithful. Admit it."

Cal: "I never said any such thing."

Me: "You didn't have to. It's totally obvious. When you say you think humans are incapable of monogamy, you mean women."

Cal: "No, I don't."

Me: "Did you cheat on her?"

Cal: "Who?"

Me: "Valerie."

Cal: "HOW DO YOU EVEN KNOW HER NAME?"

Me: "Holly told me. Did you?"

Cal: "Of course not."

Me: "See? I rest my case."

Cal: "HOW? I DON'T EVEN KNOW WHAT YOU'RE TALKING ABOUT!"

Me: "You distrust all women because of what one of them did to you. And that's made you take this anti-marriage stance. But it's not marriage that's the problem. It's ditzes like your ex who don't take it seriously or get hitched for the wrong reasons or whatever. Don't blame the institution of marriage for Valerie cheating on you. It wasn't marriage that made her cheat. She was just a ho."

Cal: "Oh my God. You are unbelievable."

Me: "Yes. But I'm right, too. There's the exit. Don't miss it."

He's acting like he's all shocked now that I would bring up this very private thing from his past.

And I guess it IS kind of rude to call someone's ex a ho. But really, that's what she is. Just like Dave is a male ho. But I haven't let Dave's predilection for humping soul-sucking Human Resource reps behind my back sour me on the idea of matrimonial bliss, or of someday finding that perfect someone, now, have I?

And really, I know that, technically, there's no such thing as matrimonial bliss . . . marriage is work, and there are no soul mates. You just have to find the person who annoys you the least (at least according to Dr. Phil), or rather, annoys you in ways you can stand.

Really, I bet there'd be a lot less divorce if people realized this. A lot less marriages, too. But that might not be such a bad thing.

Oooooh, I smell horse! The Centro Ippico! We're almost home!

✉

To: Listserv <Wundercat@wundercatlives.com>
Fr: Peter Schumacher <webmaster@wundercatlives.com>
Re: JANE HARRIS

FANTASTIC NEWS, KIDS!!!! There is going to be a wedding after all!

This just in:

JANE HARRIS has driven all the way to Roma to get the APOSTILLE that her friends need to have the marriage! YES! She walked in at approximately 21:00 hours, while my grandmother and I were sitting at the banquet table in the villa, trying to get JANE HARRIS's friends, who ate of the bad oysters but were finally starting to feel better, to drink some soup.

In walks JANE HARRIS holding up the APOSTILLE! The wedding will go on tomorrow morning as planned! The friends of JANE HARRIS, even though they are both still sickly, jump up and shout for joy! And JANE HARRIS says, "This is my wedding present to you!"

It is the best wedding present anyone has ever given to anyone, declares JANE HARRIS's friend Holly.

My grandmother opens the bottle of champagne to celebrate.

So come one, come all, to the Ufficio of the Secretario of Castelfidardo tomorrow morning at 9:00!

This is Peter, #1 Fan of Wundercat, saying GOOD NIGHT!

Wundercat lives—4eva!
Peter

✉

To: Holly Caputo <holly.caputo@thenyjournal.com >
Fr: Darrin Caputo <darrin.caputo@caputographics.com >
Re: Hello, it is your mother

Holly, this is your mother. Something horrible has happened. Your brother Darrin is going to get married. To a man. On the steps of City Hall. Where everyone will see.

You must come home at once. You know your brother has never listened to me or anyone else in this family. You must stop him from doing this. I cannot allow a child of mine to disgrace himself in this way.

I am begging you to talk your brother out of this crazy scheme. Perhaps Mark can help, as well. He's a doctor, surely he must know how wrong it is to flagrantly defy the law in this way.

Counting on you to come home and do the right thing by your poor, confused brother,

Your mother

PDA of Cal Langdon

I was right from the beginning. From the moment I first laid eyes on her—holding all those water bottles in the duty free shop back at JFK—I thought to myself, "There's a nut case."

I called it.

And yet . . . she made some very miserable people very happy tonight. I never saw a bigger pair of sadsacks than Holly and Mark, slumped at that giant dining table, when we walked through the door tonight. Mark, of course, looked particularly lost, since he's blind as a bat without his glasses. I walked in and handed them to him—I actually had to put them on his head, since he couldn't even see me holding them out to him—and then Jane slapped that form onto the table with a big, "Here's your wedding present."

I actually thought Frau Schumacher might have a heart attack, she was so excited.

And to tell you the truth, it was a little upsetting, because I could picture myself, having to give her mouth-to-mouth to revive her, while Mark pounded on her chest. And I have the disturbing idea—maybe from the way the woman hangs on my every word (though surely this is because I'm the only one here who speaks German?)—that if she came to and found my lips on hers, even giving her the breath of life, she might actually . . . well, sort of enjoy it. Maybe even slip me the tongue.

Could it be that Jane is right? Could there possibly be something to her theory that marriage is all right for some people—that it didn't work out for Valerie and me because Valerie was . . . well, a "ho"?

This seems an oversimplification of the problems Valerie and I had.

And yet . . .

Well, marriage certainly seems like it might be all right for Mark and Holly. They're happy enough about it, jumping around as much as they can, considering their still queasy stomachs. I have to say, I can't understand how anybody could be as delighted as they are at the prospect of being married by the socialist mayor of a town devoted to accordion construction, thousands of miles from their families.

But maybe there's something romantic about it that I'm missing. Valerie always accused me of not being romantic enough. The sewing machine I got her for Valentine's Day was always a bone of contention. She said she'd have preferred a diamond tennis bracelet.

But I thought a sewing machine was a much more practical gift, considering how much she was spending on clothes . . .

Now Holly's grabbed Jane and the two of them—followed closely by Frau Schumacher, who seems fairly spry for her age and apparently doesn't like to be left out of anything—have disappeared, apparently in a panicked quest to ease the wrinkles out of the wedding gown none of the rest of us is allowed to see.

With the girls otherwise occupied, Peter and I attempted to throw perhaps the lamest, most pathetic bachelor party in the history of time for Mark. Lame because of course the groom is so weak from food poisoning he can barely lift his glass to his lips. Pathetic because the only entertainment are the stray cats from last night, back for another helping of fish.

That's right. No lap dances or kamikazes for Mark.

But perhaps this is fitting for a man who has chosen such a perverse—and yet strangely right—place to wed.

Now Mark's staggered back upstairs to bed—interrupting the girls while Holly was trying on the wedding gown, judging from the indignant screams I just heard floating down from the window—leaving me alone with young Peter, who just asked me if I thought Jane Harris would be back down, or if I thought she'd go straight to bed.

How touching that this young man believes I am in any way privy to Ms. Harris's private thoughts or intentions. As this is an entirely erroneous assumption, however, I was forced to inform him that I did not, in fact, know.

Then the little malcontent had the nerve to look in my eye and ask me just what, precisely, were my intentions toward the lady in question.

Not in so many words, of course. His exact phrasing, uttered in a highly disapproving tone, was, "Are you and Jane Harris lowers?" by which I am assuming he meant lovers. I can't say I cared for the smug look that crept over the kid's face when I told him that we most certainly were not.

Perhaps I shouldn't have been so adamant?

At least he didn't say anything. Instead, he calmly produced a deck of cards from the back pocket of his jeans and asked if I cared to play a game of War.

Reduced to spending a beautiful, starlit night along the Adriatic coast playing War with a German teenager.

I can't help wondering if the man at the consulate's office wasn't right this afternoon when he expressed his belief that it's better to have a corpse in the house than a man from Le Marche. Not that there happen to be any of those in the vicinity. Just that . . . well, this place seems to *do* things to otherwise normal people. . . .

To: Cal Langdon <cal.langdon@thenyjournal.com>
Fr: Mary Langdon < m.langdon@internetcafenetwork.com>
Re: Thank You

Oh my God, Cal, thanks for the money. I really needed it. Jeff (the guy who owned the van) turned out to be a total psycho. He kicked me out just because he happened to catch me talking to another guy. I don't know who he thinks he is, anyway—the freaking Taliban? God, I hate it when guys think they own me.

But it's cool because I hooked up with this awesome group of ski-boarders. They've even got a spare room I can crash in. One of them, Malcolm, showed me how to ride the halfpipe. He let me use one of his boards and everything. He says he thinks I might have a lot of natural talent. Who knows? Maybe boarding's been my calling all along, and I just never knew it, because Mom and Dad always made us go on those stupid beach vacations, instead of taking us skiing, like normal parents.

Anyway, thanks again for the cash.

More later,

Mare

To: Cal Langdon <cal.langdon@thenyjournal.com >
Fr: Ruth Levine <r.levine@levinedentalgroup.com >
Re: Hello!

Hi, Cal! I don't mean to be a pest, but I was just wondering if you got my earlier email, and if you'd had a chance to consider what I said in it. About Mark and Holly. I know you're with Mark right now, and I was hoping you'd had a chance to speak to him about it. For reasons I'd rather not go into just now, he and I aren't really speaking at the moment. Or rather, I'm speaking to him, but he appears to be put out with me. I know it will blow over soon—you know Mark and his moods. But I just hope that, in the meantime, you'll keep an eye on him, and keep him from doing anything . . . well, rash.

I certainly don't mean I think he's going to KILL himself because he got into an argument with his mother, of course. By rash I just mean . . . well, I don't know—PROPOSE to her, or something. Holly, I mean. Not that I don't like her or wouldn't want her as a daughter-in-law. She's a perfectly affable girl. It's just that she's not one of *us*.

Anyway, I don't mean to spoil your nice vacation with my constant emails. I hope you're having a good time. I just also hope that if, you know, you find yourself in a position to maybe give Mark a little dose of reality about how difficult it can be to make a marriage work—especially when two people come from such different cultures as he and Holly do—I'd really appreciate it.

Affectionately,
Ruth Levine

Travel Diary of

~~Holly Caputo and Mark Levine~~

Jane Harris

Holly looked happier tonight than I've ever seen her. Happier even than the day Brad Toller asked her to the senior prom after she'd spent the entire year just trying to get him to notice her. Seriously. She's GLOWING. I mean, she's still pale from having spent the entire day and most of last night throwing up—and her wedding dress is hanging off her, she's lost so much weight—but tomorrow she's going to make the most beautiful bride in the universe.

We so did the right thing, Cal and I, perjuring ourselves, etc., today at the consulate's office.

Now Holly's drifted off to bed in a dreamy haze, and I just heard Mark come in to join her, and Frau Schumacher seems to have left, and I realize I'm STARVING. I mean, we haven't eaten since the Hotel Eden this afternoon, so I'm going to forage for food down in the kitchen, then go straight to bed myself, since we have to get up so early tomorrow for the ceremony.

I noticed Cal was pretty quiet tonight, while everybody else was celebrating. I can't even begin to imagine what was going through his head. That ex-wife of his totally messed him up. I wouldn't mind running into her in a dark alley someday. I bet I could show her a few things I've picked up since living in the East Village, stuff she probably doesn't run into too much in her suburban kick-boxing class. Really, where do girls like that get off? They take perfectly adequate guys (well, OK, Cal needs work, but I imagine back then he probably wasn't as much of a pompous ass) and ruin them for the rest of us. That's just wrong.

Not, of course, that I would want Cal Langdon if he wasn't

damaged goods. Please! The last thing I need is a journalist for a boyfriend.

Although he does look awfully good in a bathing suit—

No! Stop it! I do NOT need to date a modelizer! That is just setting yourself up for heartbreak and many, many pints of macadamia brittle.

PDA of Cal Langdon

This is intolerable. I am in Italy, on a warm, moonlit night by a sparkling pool, with palm fronds blowing gently in the evening breeze, a platter of olives and crumbled chunks of Parmesan and a bottle of extremely excellent wine before me, and a woman radiating a very healthy sexuality across from me . . .

And I'm playing War with her.

What's wrong with this picture?

What's wrong with ME? I shouldn't want this woman. She's everything I can't stand . . . artistic, obsessed with popular culture, set in her ways, *American* . . .

And yet . . .

I want to kiss her.

Maybe it's the moonlight. Maybe it's this damned place.

Or maybe it's because she made me laugh so many times today.

Damn. What's *happening* to me? So she made me laugh. Mark makes me laugh, and I don't want to kiss *him*. I don't even like funny women. And I especially don't like funny *artistic* women.

So why is it that I'm going to kill this kid if he doesn't get the hell out of here in the next five minutes?

One.

Two.

Three.

He's still not leaving. He's telling some story about a comic he loves. Jane is apparently familiar with it, though it's not her own. It appears to have elves and gnomes in it. Peter is gushing over the fact that the final installment is coming out in only two weeks. Jane, who knows the author, says she's heard what's going to happen, but flirtatiously refuses to tell the kid. He is delighted by this, and is begging her. She refuses to divulge what she knows, and lays down an eight. Peter's just lain down an eight.

War.

She won.

The candlelight brings out the highlights in her dark hair, and makes her eyes shine. Her skin looks like butter . . .

What is *wrong* with me? I do NOT want to get involved with this woman. Or any woman, for that matter. I have a book to write. I have to find a place to live. I don't even have a dry cleaner. I can't get into a relationship. . . .

OK, I'm giving the kid another five minutes to leave. It's nearly midnight. Doesn't he have some computer system he has to go hack into somewhere back home?

Now she's asking him about Annika. Who the hell is Annika? Oh, the girl at the mayor's office. The mayor's daughter, apparently. Peter speaks scathingly of Annika, whom he's clearly in love with, and who, judging by his insistence that he loathes her, obviously doesn't return his feelings for her.

I slap down a two. So does Peter.

War.

Oh, it's war, my boy. In more ways than you know.

Wait. What's that?

Meowing. The cats are back.

She leaps up and heads into the kitchen to find something to feed them. Peter and I are alone at last.

By the time she returns with a bowl of what looks to be the contents of several cans of tuna, Peter is gone.

"Where'd Peter go?" she wants to know.

And I can't help but believe that she genuinely doesn't know.

This is a mystery I'm only too happy to clear up for her.

Travel Diary of

~~Holly Caputo and Mark Levine~~

Jane Harris

IS HE INSANE? I mean, I know he thinks I'm silly, what with my "little cartoon" and my too-high heels that I'm always tripping over and the whole "carabinieri" thing.

But it never occurred to me that he might think I'm the STUPIDEST HUMAN BEING ON THE FACE OF THE PLANET.

Because that's exactly who I'd have to be to fall for his whole "It's just a kiss, it doesn't have to mean anything" routine.

But you know what? I'm not going to let him. Ruin the wedding, I mean. He can sulk all he wants tonight, but if he comes downstairs tomorrow morning with anything but a great big happy smile on his face, I will personally give his arm hairs a twist he won't forget.

Who does he think he is, anyway, Enrique Iglesias? "I just want to kiss you. You're an an artist. I thought you people were used to living in the moment?"

Whatever!

Apparently he thinks just because I am an unmarried woman of a certain age who lives with a cat, I must be desperate. Or retarded.

Well, I'd HAVE to be pretty desperate—or retarded—to fall into bed with HIM. What, just because he did me (well, Holly and Mark, really) a favor today, I'm going to sleep with him? Because we had a nice lunch and some laughs, I'm easy? Please.

And okay, the guy is truly, almost unbelievably hot. I'll admit I was checking out his hands as we played cards. They're all big and sinewy, exactly the kind of hands a girl wouldn't mind roaming all over her body.

And he can be charming when he puts his mind to it. Even kind of funny.

And he's definitely intelligent. At least, about stuff other than women. And he can be funny, like today at the consulate, with Rhonda.

And he's nice to cats—when he thinks no one is looking.

But I'm sorry, my days of sleeping with guys just because they happen to have nice hands and can tell a funny joke are OVER. Because you know what that gets you? Another night with a hot, funny guy who's not going to be the least interested in going with you to your office Christmas party or splitting the Con Ed bill—much less actually have the money to pay half the rent, even though he's totally moved in.

I'm over that. WAY over that.

You think that'd have been clear to him from the beginning of our relationship. I mean, I know I'm an artist, a word that to him is obviously synonomous with "wacky madcap." But could I really have struck him as the one-night-stand type? Isn't it obvious, from the way I keep bringing up *Ladyhawke* and the fact that hawks and wolves mate for life, that I am interested in monogamy and commitment?

Apparently he didn't get the message. I mean, I come out with food for the cats and Peter is gone—kind of suddenly, since we'd been in the middle of a card game when I got up.

So I'm all, "Where's Peter?" and Cal's like, "I gave him twenty euros and told him to make himself scarce."

Me: "You WHAT?"

Cal: "You heard me. About time, too. He's been keeping me from being able to do this all night."

And then he took me by the shoulders, and before I had any idea what was happening (no, really, I NEVER suspected he was attracted to me, since he's done nothing but grouse at me since the moment we first met. Well, except for putting his arm around me, back at the consulate. But that was just for show!), he pulled me to him and started kissing me.

Kissing me! Like we were in a romance novel, or something!

And OK, he's no slouch in the kissing department. Clearly, he's had some practice.

And OK, I didn't exactly hate it. Far from it, actually. All the different parts of me that usually go all melty when someone hot kisses me in a purposeful way went all melty, right on schedule, when he did it.

And I will admit that for a split second, I was all, "Oh my gosh! He likes me! He REALLY likes me!" and I entertained a quick tiny fantasy of us strolling down Second Avenue hand-in-hand and going to Veselka's for blintzes and me introducing him to The Dude. And I started to kiss him back. . . .

But then I realized . . . that fantasy? It will never, ever come true. Because he doesn't believe in love, much less marriage, and he will NEVER go to Veselka's for blintzes with me, much less stick around to meet The Dude—at least not long enough to form a meaningful relationship with him. And how long can I keep introducing The Dude to men he isn't ever going to see again? He's very sensitive, and when he does bond, it's forever. He wouldn't finish his Friskies for days after Malcolm left.

And then Holly's voice chimed into my head with *You've got to start thinking about the future, and date people who will actually stick around for a change*, and I remembered that bride we saw outside the church in Rome, and how happy she looked, and how her dad was beaming down at her—

And right then and there, I realized something that I don't think I've been willing to admit to myself since college, or whenever it was that the idea of getting married no longer seemed as cool as it had back during those Barbie games in fifth grade:

And that's that I WANT to get married someday. I do. I really do. I want the bouquet and the red carpet and the gown and the veil and the weepy dad and the flower girls and till death do us part.

So what was I doing kissing some guy who thinks marriage as an institution ought to be abolished?

So instead of wrapping my arms around his neck and kissing him back, as I'm sure he was expecting me to do, and as I have to admit I really did WANT to do—at least, my BODY wanted me to—I put my hands on his chest and shoved.

He staggered back into the metal lawn chair he'd been sitting in, and just sat there blinking up at me, like, "What gives?"

But before he had a chance to say anything, I went off.

Me: "What do you think I am? An idiot? I am NOT sleeping with you."

Cal: "Um . . . it was just a kiss."

Me: "You don't believe in love. You think it's all a result of phenyl . . . phenyl . . . whatever it is."

Cal: "Phenylethylamine. And, not to be pendantic . . . but it was just a kiss."

Me: "But unlike you, I do happen to believe in love. And marriage. So what's the point? One night, and then what? I become another name in your Blackberry. No, thank you."

Cal: "Pardon me if my memory is the one at fault here, and, keeping in mind that it was, again, just a kiss, didn't you e me not long ago that you were in no rush to get married or have children because you wanted to concentrate on your career?"

Me: "I might have. But I want to get married EVENTUALLY. So why in God's name would I fall into bed with some guy who's totally against the very idea of marriage? What's going to happen tomorrow morning, when you can't even make eye contact, and are avoiding me? And how about on the plane going back to New York, when we have to sit by each other again? And when we get back to Manhattan? Are you going to call? Am I ever even going to hear from you again?"

Cal: "Apparently, you've already decided that you aren't. Even though it was, I'd like to point out for a third and hopefully final time, just a kiss."

Me: "You know what? Holly's right. I've got to grow up. I'm not sleeping with any more inappropriate men. No more ski boarders. No more musicians. And certainly no men who hate the very idea of marriage, and who have no intention of pursuing a long-term relationship with me."

Cal: "You got all of that out of one kiss? I mean, about my not having any intention of pursuing a long-term relationship with you?"

Me: "Make fun of me all you want. But you know what? I'd rather go to bed with *Paolo* than with you."

Cal: "Who's Paolo?"

Me: "You remember. Of Paolo and Rhonda. Back at the consulate."

Cal: "PAOLO? The half-wit mechanic?"

Me: "Yeah, but at least he wasn't going around bleating that there's no such thing as romantic love. At least he believed in marriage."

Cal: "The guy didn't speak any English! I doubt he had any idea he was GETTING married."

Me: "Go on feeling all superior to us poor suckers who believe in love and monogamy and want to find someone with whom we can spend the rest of our lives. Because you know what's going to happen twenty years from now? I'm going to be with someone—someone I can have breakfast with and read the paper with and watch stupid movies with and sleep with and go on vacation with, someone who WON'T cheat on me, the way your wife cheated on you, because I'm going to marry someone who loves me for me and not my money or whatever—and you're going to be all alone. I hope you like it."

Cal: "Well, thank you very much. I'm sure I will. And I hope you and Paolo will have a happy and prosperous life together. For your thirty-fifth anniversary, might I recommend a cruise?"

Me: "Thanks, I'll keep it in mind."

Cal: "Well. I guess we have nothing more to say to each other, then."

Me: "I guess we don't. Good night."

Then I swept off the terrazza and came up here and wrote all this.

I think I made quite an impression on him.

I just wish I hadn't tripped over the threshold when I was going inside.

But I really don't think he noticed.

Now it's quiet—I guess he must still be down there, since I didn't hear him come up. All I can hear are the crickets outside.

Still . . .

I can't help wondering if I did the right thing. I mean, I think we WOULD have had a good time. He really is a good kisser.

And you know, he can be fun—like in the consulate's office—when he lets himself.

And he's obviously smart. It's not like we'd ever run out of things to talk about.

Okay, argue about. But whatever.

Maybe I shouldn't have been so hasty to shove him away. . . .

No. No, I did the right thing. Because what would have been the point? A night of bliss and then what? He'd just go back to his skanks.

Only this time, I'd be one of them! Oh my God, I wouldn't be able to BEAR the idea of him thinking of me that way. As another woman he'd scored. I couldn't. I just think I'm *worth* more than that.

You know, I'm starting to think that The Dude might actually be my soul mate. He's *everything* you'd want in a man . . . loyal, trustworthy, attentive, handsome, smart, not afraid of commitment . . . he even has a good sense of humor.

Too bad about the fish breath, though.

Oh, damn. I left my bottle of water downstairs. I wonder if I can sneak down and get it without running into him again. . . . Maybe if I don't put on any shoes.

PDA of Cal Langdon

Well.

That was . . . unusual. I mean, it was just a *kiss*. . . .

A really good one. An exceptional one, I'd have to say. I've kissed quite a few women in my day, but that one certainly stands out.

Obviously, however, I made an error in judgement. A grave one.

Still, it wasn't like she didn't kiss back. At first.

But she's right, of course. It would have been a mistake. I don't know what I was thinking. I *never* do things like that. Act on impulse in that way, I mean. I can't imagine why I thought. . . . It isn't as if it could go anywhere, she's completely right. We live in two entirely different worlds.

Still, she's an artist. You'd think she'd be a little more receptive to taking a risk.

Well, it's lucky she resisted. She's clearly one of those clingy, needy ones, if she can jump straight from a kiss—which was all it really was, no matter what she thinks—into a full-blown relationship. She'd probably have asked me to move in after our first time making love, then spend every weekend in the foreseeable future whining about wanting to take me to meet her parents.

Or worse, be her date to some friend's wedding.

Shudder.

No, I made a lucky escape with this one. She's clearly no Grazi. There'd be no more pleasure for pleasure's sake, here. Obviously, I overestimated her intelligence.

It was those damn shoes.

Why does she even wear the stupid things, when she clearly can't even walk in them?

Anyway, this is all for the best. The last thing in the world I need right now is to be saddled with some marriage-crazed cat cartoonist. I need to get to work on my next book, and it'll be much easier to do that if I'm unfettered, relationship-wise.

And despite what she might think, I happen to *like* eating breakfast alone. And I've never had to sleep alone if I didn't want to.

Well, except for tonight.

PDA of Cal Langdon

Ski boarders? Musicians? Just who has this girl been sleeping with? Must remember to ask Mark tomorrow.

PDA of Cal Langdon

I can't ask Mark tomorrow—or today, I should say. It's his wedding day. He's hardly going to be likely to want to discuss his wife's best friends's love life.

Still. It was just a *kiss*. I don't know why I did it. I couldn't help myself, honest to God. It's not like I'm in love with her. God forbid!

It was just a kiss.

So why can't I stop thinking about it?

PDA of Cal Langdon

Upon ambling through the kitchen just now on my way up to bed, I made a rather startling discovery. Ms. Harris appears to have come back downstairs to retrieve something she forgot to bring up the first time she stormed off to her room, and in doing so, has left by the refrigerator something I'm sure she didn't mean to leave behind: that little book she's constantly scribbling in, the one that says Travel Diary of Holly Caputo and Mark Levine on it.

Oddly, I've noticed she's scratched out Mark and Holly's names and inserted her own. And yet, when I—quite by accident—opened it to the first page, I couldn't help noticing the words:

Dear Holly and Mark,

Surprise!

I know neither one of you would bother to keep a record of your elopement, so I've decided to do it for you!

Surely if she really is keeping this diary for Mark and Holly, it wouldn't be wrong of me to read it. Obviously she intends to give it to them.

And I think I have every right in the world to see what's being said about me, as I imagine she's had some rather choice things to say on the subject. Perhaps there's even a libel suit in my future. Who knows?

And yet I can't help feeling that I'm overstepping some boundary here.

Hmmmm. Quite a moral dilemma.

PDA of Cal Langdon

Anal retentive?

PDA of Cal Langdon

Modelizer??

PDA of Cal Langdon

I'm going to kill Mark for the appendage thing.

PDA of Cal Langdon

Apparently I'm a sardonic bastard, as well.

PDA of Cal Langdon

I . . .

I don't know what to say. Except . . .

Except I'm starting to think it wasn't just a kiss after all. In fact, seeing it all laid out there like that in her book, in black-and-white—all of my interactions with this woman, I mean, in more or less graphic detail—I'm starting to realize that it might be . . . it could ONLY be.

But that's IMPOSSIBLE. I'm overtired, that's all. It's nearly three in the morning, for Christ's sake.

And yet there's no denying that sometimes when I look at her, I think—

No. It's the tattoo. That damned tattoo and those stupid shoes. They're DESIGNED to make a man think things like that.

Except that . . . well, that drive to Rome today, and that wait in the consulate's office . . . that drive and that wait could have been so tedious, but I actually had more fun than I've had in a really, really—

I've got to snap out of it. This CAN'T be happening. Not now. I'VE GOT A BOOK TO WRITE. I've got an apartment to find. I've got a sister to support.

My God. I think . . . I really do think . . .

So. It wasn't just a kiss.

But she thinks—because of my big mouth, she's convinced—

Only how can I show her that with her, it's different? I can't just tell her, she'll never believe me, she's obviously convinced I'm a "modelizer."

Holy crap. Grazi.

✉

To: Graziella Fratiani <grazielle@galleriefratiani.co.it>
Fr: Cal Langdon <cal.langdon@thenyjournal.com>
Re: You

Grazi, I've left two messages on your cell. I realize it's late—or early, as the case may be. Still, I wanted to let you know—about your coming out to the villa this week: I really don't think it would be a very good idea after all. I know we'd talked about it and I said I thought it would be fine, but actually, I think it might be really awkward at this point. Mark and Holly really want to make it more of a family thing. I know you understand. Thanks so much, and I'll call next time I'm in town, I swear.

Cal

PDA of Cal Langdon

How could I have been so stupid? How could I have missed all the signs? They were all there . . . I mean, I even fed those stupid *cats.* How could I for one second not have wondered what was happening to me?

I just kept blaming the prosecco.

I ought to be shot.

To: Listserv <Wundercat@wundercatlives.com>
Fr: Peter Schumacher <webmaster@wundercatlives.com>
Re: JANE HARRIS

GOOD MORNING! It is the day of the marriage of the friends of JANE HARRIS! YES!!! Come one, come all, to see the marriage of the friends of JANE HARRIS! I will be riding my motorino to get the marriage brotchen, and many other surprises! My grandmother and I have been working on many plans for the wedding couple!

Come to the Commune di Castelfidardo to see the marriage of the Americans today! It will be a marriage never to forget!

From the #1 Fan of Wundercat!

Wundercat lives—4eva!
Peter

Dear Holli and Marc,

For your marriage we wish you unlimited thirst
for a double good life that you both
grow and thrive and your luck may
increase and not burst!

Love,
Inge and Peter Schumacher

Travel Diary of

~~Holly Caputo and Mark Levine~~

Jane Harris

Oh my God, Peter and his grandmother have OUTDONE themselves. They are the sweetest people EVER. We woke up this morning to the smell of fresh coffee, and we went downstairs to find the dining table practically sinking under the weight of all the pastries, fresh fruit, breakfast meats, and fluffy scrambled eggs piled onto it.

Plus someone (Peter swears it wasn't him) decorated the front gate with wildflowers from the horse pasture and two pairs of blue socks (still not sure about the significance of this). Apparently, wearing blue socks on your wedding day is important for good luck in this community. However, since Holly's wedding dress is above the knee, I'm afraid this won't do at all.

Speaking of whom, the bride is still glowing. You can't even tell she spent all day yesterday with her head in a toilet. She just looks pretty and happy and . . . well, like a bride!

Even Mark is glowing . . . I mean, if you can say that about a man. There is a bounce in his step that I haven't ever seen before, and he can't seem to stop smiling. He was too nervous to eat—it was so sweet! He keeps looking at his watch and going, "Shouldn't we start getting ready? We don't want to be late. The mayor has that football game to coach."

Cal's the only one who wasn't downstairs on the stroke of seven, bright-eyed and bushy-tailed. He finally showed up a little before eight—from OUTSIDE. Apparently, he'd taken the car and gone somewhere.

But when Mark asked him where he'd been, he went, "To get the paper," and slapped a Herald Tribune down on the table.

Yeah. Nice job, Cal. Way to help out your friend on his wedding day. Get him the paper.

Who cares about him, anyway? Um, not me.

Now Holly and Mark are getting ready. I am on call in case Holly has a hair emergency, but I can already tell that she won't. Her hair is doing exactly what she wants it to. It's behaving perfectly, exactly the way hair SHOULD be on a girl's wedding day.

I am in charge of the paperwork (already in my bag), camera (ready), and lucky socks (ditto). Peter is in charge of the rings. Cal is in charge of driving. He appears to be taking this with the same kind of stoicism you might expect from a man preparing to step in front of a firing squad. How flattering to Holly that her husband-to-be's best friend apparently equates his marrying her to being shot.

Whatever. I'm not going to let that freak spoil the day. This is what we came here for, and everything is going so well: There isn't a cloud in the sky; Holly looks prettier than I've ever seen her; Mark is being the perfect nervous bridegroom; and someone else even made breakfast.

I bet there are a lot of brides who'd gladly sacrifice having their families attend their wedding in exchange for just ONE of the above.

Ooooh, we're leaving—

PDA of Cal Langdon

My God. The entire town has turned out for this wedding. Or at least, that's how it appears. There's nearly a hundred people gathered outside the Commune. And they're all wearing . . .

They're all wearing Wondercat T-shirts.

Seriously. Every last one of them.

Some of them are holding Wondercat banners. And have on Wondercat baseball hats. There's even a baby in a Wondercat COSTUME.

Jane looks completely mortified.

Especially when she stepped from the car, they surged forward, clamoring for her autograph.

She tried to explain to them that she's here for a wedding, and not a comic-book signing. But to no avail. It took us ten minutes just to get into the building. And most of the Wondercat fans have followed us, with the apparent intention of witnessing Holly and Mark's marriage for themselves.

I blame Peter. He's looking particularly pleased with himself. Yes, this has Teenaged Stalker written all over it.

Ah, here comes the secretario. He looks oddly surprised to see us. He keeps stammering something about how he'd heard the bride and groom were too ill to make it to Roma for the APOSTILLE. Jane's shoved our paperwork beneath his nose, but he's looking very skeptical—

Travel Diary of

~~Holly Caputo and Mark Levine~~

Jane Harris

Oh my God, this is HORRIBLE!!! THE MAYOR WON'T MARRY HOLLY AND MARK!!!! HE DOESN'T BELIEVE THE SIGNATURES ON THE APOSTILLE ARE THEIRS!!!! He says he heard that Mark and Holly were sick in bed all day yesterday, and so how could they have gotten the Apostille? He says the signatures on the Apostille have to be forgeries!!!

I'M GOING TO KILL PETER!!! THIS IS ALL HIS FAULT!!!! I know he must have posted something on his Web site or something about it. Because why else would there be all these Wondercat fans here? How else could they have known? And how else could the MAYOR have known about Holly and Mark????

Oh, God, I am DYING for them. Holly looks SO pretty, and Mark is so handsome. HOW can the mayor be so heartless? Should I confess? Should I go up there and be all, "OK, it was me, it's my signature, not Holly's, but I did it for a good cause, and you should still marry them because look how cute they are together"? Would he even go for that?

I don't think so. He was completely unmoved by Frau Schumacher's tirade, which lasted five minutes, at least.

And now he's taking his sash off! His mayoral sash! Like he's done for the day! He's heading off for soccer practice like he hasn't left a roomful of broken-hearted people behind! How can anyone be so—

Oh, no. What's Cal doing? Oh, God, he's not going to confess that it's his signature, is he? I KNEW he'd do something to ruin Holly and Mark's chance at—

Wait. Wait a minute, he's not—

✉

To: Claire Harris <charris2004@freemail.com>;
Darrin Caputo <darrin.caputo@caputographics.com>
Fr: Jane Harris <jane@wondercat.com>
Re: Holly and Mark

We're here! At the Commune di Castelfidardo, in the Municipale building, for Holly and Mark's wedding!

For a minute it looked as if it weren't actually going to happen. The mayor seemed to suspect all was not right with Holly and Mark's paperwork.

But then Cal Langdon—CAL LANGDON, Mr. I Don't Believe In Marriage Himself—stepped up and, whipping out a notepad, asked the mayor for his full name.

And when the mayor asked him just what he was doing, Cal went (according to Peter, who translated for me), "Oh, I'm a foreign affairs correspondent for *The New York Journal*, and I think my readers would be very interested in learning about how Le Marche officials treat American visitors to their region."

The mayor couldn't put his sash on fast enough! He started the wedding ceremony then and there!

CAL LANGDON SAVED THE DAY!

I wasn't the only one who started cheering, either. Half the town seems to have turned out for the ceremony, as well!

Holly looks so pretty in her dress, which is—even though I helped her pick it out, so I am sort of complimenting myself by saying this, but it's true—stunning. Her waist looks TINY, and she's got a tiny bouquet of white flowers that this kid Peter made her . . .actually they're garlic flowers from the garden, so you don't want to sniff them. But she doesn't know that, so DON'T TELL HER.

And then, solemnly, with all this dignified grace, they began the ceremony, with Holly and Mark holding hands and looking so sweet and nervous in front of them, and all of the rest of us—including, I am astonished to note, a good number of school-children, including the mayor's own daughter, who surely should be in school—crowded all around the sides of the room. Everyone seems to be on his or her best behavior.

Well, except for Cal Langdon, who despite his earlier heroics for some reason won't stop looking at my feet. I do have on my new Christian Louboutins, though—the ones with the rhinestone flowers over the toe straps—so that might be why. Possibly he thinks they aren't suitable wedding attire?

The mayor opened this big book and began to read, while the secretario translated in not very good English. It's a very moving ceremony so far, all about how they promise to live in the same house and educate their children. Marriage is obviously taken very seriously here in Italy, but they don't seem much concerned about the for richer or poorer, in sickness and in health stuff. They just seem to want everyone to live under the same roof and go to school.

This seems very reasonable to me.

Ooooh, it's the ring part, I have to start taking pictures, more later—

J

Art. 147- Doveri Verso I Figli

Il matrimonia impone ad ambedue I conuigi l'obligo di mantenere, istruire ed educare la prole tenendo conto delle capacita, dell'inclinazione naturale e delle aspirazioni dei figli

(domando allo sposo)

Sig. *LEVINE MARK* dichiara di voler prendere in moglie la qui presente Sig. *CAPUTO HOLLY ANN*? *(si)*

(ed alla sposa)

Sig. *CAPUTO HOLLY ANN* dichiara di voler prendere in marito il que presente Sig. *LEVINE MARK*? *(si)*

I testimoni hanno sentito *(si) (si)*

Io *Antonio Torelli*
Ufficiale di Stato Civile del Commune di Castelfidardo
Diacharo che il Sig. *LEVINE MARK* e la Sig. *CAPUTO HOLLY ANN* sono uniti in matrimonio

Commune di Castelfidardo
Provincia di Le Marche

Ufficio Dello Stato Civile
Certificato di Matrimonio
L'Ufficiale dello Stato Civile

Certifica

Che dal REGISTRO degli ATTI DE MATRIMONIO
atto N. 1 Parte II Serie C risulta che nel giorno
23 del mese di settembre contrassero
matrimonio in Castelfidardo

Mark David Levine	Holly Ann Caputo
Celibe	Nubile
Nato a Ohio USA	Nata a Illinois USA
Cittadino Statunitense	Cittadina Statunitense

✉

To: Listserv <Wundercat@wundercatlives.com>
Fr: Peter Schumacher <webmaster@wundercatlives.com>
Re: JANE HARRIS

IT IS DONE!!! The friends of JANE HARRIS have had the marriage! It was very beautiful. I hold onto the rings, and when the secretario say to me, "The rings, please," I give them to the friends of JANE HARRIS. JANE HARRIS took many photographs. One photograph was of me giving the rings.

Then the mayor said, *"Io diacharo che sono uniti in matrimonio,"* and everyone in the room gives big cheer!

And then the marriage couple kiss, and everyone gives bigger cheer!

And then the friend of JANE HARRIS named Cal Longdon says to everyone, "To thank you all for making this day so special for my friends, I'd like to invite everyone back to La Beccacia, where a champagne brunch is currently being set up."

Then everyone looks at Cal Longdon strange because we do not know this word, *brunch*.

Then JANE HARRIS says, "Are you serious?"

And Cal Longdon says, "Yes, I am serious. I ordered it this morning."

So now we have the lunch with JANE HARRIS and her friends! I bring my boom box so there is the music for dancing! I will dance with JANE HARRIS! YES!!!

This is Peter, #1 Fan of Wundercat!

Wundercat lives—4-eva!
Peter

WESTERN UNION
TELEGRAM

To: Ruth and Ira Levine
From: Mark Levine

Dear Mom and Dad,

Well, Holly and I did it. We're married. Wish you could have been there. Mom, stop crying. Susie Schramm has nothing on my Holly.

Love, Mark

WESTERN UNION
TELEGRAM

To: Salvatore and Marie Caputo
From: Holly Caputo

Dear Mom and Dad,

Mark and I got married this morning in Castelfidardo. Please don't be mad. We'll come for a visit when we get back to the States. I know you'll love him as much as I do someday.

Love, Holly

P.S. Darrin made up the thing about getting married to cover for me, lay off him.

Travel Diary of

~~Holly Caputo and Mark Levine~~

Jane Harris

I'm in total shock.

I can't believe he did this. When did he do this? He must have snuck out at the crack of dawn to get all this done. He couldn't have arranged any of this before this morning. I KNOW he didn't arrange it yesterday. I was with him all day yesterday. He was still vehemently opposed to marriage all the way up until last night. I KNOW that.

So the only way he could have done all this—the only TIME he could have done all this—was this morning, before eight. Before EIGHT IN THE MORNING.

How did he do it? I mean, there is enough food here for a small army. He must have had to wake people up to get them to start cooking this much food—much less get it delivered on time. What did he do, stand outside a restaurant and bang on the door until someone let him in?

You know what? He must have. He totally MUST have.

But WHY? Why would someone as ethically opposed to love and marriage as he is DO something like this?

Maybe for the same reason he stepped up and made sure Holly and Mark got their wedding after all—because he has a heart after all?

I'm serious. He MUST have one. This—and what happened back in town—PROVES it.

Cal Langdon is actually . . . well . . . nice.

Seriously! The terrazza looks so beautiful—someone's put vases of fresh flowers everywhere. There are tables set up across the lawn covered in white table cloths, and there are plastic lilies—actually, quite tasteful ones—floating in the pool. The champagne corks are still popping—it's a real party!

A party of people we never met before this week—some we never met before today—but a party nonetheless. Thrown together at the last minute by a man who, as of midnight last night, was still insisting love is nothing but the result of a chemical imbalance in the brain.

Holly looks so happy over there, dancing with the mayor! It's almost as if she were dancing with her dad after all.

And Mark, dancing with—well, whoever that is. Oh, wait, Annika called her Mutti, so she must be the mayor's wife. He looks blissfully happy too. The two of them seem to be over the moon. This is SO MUCH better than eloping down at City Hall back home. This is like . . . well, what the reception would have been like if Holly's mother had planned it.

It wouldn't have happened—any of it—without the man who's been insisting from the beginning that Mark and Holly were making a horrible mistake. Cal Langdon did it. Cal did it ALL.

This is just unbelievable. I wish I had thought of something so sweet. Why didn't he ask me? I totally would have chipped in.

But apparently I'm the enemy now, judging by the way he's avoided speaking to me all morning—except once to say that my Christian Louboutin pump had come unbuckled. Only he didn't call them Christian Louboutins. He said, "Your, um, shoe is coming undone."

I guess I can't really blame him. I mean, about the not-speaking-to-me thing. I really was pretty brutal to him last night. It was just a kiss, after all. I don't know why I had to jump to the conclusion that all he wanted was a roll in the hay. I'm so STUPID sometimes. I've blown it with yet another great guy.

But how was I to know he was planning this lovely party all along? I mean, what's someone who claims not to believe in love doing, throwing a wedding reception? Not to mention rushing in and SAVING the wedding in the first place. How could I have misjudged him so BADLY?

But the brain-chemical thing. I mean, there's still THAT—

Peter just wandered over here and asked me to dance again. This is the third time. I was like, "Peter, why don't you ask Annika to dance?"

I said it kind of loudly, since Annika is standing nearby. She doesn't exactly look like she wishes I hadn't mentioned it.

Then again, her English isn't as good as Peter's. In fact, she should probably be in school. Half the wedding guests look like they're skipping calculus to be here. Did Cal get this declared as a local holiday on top of everything else? Or is it Italian tradition for everyone in the village to abandon their schools and workplaces whenever zany Americans take it into their heads to be married in their town?

Anyway, Peter is telling me he CAN'T ask Annika to dance, as she'll just say no.

"Annika," I say. "If Peter asks you to dance, will you say no?"

Ha. Annika just shook her head, blushing. BLUSHING!

So I shoved Peter over there, and the two of them are slow-dancing to "Killer Queen."

Because of course Holly keeps insisting Peter play Cal's Queen CD over and over again. "Fat-Bottomed Girls" really IS her official wedding theme song.

Oooh, Cal is smacking one of Zio Matteo's spoons against the side of a champagne flute. He's going to make a speech!

Oh, dear. Considering how he feels about the occasion—or did until his mysterious change of heart this morning—"Down the hatch, and through the gums, look out stomach, here she comes," is about as eloquent as I imagine this is going to get.

✉

To: Darrin Caputo <darrin.caputo@caputographics.com>
Fr: Holly Caputo <holly.caputo@thenyjournal.com>
Re: I'm MARRIED!!!!

Well, I did it. Mark and I are married. I sent Mom and Dad a telegram, but they won't get it until tomorrow.

Still, I wanted you to be the first to know.

I hope you're happy for me. I'm over the moon, myself. The only thing that could possibly be better than this is if you were here.

Jane's been so great—there was a snag with our paperwork, and they almost weren't going to let us go through with it, but Jane drove all the way to Rome and perjured herself on our behalf, along with Mark's friend Cal, who's also thrown us the sweetest reception right here at Zio Matteo's. He just gave the most elegant toast, and since I know Bobby collects them, I tried to write it down as best I could. It went:

"Thanks everyone for coming here today. I know not all of you speak English, so I'll try to make this brief. I've known Mark Levine since the two of us were in OshKosh overalls. And though I haven't always approved of every choice he's made—I still think he should have gone out for the MLB instead of medical school, but he always did have a rescue complex, and wanted to save lives instead of hit homers for a living—this one—marrying Holly—is one even I can support. People in Mark's field can't leave anything well enough alone. They've even analyzed the chemical make-up of love. When we fall in love, our brains are flooded with something called phenylethylamine. It's a stimulant that can be found in chocolate, and, like the effects of chocolate on the mood, it doesn't last.

"But for the lucky few—and I believe Mark and Holly fall into this category—even as the human body builds up a tolerance to the "love" drug, other chemicals—endorphins—rush in. Endorphins are what flood the brain when long-term lovers touch. They're what give them that secure, comfortable, old-shoe feeling. But to keep things from getting TOO comfortable—and keep them exciting—a healthy dose of naturally occurring oxytocin gets released too, increasing desire, and stimulating—

"Well, I think I can leave the rest to your imagination. Right now I'd like you all to just raise your glass and say, Congratulations, Mark and Holly. May your lives together be blessed with health, happiness, and many, many endorphins."

Isn't that sweet? Everyone else really seemed to think so. I had no idea Mark's friend could be so eloquent. I think he really knocked poor Janie for a loop, too, because she just stood there staring at him with the funniest look on her face!

Whoops, Mark wants to dance again—more later. I hope you can read this, I have to admit, I'm a little tipsy!

Much love,
Holly

Travel Diary of

~~Holly Caputo and Mark Levine~~

Jane Harris

OK, I'm scared now. Something's happened to Cal Langdon.

Seriously. It's as if he snapped or something in the night. Maybe his Wellbutrin ran out. Or maybe he started actually TAKING Wellbutrin.

What gives???? First that thing this morning in the mayor's office. Then this party he's throwing for two people whom, at the beginning of the week, he didn't even think should get married in the first place. He had to have spent a small fortune on all of this champagne alone.

And Holly just came up to me—three sheets to the wind, but whatever, it's her wedding day, she deserves to enjoy it—and slurred, "Oh my *Go*', Janie, d'you know what Cal did? D'you know what Cal DID?"

And when I asked what Cal did, she said, "He booked us a shuite—Mark and me—a deluxe shuite at a five shtar hotel right—on the beach—for tonight. For our wedding night. For a little honeymoon. All inclushive, dinner AND breakfasht . . .and there's even a Jacuzzi tub in the room. AN INROOM JACUZZI. Have you ever heard of anything sho shweet in your LIFE?"

I had to admit that I hadn't.

And that toast? WHAT ABOUT THAT TOAST???? THAT was not the toast of a man who doesn't believe in love. Not at ALL. That was, in fact, an in-depth scientific DEFENSE of love. LONG-TERM love.

What was he THINKING?

Maybe he's not. Maybe he's on drugs. That HAS to be it. He got up this morning with some diabolical plan to stop Holly and Mark's wedding, and somewhere between trying to bribe the mayor into calling in sick and phoning a bomb threat into the Commune di Municipale building, someone slipped him a roofie. Or some E.

Except that if this were true, why is he currently dancing with Frau Schumacher in a completely sober (and yet completely engaging and charming) manner? He's navigating her across the terrazza—ahem, and toward me—with perfect ease. In fact, Peter's great-grandmother looks as if she just died and went to heaven, she's so thrilled by the manly embrace she's floating in. She doesn't even seem to be aware of the fact that she's dancing to "Bohemian Rhapsody."

Which is coming to its head-bobbing end shortly. Surely he's not getting any ideas. You know, about asking ME to dance. Not after the dressing down I gave him last night. LIKE THE HUGE IDIOT I AM.

Oh my God. I'm actually considering APOLOGIZING to him for not kissing him last night. That's how much he's psyched me out with this sudden about face of his. I mean, endorphins? ENDORPHINS? He never said a word to me about endorphins. He was all phenylethylamine yesterday. Now suddenly he's Mr. Endorphin?

"Oooooh, such a lowely party!" That's what Frau Schumacher just said, as Cal twirled her into a seat near me, "Bohemian Rhapsody" having come to its rousing (and second in the past hour) finish.

Me: "I'm so glad you're enjoying yourself, Frau Schumacher. I had no idea you were such a good dancer."

F.S.: "Me? I am nozing. Zees man, here" (clutching Cal's hand. He, by the way, looks ready to flee to the other side of the room again)—"he is the party animal!"

Cal: (looking—I <u>have</u> to say it—sweetly embarrassed) "Now, Frau Schumacher. Don't be modest. We know you must have been quite a party girl yourself once."

F.S.: (dismissing this with a wave of her hand) "Vell, yes, of course. But zat vas long ago. Oh, the parties zey used to zrow at the headquarters of the Führer! Zis reminds me of zem, a little. Zere the champagne flowed and flowed, just like here."

Cal and I exchange wide-eyed glances.

Me: "Excuse me, Frau Schumacher. Did you say . . . headquarters of the Führer?"

F.S.: (wide-eyed with innocence) "Yes. But of course. Zat is vhere I go as young girl to dance. Ven I vorked for the S.S.."

Cal: (stunned) "Frau Schumacher . . . you worked for the S.S.?"

F.S.: (waving her hand again) "Of course, of course. Ve all did! Vell, zat is vhat you did back then! Zere is more champagne?"

Cal hastened to refill Frau Schumacher's glass. "Under Pressure" came on over Peter's CD player, and his great-grandmother leaped back to her feet, declaring, "Zis is my fa-worite!"

Then she threw herself back onto the dance floor/pool deck.

Cal and I are staring at each other.

"We can never," I warn him, "*ever* tell Mark and Holly that someone who used to work for the S.S. made their wedding breakfast."

Cal shrugs. "Vhat's the big deal, Jane? Ve all did it," he says, in a perfect, deadpan imitation of Peter's great-grandmother.

"Swear," I say to him.

“Sworn,” he says. Then: “So. Still writing in that book, I see.”

Me: (unable to drag my gaze from his hands, which are looking even sexier holding a champagne glass than they did last night, holding playing cards) “Yes.”

Cal: “You're not going to give it to them, then?”

Me: (Is it my imagination, or do his eyes actually match the blue of the sky above our heads?) “Give what to whom?”

Cal: “Mark and Holly. As a wedding present. The travel diary you've been keeping for them.”

Me: (He's wearing a jacket and tie in honor of the occasion. Can I just say that he looks almost as good in them as he does without a shirt on?) “Oh, no. Not anymore. I changed my mind. Kind of the way you did.”

I know! Bold move on my part!

He looks confused. May I just say that confused, on him, is completely adorable?

Cal: “I beg your pardon?”

Me: “Well, this party, of course. When did you decide marriage is a good thing that ought to be celebrated instead of dreaded?”

Cal: “Oh, that. Well. Listen, would you quit writing in that book for a minute? It's kind of distracting.”

Me: “But it's my first trip to Europe, you know, and I don't want to miss a minute.”

Cal: “If your head is constantly stuck in a book, you're going to miss a lot.”

Me: “I'll quit writing if you tell me what changed your mind.”

Cal: “Changed my mind about what?”

Me: "Holly and Mark."

Cal: "Oh. Well. You, actually."

ME???

Me: "ME??? But . . . when? Not last night."

Cal: "Yes, actually. Last night."

Me: "But I was so mean to you!"

Cal: "Maybe I deserved it."

Oh my God, he DID start taking Wellbutrin! He MUST have! There's no other explanation for this!

Me: "Okay, what gives? Why are you being so nice all of a sudden?"

Cal: "I'm always nice."

Me: "No, you're not. What was all that saving the day down at the mayor's office? You blew your perfect opportunity to save your friend from a fate you USED to think was worse than death. So what happened?"

Cal: "I realized I was wrong."

Me: "About Holly and Mark?"

Cal: "About everything."

Me: "EVERYTHING? Even that whole phenylethylamine thing?"

Cal: "Well—that's a scientific fact. But everything else."

Me: "But . . . how? Why? Did you pick up a prescription for anti-depressants while you were in town this morning, in addition to hiring a caterer and all of that? Because you are NOT acting like yourself."

Cal: "Yeah, well, maybe I had a chance to see how I appear through someone else's eyes, and I didn't exactly like what I saw. Now will you put down that book and dance with me? They're playing our song, you know."

"Fat-Bottomed Girls" just came on again.

Nice one. Maybe he hasn't changed that much, after all.

Which wouldn't necessarily be a bad thing. I mean, who wants a guy who can't take—or make—a joke?

Cal: "Come on. Give me a chance to prove to you I've got one."
Me: "Got what?"
Cal: "A heart."

HOW DID HE KNOW????

And how can I say no?

✉

To: Listserv <Wundercat@wundercatlives.com>
Fr: Peter Schumacher <webmaster@wundercatlives.com>
Re: JANE HARRIS

Halloooo! I am writing to you having come home from the party for the marriage of the friends of JANE HARRIS! This was a very good party. If you were not there, I feel sorry for you! There was much feasting and champagne. Some people were getting very drunken. This was very comical!!!

Everyone has very good time when the car from the hotel come to take away the happy couple for their honeymoon. Then we decide to follow the car on our motorinos, because this is very fun. We stand beneath the terrazza of the happy couple at the hotel, and shout many comical things. Then the bride, she comes out and throws her bouquet to us! The bouquet was catched by Annika! Annika will now be the next bride in Castelfidardo (in American tradition)!

But this is not the most comical thing that happened at the party of the marriage of the friends of JANE HARRIS. The most comical thing was when JANE HARRIS was dancing with the very nice Cal Longdon (who gives me 20 euros to spend on MORE WUNDERCAT COMIX) and a very beautiful Italian lady arrive at the villa. She is called Graziella, and she come to see Cal Longdon.

Cal Longdon looked very, very surprised to see this woman. JANE HARRIS looked very surprised to see this woman, also.

Then JANE HARRIS pushed Cal Longdon into the pool.

This was most comical of all! JANE HARRIS is very hilarious—just like Wundercat!

This is Peter, #1 Fan of Wundercat, saying GOOD NIGHT!

Wundercat Lives—4eva!
Peter

To: Holly Caputo <holly.caputo@thenyjournal.com>
Fr: Sal Caputo <salcaputo@freemail.com>
Re: Hello, this is your father speaking

Hello! You didn't know your father had email, did you? Well, I'll admit we don't have much use for it down at the shop, but I do like to have one for bidding on antique Electroluxes on eBay. You never know when you might find one that just needs a little tweaking to get it running again.

Anyway, what is this I hear that you and Mark got married today at Zio Matteo's place in Marche? Is this true?

Well, if it is true, you have made your mother very sad. She is at church right now, making a novena for you. At Mass this evening she plans to petition for a prayer of the faithful to be said for your immortal soul.

I, however, want to be the first to say congratulazioni. Or should I say mazel tov? I know in the past your mother and I have expressed our concern about Mark not sharing our beliefs. But you are a big girl now, and you need to make your own decisions. I have always liked Mark. At least he understands how a motor works, unlike some of your brothers.

And, as I said to your mother, it will be a good thing to have a doctor in the family. Especially since I have a mole I would like for him to look at when the two of you come to visit.

Don't worry about your mother. I will ask Father Bob to have a word with her.

And, of course, now she'll be able to concentrate on making Mark convert. You know how she loves a project.

Much love,
Dad

To: Mark Levine <mark.levine@thenyjournal.com>
Fr: Ruth Levine <r.levine@levinedentalgroup.com >
Re: Hello!

Mark. Tell me it isn't true. Tell me that Marie Caputo, from whom I just received a nearly hysterical phone call, claiming one of her sons told her that you and her daughter have eloped, is suffering from a psychotic delusion.

Mark—what were you thinking? Do you know what you've done? What am I going to tell Gloria Schramm? I promised you'd call Susie just as soon as you got back to New York. Now you're going to call her, not to ask her to meet you at the Cub Room for after-work drinks, but to tell her you're married? The poor girl will have another one of her episodes. Last time they found her wandering around Fifth Avenue in nothing but Uggs and a pair of Spanx.

Tell me it isn't true. Do you know how far in advance you have to reserve the reception room at the country club? A year! If you had just let me know you were planning something like this, I could have put my name on the list months ago, and we might have been able to have a nice party when you two get back. Now what am I supposed to do? Have people over to the house? You know we haven't had the dining room wall replastered yet from when those stupid kitchen people accidentally drilled straight through while they were installing the new cabinets.

We *might* be able to get a room at the Marriott if they've had a cancellation. I'll have to check.

And your father says now you'll be paying taxes this year as if you were a married man for the entire twelve months, when you were only married for three of them. He says you should have waited until January.

What size coat does Holly wear? I'm going to look into having your uncle Isaac make her up a mink. And don't go telling me she's opposed to wearing fur, it gets very cold in New York, and if she's going to be having my grandchildren, I want to make sure she doesn't walk around with a headcold half the year.

You could have told us, you know, Mark. Your father and I would have loved a trip to Italy. You know the last place he took me was the Bahamas and it rained the whole time.

Love to you both,
Mom

✉

To: Jane Harris <jane@wondercat.com>
Fr: Claire Harris <charris2004@freemail.com>
Re: Holly and Mark

Honey! I'm so excited for them! I just ran into Marie at the Kroger Sav-On. She was carrying on about how God never gives you more than you can handle and that this just means more time in purgatory for Holly, you know, but I could tell she was over the moon. She was positively glowing.

Although that might have been because it's unseasonably hot here for September.

Still, she was buying Lender's bagels. Bagels! I asked her about them, and she very nearly blushed as she replied, "They're for freezing. For when Mark and Holly come to visit, Then I'll defrost them. He likes to have them for breakfast, you know."

I think that's a good sign, don't you?

Anyway, I hope you're still having a nice time. Daddy and I are fine. He did get a few acid burns while changing the battery in the Volvo, but Neosporin seems to be working just fine on them.

And just in case you got any ideas from Holly and Mark's wedding, I hope you know your father and I don't care WHO you marry, as long as you invite us.

Although I do think that Cal Langdon would probably look very nice in a tuxedo.

Love,
Mom

✉

To: Jane Harris <jane@wondercat.com>
Fr: Malcolm Weatherly <malcolmw@snowstyle.com>
Re: Ciao!

Hey, babe. Haven't heard from you in days. Hope things are okay.

Listen, I was just wondering—we're not exclusive or anything anymore, are we? I mean, it's okay to hook up with other people, right? Since I moved out? Because I sort of met someone. Just drop me a line and let me know, will ya? I don't want to do anything to piss you off. But a guy's got needs, you know?

Peace out,
Malcolm

✉

To: Jane Harris <jane@wondercat.com>
Fr: Julio Chasez <julio@streetsmart.com>
Re: The Dude

Hi, Ms. Harris. Listen, I was wondering—when are you getting back, exactly? Because The Dude, he's—well, he seems like he misses you, or something. I mean, this morning when I went in to feed him, I caught him gnawing on the screen over the window, trying to get out onto the fire escape, on account of there being a pigeon there. He made a pretty big hole in it, actually. The screen I mean. My dad replaced it, though, don't worry, and I shut the window all the way so he can't do it again.

And just now he kind of bit me again when all I was trying to do was pet him.

So I was just wondering . . . when are you coming home, again?

I hope it's soon.

Julio

PDA of Cal Langdon

It seems fairly obvious to me that I could have handled that better.

Really, Grazi's timing could not have been more unfortunate. I think I had almost gotten *her* to forgive me for my earlier, unfortunate gaffes.

Although I still insist my opinions, especially on marriage, were perfectly valid. You can't tell me there isn't an educated person alive who might, looking at the world as it is today, wonder if bringing a new life into it might not be the wisest course of action. Given the state of the global-economic—not to mention environmental—situation as it exists at this moment, what kind of person could possibly consider having children, when all that child stands to inherit is a planet devoid of adequate energy sources and (as a consequence of this rape of our fossil fuels) an ozone layer; bankrupt Social Security and Medicaid; and a community terrorized by fundamentalists who believe it is their inherent right to exert their values and beliefs on others, through physical force, if necessary?

Only a fool.

And yet, for the first time in my life, I can see how being a fool can have its advantages. Especially if what you're being a fool for is love.

God. I can't believe I just wrote that.

But, incredibly, it's true. I can see now why Mark and Holly felt they *had* to marry, in spite of their parents' opposition, in spite of what they know about this world and the dangers it holds. I can see now why it was so important to them to legalize their union—why having an easily accessible escape route from a romantic relationship isn't always necessarily the best thing, if you want the relationship to last.

I see all these things now.

Too bad I can't convince *her* of that.

Not that I thought it would be easy. But I honestly never anticipated that I might be doing it from the bottom of a pool.

Here is where the Old Cal might start bleating about how She's got some nerve, expecting me to have acted like a damned eunuch in the past, when I didn't even know her. This is when the Old Cal might think to himself, Why am I even bothering to put myself through this? I've got a perfectly beautiful, elegant, sophisticated Italian woman right here who'd be more than happy to make love with me all night long. Why am I worrying about what some American cartoonist is thinking?

Ah, there's the rub. Because I don't want the beautiful, elegant, sophisticated Italian woman. I want the cartoonist with the cat tattoo who can't seem to stop tripping over her own shoes.

God help me.

She, however, has made it perfectly clear she doesn't want me. At least, not anymore. I suppose Grazi strolling in like that, looking as if she owned the place in that hat and those stilettos, was just one strike too many against me.

Grazi was perfectly understanding about it. She apologized for not having checked her email, and said by the time she got my phone messages, she was already on her way. I believe I made quite an ass of myself, trying to explain what was going on, as I drove her back to the train station (after I'd changed into dry clothes, of course).

"I see," was what Grazi had to say about it. "You are in love. With a woman who draws a cartoon. About a cat."

Hearing her put it that way, so baldly—*You are in love*—I actually felt physically ill for a moment.

And yet—here's the strangest thing of all—I felt ill in a *good* way.

"That's not all," I felt compelled to confess. "She thinks I'm a pompous ass, incapable of feeling anything except my own sense of superiority."

Grazi seemed to find this amusing.

"You *can* be pompous," she said. Which I can't say I found particularly reassuring. "You seem to think you know everything there is to know."

"She's categorically uninterested in geopolitical dynamics," I went on, "or world affairs of any kind."

"Yes," Grazi said. "But these things are not important to most people."

"This morning," I added, feeling desperate for someone, anyone to try to talk me out of what I knew perfectly well was already a foregone conclusion, "I saw her put ketchup on her eggs. And she likes Nutella. And that television show, *ER*."

To which Grazi replied, with a calmness I'm sure she was far from feeling, "Yes, but this is a very popular show."

"It's not something I planned on happening," I explained to her.

"Who plans on falling in love?" Grazi asked, with a shrug. "It simply happens. We cannot stop it, however much we might try."

Then, exhaling a plume of blue smoke from her cigarette, she added, "Though I imagine in your case, trying not to just made you fall harder. That is the way, with men like you. When it happens, nothing can stop it. Not even ketchup on the eggs."

"She hates me," I admitted miserably.

"No, she does not," Grazi was kind enough to say. "If she hated you, she would not have pushed you in the water when she saw me."

I hope—but do not actually believe—that Grazi is right.

But even if she is, what can I do about it? By the time I got back to the house after dropping Grazi off at the train station, so she could go back to Rome, the party was over, and the house was shut up tight. *She* was nowhere to be found. I knew she hadn't left . . . her suitcase was still there. Thinking she'd gone into town with the others to terrorize the bridal couple at their hotel, I drove in, but saw only Peter and his little friends on the beach, ripping apart Holly's garlic flower bouquet in some sort of strange pubescent *Lord-of-the-Flies*-like ceremony, and throwing the petals into the sea.

Now I've had too much coffee at the café, and read every English-language paper in town. The sun is starting to set, and I know I should go back to the villa to see if she's there.

But part of me is afraid to leave this chair. Because what happens if I go back there, and she gives me the cold shoulder?

Grazi's reply, when I asked her this very question as she was boarding her train, was hardly reassuring.

"She won't," she said, with a smile, "if you make the grand gesture."

"What grand gesture?" I asked. "I already threw a party that put me five grand in the hole, and all that got me was a view of the bottom of the pool."

"What does she want?" Grazi asked, pointedly. "Besides a wedding for her friend, which you already gave her? That is what you must do, you know. Give her what she wants—what she's never had—and she'll be yours."

I had to think about that one. What Jane Harris wants. I thought about it for a long time after Grazi's train pulled away from the station.

It turned out not to be that hard. I mean, it's not like it wasn't written on practically every page of her diary.

Still, how to show her I really meant it:. that was the hard part.

Of course, if it turns out I'm wrong . . .

Well, here goes nothing.

Travel Diary of

~~Holly Caputo and Mark Levine~~

Jane Harris

I should have known, of course. That it was all too good to be true.

About him having changed, I mean.

He hasn't changed. They <u>never</u> change.

I don't know what I was thinking. I mean, just because he got Holly and Mark married, then threw them a nice party, and made a sweet toast, the way any normal man SHOULD have, I thought he'd come around.

Ha. HA!

It's so transparently obvious now that the whole thing was some kind of setup to get me into bed.

I have to admit at first I was flattered. I mean, that he went to all that trouble, just to see me naked. No man's ever gone to such elaborate lengths on my behalf. Well, Curt Shipley took me to the prom.

But knowing now that he didn't really care WHO he screwed afterwards, me or Mike Morris, has somewhat spoiled my appreciation of the fact in retrospect.

Same with Cal Langdon. I mean, it was all just a big game to him. I knew it the minute I laid eyes on that art gallery woman. Just a kiss. Ha! Exactly as I suspected, it WASN'T just a kiss. He was just lonely, and wanted to get laid. He didn't care by WHO. Or WHOM. Or whatever. Why else would he have invited her?

And I'll admit, he did look kind of surprised to see her there. He must have forgotten he'd asked her to stop by.

Well, I'm sure that baptism I gave him reminded him plenty fast.

Whatever. It's not like I even care. I mean, it's not like I was

FALLING FOR HIM, or anything. Please. Falling for WHAT? Believe me, I can do better than an egocentric jerk like him.

And okay, he DOES have those nice sinewy, tanned hands. And those blue eyes. And he likes cats. And he's a great kisser. And he's super smart, but can still be funny when he lets himself.

So what? He has a lot of faults, too. He thinks he knows everything, when, very clearly, he does not, particularly when it comes to human relations.

And he writes books I wouldn't pick up to read if I even were dying of boredom.

And, though I can't be sure of it, I think I caught him looked at me a little funny this morning when he saw me putting ketchup on my eggs.

Who needs that? Not me. No, sir. I'm sticking to nice guys. Like Malcolm. Well, not Malcolm, exactly, since he's clearly moved on, which . . . good for him.

But I mean <u>simple</u> guys, like Malcolm. Guys who don't play head games. Guys with a wry appreciation of life's vagaries. Cal doesn't appreciate anything wryly. Well, except for maybe my grammatical errors.

Oh. Wait. War.

Okay. Peter won.

Whatever.

Where was I?

Oh, yeah.

The first thing I'm going to do when I get back home is register for some kind of class at the Learning Annex. I don't know what. But some kind of class a simple guy would take. Like pottery, maybe. Or Italian! Yeah. How to speak Italian. I bet a lot of guys take that class. And then I can meet a nice, simple guy, and next time I come back to Italy, I'll bring him along.

Because even though this country has its faults—the three-hour lunches, where everything, even SHOE stores, is closed . . . not to mention the lack of toilets, like at Amici Amore, or just the seats, like that restaurant in Porto Recanati—it can also be super nice. When I made Peter drop me off in town today after the party, when he and Annika and everyone else went to harass Holly and Mark at their hotel, I walked around a little, got myself a nice gelato, sat down in a little palazzo, and just relaxed.

I haven't been able to do much relaxing since I got to Italy—well, except for like five minutes by the pool that one day—what with the sightseeing and the worrying about Holly and Mark's wedding not working out and the whole Cal thing.

But today I relaxed, and I looked around, and I . . . well, I liked what I saw. Italy, I mean. Well, Le Marche, anyway. They're all so friendly, and say hi to one another as they pass on the street.

And all of the windows have flower boxes instead of fire escapes on them, because none of the buildings is more than two stories high.

And because the buildings are so low, the sky looks HUGE overhead, like in Wyoming, or something. Only it's a blue like it never gets in New York, on account of all the pollution from the traffic. Here, most everyone rides scooters, or at most, they have tiny little Smart Cars.

Even the ice cream tastes better than back in America. That was the best pistachio I ever had.

And the pace of life is kind of catching. I mean, I definitely don't approve of three-hour lunches. But if you NEED to take that long for lunch, it's nice that it's not frowned on. Like it would be in Manhattan. I mean, can you imagine if you worked on Wall Street or whatever and you tried to tell your boss you wouldn't be back for three hours?

There's something kind of nice about the way no one hurries, and how there always seems to be time for a cup of coffee and a friendly Buon giorno.

It's a shame we have to leave Friday, really. I mean, not that I'll be sad to say good-bye forever to SOME people I've met here. But I think I'll miss this place. And Peter. And even his great-grandmother and snotty Annika (whom, when she asked me what she was supposed to do with Holly's bouquet after she caught it, I told it was traditional to shred the flowers to pieces and throw them into the sea for good luck) and the mayor and the smell of horses drifting into my bedroom window in the morning and those skinny cats and the oven that you can't turn on without the lights going out and all of the Virgin Marys and the castles on every hillside and . . .

Well, just everything.

Except HIM.

After I take that class at the Learning Annex—on how to speak Italian—and I meet that guy—you know, the simple one who'll be able to appreciate life's vagaries—we'll come back to Italy, and we'll have a fabulous time, because both of us will know what carabinieri are, and neither of us will laugh at the other's mistakes, unlike—

HIM.

Oh, my God. He's back.

He has some nerve.

Oh, and look. His face still has that same hangdog expression that he had on when I left. What happened, Cal? Did your Italian skank refuse to put out when she saw how stupid you look sitting at the bottom of the pool?

Huh. He's trying to make conversation. Yeah, nice try, buddy. But you're not going to get anywhere in front of the kid. Why do you think I invited him over here? Yeah, not because I have such a burning love for card games. No, it was because I had a feeling you'd come crawling back. And I know you aren't going to be talking about <u>us</u> if there's a third party—

OH MY GOD! THAT'S BRIBERY!

Wait, two can play at that game—

AARRRGHHH!!! WHY DIDN'T I GET CASH WHEN I WAS IN TOWN?

Fine. Whatever. So Peter's gone. A twenty, and he's off. Traitor.

I don't care. I still don't have to listen to what this guy has to say. I can just go inside and see what Holly's doing—

Um, no, I can't. Because Holly and Mark are at the hotel. The hotel room <u>he</u> bought them. We're all alone. We're all alone in this giant villa because he—

PLANNED IT THAT WAY!!!!

OH MY GOD. I AM SUCH AN IDIOT.

But whatever. Still not listening. No. Not listening to you, Mr. My Only Goal In Life Is to Break the Heart of the Stupid American Girl. NOT LISTENING.

Cal: "Jane. Seriously. Quit writing in that book and look at me. Just for a minute."

Me: "No."

Cal: "Fine. But I'm not going to go away. Not until we have this out."

Me: "There is nothing to have out."

Cal: "Yes, there is. Look, I know I've acted like a jerk almost from the first moment I met you—"

Me: "Almost?"

Cal: "Okay, from the first moment I met you. But I want you to know that I feel terrible about it now. You were right. I <u>am</u> an ass. And a creep. The things I said—the stuff I did—all of it. You were right. You were completely right about Mark and Holly, and I was completely wrong. I see that now."

Hmmm. This is an interesting turn of events. He's apologizing. And conceding wrongdoing. I've never had a guy do THAT before. What can this mean?

Oh, wait. I know. Silly me.

Me: "If this is all just an act to get me to go to the hotel too, so you can have the villa to yourself for the night for you and your skank, it's not going to work. I happen to like it here, and have no intention of leaving, even for a Jacuzzi tub."

Cal: "Jane. If I wanted to spend the night with Grazi, don't you think I'd be at the hotel with her now, and not here, trying to reason with you?"

DAMN HIM AND HIS GENIUS LOGIC!

Me: "Well, whatever you're trying to do, cut it out. It's making me nervous. I liked it better when you hated me."

Cal: "I never hated you—"

Me: "HA! HA! HA! CARABINIERI!"

Cal: "What? I can't even joke with you?"

Me: "That wasn't joking with me. That was a joke ABOUT me."

Cal: "And you haven't made plenty of those about me this past week?"

Me: "Not to your face."

 Oooooh. He just swung one of the wrought-iron chairs around, set it directly in front of me, sat down in it, and leaned forward, so that I can see the blond five-o'clock shadow dusting his jaw. Also those blue eyes.

LOOK AWAY. LOOK AWAY FROM THE HYPNOTIC BLUE EYES.

Cal: "Jane. Quit writing in that book and listen to me."

Ha. So not going to happen.

Cal: "Fine. If that's the way you're going to be, then I'm just going to say this. I will admit that when I met you, I might have been laboring under some misconceptions about male-female relations. I'm not going to tell you I've never been in love, because you and I both know that's not true. I was in love once, and it didn't work out, and because of that, I have worked very, very hard to convince myself that love doesn't actually exist. Because I didn't want to admit that I'd screwed it up. And if I couldn't have it, I didn't want anyone else to, either."

Hmmm. Nice little explanation there. Neat. Tidy. Almost believable.

Cal: "But meeting you changed all that. You made me see that two people—like Mark and Holly—<u>can</u> fall deeply, madly in love, without any ulterior motives, and that that love isn't just in their heads, a result of a chemical imbalance, but the result of attraction, mutual trust, and sheer, genuine affection. The love those two have for each other—the kind of love that would make them throw caution to the wind and get married in spite of almost everyone else in the world that they cared about being totally against the idea—that's the kind of love I've always wanted, but never thought actually existed. Until yesterday."

Hmmm. That's pretty good, too.

Wait. What the hell is he talking about?

Me: "What happened yesterday?"

Cal: "Yesterday, I was stuck in a car with you for eight hours."

Bastard. I didn't even sing along with the radio. Much.

Me: "Yeah. And?"

Cal: "Something happened."

Me: "If you're referring to my driving skills, may I just say I didn't TOUCH that truck. What you felt was just the wind. We were going pretty fast. And there wasn't even a scratch. I checked."

Cal: "I'm not talking about that. I'm talking about the fact that I fell in love with you. And I'm pretty sure you're in love with me, too."

!!!!!!!!!!!!!!!!!!!!!!!!!!!!!!!!!!!!!!!

Cal: "Can you stop writing in that book now?"

How can I stop? I mean, I can barely hold onto my pen, my fingers are shaking so badly. . . .

This can't be true. This has to be some kind of elaborate boy scheme to . . . I don't know what.

Me: "Okay, I understand that guys like you will stop at NOTHING to make a sexual conquest. I mean, telling a girl what you think she wants to hear . . . that's par for the course. But it's never a good move to presume you know what she feels for you. Because I can assure you, I am NOT in love with you."

Cal: "I'm not presuming. I know exactly what you think about me. You think I'm an anal-retentive Armrest Nazi . . . an arrogant Modelizer. You can't stand the way I talk, any of the subjects I choose to talk about, the imperious manner I order food in restaurants or tell cab drivers how much we owe them. You find my taste in women odious, the fact that I don't own a television an unforgivable sin, and the fact that I would choose to write a book about Saudi Arabia completely unfathomable. And you're also totally and completely in love with me. If you weren't, you wouldn't have pushed me into the pool earlier today when you saw Grazi walk in."

Me: Speechless.

Cal: "Now will you put that book down and kiss me?"

Me: "No, I will NOT. What are you—how did you—did HOLLY tell you all that?"

Cal: "No. I read that book you're writing in."

WHAT?

Cal: "Could you write a little bigger? I'm not sure China saw that. Yes, I read your diary. It does say, on the first page, that you intend to give it to Holly and Mark as a wedding present. I didn't think it would be any big deal for me to read something you obviously meant for them to read. It wasn't until I was much too deeply engrossed in it to put it down that I realized you'd changed your plans."

Me: "Ngh."

Cal: "Well put. Yes, I know all your darkest secrets, Jane Harris. How much you pine for Dr. Kovac, who is, I'd like to point out, a fictional character. Your mistaken impression of the size of a certain part of my anatomy. What, exactly, you think about my book—not that your facial expression whenever I bring it up doesn't say it all. I know you've got a soft spot for humpbacked dwarves, stray cats, and your friend Holly, and I know you want to go to Veselka's with me and eat blintzes. I don't know what Veselka's is, but I'm a big fan of blintzes. I've never enjoyed myself more than I have the past forty-eight hours, during which I've been trapped in a car with one of the worst drivers I have ever seen, run up the Spanish Steps and then down again so I could be on time to wait in line to perjure myself at the American consulate. And I'd like to continue doing those sorts of things with you on a regular basis for the foreseeable future. Although I would also like to include sex with you, if possible. And if none of that convinces you, perhaps this will: I have every intention of sticking around long enough to form an intense, unbreakable, long-term bond with The Dude. And to prove it, this afternoon, I went and got this."

Oh, my God. He's rolling up his sleeve. Why is he rolling up his sleeve? What could he possibly—

NO!

IMPOSSIBLE!

It's a tattoo!!! He's got a tattoo. Of Wondercat!

Just like the one on my ankle.

Me: "But—How? Where?"

Cal: "Crazy Bar and Sexy Tattoo Shop in town. They say Wondercat's one of their best sellers."

Me: "But–but–but that's PERMANENT!!!!"

Cal: "So is how I feel about you. Now. Could you put the pen down and kiss me, please?"

And suddenly, I find that I can.

Because my heart has become filled with something. Something I can't really describe.

Except that it feels like bianco frizzante.

Travel Diary of

~~Holly Caputo and Mark Levine~~

Jane Harris

Oh my God. He lied. It's totally true, what Mark told Holly about Cal's—

Travel Diary of

~~Holly Caputo and Mark Levine~~

Jane Harris

Poor Frau Schumacher. She's going to have a LOT of sheets to wash when we leave. I think we've done it in every bedroom at least once.

Oh well. I suppose she's used to hard work, considering all the time she put in over at the Führer's place.

Travel Diary of

~~Holly Caputo and Mark Levine~~

Jane Harris

Even Cal admits that Nutella on strawberries, washed down with champagne, makes a lovely midnight snack.

Travel Diary of

~~Holly Caputo and Mark Levine~~

Jane Harris

Must write fast, as he's downstairs, getting more strawberries.

He loves me! At least as much as I—I can't believe I'm admitting this—love him. YES! It's true! I love him! I could shout it from the rooftop: I LOVE HIM!

And I don't think that's the phenylethylanamine talking, either.

Endorphins? Definitely.

Oh, my God. I love Cal Langdon. CAL LANGDON.

And you know, really, the only reason he doesn't like ER is that he's never seen it. It turns out they don't have ER in Libya or wherever it is he's been all these years. I'm sure he'll come around as soon as he's caught up with everything that's happening at County.

I showed him my Wondercat sketch book, too, and he laughed at my most recent cartoon. Cal Langdon LAUGHED. At one of my cartoons!!!! And called me a comic genius!

Which I already knew. But it was nice to hear it from him.

Oops, here he comes. I promised I'd stop writing about him in here.

For now.

✉

To: Arthur Pendergast <a.pendergast@rawlingspress.com>
Fr: Cal Langdon <cal.langdon@thenyjournal.com>
Re: The Book

Hey, Arthur. I was thinking. How would you feel if my second book was on Le Marche? In case you don't know, Le Marche is one of Italy's lesser-known regions, filled with breathtaking vistas of ancient castles atop rolling picturesque hillsides, shady olive groves, curved white beaches, delicious seafood, and earthy but delicate wines like the Verdicchio, considered among the finest of the *vini da meditazione*.

This is a region in which family-run businesses thrive. It's a nearly self-sufficient area that many countries—for instance, those formerly dependent on the exportation of oil—might do well to emulate.

I'm thinking about renting a place here for a few months with my girlfriend to do some research. You might have heard of her—Jane Harris? She's the creator of *Wondercat*, that hilarious comic strip about the cat. I'm sure you've read it.

Anyway, let me know what you think.

Cal

✉

To: Cal Langdon <cal.langdon@thenyjournal.com>
Fr: Arthur Pendergast <a.pendergast@rawlingspress.com>
Re: The Book

Le Marche? What the hell are you talking about? No one's ever heard of Le Marche. Who the hell is going to buy a book about some place they never heard of?

Let me tell you something: if *Sweeping Sands* wasn't Number 2 on the *Times* Bestseller list right now, I'd tell you what you can do with Le Marche.

But as it is . . ..

Go with God.

Arthur Pendergast
Senior Editor
Rawlings Press
1418 Avenue of the Americas
New York, NY 10019
212-555-8764

PS Girlfriend? Since when do you have a girlfriend? I thought you were monogaphobic.

PPS What the hell is a Wondercat?

✉

To: Listserv <Wundercat@wundercatlives.com>
Fr: Peter Schumacher <webmaster@wundercatlives.com>
Re: JANE HARRIS

Listen up, kids! You are not believing what is happening! JANE HARRIS, creator of our beloved Wundercat, is STAYING here in Le Marche! Yes! At least, this is what she tells me today when I come in the morning to bring the brotchen.

Actually, JANE HARRIS does not come to the door this morning when I bring the brotchen. JANE HARRIS does not come downstairs until very late this afternoon to get the brotchen. And then she is looking very tired. But very good, as usual!

And Cal Longdon, who comes to the door with JANE HARRIS, asks if I know any houses to rent in Le Marche, because he wants to write a book about us! US!!!

YES! Because Le Marche RULES!!!!

And JANE HARRIS says she thinks she had better stay in Le Marche, too, to help Cal Longdon write his very important book about US!!!!

And when I ask her what I know you are thinking—"WHAT ABOUT WUNDERCAT?" she says, "Oh, I can draw Wondercat anywhere."

YES!!!! JANE HARRIS IS MOVING TO ITALY! AND YOU HEARD IT HERE FIRST. Courtesy of me, #1 Wundercat Fan Of All Time!

Wundercat Lives—4eva!
Peter

Private to Annika: When you are done with Wundercat Volume 1, tell me, and I will bring you Volume 2 on my motorino.

✉

To: Jane Harris <jane@wondercat.com>
Fr: Claire Harris <charris2004@freemail.com>
Re: Your phone call

Honey, I'm just writing because last night when you called, I could have sworn you said you were *staying* in Italy. With Cal Langdon. Permanently.

Daddy says I must have dreamed the whole thing. But I don't think I would have dreamt the part where you said if your Wondercat development deal ends up going through, of course Cal will move back to New York with you, because the two of you are in a committed relationship and fully support one another in your careers.

That's just not the kind of thing I usually dream about.

And another thing: this morning when I was at the Kroger Sav-On to buy some more Band-Aids for Dad (he put a nail through his thumb hanging up another watercolor from his sister—I wish she'd take up a new hobby), I ran into Marie Caputo, who asked me—with, I must admit, a smile I didn't care for—how it felt to be gaining a son. Gaining a son? What is she talking about, sweetheart? She can't have meant you and that Cal Langdon, can she? Are you two getting married? Does Holly know something I don't know, and maybe told her mother?

How can you marry Cal Langdon, honey? Last time I talked to you, you said you hated him. And that he wouldn't stop looking at your shoes.

None of this makes any sense to me. I don't think you ought to be staying in Italy with—much less marrying—someone you've only known for a week.

I hope Marie misunderstood. In fact, I'm SURE she must have. You've always been such a sensible girl.

Besides, what about Malcolm, that nice investment banker you've been seeing?

Daddy's right, and that phone call last night must have been just a dream. Because you would never move to Italy without The Dude.

Oh, wait, I asked you that last night, didn't I? And you said you were going to pay your super's son to bring The Dude to you there. . . .

But that can't be right. You would never do anything so silly.

Well, ignore me. Hope you have a nice time on the rest of your trip.

And try to be nice to that Cal Langdon. I'm sure he can't help being in love with you. And you always did have very pretty feet.

Love,
Mom

✉

To: Julio Chasez <julio@streetsmart.com>
Fr: Jane Harris <jane@wondercat.com>
Re: The Dude

Hi, Julio! Listen, I was wondering. How would you feel about an all-expense paid trip to Italy?

QUEEN OF BABBLE GETS HITCHED

For Benjamin

Acknowledgments

Many thanks to:
Beth Ader
Jennifer Brown

Carrie Feron
Michele Jaffe
Laura Langlie

Tessa Woodward

and especially Benjamin Egnatz

A HISTORY *of* WEDDINGS

In ancient times, weddings were a little more casual than they are today. Rival tribes, in order to increase their population, would frequently stage raids against one another, with the sole purpose of acquiring brides. That's right—they'd steal one another's ladyfolk. The raiding party was kind of what you'd consider your modern-day groom and his groomsmen.

Only, you know, they wouldn't be wearing tuxes. More like loincloths.

Sometimes the young ladies in question got wind of the raiding party beforehand and didn't necessarily put up much of a fight.

But this didn't mean there wasn't ill feeling on the part of their families and friends.

Tip to Avoid a Wedding Day Disaster

Always have more gifts on your registry than you do wedding guests. This way you can avoid receiving the same gift twice . . . and those guests who can't actually make it to the festivities will still be able to find something lovely to get for you!

LIZZIE NICHOLS DESIGNS™

Chapter 1

Whatever souls are made of, his and mine are the same.

—Emily Brontë (1818–1848), British novelist and poet

"Chaz," I say, poking the man in the tuxedo who lay sprawled across my bed. "You have to get out of here."

Chaz brushes my hand away as if it's annoying him. "Mom," he says. "Stop it. I told you, I already took out the trash."

"Chaz." I poke him some more. "I mean it. Wake up. You have to go."

Chaz wakes up with a start. "Wha— Where am I?" He looks blearily around the room until his unfocused gaze finally comes to rest on me. "Oh. Lizzie. What time is it?"

"Time for you to go," I say, grabbing hold of his arm and pulling on it. "Come on. Get *up*."

But I might as well be pulling on an elephant. He won't budge.

"What's going on?" Chaz wants to know. I have to admit, it's not easy, being so mean to him. He looks downright adorable in his tuxedo shirt, all stubbly faced and confused, with his dark hair sticking up in tufts all over his head. He squints at me. "Is it morning already? Hey—why do you still have your clothes on?"

"Because nothing happened between us," I say, relieved that it's true. I mean, stuff *happened*. But my Spanx are still on, so not *that* much stuff. Thank God. "Come on, get up. You have to go."

"What do you mean, nothing happened between us?" Chaz looks offended. "How can you say that? That's my beard burn you're wearing."

I lift a hand guiltily to my face. "What? Oh my God. You're kidding, right?"

"No, I'm not kidding. You're completely chafed." A look of self-satisfaction spreads across his face as he stretches his arms. "Now come over here and let's continue where we left off before you so rudely fell asleep, which I'm going to try not to hold against you, although I will admit it's going to be difficult, and will probably necessitate punishment in the form of a spanking if I can figure out how to get those things off you. What did you call them again? Oh, yeah. Spanx." Chaz brightens. "Hey, how appropriate."

But I've already dived for the bathroom and am examining my face in the mirror over the sink.

He's totally right. The entire lower half of my face is bright pink from where Chaz's stubble rubbed it as we made out like a couple of teenagers in the back of the taxi on our way home from the wedding last night.

"Oh God!" I cry, staggering back into the bedroom. "Do you think he noticed?"

"Do I think who noticed what?" Chaz has seized me by the wrist, pulled me over, and is fumbling with the tiny buttons to my gown.

"Luke!" I cry. "Do you think he noticed I've got beard burn all over my face?"

"How would Luke notice that?" Chaz asks. "He's in France. How do you get this thing off, anyway?"

"He's not in France!" I cry, swatting at Chaz's hands. "He was just downstairs. That was him, at the door!"

"The door?" Chaz pauses in his attempt to disrobe me, looking more adorably confused than ever. Not that I have any business noticing how adorable Chaz is. "Luke's at the door?"

"No, not anymore," I say, swatting his hands away once more. "But he's coming back in half an hour. And that's why you have to leave now. He doesn't know you're here. And I want to keep it that way." I wrestle his tuxedo jacket from beneath the knee he's resting on it and hold it out for him. "So if you wouldn't mind putting this on and kindly vacating the premises—"

"Wait a minute." Chaz raises a dark eyebrow. "Wait just a minute here.

Are you honestly trying to tell me that you and Mr. Romance are getting back together?"

"Of course we're getting back together," I say, throwing an urgent glance at the clock. Twenty-five minutes! Luke will be back in twenty-five minutes! He only went in search of a Starbucks to grab us coffees and a couple of Danish . . . or whatever it is Starbucks has available on New Year's Day. Which, for all I care, could be rancid pig fat in plastic containers. *What does it matter?* "Why else do you think I've been standing here asking you to please get up? I don't want him to know you spent the night—or that you gave me beard burn."

"Lizzie." Chaz is shaking his head. But he's putting his tuxedo jacket on. Thank God. "He's not a little boy. You can't protect him forever. He's going to have to find out about us sometime."

Icy tentacles grip my heart. "Us? What us? Chaz . . . there is no us."

"What do you mean, there is no us?" He looks up from the inside coat pocket he'd been investigating, evidently in search of his wallet. "Did we, or did we not, just spend the night together?"

"Yes," I say, with another exasperated glance at the clock. Twenty-four minutes! And I have to wash my hair. I'm sure there's confetti in it from the wedding. Not to mention, I probably have raccoon rings of mascara around my eyes. "But I already told you. Nothing happened."

"Nothing?" Chaz looks wounded. "I distinctly remember holding you tenderly in my arms and kissing you beneath a sky full of falling stars. You call that *nothing*?"

"Those were balloons," I remind him. "Not stars."

"Whatever. I thought we said we were going to work on the physical part of our relationship."

"No. *You* said that. I said we'd both just come out of painful breakups and needed time to heal."

Chaz reaches up and runs a hand through his hair, causing it to stand even more comically on end. Plus, confetti falls out of it and onto my bedspread. "Then what was all that kissing in the cab about?"

He has a valid point. I'm not sure what all that kissing in the cab was about.

Or why I enjoyed it so much, either.

But I do know one thing. And that's that I'm not going to stand here and talk about it. Not right now.

"We had too much to drink," I explain, with another frantic glance at the clock. Twenty-two minutes! And I have to blow-dry too! "We were at a wedding. We got carried away."

"Carried away?" Chaz's blue eyes look unnaturally bright in the winter sunlight filtering through my new lace curtains. "That's what you call my hand down your bra? *Carried away?*"

I rush forward to place a hand over his mouth.

"We must never speak of this again," I say, my heart booming—yes, booming—in my chest.

"Don't even tell me," Chaz says from behind my hand, "that you're giving him another chance. Yes, he made the big romantic gesture, flying back from France on New Year's Day, or whatever. But, Lizzie . . . the guy is a complete commitment-phobe. He's never followed through with anything in his life."

"That isn't true," I cry, wrenching my hand away from Chaz's mouth and flipping it around for him to see. "Look!"

Chaz stares at the third finger on my left hand.

"Oh God," he says after a minute. "I think I'm going to be sick."

"That's a nice thing to say," I point out hotly, "to the girl your best friend's just proposed to."

Although the truth is, I feel a little sick myself. But that's from all the champagne last night. It has to be.

"Lizzie." Chaz flops back across my bed and stares up at the cracks in my ceiling. "Do I have to remind you that less than twenty-four hours ago you two were broken up? That you moved out of the apartment the two of you were sharing precisely because he said he couldn't see you in his future? That you spent most of last night with your tongue down *my* throat because the two of you were supposed to be through?"

"Well," I say, looking down at the emerald-cut three-carat diamond sitting in its platinum band. It seems to catch the light just so. Luke told me the certificate authenticating the gem is blood-free is on its way. "He changed his mind."

"Because your moving out like that scared him shitless," Chaz cries, sitting up again. "Is that what you want? A guy who comes running back to you and proposes just because he's so scared of being alone, he'd rather be with a girl he knows isn't right for him than be by himself?"

I glare at him. "Oh," I say. "And I suppose you think we'd make such a better couple."

"Yeah," Chaz says. "Now that you mention it, I do. But the truth is, a monkey with a paper bag over its head would make a better boyfriend for you than Luke. Because you two are totally wrong for each other."

"You—" I suck in my breath. I can't even believe I'm having this conversation. "What . . . How can— I thought Luke was supposed to be your best friend!"

"He *is* my best friend," Chaz says. "I've known him since he was fourteen years old. I probably know him better than he knows himself. That's what makes me unequivocally qualified to say that he's got no business asking anybody to marry him right now, let alone you."

"What do you mean, *let alone me*?" I can feel tears brimming along the edges of my eyelashes. "What's so wrong with me?"

"Nothing's wrong with you, Lizzie," Chaz says in a gentler voice. "It's just that you know what you want, and Luke doesn't. You're a star. And Luke's not the kind of guy who's going to hitch his wagon to a star. He still thinks *he's* the star. And you can't have two stars in one relationship. Somebody has to be willing to be the wagon . . . at least some of the time."

"That's not true," I say, wiping my eyes with the back of one of my wrists. "Luke's a star. He's going to be a doctor. He's going to save children's lives one day."

Chaz raises his gaze to the ceiling.

"The day Luke de Villiers ever actually becomes a doctor," he says solemnly, "is the day I switch to light beer. For good."

I glare at him. "Get out," I say, pointing at the door. "I mean it. Just get out."

Chaz stands up—then instantly looks as if he regrets it. Nevertheless, when he regains his balance, he says, with as much dignity as he can seem to muster, "You know what? Gladly." He stalks out of the bedroom and into the living room, finding his coat on the floor where he'd dropped it the night before. He scoops it up—holding his head a bit woozily—then heads for the door.

"You're making a big mistake, Lizzie," he turns to say when he gets there . . . looking a little surprised when he finds me right behind him.

"No," I shoot back, pressing my index finger against his sternum. "*You* are. Your best friend is getting married. You should be happy for him. And for me. Just because things didn't work out for you and Shari—"

"Shari?" Chaz shakes his head in bewilderment. "This has nothing to do with Shari. It has to do with you and me."

"You and me?" I let out a stunned bark of laughter. "There *is* no you and me."

"That's what you think," Chaz says, tugging on his coat. "And I'll be damned if I'm going to wait around until you figure out that isn't true."

"Fine," I say "I'm not asking you to, am I?"

"No." Chaz is smiling . . . but not like he's happy. "But you would if you had the slightest idea what was good for you."

And with that, he yanks open the door and storms through it, slamming it closed behind him with enough force to cause the windowpanes to rattle.

And then he's gone.

A HISTORY *of* WEDDINGS

Once the kidnapped "bride" and her groom had safely escaped the wrath of her relatives, frantically searching for her around the outskirts of the village from which she'd been snatched, they'd lay low for a while, to avoid retaliation from her family (or any possible husbands already in existence).

This was also the period during which the "groom" exerted his dominance over his new captive, stamping out any desire she might have to escape or murder him in his sleep (a not uncommon practice in early "marriages" of this sort where the bride wasn't as happy with the situation as a groom might hope her to be).

This "laying low" period could be considered the ancient predecessor to the honeymoon. Only it probably took place in a cave, not at a Sandals resort. And there definitely wasn't room service.

Tip to Avoid a Wedding Day Disaster

Never try a new beauty product—or, God forbid, get a facial—on the day of or the days leading up to your wedding. The last thing you need is a breakout or rash! Stick to your normal routine, and you'll glow like the angel you are.

LIZZIE NICHOLS DESIGNS™

Chapter 2

Two souls with but a single thought,
Two hearts that beat as one.

Franz Joseph von Münch-Bellinghausen (1806–1871), Austrian dramatist

I blink. I have to admit: this was not the reaction I'd expected from the first person I'd told about my engagement to Luke. I'd expected Chaz to have some concerns, sure. I mean, it's true that Luke and I have been having some problems up until recently. As recently as half an hour ago, as a matter of fact.

But all those problems are over now. Because Luke asked me to marry him. That was the only major obstacle standing in the way of our being together—that he couldn't see me in his future.

But all that's changed now. He's asked me to marry him! I'm going to be a bride! Lizzie Nichols, a bride, at last!

And okay. It's a little weird that every time I think about that, I feel like I want to throw up.

But that's just all the excitement from having gotten engaged before I've had any breakfast. I've always suspected I'm a little hypoglycemic. Just like Nicole Richie.

And anyway, it's all Chaz's fault. Why, instead of being happy for me, had he had to throw that absurd little hissy fit, almost as if . . . well, almost as if he'd been jealous?

Except that that's not possible. Because Chaz doesn't like me that way. We're just friends. I mean, sure, we'd messed around a little last night.

And, I'll admit, it had been . . . well, nice.

Really nice, actually.

But we'd both been a little tipsy. Drunk, even. It hadn't meant anything. It was like I'd said: still smarting over our respective breakups, we'd sought solace in each other's arms.

But that doesn't mean there was anything more going on.

Does it?

Well, I'm not going to waste any more time worrying about it. Luke is going to be here any minute. I have to get myself cleaned up before he arrives. It's bad enough he proposed—and I accepted—while I still had morning breath. I am not going to start my first day as a newly engaged person wearing the same underwear I've had on since yesterday.

By the time the downstairs buzzer goes off, I'm as sweet smelling and coiffed as I've ever been in my life—thanks to the world's fastest shower, a quick change into a stunning 1950s Lorrie Deb pink chiffon party dress (perfect for the newly engaged, soon-to-be-certified professional wedding gown restorer), and a couple layers of undereye concealer—and ready to let in the man to whom I've just pledged my troth.

I feel lighter than air as I make my way down the twin flights of steps to the building's front door (I have to get that buzzer fixed first thing when places open up again tomorrow morning).

"Whoa," Luke says after I fling open the heavy metal door. "You look—"

"Like a bride-to-be?" I ask, holding out the three layers—one chiffon, one net, and one nylon—of my full skirt and giving him a playful curtsy.

"I was going to say hot," Luke says. He triumphantly holds up a Starbucks bag . . . and a six-pack of Diet Coke for me. "Look what I scored. I only had to walk eleven blocks to find a place that was open on New Year's Day."

"Oh, Luke! You remembered!"

Except, of course, it was Chaz who told Luke how much I love Diet Coke in the first place. That's the only reason Luke bought it for me that day in the village back in France last summer. Because Chaz told him that Diet Coke was the way to my heart.

But that doesn't mean I'm in love with Chaz, does it?

Of course not! How could I think anything so silly?

My eyes fill with tears. Really, Luke's the most thoughtful fiancé in the whole world. Also the handsomest, standing there in his Hugo Boss overcoat, with his long dark eyelashes curling so perfectly . . . and without the help of a Shu Uemura eyelash curler, even. He'd looked so cute when he'd been kneeling there in that exact spot in the slush a half hour ago, so hopeful and nervous. How could I have said anything but yes when he'd proposed?

Not that saying anything but yes had even occurred to me. Well, except for a few seconds, maybe. To punish him for that whole "I don't know if I see you in my future" thing.

"I just want to let you know that when I look into my future, I see nothing but *you."* That's what Chaz had whispered in my ear at some point during the wedding last night.

Then he'd whispered, *"And you're not even wearing Spanx."*

I shake my head. Why do I keep thinking about *Chaz*? He wears University of Michigan baseball caps nearly all the time.

In *public.*

Luke's face falls. "What?" he asks. "What'd I do? You don't drink Diet Coke anymore. Is that it? I can get something else. What do you want? Diet Dr Pepper?"

"No!" I try to laugh breezily. Oh God. What's wrong with me? "Of course I still drink Diet Coke. I'm sorry. Wow, it's really cold out here. Come in." I move out of the doorway so he can do just that.

"I thought you'd never ask." Luke gives me one of those grins that still cause my insides to go weak. He stops in the doorway just long enough to brush my cheek with his lips, letting them linger for a moment in my hair.

"It's good to be home," he murmurs before moving past me. "Which is wherever you are. I know that now."

Oh! How sweet!

And how could Chaz ever accuse Luke of not knowing what he wants? He knows exactly what he wants. *Me!*

It just took him a little while to realize it. He needed a gentle nudge. In the form of my breaking up with him and moving out of the apartment we were sharing.

"So this is the new place, huh?" Luke is looking around at the somewhat dingy and exceptionally narrow hallway.

"It gets better," I say.

"No," Luke says, his tone apologetic. "I like it. It has character."

It isn't, I tell myself as I follow Luke, Chaz's fault. Not really. He's just never known happiness—true, romantic happiness—as great as what Luke and I share. So of course when he sees it, he looks on it with suspicion. Of course he doubts our chances of success.

But when he sees us together—how happy we are, now that we're really and truly committed to each other—he'll change his mind. He'll come around. He'll see how wrong he was to say all those horrible things.

And someday Chaz will find a girl—the right girl for him—who'll make him as happy as I know I make Luke . . . and he'll make her as happy as Luke makes me.

And then everything will be all right.

Wait and see. Just wait and see.

"Here we are," I say when we reach the door to my new apartment, which I fling open. "Home sweet home."

"It's great," Luke says enthusiastically as he follows me inside.

I smile at him. "You don't have to pretend to like it. I know it's horrible. But it's mine. And as soon as I get the time—and some extra money—I'm going to fix it up."

"No, Lizzie, it really is great." Luke sets down the Starbucks bag and the Diet Coke and puts his arms around me. "It's like you. Completely whimsical and totally charming."

"I hope it's not like me," I say with a laugh. "I hope I'm not covered in big blobby rose wallpaper with slopey floors and cracks in my ceiling."

"You know what I mean," Luke says, nuzzling my neck. "It's unique. Like you. It already smells like you. God, I can't believe how much I missed you. And we were apart for only, what? A week?"

"Is that what you want? A guy who comes running back to you and proposes just because he's so scared of being alone, he'd rather be with a girl he knows isn't right for him than be by himself?"

God! Get out of my head, Chaz Pendergast!

"Something like that," I say. Luke's nuzzling is getting more serious. Or at least closer to the bateau neckline of my dress.

I jump away and reach for one of the Diet Cokes.

"So who should we call first?" I ask brightly.

"Call?" Luke's eyes, which tend to have a dreamy look about them even when he's wide awake, are heavy-lidded with a combination of jet lag and, well . . . sex. Sexual desire, anyway. "I wasn't thinking about calling anyone, to tell you the truth. I was actually thinking about trying out that bed I see over there. And I was hoping you'd get out of that dress and join me . . ."

"*Luke*," I say after I've chugged down a mouthful of restorative caffeine and potassium benzoate. "We have to call people and tell them the good news. I mean, we're *engaged*."

"Oh." Luke looks longingly back at the bed. "I guess. I mean . . . Yeah. You're probably right."

"Here." I dig into the Starbucks bag and pull out the coffee he'd ordered for himself, along with two muffins. "Drink this. Let's make a list. We should call your parents, of course."

"Of course," Luke says, taking a sip of his coffee.

"And mine. And my sisters. Well, they'll be at my parents for New Year's Day brunch with Gran, so we'll be able to reach them all with one call." I grab a notepad I've left on the tiny yellow kitchen table, while Luke peels off his coat and sinks onto one of the table's matching yellow chairs. "And I have to call Shari, of course. And you should . . . you should probably call Chaz."

Luke has his cell phone out and is punching numbers into it. An overseas number. Too many numbers for him to be calling Chaz.

"What are you doing?" I ask.

"I'm calling my parents," he says. "Like you said to."

I reach out and close his flip phone.

"Hey," he says, looking confused. "What'd you do that for?"

"I think you should call Chaz first," I say. "Don't you?"

"Chaz?" Luke looks at me as if I'd suggested he mainline heroin and then shoot his mother. "Why would I call *Chaz* first?"

"Because he's your best friend," I say, sliding onto the chair opposite his. "And aren't you going to ask him to be your best man?"

"I don't know," Luke says, still looking confused. He must be much more jet-lagged than I thought. "I guess."

"He'd be so hurt if you didn't tell him first," I say. "You know, he was so kind to me this past week, while you and I were . . . apart. He helped me move in here and everything. And last night he even went with me to the Higgins-MacDowell wedding."

Luke looks touched. "He did? That was nice of him. He must be feeling better. You know, after the whole thing with Shari turning out to like girls."

"Uh," I say. "Yeah. It was. Nice of him, I mean. That's why I think you should call him first. And thank him. For being such a good friend. And tell him how much his friendship means to you. I really think he just needs to hear your voice."

"Okay," Luke says, opening his flip phone and dialing. "I think you're right."

A second later, as I'm squeezing my fingers together and praying that Chaz is still in the subway and won't pick up, Luke says, "Chaz? Hey, it's me. I've got some news, man. Are you sitting down?"

I jump from my chair, convinced I'm going to throw up what little Diet Coke I've downed so far, and run to clutch the edge of the sink.

This is it, I think. Chaz is going to tell him. Chaz is going to tell Luke that just twelve hours ago, his hand was down my bra.

And the engagement is going to be off.

Probably I'm not going to get to keep the ring.

"What? Yeah, I'm back. I'm at Lizzie's. I got back this morning."

What is Chaz doing? He knows Luke is back. I *told* him Luke's back. Oh God. Just *do it* already, so we can get this over with.

"Okay. So you're sitting down? In a cab? Where are you going in a cab on New Year's morning? You were? You did? Who was she?"

I grab the edge of the sink. This is it. I'm going to hurl.

"What do you mean, you're not going to tell me?" Luke laughs. "Fine, you dog, you. All right. Well, here's my news: I asked Lizzie to marry me. And she said yes. And I want you to be my best man at the wedding."

I close my eyes. This is the part where Chaz tells Luke that he can't be his best man because he thinks he's making the worst mistake of his entire life.

And that, oh yeah, by the way, last night his tongue was down my throat.

"Thanks!" Luke is saying into the phone in a cheerful voice. An entirely too cheerful voice for him to be responding to the news that last night his best friend and fiancée were making out in the back of a cab. "Yeah, I do too. What? Lizzie? Sure, you can talk to Lizzie. Hold on."

I turn around from the sink just in time to see Luke cross the kitchen to hand the phone to me.

"He wants to talk to you," he says. Luke is beaming. "I think he wants to extend his congratulations personally."

I take the phone, feeling sicker to my stomach than ever. "Hello?"

"Hi, Lizzie." Chaz's deep voice rasps in my ear. "You were hoping I'd spill the truth to Luke about our illicit affair and he'd call the whole thing off, weren't you? No such luck, I'm afraid. You got yourself into this mess, and you're going to have to get yourself out of it. If you think I'm going to come sweeping in like some kind of prince on a milk-white charger to save your pretty little buns on this one, you're high."

I let out a totally fake laugh. "Thank you!" I cry. "That is so nice of you to say!" Luke continues to beam at me from across the kitchen.

"Yeah," Chaz says. "You know, when you packed up all your stuff and left his ass high and dry, I thought, finally. A woman with some moral fiber. Little did I know that all he'd need to win you back was a big diamond ring and a few crocodile tears. I really expected bigger things from you, Lizzie. Tell me something. Are you going to wait until the invitations have actually gone out before you admit to yourself that Luke is the last guy you ought to be spending the rest of your life with? Or are you going to do the right thing and call it off now?"

"Great, Chaz," I say, with another fake laugh. "It was nice talking to you too."

"This is like watching a lamb being led to slaughter," Chaz mutters. "Is getting married really that important to you? It's just a goddamned piece of paper."

"Thanks, Chaz," I say. I'm not sure how much longer I can keep up the fake laughing. Because I'm ready to start shedding real tears. "Thanks so much."

"Look, I . . . Just put him back on."

I hold the phone out to Luke. "He wants to talk to you," I say.

Luke takes the phone from me. "Hey, man. Yeah? Uh-huh."

I drift away, into the bedroom, unzipping my dress as I go. I can't believe this . . . any of this. I have what I wanted . . . what it seems like I always wanted: The man of my dreams has proposed to me. I'm going to be married.

I should be happy.

Strike that. I *am* happy. I am.

Maybe it just hasn't sunk in yet.

"What's going on?"

I look over to see Luke standing in the doorway, his cell phone closed in his hand.

"What are you doing?" Luke wants to know. His gaze falls on my dress, lying in a pink puddle on the floor. "I thought we were going to call people and tell them we're engaged."

"I changed my mind," I say, flipping the bedclothes back to show him what I have on underneath them. Which is nothing. "I think I like your original idea better. Want to join me?"

Luke tosses his cell phone over his shoulder. "I thought you'd never ask," he says. And dives into bed with me.

• • •

Luke and I are doing some postcoital spooning. It's so nice to be in his arms—a place I seriously thought I'd never be again.

"So I was talking to my uncle when I was in France this past week," Luke is saying.

"Umm-hmm?" I love the way he smells. Luke, I mean. I missed that smell so much. Being a strong, independent woman who stands up for herself and walks out on the man she feels has done her wrong is really empowering and everything.

But it's not easy. Or fun.

It's much nicer to hang out in bed with that man, completely naked.

"You know, my uncle Gerald?" Luke goes on.

"Uh-huh," I say. "The one who lives in Houston. And offered you the job with his firm's new branch in Paris."

"Right," Luke says. "Thibodeaux, Davies, and Stern. It's one of the most exclusive private client investment companies in the world."

"Mmmm," I say. I'm admiring the way Luke's bicep, even when he's totally relaxed, like he is now, is just so . . . big. And round. And satiny smooth. And the perfect place for me to rest my cheek. It's impossible to think about anything else—or any*one* else—when you're resting your cheek on a hot guy's naked bicep. "Except you don't care about that. Because you're working on your postbaccalaureate program so you can finish up the pre-med classes you didn't take in college because you were getting an MBA, and when you're done, you can start applying to medical schools."

"Yeah," Luke says. "I know. That's what's so great about Gerald's offer."

I have no choice but to reluctantly lift my head from the satiny pillow of Luke's bicep.

"Your uncle Gerald made you an offer?" I try to keep my voice even-sounding. Like I don't care at all what we're discussing. La la la, don't care a bit about STUPID UNCLE GERALD BUTTING HIS NOSE INTO MY BOYFRIEND'S—excuse me, MY FIANCÉ'S—BUSINESS. "What kind of offer?"

"That this summer I could work for him, helping to get the Paris branch of Thibodeaux, Davies, and Stern up and running."

"Oh." I lay my head back down. "Instead of taking classes in your post-baccalaureate program?"

But no sooner have I laid my head down than Luke sits up, jiggling my head to the pillow.

"It's a really fantastic offer," he says excitedly. "Considering it's for only three months. It's about half a year's salary of what I used to be making. It's really generous of him."

"Wow," I say, trying to plump my pillow up so it's as comfy as his arm was. "That *is* generous."

"Not that it won't be a lot of work," Luke says. "I mean, it will be. Seventeen-, eighteen-hour days, most likely. But it's a fantastic opportunity. And, of course, I can use the family apartment."

"Neat," I say. Luke's lucky his family happens to have all these places to live just randomly sitting around empty all over the world. Apartments in New York City and Paris, a house in Houston, a château in the south of France . . .

"And I can make up the classes I'd miss," Luke says, "in the fall. It'll just be another semester tacked on to what I've already got ahead of me."

"Oh," I say.

"And the best part," Luke says, leaning over to drape one of those tanned, muscular arms across my waist, "is that you can come with me."

I blink at him. "What?"

"Yeah," Luke says, giving me a squeeze. "I've thought it all through. You can come with me, to Paris. It'll be much easier to coordinate the wedding at Château Mirac from there than it would be from here . . ."

"Um," I say. I can't believe he's serious. "I can't just take the summer off and go to Paris, Luke."

"Sure you can," Luke says. Apparently, he thinks *I'm* the one who's kidding. "They'll give you time off from the shop. They'll have to. You're getting married!"

"Yeah," I say. "Time off meaning two weeks . . . three, maybe. But not the whole summer."

"Lizzie." Luke looks disappointed in me. "Don't you know anything about the business world? Don't let the Henris tell you how much vacation time you get. *You* tell *them*. If they really want to keep you, they'll let you take off as much time as you want."

"Luke," I say, trying to figure out how I can put this without offending him. "I don't *want* to take the whole summer off. And I definitely don't want to spend it with you in *Paris*."

But no sooner are the words out of my mouth than I realize that I've done it again. Put my foot in my mouth, I mean. God, no matter how hard I try to be tactful, I just never seem to be able to say the right thing around this guy.

"Th-that didn't come out the right way," I stammer.

Fortunately, Luke is chuckling.

"I guess I never have to worry about your not being honest with me," he says.

"I'm sorry," I hurry to say. "What I meant was—"

"You don't want to spend the summer in Paris," he says. "And you don't have to apologize. I understand. You love your job, and you want to be here for it. That's okay. The thing is, Gerald's offer is really too good for me to turn down. Especially with the wedding to pay for. Look, it's all right. We can do the long-distance thing. We're already going to be doing the separate-apartment thing"—he gives me a mischievous smile, because I'd already warned him, before I'd said yes to his proposal, that I wouldn't be moving back in with him until *after* the wedding; it just seems like the wisest thing to do, under the circumstances—"so I guess living in separate countries for a couple of months over the summer shouldn't be that big a deal."

I chew my lower lip. Am I insane? I probably am. I've got this amazing guy who's finally proposed to me, and in the past hour I've turned down an invitation not only to move back in with him but also to spend a summer in Paris with him.

"He's not the kind of guy who's going to hitch his wagon to a star. He still thinks he's *the star. And you can't have two stars in one relationship. Somebody has to be willing to be the wagon . . . at least some of the time."*

Oh! I can't *believe* it! Even a session of hot and heavy makeup sex didn't succeed in exorcising Chaz's voice from my head! What am I going to have to do to get that guy out of there?

"Come on," I say, reaching for my cell phone. "Let's call people and tell them now."

Luke looks amused. "Oh, *now* you want to call your family?"

You'd better believe it. Anything to make the voice of Chaz stop talking inside my head.

"Come on," I say, dialing. "It'll be fun. I'll call my parents first. Because I'm the bride, so you have to do what I say. Hello, Mom?"

"No," a childish voice says. "It's me, Maggie."

"Oh, Maggie," I say to my niece. "Hi, it's your aunt Lizzie. Could you put your grandma on the phone, please?"

"Okay," Maggie says, and I hear the phone thunk to the floor as she goes off in search of my mother. I can hear the voices of my sisters and their husbands in the background as they enjoy my parents' traditional Nichols Family New Year's Day Brunch. Although "enjoy" might be a strong word. Maybe "endure" is more like it. I can hear my sister Rose's husband, Angelo, bleating something about how he no longer eats eggs because of the hormones in them, and my sister firing back that maybe he could use more hormones . . . especially in bed.

"Who's this?" Gran picks up the phone and barks.

"Oh," I say, disappointed. "Gran. Hi. It's me, Lizzie. I was just trying to reach Mom—"

"She's busy," Gran says. Whoever was assigned to make sure she imbibes only nonalcoholic beer has apparently failed in his or her mission. Gran is, as always, three sheets to the wind. "Somebody's gotta feed this crew. God forbid one of your sisters should offer to host one of these things and dirty up *her* house someday."

"Huh," I say, giving Luke a sunny smile to show him everything is going swimmingly. "Well, I've got some news. Maybe you could let everyone know."

"Jesus Christ," Gran says. "You're knocked up. Lizzie, I told you. Always use a rubber. I know the boys don't like them, but it's like I always say: no rubber, no way."

"Uh," I say. "No, Gran, that's not it. Luke and I are engaged."

"Luke?" Gran sounds like she's choking on whatever drink she's just knocked back. "That no-good-nik? What did you go and agree to marry *him* for? I thought you booted that loser to the curb before Christmas."

I cough and give Luke another reassuring smile.

"Are they excited?" he mouths.

I give him a thumbs-up.

"Um, I did, Gran," I say. "But now we're engaged. Can you get Mom, please?"

"No, I am not going to get your mother," Gran says. "Trust me, I'm doing you a favor, Lizzie. She did an aquaerobics class *and* a scrapbooking class at the Y yesterday, plus all the shopping for this brunch, with no help whatsoever from those sisters of yours. This news could kill her."

"Gran." I smile at Luke again. "If you don't put Mom on the phone, I'm going to call her on her cell and tell her you've been hitting the cooking sherry. And don't try to deny it. Because I can tell."

"You ingrate," Gran snarls. "What do you want to go and get engaged for anyway, Lizzie? Husbands don't do anything but cramp your style. Believe me, I was saddled with one for fifty-five years. I would know. Get out now, while you still can."

"Gran," I warn.

"I'm getting her," Gran says. I hear her shuffling off.

I can't help noticing that Luke isn't smiling anymore. I say, "It's okay. Gran's just a little tipsy."

Luke looks at his watch. "It's *noon*."

"It's a holiday," I point out. Jeesh. Some people can be so picky.

Mom's reception of the news that I'm getting married is much warmer than Gran's. She screams and cries and calls for Dad and asks to speak to Luke and welcomes him to the family and wants to know when she's going to get to meet him. Which reminds me that it is a little weird Luke hasn't met my family yet. I've met all of his.

But oh well. They'll meet soon enough, I guess. Mom wants to throw an engagement party . . . and the wedding, which Mom immediately offers the family backyard for, a suggestion I gently brush off, saying, "Well, we'll see." I'm not sure how to break it to her that Luke's already suggested we get married at his seventeenth-century familial estate in the south of France, an offer that's pretty hard to turn down.

Except that my family's never been to Europe before . . . they've never been to *New York* before.

This might actually pose a problem.

But Luke says all the right things to them on the phone, and is as charming and gracious as if my parents were a king and queen and not a professor at the University of Michigan cyclotron and a housewife. Everything, I think, as I watch him proudly, is going to be fine. Just fine.

"This is like watching a lamb being led to slaughter. Is getting married really that important to you? It's just a goddamned piece of paper."

Okay, well, it's going to be fine after a few more phone calls. And more sex.

A *lot* more sex.

A HISTORY *of* WEDDINGS

The declaration of union between two people has long been considered by sociologists to be an important step in the development of human happiness. Societally speaking, a heterosexual male who has paired off with a heterosexual female is generally thought to be calmer and less prone to violence, and a wedded female equally less troublesome. Their offspring benefit from having both a father and a mother, and—in ancient times, at least—the entire tribe benefited from the goodwill generated from a happy union. In other words: weddings were a joyous occasion that brought about less fighting and unpleasantness all around.

I would just like to point out that none of these sociologists came to my sisters' weddings. Obviously.

Tip to Avoid a Wedding Day Disaster

Is your future mother- or sister-in-law driving you insane as you plan your special day? There's a simple way to get her off your back. Give her something to do! Allowing his family—especially the female members—to take part in the preparations for the big day will not only make them feel special but will also lift some of the burden off your shoulders.

Just make sure you don't ask them to do anything too important. That way when they mess it up (as they inevitably will), it won't matter.

LIZZIE NICHOLS DESIGNS™

Chapter 3

Happy and thrice happy are those who enjoy an uninterrupted union, and whose love, unbroken by any sour complaints, shall not dissolve until the last day of their existence.

Horace (65 B.C.–8 B.C.), Roman lyric poet

Hello, Chez Henri, please hold."

"Hello, Chez Henri, please hold."

"Hello, Chez Henri, please hold."

"Hello, Chez Henri, how may I help you?"

"Yeah, is this Henri Bridal?" The woman on the other end of the phone has pronounced it *Henry* instead of the correct French pronunciation of my boss's name, which is *En-ree.*

That I can forgive. What I can't forgive is that she's chewing gum. I can feel my toes curling. Of all the annoying personal habits a bride-to-be—or anyone, really—can have, gum-chewing is the one that aggravates me the most.

"Yes, it is," I say, glaring at all the blinking lights on my phone. It's a good thing I had all those months of reception work at the law offices of Pendergast, Loughlin, and Flynn. I can handle an overloaded switchboard like nobody's business.

And the Monday morning after Jill Higgins's New Year's Eve wedding to wealthy socialite John MacDowell—at which Anna Wintour (yes, *the* Anna Wintour, longtime editor of *Vogue*) called my restoration of the ancestral MacDowell bridal gown "cunning"—the phones at Chez Henri are ringing off the hook.

Of all the mornings for Monsieur and Madame Henri to come in late from their home in suburban New Jersey, this would not have been the one I'd chosen. I'm just saying.

"I wanna make an appointment to see that chick," the gum-chewer says.

"I beg your pardon?" I am taken aback. First gum-chewing, then a reference to me—and she can only be referring to me. I am the only employee at Chez Henri who can reasonably be referred to as a "chick," Madame Henri being in her fifties—as a derogatory slang word for "young woman"?

"You know," Gum-Chewer says. "The chick that designed that dress for Blubber."

Blubber. The nickname the press dubbed poor Jill Higgins, because she happens to work in the seal enclosure at the Central Park Zoo. And because she'd deigned to fall in love with one of New York's wealthiest bachelors, and she doesn't happen to be a size two.

"I'm sorry," I say to Gum-Chewer. "The *chick* to whom you are referring happens to dislike people who look down on others due to their weight."

Gum-Chewer appears to have swallowed her gum. "But—"

"And furthermore, that *chick* happens to dislike being called a chick."

"Um, excuse me." Gum-Chewer snaps her gum. "But do you have any idea who I am? I'm—"

"No, and I don't care to know. Good-bye," I say, pressing the END CALL button. "Chez Henri, how may I help you?"

"Elizabeth? Is that you?" The woman on the other end of the line has a heavy French accent and sounds as if she's speaking to me from inside a tunnel. No, it isn't my future mother-in-law, who is from Texas. It's Madame Henri.

"Madame, where are you?" I ask in French, the language I now routinely slip into when speaking to my employers, though I hid the fact that I could speak it—not perfectly, but well enough to understand (and be understood by) them—for months. "It's crazy here. The phones are ringing off the hook."

"Elizabeth, I'm so sorry. I meant to call earlier, but my cell phone doesn't work here. I've been at the hospital."

"The hospital?" The other lines continue to ring. Callers, impatient at being placed on hold, have hung up and are calling back. I turn away from the phone. "Is everything all right? I hope nothing happened to the boys—"

"No, the boys are fine. It's Jean, actually." Madame Henri's voice sounds tiny. She's a petite woman, but the one thing about her that's never seemed small before is just that . . . her voice. She's always had a commanding—even domineering—presence. But not now. "He didn't feel well at breakfast yesterday morning. I thought it was just too much champagne from the night before. But then he said his arm hurt—"

I gasp. "Madame!"

"Yes." Her voice sounds even smaller. "He had a heart attack. He is scheduled for emergency bypass surgery here at the hospital today. Quadruple." Then, with a hint of her old asperity, she adds, "I told him he works too hard! I told him he needed to take more time off! Well, now he's getting it . . . and look how he has to spend it! He could have taken it at our home in Provence. But no! Not him! This is what it has come to."

"Oh, Madame." I shake my head. "Well, I'm sure he's in very good hands—"

"The best," Madame Henri says simply. "But it will be weeks before he can return to work. And I as well, because who do you think will have to play nursemaid to him? His sons? Bah! They are worthless. Worse than garbage."

I'm relieved to hear her bad-mouthing her children. That means the situation is nowhere near as dire as I'd first feared from the way she'd sounded. If she can trash-talk the kids—who, from what I've observed, pretty much *are* worthless—things are okay.

"And just as the shop is doing the best business it has ever done before," Madame Henri goes on. "All thanks to you! And this is how we repay you. When he is well again," she adds matter-of-factly, "I will kill him."

"Don't worry about the shop," I say, keeping my face resolutely turned away from all the blinking lights on the phone. "I'll be fine here."

"Elizabeth," Madame Henri says. "I am not a fool. I can hear the telephone ringing."

"The phone," I admit, "is a bit of a problem at the moment. But not one I can't solve."

"Do what you have to do," Madame Henri says, with a sigh. "Even . . . even hire someone."

I can't help letting out a gasp. The Henris are almost insanely tightfisted. For good reason, of course. Until I started working for them, they barely made a profit. In fact, for the first four months I worked for them, I did it for free, just to prove I'd be worth the eventual investment of my thirty grand a year . . . and the rent-free apartment over the shop.

"Madame," I say, hardly daring to believe what I'd just heard. "Are you sure?"

"I don't see what choice we have," Madame Henri says with a sigh. "You can't do it all alone. Not the phones *and* the gowns. I'll try to stop in when I can, but it won't be often. You're going to have to get some help. It's Jean's own fault," she adds waspishly. "And I'll tell him so if he dares to complain when he hears of it . . . after he's out of the hospital, of course."

"Don't bother him about it, Madame," I say. "And don't you worry about it, either. Leave everything to me. I'll take care of the shop. I'll take care of *everything*."

I have no earthly idea, of course, how I'm going to go about this. I just know that this is a crisis, and, well, I used to be a Girl Scout. Crises are what Girl Scouts are trained for. I'll get through this somehow.

I tell her to let me know if there's anything else I can do, and also to let me know the minute her husband is out of surgery. Then I hang up and stare at all the blinking lights on the phone and listen to the shrill ring of the unanswered line. I have every confidence that I can handle this. I really do.

It's just that I don't have the foggiest notion how I'm even going to begin.

"Hello, Chez Henri, can you hold?"

"Hello, Chez Henri, can you hold?"

"Hello, Chez Henri, can you—"

"Lizzie?" a familiar woman's voice screams hoarsely in my ear, cutting me off. "Don't you frigging put me on hold. It's me, Tiffany."

I pause just as my finger is about to hit the HOLD button.

"Tiffany Sawyer," the hoarse voice continues impatiently. "From Pendergast, Loughlin, and Flynn? The office we both used to work in until you, like, got totally fired, remember? Which, by the way, was last week? God, what is the matter with you? Are you going to turn out to be one of those people who become famous and then, like, forget everybody they knew on the way up? Because if that's the case, you totally suck."

"Tiffany." I glance at the Henris' wall clock. It's barely ten, which would account for the hoarseness in her voice. Tiffany, part-time model, part-time receptionist in Chaz's father's law offices, which is where I met her, rarely makes it up before noon, thanks to her hard-core partying with her married photographer boyfriend, Raoul. "What are you doing up so early?"

"Whatevs," Tiffany says. "It's, like, the day after New Year's. The city was dead last night. But that's not why I'm calling. Do you know—do you have any fucking idea—who made Page Six in the *Post* today?"

"Tiffany." I can't take my eyes off all the blinking hold lights. "I know this might seem hard to believe, but I'm actually *working* right now. My boss had a heart attack, and I'm the only one here, and I don't have time for—"

"You. *You* did. There's a huge story about you, and a photo of you and Jill Higgins at her wedding, and about how you're the up-and-coming wedding gown designer to the stars, and how Anna Wintour—Anna fucking Wintour—said your gown for Jill Higgins was, and I quote, cunning. Do you have any idea what that *means*?"

The other line starts ringing. "I'm starting to get a pretty good idea," I say.

"You are the shit," Tiffany screams into the phone. "You have it fucking made!"

"You know," I say. "It really doesn't feel that way right now. Because right now, I can't get a thing done because I don't have anyone to ANSWER MY PHONES!"

"Jesus Christ, you don't have to yell," Tiffany says. "You need someone to answer your phones? I'll answer your fucking phones."

I blink, not certain I've heard her correctly. "What? No. Wait. I—"

"I'll be right there. Where are you again? I can stay till only one because you know I've got Pendergast at two. God, I wish I could quit that place. But the benefits are so good. As soon as Raoul gets rid of that troll wife of his and I can get on his insurance, I'm giving Roberta my two weeks' notice. God, I can't wait to see her pruny, dried-up face when I do. But I can get someone to come in at one and help you out. I wonder what Monique is doing today. I know she got booted from Chanel for doing blow in the back room. But—"

"Tiffany." I'm gripping the edge of my desk. "Really. It's fine. I don't need your help. Or Monique's." Whoever that is.

"—it's cool," Tiffany goes on, " 'cause she's in Narcotics Anonymous now. So am I. That's how I met her. Coke is for whores."

I realize there's no point in telling Tiffany that the Anonymous part of Narcotics Anonymous means you actually aren't supposed to tell people you—or other people you meet there—go to meetings. It will just go in one ear and out the other, like so much of what I tell Tiffany.

"Look, you said your boss had a heart attack, right?" Tiffany goes on. "We'll just come in and help out until he's back on his feet, or whatever. Don't act like you don't need us. I can hear the frigging phone ringing off the hook in the background."

"Um, thanks. It's just—" How can I explain that if I were stranded on a desert island and Tiffany pulled up in a rescue boat, I wouldn't get in it. Love her like a sister? Yeah. Trust her? Not so much. "I don't have the money to pay you. I mean, we're not exactly making huge profits yet, and—"

"What are we talking about here?" Tiffany wants to know. "Twenty bucks an hour?"

"Twenty?" I gasp. "Who do you think we are, UPS? I was going to call Manpower and offer ten—"

"Ten!" Tiffany lets out a bark of laughter. "I haven't made ten bucks an hour since I used to babysit my neighbor's kid back in North Dakota. But," she adds, more soberly, "I guess it'll be worth it if I can get my hands on a Lizzie Nichols original. Those things are going to be next to impossible to get by the time Raoul's green card comes in and he can finally ditch the troll, I know it. Just like I know Monique's gonna want one, too. Her boyfriend, Latrell, just popped the question at Christmas. With a four-carat square-cut pink diamond from Harry Winston. Latrell's in the music industry." Her tone becomes reverential. "He knows Kanye."

"Wait," I say. This can't be happening.

"Look, I'll be there in twenty," Tiffany says. "We can discuss it then. You want a muffin or something? I'm starving. I'll pick up muffins on the way. Fuckin' Page Six! Can you believe it? Oh my God, Lizzie, this is gonna be so righteous. You're gonna be so much of a better boss than Roberta. God, I hate her. *Ciao,* baby."

Tiffany slams down the phone. I stare at the receiver, not sure what just happened. Had I just solved the problem—or created a bigger one?

I'm taking messages from everyone on hold—with assurances that Ms. Nichols (I'm posing as her assistant, Stephanie. I've always wanted to be a Stephanie) will be calling them right back—when a floral delivery guy makes his way into the shop, barely able to see past the huge bouquet—two dozen yellow roses in a crystal vase—that he's holding.

"Delivery for Lizzie Nichols," he says.

"That's me," I cry, jumping up from Madame Henri's desk and rushing over to take the flowers from him. They're so heavy I have to stagger back to the desk with them before I can sign for them and tip him.

As soon as he's gone, I tear open the tiny envelope that accompanies them, expecting to find a note from Luke, thanking me for agreeing to be his bride . . . or maybe from his parents, welcoming me to the de Villiers family.

I'm shocked when I read, instead, the following:

Sorry for my bad attitude the other day.
I never was a morning person.
Of course I'm thrilled for you both. If you're happy,
I'm happy.
Congratulations. You'll make a beautiful bride.

Chaz

I'm so stunned, I have to sit down for a few minutes—and ignore the phones—in order to regain my composure. Can he really mean it? Can Chaz *really* be all right with Luke and me getting married?

And if he is, why do I still feel a little bit like throwing up every time I think about it? Not about Chaz being all right with it—I'm pretty sure—but about Luke and me actually going through with it?

Oh, I seem all right enough with the idea of being engaged. I don't seem to mind flashing my ring around. I'd been fine on the phone yesterday—after our prolonged interlude in the bedroom—with our parents.

It's when I actually try to picture the wedding itself—and even more oddly, the dress—that my mind seems to go blank, and the vomit rises up in the back of my throat.

That's not a very good sign.

But prewedding jitters are normal, right? Everyone goes through them. Maybe not the day after they've gotten engaged. But I'm probably just getting mine over with sooner than other people do. I've always been precocious that way. My mom said I used to put together first-day-of-school outfits for all my stuffed animals. And that was before I even started preschool.

The bells over the front door tinkle, and Tiffany, wearing dark sunglasses (even though it's overcast—and winter—outside) and a black catsuit beneath her new fox stole ("Which is totally faux, by the way," she reminds me later. "Do you know what they *do* to the poor foxes to get their fur off? It's disgusting"), walks in and says, "Whoa. Who went overboard with the roses?"

I quickly thrust Chaz's card into the pocket of the Mollie Parnis silk dress I'm wearing.

"Luke," I lie automatically.

"Luke?" Tiffany whips off her sunglasses and squints at the roses. "I thought you guys, like, broke up."

"Not anymore." I hold out my left hand. "We're engaged."

"No shit." Tiffany grabs my hand. She doesn't have to squint at all to see my diamond. "Holy crap, Nichols. That's three carats, at least. Tiffany, right?"

"No," I say. "He got it in Paris—"

"Cartier," Tiffany says, clearly impressed. "Even better. Platinum band, emerald cut. This thing cost as much as a fucking house—well, in North Dakota. He may have acted like a dick," she adds, in reference to the sewing machine Luke gave me for Christmas, which in a roundabout way became the catalyst for our realizing we wanted different things out of life, and led to our breaking up, "but you have to admit. The guy came through in the end. I'm not sure about the roses, though. Interesting color choice. Yellow means platonic friendship, you know."

Platonic friendship? Well, that's good. I mean, because they're not actually from Luke. They're from Chaz.

And that's all I want from Chaz. His friendship, I mean. Platonic is good.

"Well, because Luke and I are friends, first and foremost," I twitter. Oh my God, what am I even talking about?

Tiffany makes a face.

"If Raoul ever bought me yellow roses," she says, "I'd stuff them up his butt. So where do I sit?"

"Tiffany," I say, beginning a speech I've been mentally rehearsing since hanging up the phone with her. "I—"

"Is this good?" Tiffany asks, collapsing her nearly six-foot (and barely one-hundred-and-twenty-pound) body into Madame Henri's chair, behind the desk with the telephone (which is ringing shrilly) on it. "Here. I brought you a chocolate croissant. They were out of muffins. And a Diet Coke. I know how you are."

I catch the white paper bag she tosses to me. It's truly weird how everyone just thinks they can bring me Diet Coke and everything will be okay.

Especially since it's pretty much true.

"Hello, Chez Henri, this is Tiffany, how may I help you?" Tiffany, not skipping a beat, begins picking up calls as if she's worked at Chez Henri her whole life. "Ms. Nichols? I'm not sure. Hold, please." Tiffany places the call on hold. "Do you only do restorations, or do you do original designs? I mean, I know you're doing an original design for me, but for, like, the commoners?"

"Right now," I say, slowly chewing the end of chocolate croissant I've bitten off, "I'm only doing rehab and restoration."

"Got it. Where do I log your appointments?"

I point at the black leather appointment book on Madame Henri's desk.

"But," I say. "Tiffany, we have to talk. I can't—"

Tiffany just looks at the appointment book and snorts. "High-tech," she says, then flips it open, grabs a pencil, and hits the hold button. "Only restorations. All right. I've got an opening next week on the tenth at eleven o'clock. No? Please hold . . ."

I am starting to think hiring Tiffany might not be such a bad idea. She seems to have just . . . well, taken over.

And that's a good thing. A very good thing. For now. Maybe I should worry about how I'm actually going to pay her later.

I'm getting ready to retreat to the back room to look over what I've got to do—if I can at least get my head around that, maybe I can get my head around Tiffany working for me . . . and, oh yeah, the part where I'm engaged—when the bells over the front door tinkle once more, and my confused-looking best friend, Shari, wanders into the shop.

"Oh my God," I say, nearly dropping my can of soda as I rush to hug her. "I'm so glad you came."

"I got your message," she says, giving Tiffany a curious glance. "They said you said it was an emergency. It better have been, to have made me come all the way uptown. What's so important that you have to tell me in person? And what's *she* doing here?"

"Come on," I say, taking Shari by the hand. "I'll tell you upstairs, in my place. Tiffany, can you handle things down here for ten minutes?"

Tiffany gives me the finger while saying, "Ma'am, I'm sure your daughter is a lovely girl, but Ms. Nichols only does restorations. If you have a gown to restore, we're in business. If not, I'm afraid you're going to have to look elsewhere for your daughter's wedding dress. Oh, really? Do you eat with that mouth, ma'am?"

"What," Shari asks again impatiently, "is she doing here? What's going on? Seriously, Lizzie, this better be important. I have clients who could actually be dying as we speak. And I mean literally."

I realize that the speech I've planned for Shari, who's always been my staunchest supporter, isn't anywhere near eloquent enough. So I simply turn and show her my ring.

"Oh," Shari says. "My. God."

A HISTORY *of* WEDDINGS

When brides weren't being taken by force in ancient cultures, they were sold or bartered for gold, land, or even livestock (like a cow—can you *imagine*?).

For many centuries, it was common practice to use the weddings of offspring to bring high-ranking families together, but it wasn't until medieval times that laws were enacted that required any sort of religious rite be part of the actual ceremony (along with the exchange of goods and the signing of contracts). It was also around this time that dowries began to become more common, so that it wasn't just her lovely self the bride brought to the marriage, but some cold hard cash and maybe a few dozen head of cattle too. What's more, often the bride was expected to deliver the cash to her in-laws herself (more on this later).

Tip to Avoid a Wedding Day Disaster

The legal experts at Pendergast, Loughlin, and Flynn agree: the marriages that work best are the ones where both parties are joined at the heart and *the bank account. Couples who share their assets tend to stay together longer. Apply for a joint checking account, at least for shared expenses . . .* unless *one of you has excessive amounts of debt or other legal or financial troubles. If that's the case, the debt-free party should be seeing a lawyer . . . possibly at Pendergast, Loughlin, and Flynn.*

LIZZIE NICHOLS DESIGNS™

Chapter 4

There is no more lovely, friendly and charming relationship, communion or company than a good marriage.

—Martin Luther (1483–1546), German theologian

"Wait." Shari is staring at me over the yellow tabletop in the kitchen. "He asked you to marry him . . . and you said *yes*?"

I'll admit this is not the sort of reaction I was hoping for. In fact, Shari has a lot more in common with her ex-boyfriend Chaz than she'd probably like to know.

"I'm not rushing into anything, Shar," I say to her. "I swear. I've totally thought this through."

"You have." Shari is still staring at me. She hasn't taken her coat off, even though I offered to take it from her. Judging from her body language—arms folded across her chest, head cocked at one angle as she glares at me, legs crossed—I would say she is feeling cranky toward me . . . maybe even downright hostile. "He got home from France yesterday morning. And he proposed yesterday morning?"

"Yeee-es . . ."

"And you said yes as soon as he proposed?"

"Um . . . yes?"

"So you thought this through . . . when?"

"Well . . . since then." I can tell where this is heading, and I attempt to head it off. "I mean, you'll notice, Shari, that he's not living here. I'm not letting him move in. And I'm not moving back in with him. Nuh-uh. I'm not making that mistake again. We're living in our own separate apartments until the wedding."

"Which is?" Shari demands.

I stare at her over the cups of tea I've made for us. "Which is what?"

"Which is *when,* Lizzie?" Shari asks. "When is this alleged wedding taking place?"

"Um," I say, taken aback. "Well. Probably this summer . . ."

"Right." Shari unfolds her arms and uncrosses her legs. "You're insane. I'm leaving. Good-bye."

I pull her back down before she can abandon her chair, however.

"Shari, *come on,*" I say. "Don't do this. You're not being fair—"

"*I'm* not being fair?" Shari cries. "Lizzie, come on! Did you, or did you not, just spend a night on my couch last month because that no-good boyfriend of yours pulled your heart out of your chest and crushed it to bits when he told you he couldn't see you in his future—something he might have mentioned, by the way, *before* he asked you to move in? And now for some fucked-up reason—probably because he's gone for a week without getting laid—he's decided, *Oh, hey, I guess I can see Lizzie in my future after all,* throws a diamond ring in your face, and you're all, *Okay, Luke, anything you say, Luke.* Well, I'm sorry, but I'm not going to sit here and watch you throw your life away. You deserve better. You deserve a guy who actually loves you, Lizzie."

I blink at her. The next thing I know, I'm crying.

"How can you say that?" I ask with a sob. "You know Luke's not like that. You know—"

But that's all I manage to get out. Because I'm weeping too hard to say anything more.

After a while, tired of listening to me sniffle, Shari gets up, comes around the table, and puts her arm around me.

"Lizzie," she says in a softer voice than she used before. "I'm sorry. I didn't mean it. I just . . . I worry that the reason you said yes to Luke is because you wanted to marry him so badly, and then when you found out he didn't want to marry you, you moved on. And then when he suddenly came back and wanted to marry you after all, you thought you *had* to say yes because you'd been so adamant that that's what you wanted all along. But you know, Lizzie, it's okay to change your mind."

"I haven't!" I shout through my tears. "Why would I do that?"

"I don't know," Shari says with a shrug. "Because you grew up a little since last month, maybe? I was there, remember? I saw you do it. But look . . . If you really want to marry Luke, then of course I'll support you. If you want to marry Luke, then I want you to marry Luke too."

"No . . ." I'm crying too hard to speak clearly. "No, you hate Luke."

"Now you're just being irrational. I do not hate Luke. I do think he's got a lot to learn about being a man. And, frankly, I think you could do better. But I'll support you no matter who you love, same as you've supported me, so long as you don't stuff me into a lime-green taffeta hoop skirt that matches your sisters'—which you aren't going to do, are you?" Shari asks suspiciously.

"What?" I force a laugh as I wipe away my tears. "Oh God, no. Are you kidding?"

Except that I'd once picked out a bridesmaid dress for Shari. Dupioni silk . . . Only for some reason I can't picture it in my head anymore. It's kind of funny how, before I'd gotten engaged, all I'd ever done was sit around and planned what my wedding was going to be like.

And now that I'm actually having one, whenever I try to imagine it, my mind just goes blank.

"So, where's it going to be?" Shari wants to know. "Château Mirac?"

"Um," I say. "Maybe. My mom wants me to do it in our backyard."

Shari brightens. "That'd be nice."

I roll my eyes. "*Shari.*"

"Well, why not?"

"It would make so much more sense to do it at the château. That place was practically built for weddings. And it's where we fell in love and all. And there's the added cost-benefit of its being free, since Luke's family owns it."

"Ye-e-ah," Shari says slowly. "Except it's far for your family to travel. And there's your grandmother to consider."

"What about Gran?" I ask defensively.

"Well," Shari says as she sits back down in her chair. "She's getting up there in years. You really think she's going to make it to the south of France and back for a wedding?"

"Sure," I say a little hotly. "Why not?"

"I don't know," Shari says. "I'm just saying. She's old. And . . ."

"And what?"

"And she suffers from chronic alcoholism, Lizzie. Geez, what's the matter with you? You'd think being engaged would make you happy. But you're acting anything but."

I hang my head. "I'm sorry. It's just . . . it's been a bad day. Monsieur Henri had a heart attack and is having a quadruple bypass and is going to be out for a while and I was on Page Six this morning because of the Jill Higgins wedding and the phones are ringing off the hook and—"

"Oh, so *that*'s what Tiffany's doing down there," Shari says. "I wondered."

I take a sip of my tea. It's grown cold in front of me. "I should probably be getting back to work. There are a lot of brides who need wedding gowns restored, apparently."

"And there are probably a lot of victims of domestic abuse who need help obtaining public support and orders of protection," Shari says with a sigh.

I look at her from across the table. "How did we end up here?" I ask.

"I don't know," Shari says with a shake of her head. "But I like where I am. Do you like where you are?"

"I think so," I say, looking down at my ring. "It might take some getting used to. I think I might be better at helping other people with their weddings than I am at planning my own. Whenever I think about it, I sort of want to throw up."

"Okay." Shari points at me. "That is not a good sign. Remember what I said. It's okay for you to change your mind."

I give her a queasy smile. "I know. But . . . I really do love him."

"Do you?" Shari asks as she stands to go. "Or do you love the *idea* of him?"

"God," I say with a laugh. "What kind of question is that?"

"For you? I think it's a pertinent question. You have a history of falling in love with guys it turns out you basically didn't know at all."

"Yeah, but, Shari, come on. Luke's not going to turn out to be gay or a gambling addict." I have made some unfortunate mistakes in the guy department. "I mean, I *lived* with Luke, for crying out loud. For six months. I think I know him pretty well by now."

"Yes," she says. "You'd think that, wouldn't you? Still, people can surprise you, can't they? After all, I lived with Chaz for nearly as long as you lived with Luke, and I turned out to be a—"

"Don't say it." I fling up a hand to stop her before she can say the word "lesbian." Not that I mind. It's just that I try so hard not to remember that night at Kathy Pennebaker's when we were both sixteen. I'd been lusting after Tim Daly from the television show *Wings*. Shari and Kathy, it turned out, had been lusting after . . . well, each other. God, I'd been so *blind*. Although I suppose it's just as well they never told me. It would have been all over school in half a second. I'd have *tried* to keep it a secret, of course, if they'd asked me. But somehow I can never seem to keep my mouth shut, despite my best intentions. "I got it. Look. Don't worry. At the rate we're going, it'll be a long engagement, anyway. Luke's got school to finish, and his uncle wants him to come work for him in Paris this summer, and I've got about five thousand dresses to get through before I'll ever be able to lift my head to breathe. I'm not rushing to get married any time soon."

Shari gives me a hug. "That's my girl," she says.

It's as she's squeezing me that I notice it—this weird splotchy thing on the inside of my right elbow. It looks like a mosquito bite, only it's flat, not raised. And besides, it's January in Manhattan. How could I have been bitten by a mosquito?

I don't think anything of it. Then.

It's only later that I realize what it really is: Just the beginning of the ruination of the rest of my life. That's all.

A HISTORY *of* WEDDINGS

In ancient times, brides were traditionally expected to set forth on pre–wedding day pilgrimages from their own village to that of their betrothed. Due to the likelihood of her being set upon by thieves hoping to make off with her dowry (or the bride herself), the bride made this trip accompanied by armed maidens to defend her and her bling against marauders.

Thus was born the bridesmaid—or to be more historically accurate, the WARRIORMAID.

Tip to Avoid a Wedding Day Disaster

Today's bridesmaids perform a much different function than their ancient predecessors, from helping to organize the engagement and bridal showers to shuttling guests—I've even heard of some babysitting and doing the bride's laundry (ew).

Don't forget your bridesmaids on your special day. A special gift—such as a silver necklace or bracelet—will go a long way toward showing them how much you appreciate all their help . . . although the basic human courtesy of not turning into a Bridezilla on them would also be nice.

LIZZIE NICHOLS DESIGNS™

Chapter 5

One should believe in marriage as in the immortality of the soul.

Honoré de Balzac (1799–1850), French novelist and playwright

Gum-Chewer is sitting in the shop when I get back downstairs. Even though my only previous conversation with her was over the phone, I know it's her. I'd recognize that snap, crackle, and pop anywhere.

What shocks me is that I also recognize her instantly from *Access Hollywood* . . . and *Inside Edition* . . . and *Entertainment Tonight* . . . where she can frequently be seen wearing very little on the red carpets at the premieres of movies in which she is not starring, since she has no actual talent—none, at least, that's been detected so far. Ava Geck's only claim to fame, in fact, is that her family owns a chain of discount department stores ("Get It at Geck's"), said to be worth more than a billion dollars. She herself is rumored to have a personal net worth of more than three hundred million dollars, thanks to some savvy fragrance deals and a few less fortunate reality-television appearances.

More impressive—to me, anyway—is that she also happens to be marrying a prince. Not a prince like Luke is a prince back in his father's native France, where the aristocracy was abolished centuries ago, and no one kept track of who really was or was not a royal, and we really have only Luke's father's word for it, but in Greece, where, even if the royal family is no longer recognized as the head of state, they are nevertheless still allowed to hold and be addressed by their royal titles and are invited to state functions.

Somehow, someway, Greek Prince Aleksandros Nikolaos met—and apparently fell in love with and proposed to—Ava Geck.

It's kind of surreal to see her without a television set framing her pointy face. Although the hulking bodyguard standing with his arms crossed beside her—not to mention the enormous rock on the ring finger of her left hand and the trembling Chihuahua on her lap—quickly makes me realize what I'm seeing is all too real.

"Oh, hey," she says, with a quick glance at Tiffany when I walk in. "Is this her?"

Tiffany rolls her eyes. "I already told you, Ava. She won't see you without an appointment."

Tiffany and Ava have apparently already become acquainted. It appears to be an acquaintance of some long standing. And it is obviously not a very happy one.

"Um," I say. "Hi. What's going on?"

"Ms. Nichols." Ava leaps to her precariously high stilettos—which are attached to purple suede thigh-high boots—upsetting the Chihuahua, who tumbles to the carpet with a yelp. This does not seem to concern its mistress in any way. "I'm so, like, sorry I'm here without an appointment. It's just, like, I saw the story on Page Six about you, and the thing is, I live in Los Angeles and I'm in town for New Year's—you know, I was doing a guest spot for *Celebrity Pit Fight* at Times Square for the ball drop?—and I have to get back, but I'm getting married this summer, and I, like, really, really, really want you to do my dress."

"And I already told her," Tiffany says, from between gritted teeth, "you don't do original designs, just—"

"I know this girl keeps saying you only do restorations," Ava says, flicking a scathing glance in Tiffany's direction. "But I'm all, what's the diff? I mean, if I bring in some heinous old dress and ask you to make it over, or if you just, like, make me a new one? Why can't you just make me a new one? Okay? Because that's what I want. I want a dress by someone who's young and cool. Not some dried-up old-lady dress by someone with a freaking four-story shop on Madison Avenue. Ya know?"

Except it was kind of hard to tell what she was saying, between all the chewing sounds.

"Ms. Nichols?" Tiffany stands up. "Can I have a word with you in the back room?"

"God!" Ava cracks her gum. "What is the dealio? I have money. I'll, like, pay you."

"Um," I say to Ava. I notice that the Chihuahua is getting ready to lift a leg against Madame Henri's potted hydrangea. I dive to pick up the dog and place it gently back in a confused-looking Ava Geck's arms. "Let me just consult with my, um, assistant here, to see what the schedule for this week looks like, and I'll be right back."

Ava looks relieved. At least if that's what I'm to believe from the large pink bubble she blows.

"Whatever," she says.

I allow Tiffany to drag me into the back room.

"You cannot design a dress for her," Tiffany hisses as soon as I've drawn the black velvet curtain across. "She's a skanky crack whore."

"Let me guess," I say. "You met her in Narcotics Anonymous."

"No," Tiffany says. "But she's still a skanky crack whore. Seriously, Lizzie. Did you see her on *Celebrity Pit Fight*? She made Lil' Kim cry. *Lil' Kim*. You can't. You just can't."

"She's hugely famous," I say. "She's a bazillioniare. And she's marrying a prince. Do you have any idea what kind of press that will bring in?"

"Yeah," Tiffany says. "Skanky crack whore press. Believe me, that is not the kind of press you want."

"Tiffany," I say, fighting for patience. "You don't understand. At this point in my career, any press is good press. I'm totally doing the dress."

"But she's disgusting," Tiffany insists. "Did you see the way she treated that dog? And what is with those boots?"

"Tiffany, she's obviously deeply troubled. She needs our help, not our scorn. She's clearly had no one in her life to gently guide her on how to act like a decent human being. And she really needs that, now more than ever . . . she's marrying a prince! It's going to be a royal wedding!"

"In *Greece*," Tiffany points out. "Hel-*lo*."

"Tiffany! How can you say that? Greece is the cradle of Western civilization, the birthplace of democracy, political science, Western literature and philosophy, the Olympic games—"

"Um, Lizzie, have you ever even tasted hummus?"

"Tiffany." I glare at her. "I'm doing Ava's dress. You're either with me or you're out."

Tiffany rolls her eyes toward the ceiling. "Is this because of the prince thing? Because, like, you're marrying a prince, and so you feel like you have this moral obligation to help her, because *she's* marrying a prince?"

I ignore that. "Tiffany, we have a moral obligation to help this poor girl, because if we don't, no one will, and she'll just go on doing asinine things like pulling out Lil' Kim's hair extensions on *Celebrity Pit Fight,* and she'll never discover her true inner potential."

"And you think *you* can help her find it?" Tiffany sneers.

"Yes, Tiffany," I say gravely. "Yes, I think I can."

Except that the truth is, I don't think I can. I *know* I can.

"Fine. If you want to play Dr. Dolittle to her Eliza Higgins," Tiffany says, "it's your funeral. I'll just do what you're paying me for: answer the phones."

"It's Professor Higgins," I correct her, "and Eliza Doolittle. Professor Higgins is the guy who gives the Cockney flower girl the makeover. Dr. Dolittle is the guy who could talk to animals."

"Fine," Tiffany mutters. "I can tell this was a bad day to cut back on my Adderall."

I throw back the black velvet curtain and find Ava Geck closely examining a dressmaker's dummy wearing a House of Bianchi off-the-shoulder number I've retrofitted with sleeves for a bride who's being married in a conservative synagogue.

"I like this one," Ava says, straightening up when I come in. She's still chomping on her gum. "Can you make me something like this?"

I'm surprised. Pleasantly so. For a girl who's shown her panties so many times on television, it's a surprisingly modest choice.

"I think we can come up with a gown you'll like," I say. "Something a little more Ava-like."

Ava gasps, then claps her hands. The Chihuahua barks excitedly and spins around in circles. Even the bodyguard cracks a smile. A very small one, but a smile just the same.

"Oh, thank you!" Ava cries. "This is gonna be bitchin'!"

"Yeah," I say. "Just a couple of ground rules, though. Rule number one . . . when you enter Chez Henri, you have to de-gum. When you leave, you may re-gum." I hold out my hand expectantly.

Ava stares at me blankly. "What?"

"Your gum," I say. "There is no gum allowed in Chez Henri. You're welcome to go over to Vera Wang and chew gum, but not here. It's uncivilized to stand around looking like a cow chewing her cud. So either spit it out or leave."

Ava, looking stunned, spits her gum out into my hand. I drop the wad into a nearby trash can, which the Chihuahua quickly runs over to inspect.

"Rule number two," I say, wiping my hand off with a tissue I pluck from the box on Tiffany's desk. "You must show up on time for all fittings. If you're not going to be able to make it for whatever reason, you must call at least an hour before your appointment to let us know. Failure to do this more than once, and your contract with us will be canceled. It's not polite to stand people up. We have lots of clients and could reschedule someone else in your time slot if we know you won't be able to make it in advance. Okay?"

Still looking dazed, Ava nods. The bodyguard, I notice, is still smiling, although now he looks slightly bemused.

"All right, Ava," I say. "Why don't you step into the dressing room over here so I can take your measurements?"

Ava hurries to oblige, tripping a little over her ridiculously high-heeled boots.

It's going to be, it's clear, a long morning.

A HISTORY *of* WEDDINGS

Bridesmaids in ancient Roman times were the first to wear identical gowns—identical not only to one another's but to the bride's as well. This was in an attempt to trick demons from taking the bride's soul prior to her wedding night. Any woman who'd protected three brides from evil spirits was considered too impure to marry herself, having absorbed too much black magic. This is where the expression "three times a bridesmaid, never a bride" comes from.

So they weren't making it up about the *three times a bridesmaid* thing! And you just thought they were talking about your aunt Judy.

Tip to Avoid a Wedding Day Disaster

You love your friends because of their unique personalities. Well, their bodies are unique too. So don't squeeze your bridesmaids into identical gowns. They'll hate it, and if you're really their friend, you should hate that they hate it. Choose a shade that will flatter all of them, and let them each choose a dress in that color that they like, one that they'll really wear again.

So what if they won't all look exactly the same? It's them you love, not their look, right?

LIZZIE NICHOLS DESIGNS™

Chapter 6

Two such as you with such a master speed cannot be parted nor be swept away from one another once you are agreed that life is only life forevermore together wing to wing and oar to oar.

Robert Frost (1874–1963), American poet

Luke has promised to come over and make me a nice dinner because of the day I've had—though Madame Henri calls just after five to let me know that her husband has gotten through his surgery with flying colors—but the truth is, all I want to do is take a hot bath, read a fashion magazine, and go to bed.

Only how can I tell this to Luke, who went to the market and picked up two sirloins and marinated them (his postbaccalaureate premed classes don't start up again until after Martin Luther King Day), especially for me?

So when he calls just before six with an apologetic note in his voice and says, "Listen," it's all I can do to keep from clicking my heels together with joy. He's canceling! Alleluia! And hello, this month's *Vogue*.

"There's a Michigan game on tonight," he says. "And Chaz really wants me to watch it with him. You know how he is about the Wolverines. And the truth is . . . he seemed kind of depressed on the phone when he called to tell me about it."

"Chaz is depressed?" This is news to me. He hadn't seemed a bit depressed when he'd had his hand down my bra. Not that I add this last part out loud, of course.

"Well, I mean, it's only natural he'd be a little down, you know," Luke says. "We're getting married, and his girlfriend left him . . . for another woman. I really thought he'd have someone else by now—I've never seen him go without a date for this long."

"Shari only broke up with him at Thanksgiving," I point out dryly. I notice there's a new red splotch on the inside of my elbow where the old one, which has faded away, was. So it wasn't a mosquito bite. What could they be? Maybe an allergy to the detergent I'm using? But I haven't switched detergents lately.

"For Chaz, a month and a half is a real dry spell," Luke says. "Now his best friend is marrying the cutest girl in the world . . . No wonder he's depressed."

"Then you should absolutely stay home and watch basketball with him," I say. I'm already fantasizing about the Chinese food I'm going to order in. Moo shu chicken with hoisin sauce. Maybe I'll even eat it in the bathtub.

"Well, that's the thing," Luke says. "The game's only on satellite. We'll be watching it at O'Riordan's Sports Bar, which is around the corner from your place, on Lexington. So I thought, if you wanted to stop by later . . ."

"Gosh, honey," I say sweetly. "There's nothing I can imagine wanting to do more than sit around with you and your depressed guy friend watching sports."

"We'll be ordering chicken wings," Luke says in an effort to tempt me.

"That is so hard to resist . . ."

"Come on," Luke says in a more serious tone. "Chaz loves you, you know that. He wants to say congratulations in person. And seeing you will cheer him up. You know how much he likes teasing you about your weird outfits. Besides, if you don't show up, I won't see you all day."

Except it isn't my outfit I'm afraid of Chaz teasing me about.

Not that I'm about to mention this, either.

"Luke," I say. "The whole point of our not living together is so that we can use this time of our engagement to explore who we are as individuals, so that when we come together as a married couple we'll have a clearer idea of exactly what we want out of—"

"Lizzie," Luke says. "I know all that. I was there when you made that little speech, remember? Can't a guy just want to see his girlfriend?"

I sigh, visions of my fun evening of high-fashion photos and bubbles going down the drain. Literally. "I'll be there around seven."

The bar is crowded, but thankfully not smoky, since New York City banned all smoking indoors and actually enforces it. I find Luke and Chaz in a booth beneath one of the dozens of televisions hanging suspended from the ceiling and blaring college basketball games. Luke leaps up to kiss me hello. Chaz, I see, is wearing one of his ubiquitous (except when he's in evening wear) University of Michigan baseball hats, pulled down low over his hair. He is unshaven and looking a little rough around the edges . . . rougher, even, than when I'd seen him last, after a night of too much champagne . . .

And too much other stuff as well.

"Come on," Luke says to me, grinning his adorable grin. "Show him."

I've slid into the booth beside Luke, and am taking off my coat and unwinding my scarf.

Chaz is nursing a beer, his eyes on the game above my head.

"Luke," I say, blushing, though I don't know why. "No."

"Come on," Luke says. "You know you want to."

Chaz's gaze flicks down from the television screen and onto me. "Show me what?"

Luke lifts my left hand to show Chaz my engagement ring. Chaz lets out a long, low whistle, even though of course he's already seen it. "*Nice,*" he says.

Luke's grin is now ear-to-ear.

"Let me get you a drink," he says to me. "I'll just run up to the bar, since the waitress takes forever. White wine?"

I nod. "That'd be great . . ." I wonder if I need to remind him to get it with a side of ice. I hate warm white wine, and I can never seem to drink it fast enough. It's tacky, but lately I've started asking for my white wine with a glass of ice on the side. It also lasts longer and has less calories that way.

"Be back in a flash," Luke says before I have a chance to say anything, as I slide to let him out of the booth to go to the bar, then slip back into the seat he's just vacated.

Oh well. He'll remember about the ice.

Chaz has lifted his gaze back to the game over my head. I clear my throat.

"Thank you for the roses," I say quickly, to get it over with, and before Luke gets back. "You didn't have to do that."

"Yeah," Chaz says shortly, still not looking at me. "I did."

"Well." I see that Luke is still frantically trying to get the bartender's attention, so I lay a hand—my right—over Chaz's. "Thank you. It meant a lot to me. You have no idea."

Chaz looks down at my hand. Then he looks back into my eyes. "Yeah," he says. "I think I have a pretty good idea."

I pull my hand away, stung—though I'm not sure why.

"What is *that* supposed to mean?" I ask.

Chaz chuckles and reaches for his beer. "Nothing. God, what are you so defensive for? I thought you and Luke were so blissfully happy."

"We are!" I squeak.

"Well, then"—he tilts his beer at me in a toast—"mazel tov."

"You don't seem very depressed," I can't keep myself from remarking.

Then I immediately want to kill myself.

He seems almost to choke on the mouthful of beer he just swallowed.

"Depressed?" he echoes when he's recovered enough to speak. "Who said I'm depressed?"

I look around for a conveniently loaded pistol. Sadly, there doesn't appear to be one available, so I have no choice but to answer the question.

"Luke," I mutter shamefacedly. "He thinks you're depressed because he's getting married and you're all alone."

"Luke *would* think that," Chaz says with a smirk.

"So . . . you're not depressed?" I ask, feeling a tiny glimmer of hope that maybe suicide won't be necessary, just this once.

Chaz looks me dead in the eye and says, "Why, yes, Lizzie. I'm manically depressed because the girl I've finally realized I've always been in love with, and who I was beginning to think just might love me back, turned around and got herself engaged to my best friend, who, frankly, doesn't deserve her. Does that answer your question?"

It's the weirdest thing, but my heart seems to do a flip-flop in my chest, and for a second, I can't breathe, nor can I drop my gaze from his.

Then I realize he's joking.

And I feel my cheeks begin to burn.

He's joking. Of course he's joking. God, I'm such a fool.

"What does it matter to you?" I demand, ignoring his sarcasm. I'm furious at myself—for thinking he meant it when he said he loved me, but even more, for having felt bad that I'd hurt him. He can't be hurt. I mean, obviously he can. But not by me. Never by me. "You should be relieved you escaped my sights. You don't even believe in marriage. It's just a slip of paper, right? That's what you said, anyway."

"You got that right." Chaz has leaned back to watch the game. "You want a happy romantic relationship? Don't ruin it by getting married."

I blink at him. I can't believe he's serious.

"Since when did you start feeling this way?" I ask. "You never felt like this about marriage when you were with Shari. You two were the picture of connubial bliss. Without the connubial part. But you were always making pies and doing her laundry and stuff . . ."

"Yeah," Chaz says, still not taking his gaze off the television screen . . . although I notice he's set his jaw. "Well, she left me, remember? For a *woman.* Believe me, I won't be making that mistake again. Marriage is for suckers."

"You don't mean that," I say, a little shocked at his bitter tone.

"Don't I?" He smirks at the screen. "I think I know what I'm talking about. My dad's a divorce lawyer, remember?"

"And yet he's been married to your mom," I say, "for like, what, thirty years?"

I can't believe I'm still upset about the *I've always been in love with you* remark, which, considering all the making out we were doing in the back of that cab on New Year's, wasn't really in the best of taste. I'm even more upset about the way my heart had reacted to the information. What had *that* been about?

And how, even for one second, could I ever actually have believed him?

I know I'm a naïve Midwestern girl. But I really try not to act like one. Most of the time.

"I try to keep that on the down low," Chaz says. "The happily married parents thing doesn't really go with my whole persona. You know, newly single philosophy Ph.D. candidate, living alone in an East Village walk-up, hard drinking, hard living, kind of dangerous—"

Now it's my turn to smirk.

"What?" Chaz drags his gaze from the television screen and eyes me. "You don't think I'm dangerous?"

"Not in that hat," I say.

"Oh, I'm dangerous," Chaz assures me. "More dangerous than *Luke*."

"I don't like Luke because he's dangerous," I point out.

"Oh, right," Chaz says. "You like him . . . why? Because he's rich? Handsome? Suave? Debonair? Thoughtful? Kind? Going to save the children someday?"

"All of the above," I say, "except rich. I intend to make my own money, thank you, so I have no need of his. In fact, I just took on Ava Geck as a client today."

"The skanky crack whore?" Chaz looks horrified.

"Why does everyone call her that?" I ask in annoyance. "No one has ever actually *seen* her do crack or have sex in exchange for money, and yet everyone calls her a skanky crack whore."

"I don't have to see her do it," Chaz says. "Have you ever checked out *Celebrity Pit Fight*?"

It's my turn to look horrified. "What is a hard-drinking, hard-living, philosophy Ph.D. candidate doing watching *Celebrity Pit Fight*?"

Chaz grins. "It's a really good show," he says. "I mean, if you're ever in the mood to examine one of the bleaker examples of the depraved depths to which we as a society have sunk. Or at least the depraved depths to which the entertainment industry is determined to make us think we've sunk."

"Hey." Luke slides back into the booth and hands me my glass of wine. "Sorry that took so long. This place is a madhouse. There are five different games on."

I notice with a slight feeling of disappointment that he's forgotten to get a side of ice. Oh well. We've been going out for only six months, after all. He can't remember *everything*.

"You forgot the ice," Chaz says. "Luke, tell your girlfriend she isn't going to get ahead in the wedding gown biz if she takes on skanky crack whores as clients."

I blink, not quite able to believe Chaz remembered.

"What ice?" Luke looks confused. "Wait. *Who*'s a skanky crack whore?"

"No one," I say at the same time that Chaz says, "Ava Geck."

"Who's Ava Geck?" Luke wants to know.

Chaz guffaws. I take a hasty sip of my wine, knowing what's coming.

"Do you even *watch* television?" Chaz asks Luke. "Do you ever even read a periodical besides *The Wall Street Journal*? Tell me, because I really want to know. When you're in the dentist's office, do you ever, even by accident, pick up a copy of *Us Weekly*?"

"Stop it," I say to Chaz. I'm getting annoyed with him now. More annoyed, maybe, than the situation warrants. "Just because Luke doesn't know who Ava Geck is—"

"*Everyone* knows who Ava Geck is," Chaz bursts out.

"Who's Ava Geck?" Luke asks again.

"She's—" But suddenly I'm so tired I can't even go on. I can't take it, the voices of the announcers from the televisions and the screams of the fans and the clapping whenever someone's team scores a basket—not to mention the drunk homeless guy I can see bobbing around outside the plate-glass window a few feet away, begging for change from anyone who passes by the place.

But what I really can't take is the voice inside my head that's returned. It's a familiar voice. It ought to be. Because it's the voice of the guy sitting directly across from me . . . the big, rumpled one in the University of Michigan baseball cap.

"*Why, yes, Lizzie. I'm manically depressed because the girl I've finally realized I've always been in love with, and who I was beginning to think just might love me back, turned around and got herself engaged to my best friend, who, frankly, doesn't deserve her.*"

But simultaneously I hear that same voice saying, "*You want a happy romantic relationship? Don't ruin it by getting married. I know what I'm talking about.*"

"You know what?" I say suddenly, my own voice tight with unshed emotion. "This has been fun. But I'm really tired. Do you guys mind if I call it a night? I have a big day tomorrow, and I think I'm gonna turn in early."

"Oh, come on," Luke says. "You just got here. Don't go yet. The game just started."

I look at Chaz. His face is impassive beneath the brim of his hat. But he's looking right back at me.

"Yeah, Lizzie," he says. "Don't go yet. The game just started."

It's weird. But something in the way his gaze holds mine—not to mention his tone—tells me he isn't talking about the game on TV.

Not at all.

"Okay, I'll be seeing you guys later," I say, my own voice pitched way too high, as I all but shove Luke out of the way in my haste to leave the booth.

"I'll walk you home," a confused Luke says, but I brush this offer aside with a quick kiss on his cheek and a whispered *No, thanks, I'll be fine, stay and have fun,* then bolt for the door, where I stand gasping in the bitterly cold January air.

"Spare a quarter, miss?" the homeless drunk asks me, holding out a filthy, chipped coffee cup.

I don't even answer him. That's what a jaded New Yorker I've become. I never have a quarter to spare anymore. I need my quarters. I need all the quarters I can get. Do you have any idea how much it costs to do laundry around here?

"Fine," the homeless guy says with a sniff. "Be that way, bitch."

My eyes fill with tears. I'm not a bitch! I'm not! Any more than Ava Geck is a skanky crack whore. Any more than Chaz Pendergast is in love with me. Oh, why did he have to say that, anyway? Why does he have to be so mean? After having gotten those beautiful roses, I'd been completely ready to forgive him for all the nasty things he'd said yesterday morning . . . and then he'd had to go and say *that.*

. . . the girl I've finally realized I've always been in love with . . . who I was beginning to think just might love me back. . .

He'd only been teasing. He's always teased me, the whole time I've known him.

So . . . why does it hurt so much this time?

"You want a happy romantic relationship? Don't ruin it by getting married."

But if you don't get married . . . what's the *point*?

A HISTORY *of* WEDDINGS

The Elizabethan age brought us the flowering of poetry, literature, theater, and romance. So it's no wonder we have Elizabethan England to thank for so many of our modern-day wedding traditions, including the exchange of rings, a more traditional (i.e., non-weapons-bearing) use of bridesmaids, the exchange of wedding vows, even bridal bouquets. Most upper-class marriages were still arranged during this time, often from birth. Only the lower classes had the luxury of being able to marry for love.

But if this hadn't been the case, what else would William Shakespeare have had to write about?

Tip to Avoid a Wedding Day Disaster

Your sister-in-law-to-be might have the cutest kids in the world—and she just very well may have a point: Maybe they should *have a role in your wedding. But don't let her browbeat you into sacrificing one of your bridesmaid, ring bearer, or flower girl positions for* her *kids. Don't upset one of* your *friends or family members just to placate* his *sister. There are lots of other tasks her kids can perform throughout the ceremony, such as guest book holder, confetti or program passer-outer, or even adorable, if slightly height-challenged, usher. Use your imagination, and you'll both be happy.*

LIZZIE NICHOLS DESIGNS™

Chapter 7

Now join hands, and with your hands your hearts.

William Shakespeare (1564–1616), English dramatist and poet

"Your friend Chaz sounds like a pig" is Monique's observation when she and Tiffany overhear me relating the details about my evening to Gran (Mom, as usual, wasn't available) while the three of us are having a quick, between-fittings lunch in the shop the next day.

"She's right about that," Gran, on my cell phone, agrees. "Whoever she is."

"He's not really," I say, pausing with my Così tandoori chicken sandwich halfway to my lips. "I mean, under ordinary circumstances. That's what's so weird about this."

"Well, that's it, then," Monique says firmly. She's a beauty every bit as statuesque—and sure of herself—as Tiffany.

Unlike Tiffany, however, Monique has a British accent that makes her sound like a college professor every time she speaks.

A college professor who talks a lot about men being "wankers," I mean.

"What's it?" I ask.

Tiffany and Monique exchange glances. Tiffany nods.

"He's in love with you, of course," Monique says.

"You've never even met him," I cry.

"I have," Tiffany says, stuffing a wad of Jamaican jerk sandwich into her mouth. "And he totally is."

"She's right," Gran says. "I've always thought that boy wanted to put a load of coal into your steam engine."

I nearly spit out the bite of tandoori chicken I'd just taken.

"How can you *say* that?" I cry. "He's Luke's best friend! He's my best friend's ex-boyfriend!"

Tiffany looks at me blankly. "So?"

Monique is giving me the same blank stare. They must teach it at modeling school. "Yeah," she says. "So?"

Gran sounds impatient. "*Dr. Quinn* comes on in ten minutes. How long is this going to take?"

"So . . . so . . . ," I say, for once in my life actually sputtering to find the right words. "So . . . Look. I'm sure men fall head over heels for you two all the time. I mean . . . *look* at you. But in real life—for *real* girls, like me, that is—that just doesn't happen. Men don't go around falling in love with me. And certainly not without encouragement."

"Oh, and your letting him touch your titties in that taxi wasn't encouragement?" Monique asks.

"You let him spend the night too," Tiffany points out.

I put my finger over the mouthpiece of my cell. "Excuse me," I say. "My grandmother is listening in on this."

"Too late," Gran says. "I already heard. This is even *better* than *Dr. Quinn.*"

"We were both drunk," I insist in my own defense for what has to be the millionth time. I'm regretting ever having opened my mouth about any of this, a not unfamiliar sensation. I'm especially regretting not having hung up when Gran answered. "Look, forget I said anything. It was nothing."

Why had I even said anything, especially to these girls? I wouldn't have if I'd been able to discuss any of this with Shari. If I could just call Shari and go, *Shari. This is what my fiancé's best friend said to me. What do you think?* none of this would be happening.

But I can't do that. Because my fiancé's best friend is her ex-boyfriend.

And I can't talk about what happened with Chaz with Shari. Because it would all be too weird.

But Monique and Tiffany, it turns out, are not proving to be adequate Shari substitutes. Not at all.

"That last bit he said," Monique says, "about the game just starting? That didn't sound like nothing to me. Does it to you, Tiff?"

"No way, José," Tiffany says. "I think he's warm for our Miss Lizzie's form."

"Told you," Gran sings.

"Oh my God, you guys." I shake my head. "He is so not. And even if he is . . . it's not going to go anywhere. He's completely damaged from what happened with Shari. He says he—"

It's at this moment—fortunately—that the door to the shop bursts open, and Ava Geck comes tumbling through it, her bodyguard and Chihuahua in tow. Ava has a wild look on her face, as if she's being hunted. She's wearing short-shorts over fishnet stockings, even though it's approximately twelve degrees outside, and her lower jaw is moving rapidly . . . except that she's not speaking.

Tiffany scowls down at the book in front of her. "What are you doing here, Ava?" she demands. "Your next appointment's not for four weeks."

"Sorry," Ava says, still chewing. She collapses onto the chaise longue I insisted Madame Henri place in the far corner for nervous, waiting mothers, and peers out the plate-glass window in the front of the store, her body hidden from view by a display dummy dressed in a princess gown from the 1950s, complete with a voluminous, diamanté-dotted tulle skirt that takes up almost the entire display window. "We were in the neighborhood looking at condos and suddenly . . . paparazzi! Can we hide for a few minutes until they go away? I don't have any eyeliner on."

"Hold on, Gran," I say into my cell. I walk over to Ava and hold out my hand expectantly. "You *may*," I say.

Still crouching behind the tulle skirt, she looks down at my hand with a blank expression on her face. Then comprehension dawns. She spits her gum out into my hand. I walk over to the trash can beneath the desk at which Tiffany is sitting and dump it, then reach for a tissue.

"Little Joey," I say to the bodyguard, to whom we'd been formally introduced during Ava's last visit. "There are blinds if you want to pull them down."

Little Joey—whose hulking three-hundred-pound, nearly seven-foot frame makes it clear that his name is ironic—begins pulling down the black metal blinds I'd bought at the Manhattan Target when I'd been rehabbing Jill Higgins's gown, and she, too, had had problems with stalkerazzi.

"Why are you looking for a condo in Manhattan, Ava?" I ask her.

"It's, like, so much better here than in Los Angeles," Ava says, pulling her shivering Chihuahua onto her lap. "Except for the weather. For one thing, you don't have to drive as far to get to cool places. Which is great if you're wasted. And for another, no one asks you for autographs, or crap like that—*usually*. I mean, people stare. But they don't bug you. Except, like, teenagers at H&M."

It takes us a moment to digest this. Tiffany is the first to recover.

"So are you looking for a one-bedroom or a two-bedroom, or what?" Tiffany asks conversationally.

"She's looking for four bedrooms, three baths, and an eat-in kitchen with at least two thousand square feet of outdoor terrace, and full southern exposure," Little Joey says when Ava just blinks bewilderedly at the question.

When we all turn our heads to stare at Ava, dumbfounded by this information—since to my knowledge, no such piece of real estate exists on the island of Manhattan (for less than five million dollars, anyway)—she just shrugs and says, in her little girl voice, "I've got seasonal affective disorder. Hey, do you have anything else to eat? All I've had today is a PowerBar, and I'm, like, starving."

I hand her the other half of my tandoori chicken sandwich, but she makes a face.

"What's that white slimy stuff?" she asks suspiciously.

This causes Tiffany and Monique to dissolve into a fit of hysterical laughter from which it's clear they won't soon recover.

"Tzatziki sauce," I say. "Ava, how can you be marrying a Greek prince and not know what tzatziki sauce is?"

"I like *him*," Ava says, snatching the sandwich out of reach of her dog—whose name, she'd informed us the day before, is Snow White ("After the Disney princess")—"not his country's *food*."

"Well," I say. "You should try it, at least, before you decide you don't like it."

Ava shrugs and takes a bite. Her mouth occupied, I turn back to Tiffany and Monique, who are wiping their eyes from their shared—if disgustingly raunchy—joke.

"Seriously, you guys," I say to them, addressing my remark into the phone. "Do you think I should try talking to him? Luke thinks he's depressed. What if he's right? Maybe if I talked to him about it, it would help. To bring about closure, you know? Sometimes when things are out in the open, they don't bother people as much."

"Says the girl who can't keep a secret to save her life," says Tiffany with a laugh. Although frankly I don't see what's so funny about that remark. Also, it's not true. I've kept lots of secrets.

I can't happen to think of any right now. But I'm sure there are some.

"What are we talking about?" Ava wants to know. She's already gnawed off a quarter of an inch of the sandwich half I've given her. Snow White is busy with another quarter of an inch. It's not hard to see how the two of them stay so trim.

"Lizzie's fiancé's best friend is in love with her," Monique says lightly. She's split her vegi muffuletta with Little Joey. "And she doesn't know what to do about it."

I roll my eyes. "He's not in love with me," I say. "He—"

"Oh, that's easy," Ava interrupts, licking the fingertips Snow White's just licked. "Why don't you just fuck him?"

"Who's that?" Gran asks over the phone. "I like her."

I have no choice but to set down my Diet Coke and say, "Ava, first of all: Monique is wrong. Chaz isn't in love with me. We're just friends. Second of all, you shouldn't be driving anywhere, short or long distance, if you're wasted. I want you to know that I Googled you after I got home last night, and I know all about your DUI. You need to be more careful. With all your money, why don't you just hire a driver? And last, while I appreciate that, as feminists, we have every right to embrace whatever kind of language we choose, even words considered by previous generations to be 'unladylike' or 'coarse,' it really isn't tasteful or imaginative to use vulgarities in everyday conversation. Sure, if you're really upset about something.

But the f-word, Ava, when you're speaking about making love? I think you're better than that. In fact, I *know* you are. Besides, what would Prince Aleksandros say?"

Ava looks at me with the same blank expression she'd worn when I'd held out my hand for her gum. "He says 'fuck' even more than I do," she says.

I sigh. "Let's just drop it," I say to the room—and into the phone—in general. "Pretend I didn't say anything. Especially to Mom. Okay, Gran?"

"Tell you what you should do," Little Joey remarks, after taking a delicate sip of the Diet Peach Snapple he's produced from one of his enormous pockets. "Get this guy alone, in a darkened room. Open up a bottle of Hennessey. Play a little Vandross. That's how you have yourselves some *closure*."

"Now," Gran says approvingly, "someone is finally talking sense."

I gape at my cell. "That's . . . that's preposterous," I stammer. "I happen to be deeply—*deeply*—in love with my fiancé. I mean . . . come on, Tiffany." I turn to her for help. "You've seen Luke and me together. You had Thanksgiving with us, remember?"

"Right," Tiffany says, thoughtfully tapping on her perfectly aligned—also capped—front teeth. "But I think Little Joey might be onto something, Lizzie. I think you *want* us to say you should go talk to Chaz. I mean, why else would you have mentioned it?"

Monique nods too. "Right. You do seem to want us to tell you that you should go talk to Chaz about it."

"I think you liked having his hand down your bra and are hoping he'll do it again," Tiffany adds.

I widen my eyes at her. "Boundaries," I say, jerking my head urgently at Little Joey, who is now smirking into his Snapple bottle. "Ladies! Boundaries!"

"That's what I said." Ava, ignoring me, has turned her huge baby blues onto Tiffany. "She should just fuck him and get him out of her system. That's what I did when I found myself with feelings for DJ Tippycat on *Celebrity Pit Fight*."

I blink. Then I say firmly, "I am not going to *make love* to my fiancé's best friend, Ava. That is a totally ridiculous suggestion. For one thing, I would never betray Luke's trust like that. And I can tell you that if that's how you deal with your fiancé's friends—or . . . or DJ Tippycat—well, he isn't going to stay your fiancé for long. And for another thing, I happen to be in love with my boyfriend. Besides which, Chaz happens to be my best friend's ex-boyfriend—"

"Yeah, but it's not like she wants him anymore," Tiffany says in a bored voice. "Seeing as how she's gay and sleeping with a woman now."

Ava sucks in her breath. Little Joey looks as delighted as if he's just won the lottery. Snow White yawns and curls herself into a little ball and goes to sleep. Gran says, "I think I'll just TiVo today's episode of *Dr. Quinn* . . . how the hell do you work this thing?"

"Chaz doesn't even believe in marriage," I inform them desperately. "He thinks it's nothing but a slip of paper, and that marriage doesn't actually mean anything—"

"Okay, *now* we get to the heart of the matter," Little Joey says in a satisfied voice. "So *this* is why you aren't busting a move on the guy."

"Of *course*," Monique says, wide-eyed. "It all makes sense now. What's a woman who makes her living making women's wedding dreams come true going to do with a man who doesn't even believe in the institution of marriage? It's absurd."

"She can always make him change his mind," Ava says, as if I'm not even in the room. "It's hard. But it happens."

Tiffany looks dubious. "I don't know. This is a philosophy Ph.D. candidate we're talking about. He studies, like, existentialism and shit. I think it'd be hard to get him to change his *socks*, let alone his mind."

"Let's just forget I brought it up, all right?" I ask in an unsteady voice. "Let's talk about something else—"

"Nooooo!" Gran yells, so loudly that I have to hold the phone away from my ear.

"Let's talk about your gown, Ava," I say, ignoring Gran. "I think you're right to go a little more conservative than usual. After all, this is your wedding, and you're going to be marrying into a royal family. But since it's going to be a summer ceremony, I was thinking capped sleeves—"

"This is boring me," Gran threatens. "I'm hanging up."

"You're young and slender and can get away with them. And since it's Greece, I was thinking an empire waist . . . going a little Grecian. Here, let me show you what I mean."

The click echoes with startling finality in my ear. I ignore it, closing my cell phone and laying it aside. I'll deal with Gran later. *A load of coal into my steam engine?*

With difficulty, I finally steer them away from the topic of my love life and onto the subject of my ideas for Ava's gown—which she seems to like—until Tiffany bursts out, after a glance at the wall clock, "Crap! I have to go to work. I mean, my other work. Okay, you guys, don't talk about anything good while I'm gone. And, Lizzie, don't you dare make any decisions about Chaz without checking with me first. Obviously you can't be trusted about any of this. Just, you know. Call me first if anything new comes up, and we'll talk."

"I don't even know what you're talking about," I say with a sniff. "As I've said before—repeatedly—I love my boyfriend—I mean, my fiancé—and nothing is going to happen between his best friend and myself, because there is nothing going on between us."

"*Right*," Tiffany says with a laugh, which is echoed by everyone else in the shop, with the exception of me.

After Tiffany leaves—announcing that there're still paparazzi waiting on the corner and that Ava had better continue to lay low—I declare that I, too, have to go to work—on making some sketches for Ava's dress; plus, there's the Bianchi, which I'm determined to finish up; not to mention loads of other projects to get started, given the fact that my boss is going to be out for at least the next four to six weeks, according to his wife, who'd phoned to give me a progress report—and slink into the back.

But instead of sketching *or* tweaking the Bianchi, I find myself staring into space, wondering whether or not what the others had said—that Chaz was in love with me—could possibly be true.

"I'm manically depressed because the girl I've finally realized I've always been in love with, and who I was beginning to think just might love me back, turned around and got herself engaged to my best friend, who, frankly, doesn't deserve her."

Sure. He'd *said* that. But he'd only been teasing me. And I, like the simple Midwestern fool that I am, had fallen for it. Why *did* my heart go all jumpy when he said that? I am completely and one hundred percent committed to Luke.

Of course . . . Chaz *had* said he saw nothing but me in his future . . . and that I wasn't even wearing Spanx.

Luke still doesn't know that I wear Spanx, or even what they are. I've managed to keep them a well-guarded secret from him.

How I've kept the twenty or so pounds I've managed to gain back since moving to New York City a secret from him is much more complicated. It involves never turning my back on him while undressed, and always letting him be on top during our more, er, intimate moments, so he doesn't notice my belly. Thank God for gravity.

How much longer I'll be able to carry on this facade, I don't know. It may end up to be easier to give up tandoori chicken sandwiches in exchange for salads or—God forbid—I could start working out.

But I do want to be a slender bride. Or at least less large than I am now.

But where will I find the time to work out, now that I'm running the shop single-handedly—well, not counting Tiffany and Monique—and will be doing so for at least another month and a half . . . maybe even longer, according to Madame Henri, who explained that bypass surgery recovery times can be hard to predict and depend on the individual? I don't even have time to *plan* my own wedding, let alone get in shape for it.

Funny how just thinking the words "my wedding" makes me feel a little tight in the chest. Seriously, like I can't breathe. And what is with that itchy red splotch on the inside of my elbow all of a sudden? What *is* that? Why does it keep appearing and then disappearing, only to reappear in a new spot, sometimes more than one?

Is that . . . oh my God, is that a *hive*? No. It can't be. I haven't had hives since I was in high school, when I was put in charge of the costumes for *Jesus Christ Superstar*, and the director wanted everyone in bell bottoms. This was before bell bottoms were back in style, and I realized I was going to have to slash—and insert brightly colored panels into—the pants legs of seventy-five cast members. In one weekend. I'd broken out into such bad hives that Dr. Dennis, Shari's dad, had had to give me a shot of prednisone.

Oh my God. There's another one on the inside of my *other* elbow.

Oh no, please. Don't let me turn out to be the same way over this damn wedding with Luke as I was over the bell bottoms. *Why?* Why is this *happening*? Is it Mom, and her insistence that our backyard is just as nice a place to have a wedding as Château Mirac? It can't be . . . you know, that other thing. What Monique said, about Chaz's being in love with me. It can't possibly be *that.*

No. It has to be the thing with Mom, and the whole idea of my family descending on Luke's familial estate, and how they might act when they get there. Gran, with her drinking, and Rose and Sarah, with their bickering and their picking on me, and . . .

Oh yeah, see? Another hive. Right there on my wrist. I knew it. It's because I keep seeing Rose's husband, Angelo, in my mind's eye, wandering around the château, wanting to know where he can get a Pabst Blue Ribbon . . .

And Gran. Gran, going up to Mrs. de Villiers and asking her what time *Dr. Quinn, Medicine Woman* is going to be on . . .

Oh God. Two more.

Chaz stepping forward when the justice of the peace—or whoever marries people in France—asks if there is anybody who has any reason why this couple should not be wed, because he doesn't believe in the institution of marriage, and it's just a slip of paper . . .

Oh my God! Another one on my wrist!

Okay. That's it. That is *it.* I am not going to think about Chaz—*or* my wedding—again. Whatever happened between Chaz and me, it's done, over, finished. What would be the point, anyway? There's no future for our relationship—even if we had one—since he doesn't believe in marriage.

And I'm sorry, but—call me a simple-minded fool—I do! I really do!

No. This is it. I am not going to see or speak to Chaz ever again—it's better this way, to avoid temptation—except when I have to, because he is my fiancé's best friend and our best man, and it would look weird if I didn't speak to the best man at my own wedding.

That's it. I'm done with Chaz.

And done with thinking about my wedding. For now.

Okay. Exhale.

Now. Where was I? Oh, right. The Bianchi. Okay.

That's right. I'll just throw myself into my work. That's all I need to do, and time will fly by so fast, I won't even realize it. Before I know it, it will be June . . . time to get ready for my own wedding day.

And then nothing Chaz can say or do will be able to ruin it for me . . .
By then everything will be perfect. Just perfect.
Exactly the way it's supposed to be.
See? I feel better already.
And look at that. No new hives.
Phew. Great. Okay. So . . . work. WORK!

A HISTORY *of* WEDDINGS

Everyone knows a bride needs to wear something old, something new, something borrowed, something blue. But hardly anyone knows why. According to ancient superstition, the "something old" ensures the bride's friends will be faithful when she needs them after she's embarked on her new life with her husband and his family. The "something new" is supposed to promise success in that new life. The "something borrowed" symbolizes the love of her own family—that she may take it with her as she goes to live with the family of her new husband. And the "blue" symbolizes loyalty and constancy.

The full version of the rhyme goes on to add that the bride also needs "a sixpence in her shoe."

This was for cab fare home if things worked out badly.

Tip to Avoid a Wedding Day Disaster

You know the old saying—What happens when you assume? You make an Ass of U and Me. Don't assume everyone you've invited to your wedding knows their way to the church and reception hall. Include a well-drawn, legible map along with your invitation. Trust me, some of your guests will be so drunk—yes, even before the ceremony—they'll need it.

LIZZIE NICHOLS DESIGNS™

Chapter 8

To keep your marriage brimming,
With love in the wedding cup,
Whenever you're wrong, admit it;
Whenever you're right, shut up.

Ogden Nash (1902 –1971), American poet

June, Six Months Later

"We have a new awning."

That's the first thing Monsieur Henri says when he walks into the shop.

"Well, of course we do," I say with a laugh. "You know that. Your wife helped pick it out."

"But"—Monsieur Henri glances over his shoulder at the awning stretched over the entrance to the shop—"it's pink."

Madame Henri gives her husband a sharp rap on the shoulder.

"Don't be ignorant," she advises him in French. "Of course it's pink. I showed you the swatches. You agreed to the color yourself."

"No." Monsieur Henri shakes his head. "Not *that* pink."

"Jean, you *did*," Madame Henri insists. "Remember, you were in the garden, and I brought out the swatches, and you said you liked the salmon."

"That's not salmon," Monsieur Henri insists. "That's *pink*." He looks down, then gasps. "My God. The *carpet* too?"

"It's not pink," I rush to inform him. "It's blush. It's practically beige."

"If it's the rug he's going on about, tell him the customers like it," Tiffany says defensively as she leans over her desk to gaze at the new wall-to-wall. "It's very feminine."

Monsieur Henri glances at her.

"What," he asks in English, sounding horrified, "is wrong with your hair?"

Tiffany lifts up her hand to tug on her new, ultra-short bangs. "You like? They call it the Ava. After Ava Geck. Everybody's getting it." When she notices from his expression that he clearly doesn't understand a word she's saying, she adds, "It's all Lizzie's doing. She totally civilized her. Ava was like an animal before Lizzie got her hands on her. Seriously. She could barely formulate comprehensible sentences. And now she almost always remembers to put on underwear. Well, most days."

"Take me back," Monsieur Henri mutters. "Take me back to New Jersey," he says to his wife.

"No, Jean, don't be ridiculous," Madame Henri says, taking her husband's arm and leading him toward one of the newly upholstered chairs that sit by the fully stocked coffee bar. Monsieur Henri sinks onto the slick pink silk with a sigh. He has not snapped back as quickly—or as fully—as any of us hoped he would from his bypass surgery. His recovery has been fraught with complications, including a case of double pneumonia that had him bedridden for an extra few weeks, and he is only now, months later, making his first tenuous steps back to work.

But it's clear his heart—to borrow a phrase—isn't in it.

"Where did we get these chairs?" he whines, noticing the new material he's sitting on. "And what's that smell?"

"Those are the same old chairs you've always had," I explain. "I had them recovered. They were stained and ugly. And that smell is Colombian roast. I got a cappuccino maker so the mothers can have something to drink during their daughters' fittings—"

"How much is all of this costing me?" Monsieur Henri frets, looking around at the newly painted walls (also in blush), and the vintage dress pattern packets I've hung in elaborate gilt frames.

"It's not costing you anything, you old goat," Madame Henri chastises her husband, poking him in the shoulder. "I told you. Thanks to Lizzie, business is up almost a thousand percent since this time last year. That Jill Higgins—remember, from last year? All those society women are sending their daughters to have their gowns fitted by the same place that made hers such a standout. What's wrong with you? Don't you listen anymore? Did they forget to clean out your ears when they were cleaning out your arteries?"

Monsieur Henri hunches his shoulders. He's lost so much weight since his surgery he looks almost like a different person. He resembles his twenty-something sons much more closely now, being long and lean, like them.

Unlike them, however, he's gone entirely gray.

"I don't understand anything anymore," he says with a sigh. "Let me see the book. Lizzie . . . just give me the book."

I seize the venerable appointment book from Tiffany—despite her insisting we switch over to a computerized mode of taking appointments, we've stayed with Monsieur Henri's old appointment book.

And now I'm glad. I'm able to hand it to him, almost genuflecting as I do so.

"Here it is," I say. "All ready for you."

Monsieur Henri grunts and begins to flick through the heavily penciled—and just as heavily erased—book. His wife, meanwhile, nods her head in the direction of the curtain that still separates the front room from the back (though the curtain is no longer black, but a beautiful salmon brocade). I follow her through it.

"*Hola,* Lizzie," say the two seamstresses she finds there, sewing beading onto the organza skirt of a strapless lace A-line by hand, from the lounge chairs in which they're sitting while watching a *telenovela* on the portable television I purchased for them.

"Marisol, Sylvia," I say. "You remember Madame Henri, right?"

Marisol and Sylvia grin and wave. Madame Henri waves back.

"So they're working out, I see," she says in French.

"Fastest needles in Manhattan," I reply in her native language. "Shari gives the best job referrals."

"Yes," Madame Henri says. "Well, I suppose when given the choice between going back to their abusive husbands or working for you, they would make rather enthusiastic employees. But I still don't see why you had to tell them about the union. You could have gotten them much more cheaply."

I give Madame Henri a disapproving look. "*Madame* . . ."

She gives a Gallic shrug. "I am only saying—"

A second later, Tiffany, though uninvited, joins us.

"What the hell is *his* glitch?" Tiffany wants to know. "He's looking at the book—*my* book—and groaning."

"Postsurgical depression," Madame Henri says in English. "I'm so sorry . . . I ought to have warned you beforehand. He just has a mild case . . . mostly it's annoyance about not being allowed to eat all the cheese he thinks he ought to be able to, and do the things he used to be able to do without discomfort. He gets so bored being home all day, I thought bringing him to the shop . . . well, I just thought he might perk up, seeing it again. I guess I was wrong. You've done such a wonderful job running it while we've been gone, Lizzie. Really. Please don't take his criticism the wrong way."

I shake my head. "I won't," I say. "I'm not—"

"The place looks beautiful," Madame Henri says. "I love the fresh-cut flowers."

"Oh, we worked out a deal with the floral shop down the street," I say, tucking a loose strand of hair behind my ear. "I recommend them to brides who haven't picked out a florist yet, and they deliver a fresh arrangement to the shop every week—"

"Brilliant," Madame Henri said. "And I hope you're getting a discount on your own wedding. Oh, but then I suppose you and Luke are getting married in France—"

Tiffany starts to laugh, then, seeing my raised eyebrow, turns it to a discreet cough. Madame Henri glances at me. "Oh no," she says. "Don't tell me. Trouble in paradise?"

"Of course not," I say indignantly. "We're doing fine. Luke and I have just been so busy, him with his classes, and me here at the shop, we haven't had time to plan anything—"

"But she's going to start now," Tiffany says firmly. "Especially since, what with Marisol and Sylvia's help, she's practically caught up with all the dresses for the June wedding rush. *Right,* Lizzie?"

"Um," I say, shooting Tiffany a warning look. "Right. Totally."

"What's this?" Monsieur Henri thunders from the outer room of the shop. "*What is this?*"

"Oh, Lord," Madame Henri mutters, rolling her eyes. "What now?"

We duck back out beneath the brocade curtain to find Monsieur Henri on his feet, clutching the appointment book to his chest and looking apoplectic.

"Jean!" Madame Henri, going deathly pale beneath her neat and tasteful makeup, rushes to her husband's side. "What's wrong? Is it your heart?"

"Yes, it's my heart," Monsieur Henri cries. "I think it must be breaking, because I feel so betrayed. Tell me I'm seeing things, please . . . or is it true that Mademoiselle Nichols here has been using *my* shop to peddle her own *bridal gown design line*?"

I stare at him, my jaw sagging. I've never seen Monsieur Henri so upset . . . and I've seen him lose his cool over many a Long Island bridezilla, ripping his careful work apart with verbal abuse.

But this is something different.

"I—I just did it a couple of times," I stammer. "For a few select clients, after the Jill Higgins wedding. It's generated a lot of really positive word of mouth for the shop . . ."

"For the shop?" Monsieur Henri echoes. "Or for *you*?"

"Oh, Jean, keep quiet." Madame Henri looks annoyed. "Such theatrics! You should be grateful to Mademoiselle Elizabeth, not shouting at her. If you don't stop this nonsense, I will make you go and sit in the car like I used to do with the boys when they were young."

"I *should* go back to the car," Monsieur Henri says, his shoulders sagging again. "What's the point of my even being here? No one needs me."

My heart swells with pity for the older man.

"Of course we need you, monsieur," I cry, going to put my arms around him. "I've been running this place without you for months now. But I'd love to take a break. Do you know I haven't had a single day off—not even Sundays—since you had your heart attack?"

"Yeah," Tiffany says. "And she wants to get married this summer. So how about giving her some vacation time so she can start getting ready for it? Oh, yeah, and she's gonna need time off for a honeymoon too."

I shoot her an aggravated look. I don't need any reminders about how much—okay, basically everything—I still have to do to prepare for my wedding.

"It's no use," Monsieur Henri says with a sigh. "It's not there anymore."

My arms still around his much-thinner-than-it-used-to-be neck, I look into his eyes. "What's not there anymore, Monsieur Henri?"

"The passion," he says with a sigh, and tosses the appointment book back onto Tiffany's desk.

I draw my arms away from him and stare. "Of course it is," I say with a nervous glance in his wife's direction. "This is just your first day back. You'll feel it again when you get back into the swing of things."

"No," Monsieur Henri says. His gaze has grown far away. "I don't care about wedding gowns anymore. There's only one thing I care about now."

His wife looks toward the recently repainted ceiling. "Not again."

"Oh?" I glance at Madame Henri. "What's that, monsieur?"

"*Pétanque,*" he says as he stares wistfully out the plate-glass window at the golden sunlight pouring onto Seventy-eighth Street.

"I *told* you," Madame Henri snaps. "That isn't a profession, Jean. It's a hobby."

"So?" Her husband jerks his head back around to demand. "I'm sixty-five! I just had a quadruple bypass! I can't play a little *pétanque* if I want to?"

The phone rings. Tiffany lifts it and purrs, "Chez Henri, how may I help you?" I am the only one who hears her add, sotto voce, "Get me out of this lunatic asylum."

"That's it." Madame Henri leans down and snatches up her Prada handbag. "We're leaving. I thought we could have a nice day in the city, maybe have a lovely lunch. But you've ruined it."

"*I've* ruined it?" Monsieur Henri cries. "I'm not the one who insisted on my coming back to work before I was emotionally prepared to! You know what my physical therapist says. One day at a time."

"I'll show you emotionally prepared," Madame Henri says, shaking her small fist at him.

"Mademoiselle Elizabeth." Monsieur Henri gives me a courtly bow, but it's clear his thoughts are elsewhere . . . on his *pétanque* set back home in his New Jersey garden, perhaps. "Remember . . . life is short. Each moment you have is precious. Treasure every second. Don't spend them doing anything you don't love. If being a certified professional wedding gown restorer isn't your dream—if designing them is—then go after that dream. The way I intend to go after my dream of playing *pétanque* every chance I get."

"Jean!" Madame Henri screams. "I told you! Don't *start*!"

"*You* don't start!" her husband thunders back. "Mademoiselle Elizabeth . . . Good-bye."

"Um . . . Good-bye." I blink after the bickering couple as they leave the shop, Madame Henri making a hand motion to me behind her husband's back indicating that she's going to call me later.

No sooner has the bell over the front door stopped tinkling than Tiffany hangs up the phone and declares, "Oh my God, I thought he'd never leave."

"Now, Tiff," I say. But the truth is, I'd felt the same way.

"Seriously, though," Tiffany says. "Where does he get off? It's not like you haven't worked like a dog for him. And for what? I know how much you make, Lizzie, remember? You're being robbed working here. You should totally quit and open your own place."

"With what start-up money?" I reach into the mini fridge—artfully disguised as a wood cabinet—beneath the coffee bar and pull out a Diet Coke. "Besides, I owe a lot to the Henris. And he's still not feeling his best. You heard what his wife said."

"Well, if he comes back to work here, I quit," Tiffany declares. "I'm serious. I'm not sticking around with that old coot poking into our business."

"Tiffany," I say. "This is his place. It's called Chez Henri. He's the owner, remember?"

"I don't care." Tiffany folds her arms across her chest. "He's a guy. He totally spoils the ambience we've established."

I didn't want to admit it out loud, but Tiffany was kind of right. I mean, it's a bridal shop, after all. What's Monsieur Henri doing, getting so bent out of shape about a salmon-colored awning? Besides, Madame Henri and I spent a lot of time and money on that awning. It looks totally great, sort of Lulu Guinness meets Fauchon chocolate shop. Speaking of which . . . mmmm, chocolate . . .

"Come on," Tiffany says, as usual refusing to let the subject drop well after I've tired of it. "You know I'm right. And what's with this *pétanque* stuff? What *is pétanque*?"

"It's a bowling game," I explain, "called boules or bocce here, involving a dirt lane and a small metal ball—"

"Is that all?" Tiffany asks scornfully. "Well, what does he keep going on about it for, then? Is he going to start selling *pétanque* equipment in here?"

"No, I'm sure he—"

"What are you going to do, Lizzie? He's going to ruin everything you've been working so hard for. Everything!"

Another thing Tiffany has a tendency to do is be way overdramatic about things. Monsieur Henri isn't going to ruin *everything.*

I'm pretty sure.

Fortunately my cell phone rings, sparing me from having to discuss the matter further . . . at least with Tiffany. I see that it's Luke and pick up eagerly. Things are going really well with him—well, aside from the fact that we haven't picked a date for our wedding. Or a venue. Or really even talked about it much. Or at all, actually.

Still, living in our own separate apartments is working out really well. We each have our own space, so we don't get on each other's nerves, and we totally appreciate the time we spend together. Consequently, the sex couldn't be better.

And, okay, maybe he still doesn't know about my Spanx.

And maybe I continue to refuse to be on top when we make love. Or turn my back on him when I'm naked.

And, yeah, any time Luke says he wants to spend the night at his own place—alone—so he can study for an exam, I become convinced he must be sleeping with other girls in his classes.

And, yes, every time he says he's spending a Saturday afternoon studying at the library, I'm sure that what he's actually doing is seeing some other girl behind my back, and it's all I can do to keep myself from sneaking down to NYU to spy on him (except I don't have a student ID to get into the library).

But you know. Other than that, things are total bliss!

Of course I have no reason to suspect these things of him other than, nearly a year into our relationship, I still can't believe a guy as amazing as Luke actually wants anything to do with a neurotic mess like myself. As Shari frequently remarks, it really is astonishing that a woman with as much business savvy as I have is as insecure in her romantic life as I've turned out to be.

But I blame this on my obsession with Lifetime Television. Of which I've been watching a lot more now that I live alone and there's no man in the house to groan every time I switch it on.

"Hi," I say to Luke now.

"What's wrong?" he asks right away.

"Wrong?" I echo. "Nothing's wrong. What makes you think something is wrong?"

"Because I know you. And you sound like someone just told you Lilly Pulitzer died."

"Oh," I say, lowering my voice so Tiffany, who is picking up a call, can't overhear. "Well, actually, Monsieur Henri stopped by the shop a few minutes ago, and he wasn't too pleased with some of the changes I've made since he's been out sick. He was acting kind of . . . strange."

"What?" Luke sounds adorably indignant on my behalf. "You've worked your tail off for that guy. That place is doing twice as much business now because of you!"

It's a lot more than that, really, as Madame Henri herself said. But I don't correct him. "Well," I say instead. "Anyway. I'm sure it will all be fine. He's just still adjusting to life as a recent bypass patient, you know."

"Well, he has some nerve," Luke says. "Anyway, I'm calling with good news. Something that should cheer you up."

"Really?" I can't think what he could be talking about. "I'm all ears!"

"Today's my last day of classes—"

"That *is* good news," I say. No more going off by himself to study! No more weekend trips to the library! Not, of course, that this had bothered me too much at the time (except for the whole *Is-there-another-woman?* thing) because the few weekends Luke wasn't studying, I'd been busy working on bridal gowns. In fact, I'd been sort of glad he'd been so preoccupied with his schoolwork. What kind of guy wants to hear, *Oh, I can't, honey. I have to finish the neckline on this mermaid gown by Monday* every time he asks his fiancée if she can go away gets for the weekend?

Fortunately, this was never an issue with Luke and me. Because he never asked me to go away for the weekend. Because he was always busy too.

"And I thought I'd take you out to dinner to celebrate," he goes on. "Someplace downtown. We spend so much time eating takeout uptown, I don't think I can handle it anymore."

“That sounds fun,” I say excitedly. “I can take the subway down and meet you.”

“That’s what I was thinking,” Luke says. “We can meet at Chaz’s place.”

My heart sinks immediately. This is so not what I’d had in mind.

“Chaz?” I say. “Really? You invited Chaz along too?”

I set my jaw. The truth is, I’m not exactly thrilled at the prospect of seeing Chaz. Not, of course, that there’s ever been a repeat of anything like what happened in the back of that taxi on the way home from Jill Higgins’s wedding. Chaz hasn’t even made any more baited remarks like he did that night so long ago in the sports bar. No, he’s been a perfect gentleman. Gran, Tiffany, and Monique’s theory—that he’s in love with me—turns out to have been completely untrue. Because if Chaz were in love with me, well, he’s had plenty of opportunity to act on that impulse.

And he never has. Not even once.

But that doesn’t mean I want him tagging along on one of the last nights I have Luke to myself before he takes off for France for three months.

But I don’t mention this. Because the last thing I’m going to do is try to wedge myself between my man and his best friend. As I know from every women’s magazine I’ve ever read, that’s a major no-no.

“Well, it’s one of the last chances I’m going to have to see him,” Luke says, “before I leave for Paris for the summer. I didn’t think you’d mind. You don’t, do you? And I thought it would be a good opportunity for us to meet his new girlfriend.”

My jaw drops. Quite literally. I sort of have to lever it back in place with my hand before I’m able to speak again.

“His . . . his *what*?”

“I know,” Luke says with a chuckle. “Can you believe it? And we all thought he’d never learn to love again after Shari.”

I am totally positive I didn’t hear Luke right. I ask, sticking one finger in my ear, “When . . . when did this happen?”

“Oh, I don’t know. Apparently they’ve been seeing each other for quite a while, but they’ve been keeping it on the down low because she’s up for tenure in the philosophy department, and he’s just a teaching assistant, and technically a student—even if he’s a grad student—so it’s all sort of clandestine. And you know Chaz was never exactly one to kiss and tell. Her name is Valencia Something. I forget. But I guess she's a real knockout. And a brainiac. Well, she'd have to be, for Chaz to like her."

I hate her. I do. I hate her already.

I also feel an extreme urge to stab myself with something. There is a pair of dressmaker's shears lying nearby. I think about plunging them into my heart. Then I think about plunging them into Valencia's heart. Really, I decide, that would be much better for everyone. Me. The world. Valencia. Anyone with a name like Valencia who is up for tenure in the philosophy department of a major private university deserves to have a pair of dressmaker's shears plunged into her heart. Doesn't she?

"So," Luke goes on. "What do you say? Dinner? Just the four of us?"

"Great," I say. "That sounds great." I don't mention that I'm going to bring along the dressmaker's shears. Because I'm not going to. Not really. I also don't mention that we—Luke and I, I mean—have never, not even once, gone out as a couple with *my* best friend and *her* girlfriend. Not that Luke would object, I'm sure. It's just that Shari has never expressed the slightest interest in doing this. I sort of wish she would. But her invitations are always expressly for me, and me alone. Luke is never included.

Which isn't very surprising, considering how many hours I spent on her and Pat's couch, crying about him.

Valencia. Isn't that a type of orange? Seriously. I'm almost sure it is.

"Great!" Luke says. "So I've got reservations for Spotted Pig at eight thirty. I said we'd meet up at Chaz's place, then take a cab over to the West Village together. Does that sound okay?"

"Sure," I say. The Spotted Pig! That's one of the trendiest restaurants in the Village! I should be excited. I should be wondering what I'm going to wear. Instead, all I'm wondering is what Valencia is going to wear. Is she prettier than me? Why do I even care? *I'm not dating Chaz.* How can Chaz have started going out with someone and I never even knew it? Is he in love with her? Is he going to marry her? No, of course not. Chaz doesn't believe in marriage. "I'll meet you at Chaz's."

Maybe Valencia will make him believe in marriage. To her. Someone with the name Valencia ought to be capable of that.

A brainiac. Of course. He *would* date a brainiac.

"Okay," Luke says. "Love you."

"Love you," I say and hang up.

"So." Tiffany has ended her own phone call and is totally watching me, her eyes slitted like a cat's. "Going to Chaz's, huh?"

I ignore her attempt to bait me. "Who was that you were on the phone with just now?"

Tiffany smirks. "Who do you think?"

I widen my own eyes. "*Ava?* I thought we were done. I thought she loved it. She should be on her way to Greece by now. What could she possibly have wanted?"

"I don't know," Tiffany says. "She wouldn't tell me. She said she could tell only you. She said she'd call back."

"Great," I say. I mean it sarcastically. I am not looking forward to hearing from Ava Geck. My relationship with the heiress has vastly improved since our first acquaintance, in that she no longer chews gum in my presence and has consistently remembered to wear panties during our last few meetings. And she seems to have benefited from our—meaning the shop's—tutelage in other ways as well, since she's abandoned her bleached-blond hair extensions in favor of a flattering pageboy and has started dressing less like a prostitute.

But there's still some speculation as to whether or not her wedding to Prince Aleksandros will actually take place. The odds in Vegas are twenty-five to one that the nuptials will be called off.

I personally think the two of them are going to be fine.

So the fact that there's been this last-minute phone call is freaking me out. Just a little.

Not more than the fact that Chaz has a girlfriend named Valencia, though. A girlfriend named Valencia who is up for tenure.

Still, Ava has my personal cell phone number. She'll call it if she needs to.

"So," Tiffany says. "Another night of romance with you, Loverboy, and Loverboy's best friend? Hey, so what's going to happen," Tiffany wants to know, "when Loverboy heads off to France, leaving you and the best friend all alone in the big, lonely city during the long, hot summer?"

"Nothing," I say, leaning down to snag two more Diet Cokes from the mini fridge for Sylvia and Marisol. "As you know perfectly well. Chaz and I are just friends."

"Right." Tiffany smirks. "I give you guys three weeks after Luke leaves before you two hit the sheets."

"Right," I say. "Do you have this week's time sheets? Because I have to do payroll."

"Oooh," Tiffany says, reaching for the phone. "Make that three days. I'm calling Mo. I bet she'll want to put money on this."

"Don't bother," I say. "Chaz has a girlfriend. Her name is Valencia."

Tiffany narrows her eyes. "Isn't that a type of orange?"

"She has a Ph.D. in philosophy, and she's up for tenure."

Tiffany snorts. "So? Does she make him laugh?"

"Tiffany!" I am practically screaming. "What does it matter? Are you even listening to me? He has a girlfriend! And I'm engaged! Engaged to his best friend!"

"Who you don't even love," Tiffany says.

I stalk out of the front room without another word. I have no need to listen to this. I know—even if Tiffany doesn't—the truth. I love my fiancé, and he loves me. Sure, we may not have set a date yet, and yeah, okay, he's never even brought it up since New Year's, when we called our families to tell them.

And yes, whenever I think about it, I still get a tight feeling in my chest and break out in hives.

But all brides-to-be are nervous wrecks. Look at Ava Geck, on her way to marry a prince, and calling *me,* her wedding gown designer, from the private plane on her way to Greece! It's natural! It doesn't mean you're with the wrong guy! It doesn't mean that at all.

Especially when the guy everyone's been saying for months is the right one doesn't even believe in marriage in the first place. If that's not Mr. Wrong, I don't know who is.

A HISTORY *of* WEDDINGS

Weddings in colonial times were replete with customs, none of which included engagement rings. A couple intending to "tie the knot" would do so literally—the man would present his intended with a handkerchief, into which he'd tied several coins. If the woman untied the knot, it was seen as her giving the okay to get hitched. The banns—a petition to marry that was printed up and posted at a church or meetinghouse so that anyone with an objection to the union had time to say something—were posted, and the couple would wed within a few days. Women who waited to wed past the age of fourteen were pretty much considered to be old maids.

But since most of them lived to be only about thirty-five, this isn't too surprising.

Tip to Avoid a Wedding Day Disaster

You want your wedding guests to get up on the dance floor. But they're just sitting there! Maybe it's because your DJ isn't playing what they want to hear. Make sure your DJ has the following songs on his playlist, which have been scientifically proven to be irresistible to even the stodgiest partygoers everywhere:

1. Abba—"Dancing Queen"
2. Prince—"1999"
3. Gloria Gaynor—"I Will Survive"
4. Dexy's Midnight Runners—"Come on Eileen"
5. Madonna—"Holiday"
6. Deee-Lite—"Groove Is in the Heart"
7. Kanye West—"Gold Digger"
8. The Weather Girls—"It's Raining Men"
9. The B-52's—"Love Shack"
10. Village People—"YMCA"

LIZZIE NICHOLS DESIGNS™

Chapter 9

When you meet someone who can cook and do housework—
don't hesitate a minute: Marry him.

Unknown

Chaz is late. So, for that matter, is Luke. I've buzzed Chaz's apartment, but no one has answered. I'm sitting on the front stoop of his building, having carefully spread a handkerchief from inside my purse out on the step so as not to mess up my skirt. And yes, I do carry handkerchiefs. This city is filthy and you never know when you're going to need one.

And I'm waiting.

It's a gorgeous evening, so waiting on a stoop in the East Village isn't that bad. There are a lot of people out—some still hurrying home from work, some strolling around after an early supper, some just wandering with no apparent purpose. Some of them acknowledge me with a nod or smile, but many walk on by without making eye contact, like most New Yorkers, afraid that if they look you in the face, you'll ask them for money. (Though do I look like a homeless person? This is a genuine Alfred Shaheen 1950s Hawaiian sundress with a halter-style top and a full skirt with a crinoline. Would a homeless woman really be wearing that? I'm carrying a vintage Halston bag and sporting platform espadrilles too. No offense, but I look too good to be homeless.)

A group of kids have started up a rowdy game of stickball, right in the middle of the street, calling, "Car," every time a taxi turns the corner. From a window a few floors above, I hear opera being blasted.

And I can't help thinking to myself, in spite of Valencia Whatever Her Name Is . . . *I love New York.*

I do.

I didn't always. It was grim for a while. I didn't think I'd make it here, that, like Kathy Pennebaker from my hometown, I'd have to go slinking back to Ann Arbor and end up married to my high school sweetheart (except that he's gay) and shopping at the Kroger Sav-On with a couple of runny-nosed toddlers.

Not that this is the worst fate that can befall a girl. It's a perfectly fine fate, actually.

Except that the last time I saw Kathy she was buying way more cold medicine than I think anybody would need for normal, everyday use.

But I did make it in the big city. At least mostly. Oh, sure, I can't afford to eat out every night, and I had to take the 6 train to get down here, not a taxi.

And I haven't exactly got a summer share in the Hamptons like so many New York singletons my age, and I don't own a single item made by Prada.

But someday I will (well, not the Hamptons thing, because I saw what they do there on MTV, and throwing up copious amounts of Bacardi and Coke and sleeping with a different guy every weekend is not for me. And who needs Prada when you can have vintage Lilly Pulitzer?). But I mean about the taxi and eating-out thing. I'll have moo shu chicken every night! And take cabs everywhere!

But until then, I'm doing fine. And I love it here. I really do. I never, ever want to leave.

And then suddenly three of the boys from the stickball game get into an argument, and a much smaller boy tries to intervene, and one of the bigger boys says, "Suck it, Shorty," and pushes the smaller boy, making him fall down, and I cry indignantly, jumping to my feet, *"Hey!"*

"Stay out of it, lady," Shorty says, springing back up, like a top. "I can handle this."

And he bursts back into the argument his friends are having, only to be knocked down again.

"Hey," I say, coming down off the stoop. "If you kids can't play nicely together, I'm going to get your mothers!"

"And they'll knife you," a man's voice informs me. "Not the kids. The mothers."

I turn around, and my heart gives a swoop inside my chest.

But it's not Luke. It's not my fiancé, standing there in the last golden rays of the setting sun, looking impossibly handsome in a charcoal suit and yellow power tie.

It's his best friend.

Chaz is the one who's just made my heart do a loop-de-loop. I'm not even going to try to figure what that was all about.

I'm so flustered, I say the first thing that pops into my head.

"Why are you so dressed up?" I ask him, my voice gruff. I don't know why I sound so unfriendly. It's not *his* fault my heart reacted that way on seeing him without a baseball cap.

But I'm so shocked at my physical reaction to the way he looks, I can't help sounding like a twelve-year-old boy suddenly going through puberty.

"Departmental cocktail party," he says as he reaches into his pocket and pulls out his keys. His dark hair—in need of a trim, as always—falls over his eyes as he does so. I take advantage of the fact that he can't see me to take in other details about him . . . the fact that he's wearing dress shoes—Italian leather, from the looks of it, in the five-hundred-dollar range, at least—and that the suit is exquisitely and expensively cut, perfectly framing his broad shoulders. He looks totally out of place on his street, which includes a run-down offtrack-betting place on the corner, a Japanese noodle shop one building in, and a dive bar next door to that. Him standing there in a suit like that? It's as if James Bond suddenly pulled into a suburban cul-de-sac.

"Sorry I'm late," he says, looking up. I glance away the second his gaze meets mine and feel my cheeks begin to burn. I hope he won't notice. "You weren't waiting long, were you?"

"No," I lie hastily. "Not at all."

Oh God. What's *wrong* with me?

"Well, at least it's not raining," Chaz says. "Come on in and let me get you a drink."

He unlocks the outer door to his building's vestibule, and I follow him as he stops to open his mailbox and pick up his mail. It's weird, but I'm feeling strangely shy. I'm not sure if it's the loop-de-loop incident, the fact that I know about Valencia, or that Chaz is looking so unlike his usual self, but I feel almost as if I'm with a stranger, and not a guy I've known since my first day of freshman year of college, who used to make me laugh so hard over my Cap'n Crunch in the McCracken Hall cafeteria that milk would come out of my nose.

"So what's going on with you?" Chaz wants to know as he climbs the stairs to the walk-up he used to share with Shari, and now lives in solo. "Seems like this is the first time I've seen you in ages without the old ball and chain in tow."

Because I've been assiduously avoiding seeing you without Luke for protection, to keep exactly what just happened—that whole heart-flippy thing—from happening.

Only I don't say this out loud, of course.

"Oh," I say airily. His building's hallway is, if anything, even more industrial looking and depressing than my own. Although at least I'm the only one who uses mine, so it's not littered with Chinese food menus and alternative press newspapers. "Well, I've been really busy. Working. This is my busy season, so things have been crazy."

"I imagine," Chaz says. We've reached the door to his sprawling—and slope-floored—two-bedroom (if you can call an alcove a bedroom), and he's undoing the many various locks. "According to Luke, you work harder than any woman in Manhattan. He says he hardly ever sees you anymore. What with your own wedding to plan and all, things must be busier for you than ever."

Where, I'm wondering, is Valencia? Are we meeting her at the restaurant? Or is she meeting us here, at the apartment? I want to ask, but at the same time, I don't want to bring her up. I can't seem to bring myself to mention her name. Valencia. God. I hate her.

"That's me," I say instead. "Busy, busy." I let out a laugh that sounds not unlike a pony's whinny.

Chaz pauses mid-lock.

"Excuse me," he says. "But did you just whinny?"

"No," I say quickly.

"My mistake," he says and goes back to work on his locks.

He finally gets his door open, and I follow him inside, pleased by the blast of cool air that greets me from his many window units. Unlike Luke's mother's apartment, which took on a sort of fetid quality to it once I moved out (Mrs. de Villiers eventually started sending around a cleaning agency, after a weekend visit to the city proved that her son couldn't be trusted to handle the responsibility of doing the dishes or cleaning the toilet on his own), Chaz's is super-clean . . . except for the stacks of books and student papers piled everywhere.

But at least they're very tidy piles.

"So what'll you have?" Chaz asks, going into the eat-in kitchen (a rarity in Manhattan; apparently it makes up for one of the advertised bedrooms being no larger than a closet) and opening the refrigerator. "I got it all. Beer, wine, soda, vodka, gin, juice . . . what do you feel like?"

"What are you having?" I ask, leaning my elbow up against the pass-through, on which are balanced several stacks of library books.

He grabs a Corona from a six-pack on the bottom shelf and looks at me questioningly. I shake my head and say, "White wine would be good."

"Coming up," he says, and pulls out a bottle of pinot grigio from inside the refrigerator door. It's already uncorked. It's probably what Valencia drinks. That bitch. He just has to pull the stopper and pour. "So I've been meaning to ask you. What did you do to Ava Geck?"

I take the glass he offers to me. "What do you mean? I didn't do anything to her."

"Yeah, you did. She's not slutty anymore. She hasn't been on the cover of *Us Weekly* with a big 'Censored by Us' over her crotch in months."

I smile and take a sip of my wine. "Oh," I say. "*That.*"

"Yeah." Chaz, to my surprise, sets a glass of ice down next to my elbow. To go with my wine.

He remembered. He remembered that I like my white wine with a side of ice.

I tell myself it doesn't mean anything, though. Just because Luke never remembers, and Chaz does, doesn't mean a thing. It's Luke's ring I'm wearing on the third finger of my left hand, not Chaz's.

Because Chaz doesn't even believe in engagement rings. Or weddings.

"So what'd you do to her?" Chaz wants to know. "She's boring now."

"She's not *boring,*" I say. I try to keep speaking in a normal voice so he won't notice how nonplussed I am by the ice. "She's classy. She's acting more the way someone who is about to be married to a prince *should* act. I'm sure his parents are pleased."

"They might be," Chaz says. "But millions of *Us Weekly* subscribers like myself aren't. How'd you do it, anyway?"

"I merely suggested to her that it might be in her best interest not to be photographed climbing in and out of cars and boats with her legs completely spread apart," I say.

"Like I said." Chaz shrugs. "Boring. You've personally robbed thousands—perhaps millions—of teenage boys who spend their time combing the Internet looking for glimpses of Ava Geck's Brazilian of their only chance at seeing one. May I just say, on their behalf, a collective and sarcastic thanks. A lot."

I tip my wineglass in his direction. "You're welcome. They can just learn about feminine hair removal by looking at their dads' *Playboys*, the way the rest of us did."

"Oooh," Chaz says, coming out of the kitchen and into the living room, then sinking down into one of the gold couches, which are left over from his father's law offices before they got a makeover. "Is that how you found out about it? This is getting interesting. Tell me about it. What was that like for you? Did you and Shari used to look at your dads' *Playboys* together?"

I laugh. Infuriating as he is sometimes, Chaz really *can* be funny.

"Speaking of Shari," I say, joining him on one of the matching couches. "What's going on with *you*? I hear y-you're—" Here it goes. I take a long, fortifying gulp of my wine, hoping it will keep me from stammering more. "Seeing someone."

"News travels fast," Chaz says. "Yeah, I am. A woman from my department, Valencia Delgado. She's meeting us at the restaurant tonight. I think you'll like her."

Uh, no, I won't.

Where is *this* feeling coming from? The same place the loop-de-loop came from? What's happening to me? How could I have been so good for so long—six *months*—only to start falling apart now, so close to the finish line . . . or what would be the finish line, if Luke and I had ever actually gotten around to making any wedding plans? Why am I freaking out over this Valencia Delgado person? Just because she's bound to be incredibly beautiful and well read. Not at all like me. The last book I read was—God! An Agatha Christie novel someone left in the shop! What would someone getting his Ph.D. in philosophy ever see in a girl like *me*?

But wait . . . what does that matter? *I'm* not dating Chaz. He isn't even my type! My type being the kind who actually believe in marriage.

"Wow," I say, trying to sound unconcerned, although the truth is I'm consumed with gut-wrenching anxiety over meeting this woman. Which doesn't even make sense. "That's so great. I'm glad you're not still upset over what happened with Shari . . ."

"Actually," Chaz says, "Shari and I are good now. We had lunch the other day—"

"Wait." I am so astonished I completely interrupt him. "You and Shari *had lunch* the other day?"

"Yeah. And her friend, Pat," he says. He's reached up and is undoing his tie. His lovely yellow silk tie, the one that practically caused my heart to stop. "Sorry," he says when he notices the direction of my gaze. "But this thing is driving me insane. I have to go change into real clothes. Do you mind?"

I shake my head. "Go ahead," I say. Then, as he disappears down the hall, I call after him, because I can't stand not knowing more, "You had lunch with your ex-girlfriend and her new girlfriend?"

"Yeah." Chaz's muffled voice floats toward me from his bedroom. "Only Pat's not really Shari's new girlfriend, is she? They've been together, what, like half a year now. Or more, actually."

I am having trouble absorbing all of this. I dump some ice into my wine and stare at a pile of student papers sitting on the coffee table in front of me.

"So you guys are like . . . *friends* now?" I ask.

"We were always friends," Chaz calls back to me. "We just had a period where we didn't talk as much as we used to. And, of course, we no longer make the beast with two backs.

"So anyway," Chaz says, coming back into the living room. He's changed into jeans and a University of Michigan Wolverines T-shirt. One of his many baseball caps is back in its usual place. I know I should feel relieved that he's out of his heart-fluttering finery, but strangely, all I feel is confused.

This is mainly because he looks as good to me in the baseball cap as he had earlier in the suit.

"She seems good," Chaz goes on. "Shari, I mean. And Pat's nice. For someone who clearly considers me one of the hetero male oppressors."

"So," I say, unable to stop myself. I try. I really do try. But before I can clamp my mouth shut, words are pouring out of it—words I'd give anything to stuff back inside it. "I know it's none of my business, but I was just wondering if you had told Valencia your opinion on the whole marriage thing—"

"Lizzie."

It's no good, though. As usual, the words are just streaming out of me, like water from a fountain. And nothing can plug it, not even me.

"Because it really isn't a good idea to lead her on," I prattle away. "I'm just warning you for your own good, you know. I imagine a female tenure-track philosophy professor scorned is not a pretty—"

"Lizzie."

For the first time in my life, something in another human's voice actually causes my own to dry up. I close my mouth and stare. His eyes, for some reason, seem bluer than normal. His gaze blazes into mine from where he stands, looking at me from behind the pass-through.

"What?" I ask, my throat suddenly going dry. I realize, from the intensity of his gaze, that we've somehow passed from ordinary—or, in my case, anyway, mindless—conversation to something much more serious.

And, incredibly, I feel myself blushing to my hairline, my cheeks flaming hot as the asphalt outside had been before when Chaz had come walking up.

Anything, it seems, might be brought up at such a moment. The fact that for the past six months we've barely talked . . . except politely, and always in the presence of someone else (Luke).

Or the fact that six months ago, we had our tongues down each other's throats.

Is he going to bring up one of those things? And if so, which one? I'm not sure which I dread him bringing up more—the fact that I've been trying so assiduously *not* to be alone with him so we can't have a repeat performance of what had happened on New Year's Eve . . . or discussing what *actually* happened on New Year's Eve . . .

What if he comes out from behind the pass-through and tries to reenact what happened on New Year's Eve? Will I try to stop him?

Wait. Of course I will. Won't I?

Yes! Yes, of course I will! I'm engaged! To his best friend!

Except . . . his eyes are so blue right now . . . I feel as if I could go swimming in them . . .

"I swore I wasn't going to ask this," Chaz says.

I gulp. Oh God. Here it is. I try not to remember that loop-de-loop my heart gave when I saw him coming toward me down the street. I swear I don't even know what that had been about. I am not in love with Chaz. *I am not in love with Chaz.*

"Are you—"

Then I jump as the buzzer to the front door to Chaz's building goes off.

My shoulders, which I'd clenched with nervousness, sag. Whatever it was he was going to ask me, he evidently decides to drop the subject, since he says, "Huh, speak of the devil."

And he goes out into the hallway to buzz Luke in without another word.

I find that I've been clutching the sofa cushions. Slowly I release my fingers . . . as well as the breath I've been holding. I'm sweaty, as if I'd just been running a mile.

Not that I've ever *actually* run a mile. But *as if* I have.

What's going on? Why am I such a bundle of nerves? This is dinner with my boyfriend and his best friend. And his best friend's new girlfriend, the woman I'm going to murder. Nothing to worry about. What is *happening* to me?

And when is this evening going to end, so I can go home and kill myself?

A HISTORY *of* WEDDINGS

Weddings farther west in postcolonial America were short on ceremony and heavy on the partying. It was around this time that the shivaree, or charivari, became popular, a tradition based on an old French custom that included the wedding guests gathering beneath the bride and groom's bedroom window on the first night of their honeymoon and banging on pots and singing drunkenly, allegedly to drive away evil spirits . . . but mainly with the intention of forcing the groom to throw money down to them in order to make them go away. Occasionally the festivities would reach such a fevered pitch the groom would be pulled out the window, and the bride would be forced to pay a ransom if she actually wanted to enjoy her honeymoon in the company of her new husband.

They didn't call it the Wild, Wild West for nothing.

Tip to Avoid a Wedding Day Disaster

Do you need a wedding planner? While they can often save you a bundle by getting you discounts, not every bride needs one. If you're planning a large wedding, have a demanding job, or don't have a mom or sister to whom to delegate the many tasks involved in planning your dream nuptials, then hiring a wedding planner might make sense. Look for one who does wedding planning as a full-time job, who has insurance and good references, and be sure to ask how much she charges (hourly, fixed fee, or a percentage of your wedding budget).

Your wedding planner isn't supposed to be your best friend . . . but she could just save your sanity—not to mention your life!

LIZZIE NICHOLS DESIGNS™

Chapter 10

A successful marriage requires falling in love many times, always with the same person.

Germaine Greer (b.1939–), Australian-born feminist writer

I'm having a hard time picturing *The Office*'s Jim Halpert dining at the Spotted Pig, which he allegedly did once on a date with Karen. I know it's just a TV show and fictional and all, but this place is super-trendy, and part of what makes that show so endearing is that everyone on it is so tragically *un*hip.

But there are people here with the kind of glasses they wear only in Scandinavian countries and tattoos all up and down their arms and I heard a guy at the bar telling another guy that he just got late admission to Harvard Law School, and saw a girl lifting up her skirt to show her friends her new thong. Plus everybody standing outside smoking in their camouflage cargo pants with their carefully messed up—but really loaded down with product—hair is also checking their e-mail on their BlackBerries.

"*Why* are we here again?" Chaz keeps asking. We got a table only because someone Luke knows from one of his classes—a girl, Sophie—knows the guy who is seating people tonight.

"It's supposed to be good," Luke says cheerfully. "Oh, look. Sweetbreads."

"That's guts," Chaz says. "I had to stand for an hour outside to sit at a bench at a tiny table at a place that's going to serve me guts. We could have gone to the Polish place in my neighborhood and gotten guts for five dollars and no waiting. And I could be sitting in a chair and not on a bench."

"But then you wouldn't have seen that girl's thong," Valencia points out cheerfully.

"True," Chaz agrees.

I shoot Valencia a dirty look. It's not her fault, of course, that she's so perfect—tall and tan and thin with perfect straight dark hair that she's caught up in a classy single silver barrette—a lovely complement to her ruby red sleeveless sheath dress. She can't help that she's witty and charming and intelligent too. Even her pedicure is perfect.

I want to reach across the velvet banquette we're sitting on and grab her by that perfect hair and pull until her face hits the tabletop and then keep pulling until I've dragged her across the restaurant and then maybe when we've reached the bachelorette party at the table next to ours (when did the city become so full of bachelorette parties that you couldn't seem to go out without encountering one?) I'll turn her loose and say to the bachelorettes, "Have at her, girls—oh, and by the way, she's a tenure-track professor at a major private university." Then maybe, when they're done with her, I'll give her back to Chaz—if he still wants her.

Oh, wait—did I think that?

No, I didn't. Because I'm way too busy exchanging text messages with Ava Geck to think things like that.

Ava: LIZZIE, WHERE R U?

Me: *I'm at the Spotted Pig in the West Village. Why?*

Ava: I'M COMING.

Me: *What? Ava—Why aren't you in Greece?*

No response. Calls to her cell phone go immediately to voice mail. I'm not sure her "I'M COMING" actually meant that she was coming to the restaurant. Knowing Ava, it could just as easily have meant she was *coming* . . . literally, in the throes of passion, and also happened to be texting me.

It's not something I'd put past her.

"So I've been meaning to ask you guys something," Chaz says as the waitress brings the dozen oysters Luke has ordered. I'm not eating oysters tonight. Not because I don't like them, but because it's June and I can't risk a bout of food sickness. I've got twenty gowns to get to twenty nervous brides, or my name will be mud in this town.

I mean, Chez Henri's name.

"Hit me," Luke says. He's in a good mood because his classes are over. He's not sure he exactly aced his exams—he thinks he might have tanked his bio final, actually—but that doesn't seem to be bothering him too much. He's just relieved they're over, and that he's going to be getting on a plane for Paris in a couple of days.

If I weren't feeling so guilty over the fact that I've barely had two minutes to spend with him all month anyway—and won't for the next two days he's in town, either—I'd be a little miffed over just *how* excited he is to be leaving me for the summer.

"So, are you guys ever actually going to set a date, or is this just going to be the longest engagement in the history of mankind?" Chaz wants to know.

I choke on the sip of white wine I've just taken. I can't believe he asked that. I mean, it's refreshing, on the one hand, that someone is actually asking Luke *and* me—instead of just me—about the engagement for a change. Luke's the one who always seems to escape this kind of questioning—and who also seems so perfectly content with how things are going, him living in his mother's doorman building on Fifth Avenue and me living in my hovel on East Seventy-eighth, where I have to answer the door with a lighter and a can of hair spray just in case it's a rapist and not the UPS man after all.

And okay, true, I still can't even think about my own wedding without telltale hives showing up—oh God! There's one on the inside of my elbow now!

But still. Why is it that when it comes to the wedding planning, people always ask the bride how it's going and never the groom? My family's been hounding me for months. I haven't heard a peep out of the de Villierses about it. Are any of them throwing me showers or engagement parties? Um, no. At least my family's offered. Even though I've turned them all down, since I'm too busy with work even to think about that kind of thing.

And I seem to break into hives at the mere mention of the word "engagement."

"Charles," Valencia says.

That's the other thing about Valencia. She calls Chaz *Charles*. No one calls Chaz *Charles*. Except his parents.

Chaz can't stand his parents.

"No, no, it's okay," Luke says, after slurping down one of the Caraquets. "Of course we're going to set a date. We were thinking September, right, Lizzie?"

I stare at him in total astonishment. This is—literally—the first I've heard of this. "We were?"

"Well, that's when there's an opening in the rental schedule at Mirac," Luke says. "And it won't be too hot then. And that's when most of my parents' friends will be back from their summer places. We want to make sure they can come, because they're the ones who are going to pony up with the best gifts." He winks at me.

I continue to stare at him. I have no idea what he's talking about. I mean, I do, but I can't believe he's saying it. Out loud.

"And that should give you plenty of time to start planning things," he goes on. "Three months is enough time, right?"

I look down. It's amazing. But there's another hive popping up inside my other elbow.

"I . . ." I can't stop staring at the angry red welts in the romantic restaurant lighting. The walls are red. Just like Valencia's dress. Just like my hives. "I don't know. I guess. But . . . don't you have to be back for school?"

"I can miss the first couple weeks of classes," Luke says with a shrug. "It's no big deal."

Something in his tone causes me to look up from my hives—there are two new ones—and into his face.

"Wait," I say. "You *are* going back to school in the fall. Aren't you, Luke?"

"Of course." Luke grins at me, that handsome, easy smile that so enchanted me from that first moment I met him on the train to Sarlat. "Lizzie . . . you look like something just went down the wrong way. Is everything all right?"

"She's been working too hard," Chaz says, speaking for the first time since popping his most unwelcome question. "Look at her. She's got those dark circles under her eyes."

I fling my hands to my face, horrified. "I do not!"

"Charles," Valencia says again, grinning. Her teeth are perfectly white and even. I wonder how she has time for tenure-tracking between flossing.

"Does she even sleep anymore?" Chaz wants to know.

"She's like a machine," Luke says. "I've never seen anybody work so hard."

"Of *course* I'm working hard," I say, flinging open my handbag and digging through it for my compact mirror. "It's June! What do you think happens in June? That's when people get married. Normal people, I mean, who actually *talk* about when they're going to get married, instead of avoiding the subject like it's a ticking bomb that has to be defused the way *we* do, Luke. I've been working on twenty gowns, all at the same time. I'm trying to start a name for myself, you know. Single-handedly, I might add, since my boss has been out sick for the past half a year. And having you guys tell me I have circles under my eyes and that I work too hard totally doesn't help!"

"Lizzie," Chaz says. I can see him staring at me from behind the compact, which I hold up to check on the circles. "I'm totally teasing you. You look beautiful. As always."

"Really, Lizzie," Luke says. He picks up another oyster and swallows it without chewing. "What happened to your sense of humor?"

"She's terribly solipsistic, isn't she?" I hear Valencia murmur, though I know she hadn't meant me to. I'll have to look up the word "solipsistic" later.

I feel tears prick the corners of my eyes. I don't know what's wrong with me. But I do know I want to kill everyone at the table. I really do.

Starting with Valencia.

"And the only reason I don't talk about the wedding," Luke goes on, "is that you always seem to stress out about it so much whenever I bring it up. I know your family wants to have it at their house. I also know you'd rather die . . . but you can't seem to figure out how to tell them that. So I thought it would be better for me to leave it alone until you figure it all out for yourself. That's it. It's not that I don't want to marry you anymore, or anything like that, you knucklehead."

Luke reaches over, drags me toward him, and kisses me on top of my head. I keep my gaze on the tabletop. I'm afraid that if I look up, everyone will see the tears—and shame—in my eyes.

I can't believe I wanted to kill him.

Also that I still sort of want to.

I don't even know why. Or what's wrong with me. Oh God.

What's wrong with me?

"Aw," Chaz says about the kiss. "That is just so sweet."

"Shut up, Chaz," I say, still not meeting anyone's gaze.

"Yeah, shut up, Chaz," Luke says. He's grinning again and helping himself to another oyster.

"So, September," Valencia says. "That's quite soon, isn't it?"

"I don't know about September," I say, digging through my purse again. I'm looking for my lip gloss. "I have a couple of gowns due in September. I don't know if I'll have them ready in time . . . let alone my *own* gown." The words "my own gown" cause my stomach to give a lurch. If there'd been anything but wine in it, I'm pretty sure it would have come up.

"Lizzie," Luke says in a warning voice.

"Well, what do you want me to do, Luke?" I ask, knowing I sound petulant, but not caring. "I'm just saying, things are going really well at the shop and if it keeps up like this, September should be a busy time for me as well—"

"When *isn't* a busy time for you?" Luke wants to know. "I feel like I hardly ever see you anymore."

"Well, you're not exactly Mr. Availability yourself, taking a job in *Paris* for the summer," I snap.

"Hey now, kids," Chaz says. "Can't we all just get along?"

"I took that job for *us,*" Luke says. "To pay for our wedding."

"Oh, right," I say. "A wedding we're having at your house, apparently. Which is a *vineyard*. The booze and venue are already paid for. How much can it cost? Stop using the cost of the wedding as an excuse for why you're leaving."

Luke stares at me. "Hey," he says, looking hurt. "Where'd *that* come from?"

The truth is, I have no idea. I really don't. I just know the words are out there, floating around, already said.

And there's nothing I can do to stuff them back into my mouth.

And I don't really feel like apologizing for them this time.

"Has it ever occurred to you," I demand instead, "that I might rather have a smaller wedding, one that doesn't require my fiancé having to be gone for the whole summer, working in France, to pay for it?"

"Is that really what you want, Lizzie?" Luke asks, a bit of acid in his tone. "Because I think that can be arranged. I think your mother already said we could get married in your family's backyard, with your sisters fighting over who can make the tackiest Jell-O mold, or whatever it is, and your grandmother passed out on the lawn for the entertainment."

For a second, it's as if all activity in the restaurant freezes. I suck in my breath.

Then Chaz groans, dropping his face into his hands, "Tell me you didn't just go there, man."

But Luke only glares at me across the table, his expression defiant. He's not backing down.

I am, though.

Because suddenly, I know what's going on with me. I know *exactly* what's going on with me.

And what's going on with me is that I'm done. I can't take it anymore.

I snatch up my bag, scoot out from behind the table, and say, "You don't even *know* my family. Because in all this time, you've still never even bothered to come home with me to meet them."

Luke's expression has lost some of its defiance.

"Lizzie," he says. "Look—"

"No." I thrust a heavily callused finger in his face. I may not have a pretty manicure like Valencia, but I bet my fingers have created way more lace ruching than hers ever have. I've worked my ass off for these calluses. And I'm damned proud of them. "No one disses my grandmother. Especially if they've never even met her."

"Lizzie," he says, his expression contrite. "I'm—"

"No," I interrupt him. I can barely see him, my vision is so cloudy with tears. But I'm hoping he isn't noticing that part. "If that's how you feel about my family, Luke, why don't you just go marry *yourself*? Since that's who you're obviously so in love with anyway."

Okay, not the wittiest of comebacks. But it's all I can think of in the heat of the moment, what with the tears and all.

I do see Chaz raise his eyebrows, as stunned as I am by my outburst. Valencia can't seem to raise her gaze from her wineglass, she's so embarrassed to be seen with me. But I can't back down now. I don't *want* to back down. Instead, I turn on my heel and stalk out of the room, ignoring Luke as he stands up and says, "Lizzie. *Lizzie,* come on."

Fortunately a waitress bearing a huge tray of Cosmopolitans swoops past me, blocking his path, and I hurry downstairs and outside, toward Perry Street . . . where a black stretch limo is pulling up just as I step off the curb to look for a cab to flag down. As I peer past the limo, hoping to see a cab with the TAXI sign lit up, meaning it's available, one of the limo's rear smoked windows rolls down and a familiar voice calls, "Lizzie? Oh my God."

And Ava Geck, wearing a spangled pink tube top beneath a pair of what appear to be white rubber lederhosen, leans out the window and says, "Get in, quick, before anyone sees me."

"Ava, what are you doing here?" I am not unconscious of the fact that everyone has already seen her. Everyone gathered in front of the Spotted Pig has looked up from his or her BlackBerry and is whispering, *Oh my God! It's Ava Geck! You know, Get it at Geck's!*

"Why," I ask, thoroughly confused, "aren't you in Greece, Ava?"

"I'll tell you in the car," Ava says. "Please. Just get in."

"Ava." I rub at the tears still sliding around in the corners of my eyes. "What happened? You're supposed to be getting married *tomorrow*."

"I know," Ava says. "Just get in, and I'll explain."

"Lizzie!"

I throw a frantic glance over my shoulder and see Luke coming out the door of the Spotted Pig, his napkin still in one hand.

I'm surprised—I really hadn't thought he'd follow me—but I don't hesitate a second longer. I fling open the closest door to Ava's limo and dive in.

"Go," I yell to the driver. "Please, just go!"

"Hey," Ava says as I scramble over her in my haste to grab a seat. "Is that your boyfriend? He's cute."

"Yes," I say. "Please, can we go? I have to get out of here."

"Lizzie." Luke hurries up to the limo's still-wide-open window. "Where are you going?"

"Please go," I beg Ava's driver, who surprises me by doing just that.

And soon Luke, the Spotted Pig, and all the hipsters standing outside it, busily texting with their BlackBerries, are just tiny specks in the distance.

A HISTORY *of* WEDDINGS

The Victorians were the ones who took weddings—as they did almost everything—to a whole other level. The industrial revolution proved that just about anything could be mass-produced, and soon savvy merchants realized that they could convince their wealthier customers not to be content with mere home-baked wedding cakes and homespun bridal gowns . . . no!

Now, instead of needing bridesmaids to trick evil spirits or as armed warriors, the modern bride needed them to help with invitations, choosing the cake, floral arrangements, her gown, *their* gowns—you name it.

Pretty crafty of those shop owners, huh?

And so the wedding as we know it today was born. Alleluia . . . or curses, as the case may be.

Tip to Avoid a Wedding Day Disaster

Wedding costs breakdown, or—who pays for what (Remember, this is traditionally. With today's more modern couples opting to pay for their weddings themselves, things are changing. But up until recently, the norm was the following):

The Bride:

Thank-you gifts for the maid of honor, bridesmaids, and hostess

The wedding gown, headpiece, and accessories

The groom's ring

Flower-girl basket and ring-bearer pillow

Hotel accommodations for any attendants who will be arriving from out of town

The Groom:

The marriage license

Thank-you gifts for the best man and groomsmen

The bride's engagement ring

The bride's wedding ring

Clothing (tuxedo rental) and accessories

The bride's flowers

Corsages for mothers/grandmothers and boutonnieres for groomsmen

Clergyman/officiant fee

Limousine service/transportation to and from the wedding and reception

Hotel accommodations for any groomsmen who will be arriving from out of town

The Bride and Groom:

Wedding pictures

Miscellaneous accessories (wedding favors, goblets, napkins/printed items)

Thank-you gifts for the flower girl and ring bearer

Thank-you cards

Any overnight accommodations for themselves

Their honeymoon arrangements, unless another relative or friend offers to pay for it as a wedding gift

Parents of the Groom:

Dress/suit and accessories

The rehearsal dinner

Their hotel accommodations

Bridesmaids:

Dresses and accessories

Wedding shower

Groomsmen:

Clothing (tuxedo rental) and accessories

Bachelor party

Parents of the Flower Girl/Ring Bearer:

Dress, suit/tuxedo rental, and accessories

Hotel accommodations if arriving from out of town

Parents of the Bride:

Everything else

LIZZIE NICHOLS DESIGNS™

Chapter 11

Marriage is the perfection of what love aimed at, ignorant of what it sought.

Ralph Waldo Emerson (1803–1882), American essayist, poet, and leader of the Transcendentalist movement

"What are you and Luke fighting about?" Ava wants to know. She's cradling Snow White on her slim, tanned thighs. Besides the tube top and white rubber lederhosen, she is also wearing pink suede platform boots. I suppose I should be grateful that both her boobs and crotch are completely covered for once, but rubber *and* suede . . . in late June?

"Just wedding stuff," I lie to her, although I know I should be nicer and tell her the truth, since she has, in a sense, just rescued me. The only problem is . . . I don't know what the truth is, exactly.

And I actually have more pressing concerns at the moment. Like why I'm in a stretch limo with Ava Geck.

"Ava, what are you doing here?" I ask. "Why aren't you in Greece?"

"I couldn't go through with it," Ava says simply, then gasps and seizes my arm. "Oh my God! What happened to you? Lizzie—has Luke been *beating* you?"

I look down at the hives, which have now broken out all over the insides of both my arms. In a way, they do resemble bruises.

"No," I say with a laugh, because the idea of Luke ever hitting me is so absurd. I could probably knock him clear into New Jersey. "They're just hives. I get them every time I think about . . . you know."

"Butt sex?" Ava asks understandingly.

"No," I cry, ripping my arm from her grasp. "My wedding. And what do you mean, you couldn't go through with it? You mean you just . . . *canceled* your wedding to Prince Aleksandros?"

"That's about it," Ava says with a sigh, patting Snow White on the head as the poor dog trembles in the icy blast from the limo's air conditioner. "I was just boarding Daddy's private jet, and suddenly it hit me: I'm about to become someone's wife. I was like . . . are you *shitting* me? I'm only twenty-three! I haven't even been to *college.* What am I doing, becoming someone's *wife*? So I jumped back into the car and I've been riding around ever since, trying to get my head together."

I gaze at Ava, truly touched by her words. Especially since I'm twenty-three too. "So you've decided to go to college? Ava, that is so great!"

"Hell, no, I'm not going to college," Ava says, looking shocked. "Are you kidding me? I'm just saying there's so many things *like* going to college that I haven't done. I'm not throwing my life away yet on some guy, even if he *is* a prince. I have shit to do. I don't know what, but . . . like, I was thinking I should cut an album. Something classy, you know? Like Hilary Duff."

I blink at her. "Well . . . yes. Yes, that is definitely something you could do."

"And I don't even have my own clothing line yet," Ava goes on. "My parents own one of the biggest discount department store chains in the world, and I don't have my own clothing line yet? What the hell am I *thinking*?"

"Exactly," I say. "What the hell *are* you thinking? Although, Ava . . . you can do all these things and still be married, you know. It's not like Prince Aleksandros would try to stop you. Not if he really loved you. He'd probably be proud of you."

"But that's just it," Ava says, looking down sadly at Snow White. "I don't think he would be. You know . . . this is partly your fault, Lizzie. My having to cancel my wedding, I mean."

"Me?" I gape at her, horror-struck. "What did *I* have to do with it?"

"Because since I've been coming to you, and you've been, like, helping me with my public image and stuff, Alek's kinda . . . I don't know. Lost interest in me. Like he keeps asking me how come I don't show my cootchie anymore. I think he *liked* it when I did stuff like that. Because it drove his parents completely insane. They were totally against his marrying me, you know. Which I think only made him *more* into me. But now that I've started to act a little classier, they've been a lot nicer to me. And that's made Alek completely lose interest."

My jaw sags. Although I guess I shouldn't be surprised. This explains so much about Ava's very conservative choices when it came to her wedding gown. And why she'd come to me in the first place. Sure, she could have gone to Vera Wang, but there'd been a small part of her that had still been rebelling . . . just a little.

It's all beginning to make sense. She'd wanted to please her fiancé's parents while still retaining some small part of herself.

But in doing so, it sounded like she'd turned off her fiancé.

Oops.

"So you're calling it off," I say, "before Aleksandros can?"

"That's just it," Ava says in disgust. "I don't think he ever was going to call it off. That's how gutless he is. Like, he'll stand up to his parents by marrying a total slut. But he would never *call off* the wedding to that slut, because that would make him look bad in the press."

I reach over and give her warm, bare shoulder a reassuring pat. "Ava," I say. "You're not a slut."

"Oh, I totally am," Ava says matter-of-factly. "But that's okay. I'd rather be a slut than a dickless hypocrite, like Alek. I'm just sorry about your dress."

I shake my head. "My dress?"

"The beautiful wedding dress you designed for me," Ava says.

"Oh," I say, laughing. "Don't worry about *that*! I'm sure I'll find someone else to buy it. Ava Geck's wedding dress? Are you kidding? I'll probably be able to sell it for a fortune on eBay."

Ava pouts at me. "I'm not giving it back," she says. "That thing is mine. I was thinking maybe you could make it shorter, dye it purple, slap some sequins on it, and I could wear it to the MTV Video Music Awards in September. That way tons of people will see it, and you'll still get the exposure you deserve. I should get lots of airtime, because I'm giving out the Viewer's Choice VMA. And Tippy asked me to go with him 'cause he's still got that restraining order out on his wife. That was going to be a problem before—you know, being his escort if I was married to Alek—but now that I'm not, it should be all good."

"Oh," I say, taken aback. "Um . . . sure. I could do that. No problem."

"Awesome." Ava looks a lot happier. The limo has made its way uptown via Sixth Avenue, and now we're snaking our way through Central Park, one of my favorite drives in Manhattan—which I certainly never thought I'd be making via limo. We're gliding past couples taking romantic horse and carriage rides, and less romantic pedicab rides. I wonder if they're looking at the smoked-glass windows of the limo and trying to guess who the celebrity is inside.

I'm betting none of them is guessing Ava Geck and her wedding gown designer.

"So what are you going to do now?" I ask, conscious that my stomach is growling a little. There's nothing in it but white wine. I'm hoping Ava's going to say that she's dropping me off at home so I can get something to eat . . . or at the very least, that she's going to suggest the two of us grab something somewhere. I don't know how much longer I can go without sustenance of the nonalcoholic variety. Ava may be able to go for hours on just a PowerBar, but I'm not that kind of girl.

"Um," Ava says. "Yeah. That's why I was trying to reach you."

I perk up. "You want to grab some dinner? You want to get some sushi or something?" Another thing Tiffany, Monique, and I have managed to do is expand Ava's dining horizons, so that she now eats more than just cheeseburgers and protein bars. She has consequently developed an almost pathological love for sushi . . . which isn't actually unusual for someone who's never tried it before. Wasabi has known addictive qualities. "There's Atlantic Grill right over on Third Avenue. Or Sushi of Gari . . ."

"Not exactly," Ava says. "I mean, we can totally get something to eat if you want. But I actually need a favor."

"Oh sure," I say. "Anything you want."

"Oh goody," Ava says, grinning widely. "Joey, she said yes!"

Little Joey, I realize belatedly, is sitting in the front seat beside the driver, half hidden by the privacy screen, which Ava lowers to deliver this news.

"Oh, hey, Lizzie," he calls to me from the vast expanse of leather seats and twinkling halogen lights in the ceiling between us. "How you doing?"

"Hi, Joey," I call back a bit hesitantly, since I'm suddenly realizing I have no idea what I've just agreed to. "I'm good. Um, Ava?"

"What?" she asks a little distractedly, having dug out her Sidekick, into which she is tapping with some urgency.

"What, exactly, did I just promise to do for you?"

"You're letting me stay at your place, of course," Ava says with some surprise, not even looking up from the screen.

I stare at her. "My place? You mean . . . in my *apartment*?"

"Well, I can't stay at my place," Ava says, finally looking up. Ava's condo, which is on East End Avenue near the mayor's house, Gracie Mansion, is within easy walking distance of mine (not that Ava ever walks). Ava chose to move to the Upper East Side—to the consternation of many a poodle-toting matron there—because that's where she happened to find the only condo that met her exacting standards (the aforementioned four bedrooms, three baths, and an eat-in kitchen with at least two thousand square feet of outdoor terrace and full southern exposure).

But she'd also fallen in love with the nearby Carl Schurz Park, which is right by the river, and includes a dog run built especially for small dogs.

"My place is crawling with paparazzi," she goes on. "Word's already getting out that I left Alek at the altar. They've got all the hotels staked out too, and my parents' and friends' places, as well. You're my only hope, Lizzie. I figured you could just stay at Luke's."

I'm shaking my head before the words are fully out of her mouth. "No," I say. "No, I can't stay at Luke's." The thought fills me with panic. I don't want to see Luke. I . . . I can't see Luke. Not again. Not this soon.

"Well," Ava says, looking slightly annoyed. "Fine. Then I'll stay at Luke's, and he can stay with you."

"No," I say, still shaking my head. "You can't stay at Luke's either. Because Luke and I are . . . we're . . . we're in a fight. Remember? Remember how he came running out of the restaurant after me just now, and I was like, *Drive*? *Please drive?* Remember that?" My eyes fill with tears again at the memory. Oh God. What's happening to me?

Little Joey says, from the front seat, "She did say that."

Ava screws up her face, trying to remember. "Oh yeah," she says. "Well.

Can't I just stay at your apartment with you, then? It'll just be for a few days. Until all this blows over. You'll hardly know I'm there. Snow White and I don't take up much room."

I glance at Little Joey. Ava, noticing the direction of my gaze, laughs.

"Oh, don't worry about him," she says. "*He* won't be staying there. He has his own place in Queens."

I want to suggest that Joey's place in Queens might be the ideal hideout for Ava. The paparazzi would never think to look for her there.

But then I remember what she said, about all of this being my fault. And so instead, I say, "Ava, my place . . . it's just a one bedroom. There's only one bathroom. And it doesn't have southern exposure. Believe me, it's not luxurious—"

"I don't mind, I'm used to roughing it. I served forty-eight hours at CRDF, you know," Ava assures me, referring to the Century Regional Detention Facility in Los Angeles, which housed her when she did her time for driving under the influence.

"My place isn't as bad as *prison,*" I say, slightly annoyed.

"Oh, I knew you'd say yes," Ava says, throwing her spindly arms around me and giving me a hug, and partially suffocating Snow White in the process. "This is gonna be so fun! Like camping out or something! We'll order in, and do our nails, and watch me on TV, and stay up all night talking bad about our boyfriends. Your having a fight with Luke makes it just perfect!"

I say in a strangled voice, since her deathlike grip is cutting off my oxygen, "I can't stay up all night, Ava. I have gowns I have to get finished."

"That's even better!" Ava cries, releasing me suddenly. "I can help!"

"Okay," I say. I massage my neck where she's squeezed it. I can't believe this is happening. "I guess."

"I'm so excited," Ava declares. "Vincent, make the turn onto Seventy-eighth. We're getting out there!"

Sooner than I could have imagined possible, Ava Geck, her Chihuahua, and seven of her suitcases are in my apartment, and her bodyguard is saying good night, while assuring me he'll be by at nine tomorrow morning to pick Ava up to take her to the New York Health and Racquet Club to meet her trainer for her workout. She's on my couch—though we've already established that she'll be sleeping in my bed, and I'll be on the couch, thanks to her sciatica—flipping channels with the remote, trying to see if news of her broken-off royal wedding is on E! yet. I'm supposed to be ordering dinner—moo shu chicken is out. Ava wants a Caesar salad and fettuccine Alfredo from Sistina, which is a four-star Italian restaurant on Second Avenue that doesn't deliver . . . except apparently for Ava.

I'm on the phone with the restaurant's maître d' when the buzzer to my apartment goes off, causing Snow White to burst into a cacophony of yips and Ava to squeal excitedly, "The food's here!"

"The food can't be here," I say. "I'm still on hold with Guiseppe."

Ava throws me a panicked look. She's changed from her rubber lederhosen into a pink velour sweatsuit. Although she has the word "Juicy" written across her rear end, I find this preferable to her many outfits that actually reveal her rear end, or at least the brown-cheeked moons of it. And so I am allowing her to wear it. But only indoors.

"It's the paparazzi!" she cries. "They've found me! Already!"

"It can't be the paparazzi," I say. "Unless you told someone you're here."

"Only my mom," Ava says. "And Tippy. And he wouldn't tell anyone. He knows what it's like to be hounded mercilessly by the press."

I still don't have the slightest idea who DJ Tippycat is, but I take her word for it that he wouldn't rat her out. I hand her the phone and go to the wall intercom and push the TALK button. "Who is it?" I ask in my meanest voice, which I reserve only for answering the intercom.

"Lizzie, it's me," Luke says. "Can I come up?"

I stare at the intercom as if live snakes have suddenly come bursting out of it. Luke? In all the excitement with Ava, I'd completely forgotten about my fight with him.

Ava hasn't, however. She bolts upright. "Is that Luke?" she asks, her bright eyes wide. "Are you gonna buzz him in? I can totally make myself scarce. You won't even know I'm here. I'll hide in the bathroom."

I continue to stare at the intercom, uncertain what to do. On the one hand, I'm still really, really mad at him. On the other hand . . . it's Luke. I love him.

At least . . . I think I do.

And yet . . . could he have been a bigger jerk?

"Unless you want me to pour water on his head," Ava offers generously.

She's gotten up from the couch and gone to the window, where you can look down and see whoever is standing in the doorway—providing they aren't hiding beneath the awning, as the UPS man is wont to do when it's raining. "Because I could totally do that for you, if you want me to. Or pee. I could pour pee on him. I haven't gone yet. I could go in a cup and dump it—"

"That's okay," I say quickly. "I—I'll just go talk to him outside. You go ahead and order. I'll have whatever you're having."

Ava looks dubious. "Are you sure? Because I've been holding it all day—"

"I'm sure," I say. "And you really shouldn't hold it, Ava. You could give yourself a urinary tract infection that way. I'll be right back."

I grab my keys and hurry out of the apartment and down the stairs, a little leery of leaving Ava to her own devices in my place . . . but also a little relieved to have a moment to myself. Even if, the next minute, I know I'm going to have to be dealing with Luke.

Who says, "Oh," when I undo the many locks to the outside door and step onto the stoop into the warm evening air beside him. "I thought . . . I thought you might buzz me up."

"I can't," I say unsmilingly. "I have company."

Luke looks surprised. I'm pleased to see he isn't smiling, either. At least he's taking this thing seriously. So often, when we argue, he seems to think my anger is amusing, as if I'm a kitten who's upset about someone hiding her catnip mouse. I'm not a kitten.

And I'm tired of being treated like one.

"Company?" he echoes. *Now* he's smiling. "What, did you and that girl from the limo go and pick up some sailors while you were out cruising around or something?"

"No," I say, still not smiling. "Ava's going to be spending a few days at my place. She and her fiancé just broke up, and she can't go back to her place because it's being staked out by the paparazzi."

Luke's smile vanishes. "Lizzie," he says. "Jesus. So, you're just letting her stay with you? Why can't she stay in a hotel?"

"Because—" I break off and glare at him. "You know what? Who cares? She's not. She's staying with me. What's the big deal?"

"The big deal," Luke says, "is that she's a client. And you're treating her like she's a friend. You can't get business mixed up with your personal life, Lizzie. This is exactly what we were just talking about, back at the restaurant."

"Oh, really," I say. I'm ignoring, with effort, a man who is walking by with an Italian greyhound on a leash. The man is pretending he's not listening to our conversation, but he totally is. I don't care, really, except that the dog is distracting. It's so . . . skinny. I know it was born that way, but it's still freakish. How does it digest its food with such a tiny stomach? "And just what does my grandmother's drinking problem have to do with the fact that I refurbish wedding gowns for a living?"

Luke reaches out to grab both my shoulders in his hands and gives me a gentle shake.

"Hey," he says in a gentler tone than he's used until now. "I'm sorry about that. Okay? I know I was out of line, and I apologize. I tried to apologize there in the restaurant—I chased after you and would have told you so right there, but you jumped into that limo and were gone. If everyone standing out there hadn't told me that was Ava Geck you were with, I would have . . . well, I totally would have thought you'd been kidnapped or something."

"No, I wasn't kidnapped, Luke," I say, trying not to notice how good his hands feel on my skin. I can't let sensations like that distract me. "I just . . . we just . . . I want . . ."

What am I saying? What *do* I want?

Where am I going with this?

Why won't that man take his dog and go somewhere else? Seventy-eighth Street is really long. Does his dog *have* to pee right there in front of my shop?

"Luke . . . I've been thinking. And I think . . ." The next thing I know, words are coming out of my mouth that I honestly don't remember thinking. They just come out of my mouth. Like air.

Or vomit.

"Luke," I hear myself say. "I think we need to take a break."

Oh. My. God.

A HISTORY *of* WEDDINGS

The first hand-printed wedding invitations in the Middle Ages were done in calligraphy by monks, who were commissioned to do so by royalty. By the time metal plate engraving had been invented, engraved invitations—the kind that come with a fancy sheet of tissue paper on top, to keep the print from smudging—became more popular than calligraphy. This same kind of engraving is still used today (and is why you still get tissue paper with fancier wedding invitations). The traditional double envelope in which wedding invitations are so often sent stems from the fact that in olden times, mail was delivered via horse, and no one wanted the dainty hands of the recipient to be dirtied as she opened her invitation. It was assumed a butler would open the icky outer envelope and hand the clean inner envelope to his mistress.

How sad for us modern, butler-less mail openers, daily soiling our hands on germy outside envelopes!

Tip to Avoid a Wedding Day Disaster

Remember, your wedding invitations should never *be mailed at the last minute . . . but you don't want to mail them out too early, either! The ideal time is somewhere between eight weeks and one month before the actual wedding day. Six weeks in advance is perfect.*

And please, never *use a laser-printed address label on your invitations. That's considered beyond tacky.* Hand-written only! *Yes, you* can *advertise for and hire an engineering student with impeccable handwriting for this task.*

LIZZIE NICHOLS DESIGNS™

Chapter 12

A good marriage is that in which each appoints the other guardian of his solitude.

—Rainer Maria Rilke (1875–1926), German poet

Luke stares at me. "You think we need to *what*?" he says, his grip on my shoulders loosening.

"Oh!"

I let out the sound in a whoosh. At least I think it was me. I realize I can't even be sure what sounds are coming out of my mouth anymore. That's how little control I have.

I sink down onto the top step of the stoop and hug my knees to my chest. The man with the dog, I notice, has hurried away. Apparently, he is no longer enjoying the show—the show of a girl in vintage Shaheen going crazy right in front of him.

"Lizzie." Luke sits down on the step beside me. "What do you mean, you think we need to take a break?"

"I don't know," I groan into my knees. God, what is happening to me? "I just . . . I mean, you're going to France for three months anyway . . . so we're kind of taking a break, whether we want one or not."

What am I saying? *What* is coming out of my mouth? I do not want a break from Luke. I do not. I love Luke.

Don't I?

"It's just," I hear myself saying, though at no point did I formulate the words in my head beforehand, "I know that you love me, Luke. But I don't always feel like you *respect* me. Or at least . . . not my job. It's like you think it's just this hobby I have that I'm doing for fun until something more serious comes along. But that's not what it is. This is really what I do. What I want to do for the rest of my life."

Luke blinks down at me with his gorgeous, sleepy eyes. "Lizzie, I know that. And of course I respect what you do. I don't know what would ever have given you the impression that I don't. All I meant, when I said that about Ava, was that I've worked in the business world for a lot of years, and we just never let our clients take advantage of us the way I think you sometimes do."

"It's not what you said about Ava," I explain. "It's the way you just thought I could leave with you to go to Paris for the summer. You know. When you brought it up."

Luke stares at me. "Last *January*? You're bringing up something I said in January? *Now?*"

I nod. "And maybe I do business a different way than you do," I point out. "But I'm not you. Different doesn't mean it's wrong."

"Point taken," Luke says. "Listen, Lizzie—"

"And," my mouth goes on. Why, oh, why, won't it just shut up? "I don't think you respect my family very much, either. I know they aren't as sophisticated as your family is. But you've never even met them. So how do you even know? And that's another thing. You've been going out with me for a year. For six months of that year we've been engaged. And you've never met *anyone* in my family. And yet you make remarks like the one you did tonight—"

"I apologized for that already," Luke says, moving to put his arm around me. "I know what your grandmother means to you. And if I hadn't—well, let me tell you, Chaz really let me know, back at the restaurant. But, Lizzie, you have to admit, you complain about your sisters a lot. And your grandmother . . . well, everyone talks about her drinking problem. And you know the only reason I haven't met your family is because I've been busy with school—"

"You could have come home with me at Christmas," I interrupt, "instead of going to France with your family. Or at spring break. But instead, you went to Houston to see your mother. And my family isn't rich like yours. It's not like they can go jetting off to New York to meet you like yours can."

I glance at him to see how he reacts to this. He isn't looking at me, however. He's looking at the Honda Accord parked across the sidewalk in front of us.

"Yes," he says in a quiet voice. "You're right. I probably should have."

"Because meeting my family isn't important to you," I say. I don't want to say it. It's like the words are being wrenched out of me. Like Gran, that time she got completely wasted on cooking sherry and decided to finally go after that balky kitchen pipe with Dad's giant wrench. The sherry had given her superhuman strength, and she'd managed to loosen the joint and remove all this gunk that had been trapped inside for six months. It just started spilling out.

Just like all this gunk is pouring out of me. Gunk that probably should have come out of me last January. It's all spilling out now. Even though I don't want it to. I really don't. Not on my nice clean relationship.

But I guess that's what gunk is. Stuff that sort of has to come out eventually.

"That's not true," Luke begins to protest, but I cut him off.

"Don't say you didn't have time," I say. "If it had been important to you, you could have made the time. It was important to me," I go on. "And it's important to them. They keep asking me when they're going to meet you. It would be nice if they could meet you before the wedding."

Luke opens his mouth to say something, but I barrel on.

"But it's too late now. Because you're leaving for France the day after tomorrow. And so," my voice adds ruthlessly, without my consent, "whether you want to call it that or not, we're taking a break. Because I need to think, Luke. I need to think about what's going on here. What we're doing. What *I'm* doing."

"Right," he says.

And he removes his arm from around my shoulders.

We sit for a moment in silence. But the city isn't silent, of course. Taxis rumble by, and a siren sounds over on Third Avenue. I'm not sure, but I think I hear a window open above our heads. Ava is eavesdropping.

That's all I hope she's dropping, anyway.

There's another thing I think I hear in the silence that's fallen between us as well: the sound of my heart breaking.

* * *

When I get back upstairs to the apartment, Ava is on the couch again, innocently flipping channels while still holding the phone to her ear. She looks up and smiles at me as I come in, fending off Snow White's enthusiastic mini assault.

"So?" she asks. "How'd it go?"

"Like you weren't listening," I say, dropping my keys in the fruit bowl I keep for this purpose on the bookshelf by the door.

"I was not," Ava says with a sniff. Then, seeing my expression, she says, "Well, okay, I totally was. But I couldn't hear. I was all ready to pour orange juice on his head if you started crying, though. Did you? I didn't think you did."

"I didn't," I say, and flop down onto the couch beside her. Snow White leaps up onto my lap, and I pat her distractedly. "We're taking a break."

"Really?" Ava stares at me, bug-eyed. "What does that mean?"

"I don't know." I shrug. "I just heard the words coming out of my mouth, and I went with them. That happens to me sometimes." Try all the time.

It hadn't made any sense, either. I mean, that I had said what I had to Luke. What had I been thinking, asking for a break? I love Luke. At least . . . I'm pretty sure I love Luke. I know I love waking up in the morning before he has and just staring at him and his incredible eyelashes, resting so dark and sooty against his cheekbones. I love how, when he's awake, those dark eyes still look so sleepy, like they hold the promise of a thousand secret dreams.

Most of all, I love that I'm one of those dreams, me, Lizzie Nichols, who no boy in my high school ever even asked out, because I just wasn't the kind of girl you asked out in high school . . . unless you were a gay boy and you didn't want anyone to know that, of course.

Oh yeah. I forgot. Gay boys asked me out. A lot. I was always the fat girl gay boys asked out to make their mothers happy.

So what was I doing? What was I doing telling this guy—this guy that I love so much, and who, more important, loves me back—that I wanted to take a break? Am I crazy?

Why couldn't I, for once in my life, have kept my mouth shut?

But the words just came out, and once they were spoken, I couldn't stuff them back. Well, I mean, I *could* have, but . . .

I didn't want to.

And that was maybe the weirdest part of all.

"Oh my God," Ava gasps. "How did he take it?"

"He was okay with it, I think," I say. Actually, maybe *that* was the weirdest part of all. "I mean, he says he understands that my work has to come first right now, and that I don't have time to be planning a wedding at the moment. But . . . he's still leaving for France. It's not like he offered to stay. Even though I told him I'd be happy with a much smaller wedding that didn't cost as much, so he wouldn't have to go work there. He's still going."

Is it wrong that this bothers me as much as it does?

Ava makes a face. "Men are all such dicks."

Yeah, okay. So . . . not wrong.

"Tell me about it," I say. I look at the phone Ava is holding to her ear. "Are you still on hold with Sistina?"

"Oh, no," Ava says. "They'll be over with the food in half an hour. This is your grandmother. She wanted to know how to record something with a season pass on TiVo. So I told her how to do it. It *is* tricky, after all. Then when she told me how much she likes Byron Sully from that old show, *Dr. Quinn, Medicine Woman,* I told her how to do a Wish List for the actor, so that anything with him that comes on will be recorded. She seemed really grateful. I told her you were downstairs with Luke, so she said she'd hang on till you got back upstairs. Do you want to talk to her?"

I take the phone from Ava, feeling more stunned than ever. "Sure," I say. "Hello?" I murmur into the receiver.

"So," Gran's voice crackles into the phone. "You haven't shtupped him yet?"

I nearly choke on my own spit, I'm so shocked by the question. "I beg your pardon?"

"Sorry," Gran says. "This Chaz character. Why haven't you shtupped him?"

"Because," I say, horrified, "I happen to be engaged to his best friend."

"Is she asking about Chaz?" Ava wants to know from the couch. "I was wondering the same thing. I mean, when are you two going to get busy? Now that you're on a break."

"It's not *that* kind of break," I say, irritated.

"Well, what kind of break is it?" Ava wants to know. "I mean, if you can't fu— I mean, make love with other people, what's the point of it?"

"It's just . . . it's to . . ." I stare blankly at the television screen. Ava is watching an old rerun of *Celebrity Pit Fight,* in which Ava is wrestling with Da Brat in what appears to be an outdoor vat of pudding. "It's so that we can concentrate on our professional goals at the moment, and not be bogged down with romantic problems."

"Oh God," Gran groans over the phone.

"Oh," Ava says, brightening. "Like me and Alek. Well, like me, I mean."

"Exactly," I say. "Only Luke and I aren't broken up. We're just on a break."

"Who *is* that I was just talking to?" Gran wants to know.

"No one you know," I assure her. "Just a friend of mine. Her name is Ava."

"She sounds just like Ava Geck," Gran says with a snort. "You know, the skanky crack whore. What's Ava Geck doing in your apartment?"

"She's just staying here for a few days," I say. The call waiting goes off. I say, "Gran, can you hold on a sec? Someone's on the other line."

"What else have I got to do?" Gran wants to know.

So I pounce on the other call. "Hello?"

"Lizzie?" It's Shari. "Are you all right? I called as soon as I heard."

I blink. On the television screen, Da Brat has seized a handful of Ava's golden hair (extensions) and is using it to drag her through the pudding.

"Of course I'm all right," I say. "What are you talking about?"

"I was just talking to Chaz," Shari says. "His call waiting went off, and it was Luke saying you two are breaking up. I called as soon as Chaz told me. I thought you'd be upset. But you seem awfully calm about it."

"Because we're not breaking up," I say through gritted teeth. "We're *on a break*. Of course I'm calm about it. It was my idea."

"Oh," Shari says. "A break. I thought Chaz said a break*up*. He was talking so fast. He wanted to get off the phone with me so he could talk to Luke—"

"Oh, watch this part," Ava says, pointing at the television screen. "This is where I make her eat it. The pudding, I mean."

"Who is that with you?" Shari asks.

"That's Ava Geck," I say. When Ava makes a frantic slashing motion at me, I roll my eyes and say, "But don't tell anyone she's staying here. She's hiding out from the paparazzi. She just ditched her Greek prince boyfriend, who she was supposed to marry this weekend."

"Holy crap," Shari says. "And she's staying at *your* place? Can't she afford to hole up somewhere a little nicer?"

"Thanks," I say sarcastically.

"Well, sorry. But you know it's true. So . . . you're really all right with this break thing with Luke? I thought you'd be in hysterics."

"I'm really all right with it," I say. "Like I said, it was my idea." I pick up the orange juice container and head to the kitchen with it. "It's like all this stuff that had just been festering in me for months came pouring out. I even told him about my Spanx." My cheeks begin to burn at the memory of it.

There is silence at the end of the line. Then Shari says, "Lizzie. Are you telling me your fiancé didn't know that you wear control top panties?"

"No," I say, opening the refrigerator door. "He didn't know. No wonder he doesn't respect me. What is there to respect? I'm a complete fake."

"Oh, honey," Shari says. "I don't think you're fake. Just . . . complicated."

"Face it," I say, slamming the refrigerator door with my foot. "I'm a fake, Shari. A big, shallow fake who would rather spend time renovating wedding dresses than with her own fiancé." I wasn't making that last part up, either. What does that say about me?

Shari sighs. "I think this break is a good idea. Both of you can spend the summer getting your heads together, putting things in perspective. Giving yourselves some space. It's been a very intense twelve months since you met on that train."

"Right," I say. I know what she's saying makes sense. I know what I've just said to Luke, out on the stoop, makes sense. It all makes perfect sense.

So why does my heart hurt so much all of a sudden?

"I have to go," I tell her. "Gran's on the other line. It's just—" My voice cracks a little. "Luke and I are breaking up, aren't we?"

"No, Lizzie," Shari says. "Not at all. I mean, I don't think so. Not necessarily. Not if you don't want to be. Do you want to be?"

"I don't know," I admit miserably. I'm so confused. I remember how he kissed me good-bye out on the stoop. Was it my imagination, or had there been something like relief in that kiss? Not relief that we weren't breaking up, either. But relief that maybe . . . just maybe . . . we were a little bit closer to doing so?

That has to have been my overactive imagination. Luke is the one who proposed, after all. I broke up with him last time, remember? He's the one who came crawling back, begging my forgiveness. He'd done the same thing again tonight. If he wants to break up so badly, why does he keep coming back, every time I give him what he wants?

Do I want to break up with him?

What is it Shari said, all those months ago in this very kitchen? *I worry that the reason you said yes to Luke is because you wanted to marry him so badly, and then when you found out he didn't want to marry you, you moved on. And then suddenly when he came back and wanted to marry you after all, you thought you had to say yes because you'd been so adamant that that's what you wanted all along. But you know, Lizzie, it's okay to change your mind.*

No. Not that . . . the other thing. That I love the *idea* of Luke, not Luke himself.

But that's ridiculous. Isn't it? I mean, how can you love the *idea* of someone, and not the person himself? Of course I love Luke. I love that he wants to be a doctor and save the children, and I love his eyelashes, and that he always looks so impeccably put together, and smells so nice when he gets out of the shower . . . those aren't *ideas*. Those are real . . .

Aren't they?

"Fights like this," Shari goes on, "can sometimes make couples stronger. They're almost always a good thing. Getting things out in the open can only make things better. Chaz says—"

"What?" I ask, snapping back into the present at the mention of Chaz's name. "What did Chaz say? I can't believe he called you. Since when are you and Chaz so chummy all of a sudden?"

"You know Chaz and I always stayed friends," Shari says. "I love him . . . as a pal. I always will. And he adores you, you know. He always has. He was worried about you. He says you ran out of the middle of a restaurant and jumped into some limo—"

"Ava Geck's," I say.

Ava, in the living room, looks up and calls, "Seriously, you have to watch this part. This is where Tippy comes in and starts shaving his legs! With pudding!"

I head obediently back into the living room. "Really," I say into the phone. "I was fine. I just got so mad at Luke. You know? He said the shittiest thing to me, and right in front of Chaz's new girlfriend, Valencia. Who's perfect by the way. You should see her, no cellulite whatsoever and tan all over. Plus, she's got a Ph.D. She called me solipsistic."

"She called you what?"

I try again. "Solipsistic."

"She *said* that?"

"Right in front of me," I say, nodding vigorously, even though Shari can't see me. "Why? What does it mean?"

"Um. I'm not sure," Shari says. I can tell she's lying. "Look, just call me back after you're done talking to Gran. Pat and I are having a Fourth of July barbecue next week, and we want you to come."

"Really?" I'm touched. "Shari, I'd love to."

"Great. It's going to be fantastic. We've got the back garden to ourselves, you know, for the barbecue, and then we've also got roof rights, so everyone can go upstairs after nightfall and watch the fireworks. We've got a great view."

"Oh, Shari, it sounds perfect. Can I bring anything?"

"Just your lovely self. Chaz is bringing a strawberry rhubarb pie, and maybe a blueberry pie too, if he can wing it—"

"Wait." I can't believe what I'm hearing. "You invited *Chaz*?"

"Of course I invited Chaz," Shari says. "You don't think I'd let him be alone on Fourth of July—or go off with that horrible Valencia—do you?"

"No," I say, thinking that there was no way, if Luke had been in town, she would have invited me to her place. Not if she thought there was a chance I'd bring him. Not in a million years. "I just didn't know you guys were *that* tight."

"Hey, I didn't break up with the guy because I don't *like* him anymore," Shari reminds me. "I broke up with him because I fell in love with someone else. He's a great guy. I just hope he finds somebody who can appreciate him, you know? He's got a lot to offer."

"I think he already found somebody," I say gloomily. I don't mention the loop-de-loop my heart gave earlier in the evening when I saw him. I still haven't figured that part out. I'm not sure I want to, either.

"I mean somebody *nice,*" Shari says. "Not vile cellulite-free philosophy department skanks. Don't tell him this, but there's a cute new girl in my office I'm hoping to set him up with at my party. I specifically told him to come stag so I could fix them up together. I think they'll get along great. She loves college basketball too. I don't think she cares about baseball caps. And I *know* she's never used the word 'solipsistic' in conversation."

I feel as if Shari's just shoved a steak knife through my heart. Really. My best friend. I can barely breathe, in fact, I'm so wounded.

"Is she pretty?" I hear myself wheeze. It's surprisingly hard to talk with a steak knife in your chest.

"What?" Shari asks. "Did you just ask me if she's *pretty*?"

"No," I say quickly. "I said is she witty. Because you know Chaz likes only witty girls. Because he's so . . . smart."

Oh. God. What's wrong with me? How can I even be worried about this? I'm possibly—okay, probably—breaking up with my long-term fiancé, the man of my dreams, right now. Why am I even giving a moment's thought to the fact that Shari is setting up Chaz with some girl from her office?

I'm engaged to Chaz's best friend. Even if we *are* on a break.

"That's great," I say with forced enthusiasm.

"I know. Anyway, so we'll see you on the Fourth, around seven?"

"I'll be there," I say, and after Shari asks me one more time if I'm okay, and I assure her that I think I am, even though I'm pretty sure I'm not, we say our good-byes, and I hang up.

"Oh shit," I say, remembering Gran when I hear her breathing.

"Yeah." Her cranky voice fills my ear. "Still here. Remember me? The grandma?"

"I'm so sorry," I say. "That was Shari."

"Of course it was," Gran says in a bored voice. "You still haven't answered my question. Why haven't you shtupped him?"

"I did answer your question," I say. "Because I'm engaged to his best friend. And where did you learn a word like 'shtup'?"

"TV," Gran says, sounding wounded. "Where else? And what should it matter who you're engaged to? When it's right, it's right. And with that one, it's right."

"Gran," I say tiredly. "How do you even know?"

"Because I've been alive a lot longer than you have. Now, what are you going to do about it?"

"Nothing, Gran," I say. "He has a new girlfriend. She's really pretty and smart. Her name is Valencia."

"Isn't that a type of orange?"

"Gran. You know what I mean. She's perfect for him."

"So?" Gran sounds offended. "And you're not?"

"No, Gran," I say miserably. "I'm not. I'm just . . . I . . . I—"

I don't know how to go on, really, or what more there is to say. I find myself, for one of the first times in my life, at a loss for words. How can I explain to her just why it is that Valencia is so perfect for Chaz—for any guy, really—whereas I, on the other hand, am not? So not.

Gran, however, comes to my rescue.

"Yeah, yeah, yeah," she says. "I know. You're engaged. I heard. Engaged isn't married, you know. Engaged isn't dead. Listen, I gotta go. My show's coming on. I've seen it before. I've seen them all before. But that's one of the good things about getting old. I can't remember how a single one of these goddamned episodes turns out. I'll talk to you later."

She hangs up. I do the same and turn around to find Ava looking up at me with a wounded expression on her face.

"You're going somewhere on the Fourth of July?" she asks sadly.

It takes me a minute to register what she's saying. Then I shake my head.

"Just to a barbecue," I say. "At my best friend's house. In Brooklyn." When Ava continues to look stricken, I add, "Ava . . . you can come, if you want to. But . . . won't you have other plans? I mean, the Fourth of July isn't for another week. You'll probably have gotten a better invitation by then." And, please God, you won't still be staying at my place.

"I don't know," Ava says. "Maybe. Chaz is going to be there?"

"Yes," I say slowly, wondering what she's getting at.

"I kind of have been wanting to see this guy," Ava says. "You talk about him so much. Maybe I'll just stop by. Oh, *there he is*!" She points a French-manicured finger at the screen.

And I have the privilege of gazing, for the first time, at DJ Tippycat.

He is surprisingly normal looking—a bit on the short side, slightly balding, and wearing a shirt with the word "Wonderbread" written on it. In fact, if Shari were here, she'd accuse him of being a nebbish.

"Wow," I say. "He's . . . that's . . ."

"I know," Ava says with a sigh. "Isn't he *hot*?"

And I realize that there really is no accounting for taste. At least when it comes to DJs. And, I'm pretty sure, princes.

And philosophy Ph.D. candidates.

A HISTORY *of* WEDDINGS

When, during medieval times, marriages represented not only the joining of two people but of two families, or even two countries, it was necessary for the bride to dress to impress, meaning layering on the bling . . . not just jewels, but the costliest furs and materials that could be found, as she was representing her noble lineage.

So were introduced the first wedding gowns . . . the richer and more powerful the bride's family, the wider the sleeves and the longer the train.

Obviously, those on the lower social rungs attempted to copy the richies until . . . well, *everyone's* wedding gowns were long and flowing.

It wasn't until Queen Victoria chose to wear white to her wedding to Prince Albert that the color became the most popular choice for wedding gowns. Until then it wasn't thought to represent brides or purity—blue was!

But white has stood for brides ever since, and we have the Victorians to thank for it . . . along with the concept of evolution, free public education, and don't forget Jack the Ripper!

Tip to Avoid a Wedding Day Disaster

While starlets such as Sarah Jessica Parker might be able to get away with a black wedding gown, a touch of white to acknowledge the special nature of the day is generally appreciated. Wearing all black on your wedding day is actually considered bad luck. While it hasn't appeared to affect Sarah (as of this writing), really—why risk it?

LIZZIE NICHOLS DESIGNS™

Chapter 13

There are three things that last: faith, hope and love, and the greatest of these is love.

I Corinthians 13:13

I wake the next morning to the sound of a horrified gasp.

I spring from the couch—ignoring the crick in my neck, brought about by having spent the night on a less than comfortable sleeper sofa that does not, in fact, fold out—and lunge for the window, where Ava is standing.

"What?" I demand, expecting to find a dead body, at the very least. But all I see are a few dozen paparazzi lying in wait below.

Ava points a trembling finger at them. They haven't yet noticed that she's spotted them; they are leaning against parked cars, smoking cigarettes and sipping coffee from Starbucks cups.

"How," Ava demands, in a sleep-roughened voice, *"did they find me?"*

I blink down at the rough-and-tumble cameramen, with their beards and their cargo pants and their multiple lenses.

"How should I know?" I ask. I try not to sound as cranky as I feel. I'm not really a morning person, and feel even less so after my night on the couch. "I didn't tell anyone you were here."

"Well," Ava says. She's scooped up Snow White and is clutching her to one silk pajama–ed breast. "*I* certainly didn't tell anyone I was here."

"Little Joey?" I ask.

Ava shakes her head. "No way. Are you sure you didn't tell anyone?"

Ava has begun tearing about the apartment, gathering up her things and stuffing them back into her seven suitcases—as much as she can do so one-handed, since she's still hanging on to her dog. "What about Luke? Could Luke have told anyone? Maybe he's mad at you for breaking up with him."

"We're not broken up," I remind her. "I told you, we're just on a break. Besides, he doesn't even know who you are."

I notice Ava's lower lip jut out a fraction of an inch, but she chooses to ignore this ill-timed reminder that not everyone is addicted to Google Entertainment News.

"Well, what about your friend Shari?" she asks. "You told her not to tell anyone I was here, didn't you?"

"Of course I did," I said. "She'd never say a word. What about your limo driver? Would he have told anyone?"

"Absolutely not. They all sign a confidentiality agreement with the company they work for. He'd never breathe a word, not if he didn't want to lose his job." Ava pauses as she's jabbing numbers into her cell phone. "What about your grandmother?"

I immediately begin chewing my lower lip. Gran. I'd forgotten to tell Gran not to tell anyone that Ava Geck was staying in my apartment. But surely she wouldn't—

"Yeah," Ava says, looking away from me. "That's what I figured." Someone picks up on the other end of the line she's dialing. "Joey?" she barks into the phone. "Code one. We're compromised. Come *now*."

"But she wouldn't have told anyone," I insist, trailing after Ava as she heads into the bathroom. "I mean, Gran didn't even know for sure it was you. And she wouldn't have known who to call. She doesn't exactly have TMZ or whoever on speed dial!"

"Yeah," Ava says, looking tight-faced. "Well, she sure seems to have caught on fast, hasn't she?"

It's all I can do not to burst out with, *You're the one who picked up the phone! You're the one who taught her how to program the season pass on her TiVo!*

It's not Ava's fault, though, I know. It's mine. Me and my big mouth. As usual.

"Ava," I say. "I'm so sorry. I'm really just so, so sorry."

"Whatever," Ava says, with a shrug of her slim shoulders. I notice she can't seem to make eye contact with me. "I'm going to take a shower. When Joey gets here, will you buzz him up? He'll buzz three times quick in a row, then twice, real slow, so you'll know it's him. Okay?"

I nod. I feel terrible. "Ava—"

"Just let him in," Ava says. "Okay?"

I nod again, then back out of the bathroom so she can close the door. A second later, I hear the water turn on.

I can't believe this. What a disaster! The integrity of Chez Henri has been totally compromised. Not to mention my own personal integrity. Not that I had much of it to begin with.

Still, I can't believe Gran of all people had been the one who'd called the paps on Ava. She wouldn't even have known how to do it. It's not as if it matters—the damage is done, obviously—but I have to know. I have to know if it's really my fault. I pick up the phone and call my parents' house. Gran picks up on the first ring.

"What?" she demands.

"Gran," I say. I keep my voice low, in case Ava hasn't gotten into the shower yet and is eavesdropping, as she is all too wont to do.

"Who is this?" Gran demands. "Lizzie? No one's here. Your dad's at work, and your mom's at the Y. Your sisters are all God knows where—"

"That's okay, it's you I want to talk to, anyway," I say. "Did you say anything to anyone about Ava Geck staying at my place?"

"Well, good morning to you too," Gran says. "Did you shtup him yet?"

"Gran," I whisper. "I'm serious. Did you tell anyone about Ava?"

"Of course not," Gran says, sounding annoyed. "Who would I tell? No one talks to me except you. I'm just crazy old Gran, too drunk for anyone to take seriously—"

I feel myself begin to relax. It hadn't been my fault after all. For once in my life, it hadn't been me—

"Although," Gran says, in a different tone, "your sister Rose was skulking around last night while I was talking to you."

I feel my blood run cold. If it had been Sarah, I wouldn't be worried. But Rose is a different story.

"Do you think she heard you?" I ask.

"I *know* she heard me," Gran says. "She asked a lot of questions after I hung up, like why I was asking about Ava Geck, and what Ava Geck was doing at your place. I just told her what I knew—"

I let out the worst curse word I know. Gran, being Gran, is unimpressed.

"Well," she says. "You can't exactly blame her. It's not like she doesn't need the money, the way she's maxed out her credit cards on clothes over at the discount places . . . especially that T.J. Maxx. Plus that no-good bohunk of a husband of hers got laid off again, and he's not exactly impartial to the jewelry counter over at JCPenney. You should see how many gold neck chains I saw him wearing at the pool the other day."

I close my eyes, trying to summon the strength I need not to burst into tears on the spot. I'm sure Rose is swimming in debt.

That doesn't mean I don't want to hop on a plane to Ann Arbor and strangle her.

"If you see Rose today, Gran," I say, "can you give her a swift kick in the pants for me?"

"Don't worry," Gran assures me, relishing, as usual, being in the middle of a cat fight between me and one of my sisters. "I'll remind her of how fat her arms looked in that slutty dress she wore for her senior prom. That always makes her cry. Like goddamned Niagara Falls."

"Thanks," I say, and hang up feeling only slightly better. Really, could things get any worse?

And yet they do when, a half hour later, Ava emerges from my bathroom looking perfectly coiffed in a purple animal-print catsuit with bright orange stilettos, and finds Little Joey and me waiting for her on the couch.

"Ready?" she asks him, not even glancing at me.

"Ava," I say, leaping up. "I'm sorry. It was me. I mean, I told my grandma. But it wasn't her fault. My sister—"

"It's okay," Ava cuts me off. But I can tell from her pinched expression it's not. It's not okay. It's far from okay. "We're going now. Right, Joey?"

Joey heaves his three-hundred-pound girth up from the sofa. "You got it, Miss Geck. I already took down the suitcases."

"Ava," I say, trying again.

"It's *okay,* Lizzie," Ava insists.

But I know it isn't. Nothing is okay.

Nothing is ever going to be okay—at least between me and Ava—again.

I watch them leave through the living room windows. The paparazzi throw down their cigarettes and coffee cups—I'm going to have to sweep them all up before the shop opens—and surges forward to virtually attack Ava the minute she walks through the front door of my building. Little Joey shields her the best that he can, using his elbows and sizable belly to forge a path for her to the waiting limo. Ava climbs inside, Little Joey follows, and they speed off, the photographers in hot pursuit.

And then my street is quiet again. If it weren't for all the litter on the sidewalk—and the wad of blond hair in my drain—it would almost seem as if they hadn't been there at all.

But I know I've just messed up an important client relationship. Worse, I've messed up a budding friendship.

And honestly, I have no one to blame for it but myself. Just like all the other messes in my life at the moment. Great.

Just great.

• • •

I had never been up to Shari and Pat's roof before, but it turns out they've built a little garden oasis there. On a redwood deck, surrounded by overflowing flower boxes bursting with geraniums and delphiniums, you can stand and look out at the skyline of Manhattan, rising in all its glory out of the East River. It's an amazing view. And it's all theirs.

Well, along with all the other tenants in their building. And all the other neighboring rooftops along their street. All of whom are having Fourth of July parties at the same time as theirs.

But they aren't about to let all the dueling stereo speakers bring them down. Shari, at least, has a lot of other issues to worry about.

"I can't believe he brought her," Shari keeps saying, casting dark looks in Chaz's direction.

"I told you he would." I'm downing ice cream like there's nothing else being served, which isn't true, because there are also burgers, hot dogs, chips, about ten different kinds of pasta salad, and, of course, the two pies Chaz brought.

But somehow, the only thing that is making me feel better is ice cream. It's been a long week. A looooooong week.

And the sight of Chaz sitting over there with Valencia—who is looking cool and serene, in spite of the ninety-degree heat, in white linen gauchos and a black tank top that shows off her perfectly toned arms—isn't doing much to make me feel better.

"So, is that the girl?" I ask between gulps of rocky road.

"What are you talking about?" Shari wants to know.

"The girl you're trying to fix Chaz up with. Is that her?" I point to a pretty girl who has joined Chaz and Valencia over by the beer cooler they're both sitting beside.

"Yeah," Shari says, looking annoyed. "See how cute they look together? They'd be a perfect couple—if he hadn't brought that ice bitch with him. And what's Tiffany doing over there with them? She's totally monopolizing the conversation, it looks like."

I take an enormous bite of my ice cream. "I don't know," I say, my mouth too full to say more. Fortunately.

I don't mention that Tiffany, in the car service her fiancé, Raoul, insisted we share on the way over, had sworn to me that she was going to keep Chaz from making a love connection with "that ho from Shari's office, because he's totally right for you. And, furthermore, I am going to split him and that orange-name lady up too."

I didn't bother reminding her for the millionth time that it doesn't matter to me who Chaz dates because I'm actually engaged to someone else, because she'd just have brought up, as she usually does, that I'm "on a break," and people who are happily engaged don't tend to ask for one of those.

"Hey, so what's up with Ave Geck?" Shari asks, distracting me from my gloomy thoughts. "Is she still mad at you for outing her to the press?"

I wince. The fallout from the Ava situation turned out to be worse than even I could have imagined. The Henris had not been too happy to see the front of their shop in photos plastered all over the press the morning after it was announced Ava Geck's high-profile royal wedding had been canceled. I'd tried to convince them there was no such thing as bad press, but they hadn't really gone for it. They couldn't understand what Ava was doing spending the night in my apartment in the first place. Like Luke, they didn't think an employee inviting a client to stay with her was particularly professional.

In retrospect, maybe they were right. But then, Ava had pretty much invited herself.

"Yeah," I say. "She's not speaking to me. Which I can understand."

"Well, she's the only person I know who *doesn't* want to be a member of Lizzie Nichols's entourage these days." Shari points at the small cluster of people gathered around Chaz's pies—he'd brought both a strawberry rhubarb *and* a blueberry—running their fingers around the empty tins and then licking them, and then running them around the rims again. Tiffany's fiancé, Raoul, and Monique and *her* fiancé, Latrell, have already handed out the bottles of champagne and boxes of sparklers they brought along with them, to contribute to the festive party mood. And to make up for the fact that they hadn't exactly been invited.

"Okay," I say sheepishly. "I realize four people is a lot. But they all *really* wanted to come." I don't mention that Shari's fantastic view of the fireworks—and the fact that the Fourth of July happened to fall on a Wednesday this year, making it hard to go out of town—had something to do with it.

"I'm not complaining," Shari says. "It's just that if you get any more popular, I may have to move to someplace bigger in order to accommodate all your fans every time I have you over."

"I'm not *popular,*" I say, abashed. "I'm just . . ."

"Admit it," Shari says with a smile. "They're the misfit toys, and you're the island. How are things going with Luke, anyway?"

I shrug. "Fine," I say, speaking around the red plastic spoon hanging from my mouth. "I mean, as well as can be expected, seeing as how he's in Paris and I'm here and we're on a break."

Shari points at the ring finger of my left hand. "You're still wearing it."

"Well," I say, neurotically shoveling more ice cream into my face, "we're still engaged. He's acting like everything is fine."

"Ooooh!" shrieks Tiffany suddenly, jumping to her four-inch stilettos and pointing into the twilit sky. "They're starting!"

We hear a muffled boom, and the next thing I know, a huge carnation of light is exploding in the sky.

"Zee One Hundred," Shari screams. "Switch it to Zee One Hundred!

We're missing the musical accompaniment!" She dives for the radio while two dozen people look at her as if she's lost her mind.

A second later, Tiffany sidles up to me and says, "Okay, so here's the L.D."

I screw up my face at her in confusion. "The what?"

"The L.D.," she says. "The *lowdown*?" When I nod, she goes on, "Don't look at me. Look at the fireworks. *Pretend we're talking about the fireworks.* Her name is Mae Lin, and she's got some kinda like master's degree in like social work or something. She lives in Alphabet City and she loves the Buckeyes—that's a basketball team—and collects vintage Fiesta Dinnerware. You are so fucking dead."

I look at Tiffany. "Tiff," I say as the fireworks boom along the skyline behind me, "I told you. I don't care. I don't like Chaz that way."

"Yeah, right," Tiffany says with a hoarse laugh and takes a swig of her champagne. "*Whatever!* If he were the marrying kind, you would so have screwed him already. Just admit it."

Z100 is blasting "Born to Run." Shari's girlfriend, Pat, is saying, "No. Just . . . no. Are you kidding me with this?" While Shari says, "Honey, it's the Boss. What are you gonna do?"

"Here's what you do," Tiffany says, taking my empty ice cream bowl from me and setting it on a nearby picnic table. "Go over there—both Mae Lin and Valencia are gone now, it's okay, they went downstairs to dry off. I 'accidentally' spilled my bottle of champagne on them—and tell him his pies were good."

"Tiff." She's pushing me toward Chaz. I lock my knees, refusing to budge. "No. I'm engaged. And he doesn't . . . what you just said. About marriage. Remember?"

"God!" Tiffany gives me another shove. "Why are you being so fucking stubborn? You can *change* him! I know all your *other* girlfriends are always telling you men can't change, and in general it's true. But not in this case. With you. And him. *Believe me. I know.* Come on, Lizzie. You're always helping other people. Why won't you let *us* help *you* for once?"

"Because you aren't helping me," I say from between gritted teeth. I have to raise my voice a little, because the boom of the fireworks—and the swell of Z100, playing from so many rooftops—is so loud. I notice two leather-braceleted men looking over at us in amusement.

I turn my back to them. "I told you, Tiffany, I love Luke. *Luke,* not Chaz."

I almost completely believe this as I say it too. To the point that I even manage to convince myself that I have not spent the whole of the party trying not to look over to where Chaz is sitting and wondering how he's managed to get such a dark tan so early in the summer, or why he insists on wearing khaki shorts. They're so undignified for the urban male.

Although with muscular legs like his, he can, of course, get away with it . . .

"I don't think you do," Tiffany insists. "And I'm sorry, but I don't think Luke loves you, either. He wouldn't have gone to France—or agreed to your stupid fucking break idea—if he did. I think you two are both just afraid to admit it's been over between you for a long time already. You had a summer fling that's gone on way, way too long. Believe me, Lizzie, I know what real love is, and I see it standing over there by that fuckin' beer cooler in a baseball cap. Now *go . . . over . . . there . . .*"

Tiffany shoves me with a strength surprising in so thin a person—well, she *does* work out—and I find myself stumbling in my lace-up platform espadrilles . . . only to end up stumbling practically *into* the beer cooler. I'd have fallen inside it if Chaz hadn't reached out and grabbed my arm.

"Hey," he says, looking concerned. "You okay?"

"Yeah," I say, turning beet red. "I'm fine. Tiffany wants me to tell you that, um. She liked your pies."

Chaz stares down at me, his dark eyebrows raised.

"Oh," he says. "Well, that's nice."

"Yeah," I say, trying to regain my composure. "I did too. Good . . . pie. Both of them."

Am I? I ask myself. Am I *really* the stupidest human being on the face of the planet? Or does it just feel that way sometimes?

"Great," Chaz says. "So. How's the break going?"

"The break?" I echo lamely.

"Yeah," Chaz says. "The break you and Luke are on."

"Oh, the *break*!" Behind Chaz's head, fireworks are exploding into amazing shapes, like apples and kissing lips. And he's not even looking. His gaze is riveted to my face. Which I hope he can't tell is still burning as brightly as the lights of the skyline behind him. "Um, fine. I guess. Luke really seems to like it over there. It's a lot of work. But then he knew it would be."

"Well," Chaz says, picking up his beer and taking a sip of it, "he's always had a thing for numbers."

"Yeah," I say. "Well, he's just doing this as a favor for his uncle."

"Yeah," Chaz says. "Right."

I glance up at him sharply. "What do you mean by that?" I snap.

"What do you mean, what do I mean?" he asks defensively. "I don't mean anything. I just said you were right."

"You sounded like you were being sarcastic," I say.

"Well, I wasn't being sarcastic," he says.

"You think he was desperate for any excuse he could get," I say, clarity breaking over me suddenly like a crystal ocean wave, "to leave town and get away from me. Because I'm smothering him."

Oh my God. It's happening again. My mouth, I mean. Running away without me. What am I even talking about? I mean, I know, of course . . . it's what I stay up nights—when I should have fallen asleep hours before, exhausted from adjusting seams all day with Sylvia and Marisol—worrying about.

But why am I mentioning it to *Chaz,* of all people?

Chaz seems to be wondering the same thing.

"How much wine have you had?" Chaz asks, laughing with disbelief.

"None," I say. Amazingly, it's the truth. Also, I'm wishing I'd shut up. But my mouth keeps on moving without me, as usual. "And you're wrong. I don't smother him at all. If anything, I don't pay *enough* attention to him. And besides, that would completely fly in the face of what you said that day."

"What day?" Chaz asks, looking more confused than ever.

"The day I told you he proposed. You said he was proposing only because he's so scared of being alone, he'd rather be with a girl he knows isn't right for him than be by himself."

Shut. Up. Lizzie.

Chaz blinks at me. "Well . . . I still think that's true."

"But you can't have it both ways." In the distance, the fireworks are still going off, in much quicker succession than before. *Boom. Boom. Boom.* Each blast seems to be timed to go off with my heartbeat rather than the Bon Jovi song that's now blasting from the radio around us. I'm standing so close to Chaz that I can see his chest rising and falling in the same rhythm through the front of his short-sleeved polo. It's hard not to put my hands on his chest to see if his heart is beating in time to mine as well.

God, what is *wrong* with me?

"Either I'm smothering him or he's scared to be without me," I blurt out instead. "Which is it?"

"You are completely insane right now," Chaz says to me, still laughing a little. "You know that, don't you?"

The truth is, I do know that. But knowing it doesn't help.

"You're his best friend," I point out. "You've known him longer than I have. And you seem to have so many opinions on our relationship. Or at least you used to. I realize we haven't talked about it in a while because you've been so busy with *Valencia,* but I assume you must have some new theories on the matter. Go ahead. Let's hear them."

"Not now," Chaz says, looking down at me with a grin I can only call suggestive. "Too many people around. Why don't you come back to my place after this? I'll be happy to tell you every theory I know. And illustrate them, as well."

The grin has caused my breath to catch in my throat. Not that I'm about to let him know that.

"Oh, you'd like that, wouldn't you?" I demand. I'm standing so close to him now that our faces are just inches apart. "Is that the only way you can relate to women? As sexual objects?"

"As you know perfectly well," Chaz says, looking mockly offended, "no. What is the *matter* with you tonight? Is this about Valencia? Are you jealous or something? I don't think I should have to remind you that you're the one who's engaged."

"Right. To your *best friend.*"

"Hey, he's *your* fiancé. As you seem to feel the need to keep reminding yourself."

"At least I *have* a fiancé," I say. "At least I'm not an emotional cripple who is afraid to commit myself to someone just because the girl I liked turned out to like girls."

"Oh yeah?" Chaz's blue eyes flash more brightly than any of the fireworks that have exploded in the night sky so far. "Well, at least I didn't get myself engaged to the first guy who asked me to marry him just because I'm in the wedding gown business and I couldn't stand seeing all my clients getting pretty diamond rings on their fingers and not have one for myself."

I suck in my breath, outraged—just as my cell phone vibrates in the pocket of my gingham sundress. I have to keep the stupid thing on all the time these days because of bridal gown emergencies. Although I have no weddings scheduled for today.

"That," I snap at Chaz, "is so untrue. I happen to love Luke. And I want to spend the rest of my life with him."

"Yeah," Chaz sneers. "Keep telling yourself that. Maybe someday you'll even start to believe it."

I slide the phone out, thinking maybe Luke is calling—although it's close to two in the morning in France—then see that it's my mom.

"And I suppose," I say to Chaz, "you think you're so much better for me than he is."

"I'll tell you one thing," Chaz says. "I wouldn't be stupid enough to go off to *France* for the summer and leave a girl like you on your own with guys like me around."

Flustered by this, I fumble with the phone, nearly hanging up on my own mother in my attempt to answer her call.

"Mom?" In the background, the fireworks are reaching their crescendo. It's the show's grand finale. "I can't talk right now. I have to call you back—"

"Oh, Lizzie, honey," my mom interrupts. "I'm so sorry to bother you. I know you're at Shari's party"—we'd talked earlier in the week, and I'd mentioned that I'd be attending a party at Shari's today—"and I don't want to spoil it for you. But I wanted to tell you before you heard it from anybody else: Gran died."

The fireworks are so loud, I don't think I've heard her correctly. I put one finger in my ear and yell, "WHAT?"

"Honey, GRAN DIED TODAY. Can you hear me? I just wanted to make sure you didn't hear it on your machine or from the Dennises or anything like that. Honey? Are you there?"

I murmur something. I don't know what.

I think I'm in shock.

What had she said?

"Lizzie?" Chaz is looking down at me with a funny expression on his face. "What is it?"

"Can you hear me now?" Mom is asking in my ear. The ear I can hear out of. When I say yes, she says, "Oh good. Anyway, it was very peaceful. She went in her sleep. I just found her there this afternoon, in her chair. She must have dozed off watching *Dr. Quinn.* You know she figured out how to TiVo it. She had a beer in one hand, I don't know how she got hold of it. Well, we had a Fourth of July barbecue, she must have sneaked one . . . Anyway, I just wanted to let you know, we're planning a memorial service for this weekend. I know how busy you are, but I hope you'll be able to come. You know how fond she was of you. It wasn't right that she played favorites with you girls, but you really were always the one she liked best out of all the grandkids—"

The world seems to have tilted. Suddenly, I can't stand up anymore. I feel my knees give out . . . but it's all right, because Chaz has his arm around me and is steering me toward the beer cooler, the lid of which he's snapped closed. He sits me down on it, then sinks down beside me, one arm around my shoulders, going, "It's okay. Take it easy. I've got you. Just breathe."

"Gran's dead," I say to him. I can't see him very well.

Then I realize it's because I'm looking at him through a veil of tears. I'm crying.

"I'm sorry," he says. "Lizzie, I'm so sorry."

"She was watching *Dr. Quinn,*" I tell him. I don't know why. It's all I can think about. "And drinking beer."

"Well," he says. "If you're Gran, and you have to go, that's the way to do it."

I let out a hiccupy sound, halfway between a sob and a laugh.

"Lizzie?" Mom's voice sounds in my ear. "Who's that with you?"

"Ch-Chaz," I say with another sob.

"Oh, honey," Mom said. "Are you crying? I didn't think you'd be so upset. Gran was ninety, you know. It wasn't as if this was entirely unexpected."

"It was by *me,*" I wail. I realize dimly that the booming of the fireworks has ceased, and that it's grown very quiet all of a sudden. I realize, as well, that the pale blobs I can see through my tears are faces . . . the faces of everyone at Shari's party. And that they're all turned toward me. I fight to regain my composure, reaching up and trying to wipe away my tears with the back of my wrist.

But they won't stop. They just seem to come faster.

Chaz, seeming to realize the problem, pulls me into a hug. And suddenly I'm weeping against his chest.

"Oh," Mom says comfortingly into my ear. I'm clutching my cell phone tightly in one hand, and the front of Chaz's shirt with the other. "Good. I'm glad Chaz is there. He's a good, old friend and will take care of you." I don't mention that my "good, old friend" not five minutes ago was making lewd suggestions about "theories" he was going to illustrate to me back in his apartment.

"Yeah" is all I can manage to choke out.

Because the truth is, until she'd called, I had pretty much been going to accept his invitation.

"Mom," I choke. "I'm gonna go now."

"Okay, honey," Mom says. "I love you."

And then she's hung up, and I've hung up, and Chaz is saying, "Shhh," into my hair, and Tiffany has come over and is asking what's wrong, and Shari is stroking my arm and going, "Oh, Lizzie. It's going to be all right."

But it isn't. How can it be?

Gran is gone.

I never even got to say good-bye.

A HISTORY *of* WEDDINGS

Why is the third finger of your left hand considered the ring finger? Ancient Egyptians and Romans both believed that a vein from that finger led directly to the heart, so it seemed like the logical position for the placement of the wedding band. Science has since proved this not to be strictly accurate.

But tradition lives on, and that finger is still universally known as the ring finger. And isn't it romantic to think that our wedding rings are linked to our hearts? Well, by a creepy vein of blood, anyway?

Tip to Avoid a Wedding Day Disaster

It may sound obvious, but try on your rings—both bride and groom—in the days leading up to your wedding. The last thing you want to be doing during your wedding ceremony is squeezing a ring that won't fit over fingers that have swollen due to nervous last-minute binge eating.

LIZZIE NICHOLS DESIGNS™

Chapter 14

You were born together, and together you shall be for evermore . . . but let there be spaces in your togetherness. And let the winds of the heavens dance between you.

Kahlil Gibran (1883–1931), Lebanese-American artist, poet, and writer

"Here's another one," my sister Rose says, dropping the casserole plate down on the kitchen table in front of me unceremoniously. "I think it's green bean. Or something green, anyway."

My other sister, Sarah, looks up from the notebook into which she's recording the names of everyone who has brought something over for us to eat, since we are supposedly so consumed with grief over Gran's death that we can't cook. For some of us, this is actually true. The kitchen table is covered with casserole dishes.

"Who's it from?" Sarah wants to know.

"I don't know," Rose says crabbily as she digs through her purse, which she's left on the kitchen counter next to the sliding glass door to the deck. "I found it on the front porch. Check the card, nimrod."

"Suck my dick," Sarah says, snatching the card off the top of the casserole dish.

"Do you kiss your husband with that mouth?" Rose wants to know. Then she lets out a tinkly laugh. "Oh, that's right. He left you. So where's Luke, anyway?" Rose turns her attention to me.

"Don't talk to me," I say to Rose.

Rose looks at Sarah. "What's her glitch?" she wants to know.

"She's not speaking to you," Sarah says. "Because you called TMZ on her client. Remember?"

"Oh, please," Rose says with a laugh. "You're not still mad about that, are you? That should be water under the bridge. Our grandmother is dead. Now, come on. Where's Luke? Your fiancé? Isn't he going to come to your own grandmother's funeral? Or is he too busy with school or whatever? As usual."

"He's in France," I say from between gritted teeth.

"Oh, *France,*" Rose says with another laugh. "Sure. Why not. *France.*"

"He *is,*" I say. Why can't I not speak to people I've resolved never to speak to again? "He's helping his uncle set up a new investment office. Not that it's any of your business. He wanted to come. He's really sorry. But he can't leave right now." And besides. We're on a break. I don't mention this to Rose, who doesn't deserve to know any of my personal business. But it's true.

"Of course," Rose says. "You know, we're all starting to wonder if this Luke guy even exists, or if he's just some guy you've made up to make us think you finally got a boyfriend. As if." Still laughing, Rose opens the sliding glass door and steps out into the cool evening air, not bothering to close it behind her, so all the mosquitoes come buzzing in.

"I hate her too," Sarah informs me matter-of-factly as soon as Rose is out of earshot. "Don't pay any attention to her. You have no idea how lucky you are you got out of here. Seriously."

I am sitting with my arms crossed in front of my chest, holding on to both my elbows. I have been sitting like this since I got home.

I just can't believe she's really gone. Gran, I mean. The thing is . . . I knew she was old. I did.

I just never thought she was *that* old.

"Well, she just died, Lizzie" is what Shari's dad had said when I'd asked him how it had happened when he stopped by to drop off a plate of Mrs. Dennis's Heath Bar Crunch cookies a little while ago. "She was old."

"But—" I'd been going to ask if there was going to be an autopsy. But a warning look from my mother had stopped me. Mom doesn't want people talking about cutting up his mother in front of Dad. Which I guess I can understand.

And okay, Gran *was* ninety, after all. I guess *how* she died isn't any big mystery.

But why *now*? When I need her most? I mean, not to be selfish or anything. But couldn't she have waited a month or two, for a time when I wasn't so . . . confused?

Everyone seemed kind of relieved when Dr. Dennis gave me a little bottle of pills.

"Shari asked me to prescribe you these," Shari's dad said, uncomfortably handing them over. "They're to make you feel better. Now, remember . . . no drinking alcohol while you're on those, Lizzie!"

Everyone laughed like Dr. Dennis had made a great joke. And looked at me expectantly, waiting for me to take one of the pills. Which I pretended to, just to get them off my back.

But if they think doping me up is going to keep me from asking the hard questions—like are they going to play Gran's favorite song, "Highway to Hell," at the funeral, or aren't they?—they can just think again. I'm not going to be dismissed that easily. Gran might have been happy to ride through life in an alcoholic haze—she might even have been good at it—but not me.

Never me.

"Really," Sarah is going on. "You wouldn't believe what a bitch Rose has turned into. Well, not turned into, because she was always a bitch. But she's gotten worse with age. You think that thing with her calling the paparazzi on your friend is bad? Just wait. Maybe it's perimenopause. I saw something about it on *Oprah.* So Chuck and I are having some problems? He didn't *leave* me. He's just taking some time to work through a few things. Like Rose and Angelo have it so perfect. He doesn't even have a job. She's still supporting both of them."

"Huh," I say. I still can't believe my own sister thinks my fiancé is made up. Like I would even go to the trouble. For *her*.

And, okay, so Luke didn't even *offer* to fly back and meet me here for the funeral. But I'm the one who asked for the break. Maybe he thinks he wouldn't be welcome. That's a natural assumption, right? It's my fault, really. The poor guy probably thinks I don't want him anymore.

Besides, he doesn't have any living grandparents. They all died when he was little. He doesn't know what it's like to lose a grandparent as an adult. A grandparent I was as close to as Gran. Luke doesn't have any idea what that's like.

Neither do I, actually. I'm just going through it now for the first time. Without my fiancé's shoulder to lean on.

"And you should see what she's doing to her kids," Sarah goes on. "You have never seen kids so overextended. Ballet, tap, karate, gymnastics, French—*French,* for Christ's sake. They live in Michigan. When are they going to need to speak French? Except maybe at your wedding, if it ever takes place. They never have a minute to themselves, just to be kids. No wonder they're so weird."

At that minute Maggie, Rose's eldest, wanders into the room, holding a reporter's notebook, a pencil poised in one hand.

"Excuse me," she says. "I'm starting my own newspaper. Do you have any news?"

Sarah and I blink at her.

"What?" I say.

"*News,*" Maggie yells. "I'm starting my own newspaper. A kid's newspaper. I need some news to put in it. Do you have any *news*?"

"Your great-grandmother just died, for Christ's sake," Sarah says. "That isn't enough news for you?"

Maggie looks at me. "Aunt Lizzie," she says. "How do you feel about Gran being dead?"

Tears prick my eyes. Trying not to weep openly in front of my niece, I say, "I'm very sad about it. I'm going to miss her very much."

"May I quote you on that?" Maggie wants to know.

"Yes," I say.

"Good. Thank you." Maggie turns around and leaves the room without another word.

"See?" Sarah says as soon as she's gone. "There's something wrong with that kid."

Rose chooses that moment to reenter the kitchen, reeking of cigarette smoke. She closes the sliding glass door behind her and drops a pack of cigarettes and her lighter back into her purse.

"Something wrong with what kid?" she asks.

"Your kid," Sarah snarls. "Maggie. She just came in here and announced she's starting a newspaper and asked us if we had any news."

"At least," Rose says mildly, peeling the aluminum foil back on a peach cobbler someone has brought over and plunging a spoon into it, "she's not an unimaginative, nose-picking moron like some people's kids I could mention."

Sarah sucks in her breath, but before she can say anything, I ask, "So what did you do with the money, Rose?"

Rose looks up from the cobbler. "Excuse me?"

"The money you got from spilling the fact that Ava Geck was hiding out in my apartment." I stare at her. "What did you spend it on? It couldn't have been liposuction for your upper arms, because they're looking as enormous as ever."

Rose's shriek of outrage causes Mom's china collection to tinkle. I take that as my cue to get up and leave.

"What's going on back there?" Mom asks me as I drift into the living room, where she and Dad are meeting with Father Jim, who'll be conducting Gran's memorial service.

"Nothing," I say and collapse onto the couch beside her. "Just sister stuff."

Mom gives Father Jim an apologetic smile and says, "I'm so sorry. Go on, Father."

I sit and listen to their conversation, barely able to register what they're saying through the miserable haze into which I've sunk. I can't remember ever feeling quite so horrible. I want to die. I do. Why won't someone just kill me already? How can everyone just go on talking like nothing is wrong when it's the end of the world, already?

"Well," Father Jim says. "I was thinking a mass would be a lovely gesture."

"Oh, a mass," Mom says, looking over at Dad. "Yes, that would be lovely."

Dad looks skeptical. "I don't know," he says. "A mass. That'll make it an hour longer." I wonder if Father Jim caught the fact that my mom kicked my father under the coffee table. "Ow. What I mean is, my mother wasn't a particularly religious woman."

Even through my misery, I'm able to register the fact that Gran wasn't religious. She'd want a Byron Sully tribute at her memorial, not a tribute to God. Because to her, Byron Sully *was* God. I feel myself perking up. Just a little. Because I'm starting to feel something besides sadness. And that's anger.

"That just makes it all the more important," Father Jim goes on, "to have a mass. Your mother's attendance at our church was, especially in her later years, sketchy at best. But I know, had she been in full possession of her faculties at the end, this is what she'd have wanted."

She *was* in full possession of her faculties, I want to shout. Fuller possession of her faculties than any of you.

"Now," Father Jim continues. "About the musical selections—"

"Her favorite song was 'Highway to Hell,'" I surprise myself by saying.

My mom glares at me. Dad bursts out laughing, but stops when my mother transfers her glare to him.

"Er," Father Jim says. "Yes. Well, be that as it may, I find a more traditional selection tends to please parishioners—"

"But it's her favorite song," I interrupt. I don't blame my mother for glaring. She's right. Why am I interfering? At the same time, though— "Surely you'd want to play someone's favorite song at her *funeral*."

"Well, maybe not *that* song," Mom says, looking flustered. "It's about . . . well, going to *hell*, Lizzie."

"Maybe we could find an instrumental version," Dad says thoughtfully.

Mom gives me a "see what you started" look. Then she says, "Lizzie, Mrs. Brand said she'd be stopping by with a Brunswick stew. Could you wait on the porch for her? She twisted her ankle recently and I don't want her trying to get out of the car while holding a large pot. It would be lovely if you could meet her in the driveway and take the stew from her directly."

I stare at my mother as if she's lost her mind. When it becomes clear from the unblinking way in which she stares back, however, that she's not kidding, I sigh and get up from the couch. I'm almost all the way out of the house when I overhear her say, sotto voce, to Father Jim, "Lizzie and her grandmother were very close. I'm not sure having her here while we plan the service is really the best idea. Lizzie's always been the most . . . well, *emotional* of my children."

Tears fill my eyes. I stagger out onto the night-darkened porch—no one has thought to flick on the light—and sink down onto the steps, burying my head in my knees. *Emotional?*

Well, I guess that's me. Is it *emotional* to be sad that my grandmother is dead? Is it *emotional* to wish that the person who was conducting her funeral was someone who actually knew her, who could maybe say a few words about her that might actually *mean* something?

Is it *emotional* to feel as if I'm a stranger in my own family, as if these people I've known my whole life don't actually know me—or care about me—at all? Gran was the only one—the *only one* of them—who ever said anything to me that was actually worth a damn.

Not that I ever told her that.

And now she's gone. And I'll never have the chance. Never have the chance to talk to her again.

No wonder I'm so *emotional.*

God. Maybe I should take one of those pills Dr. Dennis prescribed after all. I can feel them, rattling around in their bottle in the pocket of my jeans. Will they make me feel less *emotional*? Will they stop me from feeling anything at all? Because right now that's what I'd really, really like.

Headlights flash, and I raise my head. Mrs. Brand and her Brunswick stew. I swipe at my cheeks with my wrists. I don't want Mrs. Brand—whoever she is—to see me looking like such an unholy mess.

But the car doesn't turn into the driveway. It pulls over and parks down the street. It's so warm and humid outside, a sort of mist has settled over the street, making it look as if a fog has rolled in. I stare at the red taillights through the fog, breathing in the summer air, so familiar and yet so strange after so many months in the city. The smell of fresh-cut grass, the whine of cicadas, the chirp of crickets . . . these are summer scents and sounds that are almost foreign to me now, I haven't experienced them in so long.

Someone gets out of the parked car. Even though it's pretty dark out, and the mist is pretty thick, I can see it's not a woman. It's a man, tall and broad-shouldered. I look away, through the fog, into the dark sea of our yard—the yard where Rose and Sarah forced me to hose off Mom and Dad's bedspread that time Gran was babysitting us and ended up vomiting cooking sherry all over it.

Yeah, that hadn't been much fun.

But before that—before the vomiting—Gran had told me the story about working in the munitions factory during World War II, while Gramps had been off fighting the Nazis in France (every single man in his platoon had died when they'd found a bottle of wine in an abandoned farmhouse in Marseille and drank from it, not knowing it had been poisoned by Nazi sympathizers. Gramps, being a teetotaler, was the only one to survive), and how she and the other girls had painted black lines on the backs of their legs to make it look like they were wearing stockings with seams when they went out on Saturday nights, because all the silk had been used up for parachutes.

That's the kind of thing we should be talking about at her funeral. The happy times. The incredible sacrifices her generation made—without complaint. Not some stupid biblical passages that have nothing to do with Gran and never did.

I notice through the fog that the man is walking toward our house. I also notice he's the same shape and size as . . . my fiancé.

My heart seems to freeze inside my chest.

But what would Luke be doing here? I mean, it's true my grandmother—the family member I cared about most in the world although I might not have realized it until it was too late—is dead. And it's true I'm really disappointed in him because he's made no effort during the course of our relationship so far to meet anyone in my family.

But he's in France. He wouldn't have flown all the way to Ann Arbor just for the funeral. *We're on a break.*

And then, as the mist swirls and tumbles around the man's legs as he turns into our driveway, I see something that causes my heart, which a moment ago was frozen, to explode into what feels like a million tiny pieces of flame—like fireworks, only inside my chest, instead of up in the night sky: *he's wearing a baseball cap.*

A second later, I'm on my feet and I'm running. I'm running toward him through the fog, and a second later, I skid to a halt in front of him. He stops too.

So, it seems, does time. All I can hear, in those few heartbeats, is the sound of the cicadas. And our breathing.

"What are you doing here?" I demand. My voice sounds gravelly for some reason.

"What do you think I'm doing here?" Chaz shoots back. His voice sounds gravelly too. "I came to see how you're doing."

I scan the street behind him. I see no one else in the mist.

"Where's Valencia?" I ask him.

"Fuck Valencia," he says.

"I'd assumed you already took care of that," I say.

"You know what?" Chaz says, starting to turn back toward the car. "I can leave, if that's what you want."

My heart gives a twist, and I take a quick step forward, laying my hand on his arm.

"Don't go," I say. "I'm sorry. I just . . ." A sob catches my throat. "Oh, Chaz. Everything is so screwed up."

"I know," he says. I can't see his eyes because they are hidden in the shadow of the brim of his baseball cap.

"No," I say, my own eyes swimming in tears. "I mean, it's not just—it's not just Gran. It's a lot more than that."

And then, just like that, it happens. My mouth takes over from my brain, and the words just come spilling out before I can stop them.

"It just sucks," I hear myself saying in that same strange, gravelly voice, "because . . . because I think I'm in love with my fiancé's best friend."

"So?" Chaz says without skipping a beat and sounding completely unsurprised. "I've got it worse. I'm in love with my best friend's fiancée."

For a moment there's no sound at all. Neither of us seem to be breathing, and even the cicadas have fallen silent.

I'm not sure I heard him right. His best friend's fiancée? But that . . . that's *me*! Chaz means he's in love with *me*!

That's what he's doing here at my parents' house on this foggy summer night. That's why he's standing here in front of me with his arms at his sides, palms open, nothing to hide, no more sarcasm, no more biting remarks, no more Luke, no more Valencia, no more nothing. Just us.

All it took was a few thousand miles of separation, the stripping away of all but the rawest of emotions, and the death of one of the people I love most in the world.

Then, as if by some unseen cue, we both take a step forward until our chests collide, and he says, "Oof," and then, "Lizzie—" and I throw my arms around his neck and drag his head down so that I can press my lips to his.

And then neither of us says anything for quite some time.

A HISTORY *of* WEDDINGS

The first bridal registry was established by the department store Marshall Field's in Chicago in 1924. It was created in an effort to help couples keep a list of wedding gifts they desired for their households and soon caught on in shops worldwide.

The first electronic or online registry was introduced by Target in 1993.

When the first jealous ex logged on to mock the bride's choice of flatware in front of all her coworkers was not recorded.

Tip to Avoid a Wedding Day Disaster

No one ever wants to think that a wedding could be canceled. But these things happen. That's why proper wedding etiquette calls for wedding and shower gifts never, ever to be used before the wedding actually occurs. That way, if the wedding does not actually take place, these things can be easily returned to the giver, as is the appropriate action in such a case.

LIZZIE NICHOLS DESIGNS™

Chapter 15

Come live with me and be my love,
And we will some new pleasures prove
Of golden sands and crystal brooks,
With silken lines and silver hooks.

John Donne (1572–1631), English poet

"This is so wrong," I say as I sprawl naked across Chaz's equally naked chest.

"Is that why it feels so right?" he wants to know.

"If there's a hell," I say, "we're going straight to it."

"At least we'll be together," he says. "And I'm pretty sure Elvis will be there. And Einstein. He was an adulterer too, right?"

I groan and turn my head only to find that I'm looking at a mural on the wall of a castle on a hill. It's not even a very good mural.

But I don't turn my head again because on the other wall is an even worse mural of a knight riding a white horse. Chaz is staying at the Knight's Inn, which has windows with imitation diamond panes and a turret to make it look like a castle. When I asked him why in God's name he would choose to stay at a Knight's Inn out of all the hotels in Ann Arbor, he'd said, "Lizzie. I've got a *turret* in my room. How can you even ask me that question?"

"And Shakespeare," Chaz says now. "He was an adulterer. So at least hell won't be boring."

"I'm not an adulterer," I say. "I'm not married. I'm just engaged. And we're on a break."

"Did you specify the parameters of the break?" Chaz asks. "Did it include rampant monkey sex with your fiancé's best friend?"

"Stop it," I say. "You took advantage of me when I was in a weakened emotional state."

"Me?" Chaz starts to laugh, his stomach muscles causing my head to bob up and down. "You assaulted me in your parents' driveway. I was just coming by to pay my respects, and the next thing I knew, your tongue was in my mouth, and your hand was down my pants. I was so scared, I almost called nine-one-one to report a sexual predator on the loose."

"Seriously," I say. "What are we going to do now?"

"I can think of a few things," Chaz says, lifting the sheet that's covering us and looking under it.

"We can't let animal lust get in the way of our friendship," I say.

"I don't want to be friends with you," Chaz says matter-of-factly. "I stopped wanting to be friends way back last New Year's Eve. Remember? You're the one who had to go and ruin everything by getting yourself engaged to someone else. While I was sleeping, I might add."

I roll off him and lie on my back, staring at the ceiling, which is made out of that hideous stuff that has sparkles in it. There's an overhead light that has been crafted to look like an old-fashioned lantern. I wouldn't be surprised to learn that it has a lipstick camera in it that has been videotaping our every move for the past two hours. The Knight's Inn seems like it might be that kind of hotel.

Which makes it the perfect place for my tawdry affair with my best friend's ex-boyfriend and my fiancé's best friend.

"You don't even believe in marriage," I wail miserably to the lipstick camera. If there is one.

"Well, if I did, I certainly wouldn't marry you, that's for sure," Chaz says. "You'd just go around sexually assaulting my best friend behind my back while I'm in France and you're at your grandmother's funeral. You'd make the worst wife ever."

I lean over to hit him, but he rolls over on top of me, pinning my arms down beneath the sheet. A second later, he's staring deeply into my eyes.

"Lizzie," he says, looking serious for a change. "You need to stop beating yourself up about this. You and Luke have been over for a long time. You should never have said yes when he asked you to marry him. I told you that that morning in your apartment. If you had listened to me then, you could have saved everyone a lot of heartache. Especially me. And yourself."

I glare at him. "Do you think I don't know that?" I demand. "But you didn't exactly go out of your way to act like Prince Charming that morning, you know. You could have just told me you loved me then, you know."

"I seem to recall that, number one, you never gave me the chance . . . you were already engaged to someone else by the time I woke up, and that, number two, I did tell you I love you, and you took it as a joke and walked out."

I blink. Then say indignantly, "You mean at the *sports bar*? But you were so nasty! I didn't think you were serious."

He looks hurt. "I bared my soul to you, and you thought it was nasty. Nice."

"Seriously," I say. "You were horrible. You couldn't possibly have expected me to think you meant a word that you said—"

"I was mortally wounded!" Chaz insists. "The woman I loved, and whom I thought loved me in return—don't lie, you even said at Jill Higgins's wedding the night before that we were going to try taking things to another level—had just pledged herself to another!"

"Now you're just being ridiculous," I say. "Agreeing to take things to another level and saying that I'm in love with you are two completely different things."

"*If* I was nasty, like you say, I had a right to be," Chaz says. "You were acting like a crazy woman. Getting yourself engaged to a guy who is so completely wrong for you—"

"You didn't seem to have any objections when Luke and I got together last summer," I point out.

"Sure, I had no objections to your sleeping with him," Chaz says. "I never thought you'd want to *marry* the guy. Especially when I knew perfectly well you weren't in love with him."

Still pinned beneath his body weight and the sheet, I can only glare at him some more. "I beg your pardon," I say. "But I most certainly was."

"*Before* the Great Christmas Sewing Machine Incident, maybe," Chaz says. "But not after. It just took you awhile to admit it to yourself."

I blink at him, trying to figure out if what he's saying is really true. There's a part of me that's sure it isn't.

But there's another part of me that's equally scared it is.

"But you finally came around to admitting you're in love with me now," Chaz says as he reaches for the room service menu. "So what does it matter? Now I need sustenance. All of this cuckolding makes a knight hungry. What should we have? Beef nachos supreme? Or . . . ooh, bacon and cheddar potato skins with sour cream. Such fine fare this establishment offers . . . oh, wait. Cream cheese and turkey pinwheels. Who could resist?"

"I can't tell him," I burst out.

Chaz stares down at me. "About the cream cheese and turkey pinwheels?"

"No," I say, poking him through the sheet. "Get off me, you weigh a ton." Obligingly, Chaz slides off me. "Luke. He can never know."

Chaz leans up on one elbow, his head in his hand. "I can see why," he says, regarding me, his blue eyes expressionless. "Who eats turkey with cream cheese? That's a disgusting combination."

"No," I say, sitting up. "About us. He can never know about *us*."

Chaz's tone doesn't change. "You're going to marry Luke and keep me around as a boy toy? How twenty-first century of you."

"I . . . I don't know what I'm going to do," I say. "How can I . . . I mean, he loves me."

Chaz taps the menu. "Lizzie. Let's just order. We don't have to figure it all out tonight. And they stop serving at eleven."

I chew my lower lip. "I just," I say. "I . . . I'm not very good at this. At being . . . bad."

"Oh, I don't know," Chaz says with a grin. "I think you did an exemplary job of it earlier."

I lift up one of the flat, uncomfortable Knight's Inn pillows and smack him with it. He laughs and tugs it away from me, then wrestles me back down to the mattress.

We barely order our nachos in time to make the eleven o'clock cutoff.

• • •

"Where were *you* last night?" Sarah wants to know when I come tromping into the house the next morning.

"And aren't those the same clothes you were wearing yesterday?" Rose asks cattily.

Their eyes light up a second later, however, when Chaz follows me through the screen door.

"Chaz!" my mom cries, looking genuinely delighted. "What a surprise!"

"I'll say." Rose shoots me a look so laser sharp, it might have melted steel. "When did *you* get into town, Chaz? Don't tell us . . . last night?"

"How sweet of you to come," Mom says, going to give Chaz a hug. Having dated Shari for so long, he's an old family favorite. Well, with my parents. My sisters don't play favorites. Except among their kids.

"Of course I came," Chaz says as my mom releases him and my dad wanders in from the den, his reading glasses perched on top of his head and the newspaper dangling from his fingers. "I was a big fan of Mrs. Nichols."

"Well, my mother was something of a character," Dad says, shaking Chaz's hand. "Good to see you."

Rose and Sarah, meanwhile, are taking in the beard burn that no amount of foundation on my part has so far been able to cover up. Chaz's five o'clock shadow starts growing at approximately ten in the morning, and any kissing after that takes its toll. Conscious of their scandalized yet delighted gazes, I check out the new offerings—a pie from one of the neighbors, a floral arrangement from Gran's dentist—while Chaz accepts Mom's offer of coffee and a piece of the coffee cake the Huffmans brought over.

As soon as they're out of earshot Rose takes two quick steps toward me and hisses, "Sssssslut," in my ear while giving me a quick pinch on the butt as she heads into the kitchen to refill her own coffee mug. I let out a yelp—she always gives the most painful pinches.

Then Sarah moves in to whisper, "I always did think he was cute. You know, not, like, traditionally cute, but tall, at least. A little too hairy for me, though. But isn't he still in school? Does he not have a job? How's he going to support you without a job? Are *you* going to have to support *him*? I'm all for being a feminist, but not *that* feminist. Look what happened to Rose."

My eyes are still filled with tears from Rose's pinch. I have to sit down because I can't see to navigate the living room furniture, which my mother has rearranged to make space for all the floral arrangements that have been arriving. The next thing I know, a sheet of paper is thrust into my hands.

"Here," a child's voice says.

"What's this?" I ask.

"It's my newspaper." When my vision clears a little, I see that my niece Maggie is standing in front of me. "That will be one dime, please."

I reach into my pocket, find some change, and give Maggie a dime. She walks away without saying thank you.

I look down at the sheet of paper. It is printed in sixteen-point type and arranged to look like the front page of an actual newspaper. She's clearly had someone's help with it, since, being in the first grade, she'd only just learned to read and write. The headline, which is in twenty-six point, screams, "*GRANDMA NICHOLS DIES!!!!*"

Below that, the article goes on to describe Gran's death in grisly detail, with a line about how Elizabeth Nichols is quoted as being "very sad."

"Now, Lizzie," Mom says, coming out of the kitchen with Chaz in tow, holding a steaming mug of coffee and a plate of coffee cake. "I wanted to let you know, we've selected a reading for you to do at the service this afternoon."

"A reading?" I look up from the paper. "What kind of reading?"

"Just a passage from the Bible that Father Jim picked out," Mom goes on as Rose drifts out from the kitchen and takes a seat by the piano. "I'll get you a copy so you can practice. Each of you girls is doing one."

"Gran never read the Bible," I say, "in her life."

"Well, you can't have a funeral without Bible readings," Sarah says.

"And these are very tasteful Bible passages, honey," Mom says. "Don't worry."

"Tasteful Bible passages," Chaz says, putting his plate of coffee cake down on a side table. When Mom looks at him, he grins and raises his mug of coffee toward her in a salute. "Great coffee, Mrs. Nichols!"

Mom smiles. "Why, thank you, Chaz."

I'm too miserable to smile. "Mom," I say. "This funeral . . . it's like it doesn't even have anything to do with Gran. We should be having a celebration of her life. The things in it should represent things she really loved."

"Like what?" Mom asks with a tiny snort. "*Dr. Quinn, Medicine Woman* and beer?"

"Yeah," I say. "Exactly."

"Don't be ridiculous, Lizzie," Rose says. She shoots a look at the kitchen door, through which my dad hasn't reappeared, apparently still being busy getting his own coffee and cake to go with it. She drops her voice to a whisper as she hisses, "Grandma embarrassed us enough while she was alive. Let's not have her embarrass us in death too."

I widen my eyes and swing my head around to look at Chaz, who's choked a little on the mouthful of coffee he's just swallowed.

"So, Chaz," Dad says as he comes into the room, followed by Angelo, Rose's husband, who is wearing a black suit with no tie and a black shirt unbuttoned almost to midchest. "Are you still in school?"

"Yes, sir," Chaz says. "I have about three more years of course work left, then I have to start writing my dissertation, and then I'll have to defend it. I hope after that I'll be able to find a job and start teaching."

"Oh?" Mom makes room on the couch for Dad to sit down beside her. "And where are you hoping to find a position? Back here in the Midwest? I know how you feel about the Wolverines. Or out East?"

"Doesn't matter," Chaz says with a shrug. "Wherever Lizzie is."

Mom pauses with her coffee mug halfway to her lips, looking as if she's not quite sure she's heard Chaz correctly. Rose narrows her gaze and directs it pointedly to the ring on my left hand, while Angelo looks confused. Sarah coughs. Dad just grins affably and says, "Well, that's nice," and shovels the rest of his coffee cake into his mouth.

"I don't get it," Angelo says. "I thought Lizzie was engaged to that Luke guy. Chaz, weren't you goin' out with that lesbo friend of hers?"

"Who's Luke?" Dad wants to know.

"Oh, you remember, dear," Mom says. "We talked to him on the phone. That nice boy Lizzie met in France."

"I'm still engaged to Luke," I say quickly. "Things are just . . . complicated right now."

"Are they ever," Rose says, getting up and grabbing Chaz's and Dad's empty plates. "Too bad Gran's gone. She'd have *loved* this."

And I realize, a little belatedly, that Rose is right. Not only would Gran have loved what's going on between me and Chaz, but she'd have been rooting for it. She was the one who'd urged me not to get engaged. She was the one who always thought Chaz was my boyfriend all along.

And a hunk too, if memory serves.

Gran had been right.

About a lot of things, it turns out.

A HISTORY *of* WEDDINGS

The first wedding rings were worn only by brides, not grooms. That's because the first brides were considered possessions by their husbands and once "ringed" (or captured), they were considered their husbands' property. The ring—though still worn on the fourth finger of the left hand, the finger with the vein thought to lead to the heart—was a symbol of the husband's ownership. It wasn't until World War II, in fact, that it became popular for men as well as women to wear wedding rings, and not until the Korean War that it became standard.

Why is this? Why, so women could be sure that their menfolk, when away from home, were reminded that they were not available!

Tip to Avoid a Wedding Day Disaster

When canceling a wedding, it is appropriate, but not mandatory, to send out formal announcements. Informing friends and family verbally that your plans have changed is fine. If, however, you are postponing the wedding, it is necessary to send out a card simply stating the rescheduled date and location of the wedding. If calling all the guests on your list to tell them that your wedding is canceled is too painful for you, have someone else—such as your wedding gown designer—do it for you. That's what we're here for! Well, what our receptionists are here for, anyway.

LIZZIE NICHOLS DESIGNS™

Chapter 16

I have spread my dreams beneath your feet;
Tread softly because you tread on my dreams.

W. B. Yeats (1865–1939), Irish poet and dramatist

Honey, where have you been?" Mom demands as Chaz and I enter the church, late. This was a deliberate ploy on Chaz's part to spare me what he'd declared to be a barbarous practice—the viewing, which had been scheduled for the hour prior to the funeral.

Unfortunately, I discover as Mom grabs my hand, they've kept the casket open just for me.

"Hurry," she says, tugging urgently. "They're about to close it."

"Uh, that's okay," I say. "I'm good."

"No, honey," Mom says. "You, more than anyone, need the closure of seeing Gran at peace."

"No," I say. "I really don't, Mom."

But Mom evidently doesn't believe me, because she rips me from the safety of Chaz's protective embrace and drags me to the side of Gran's coffin, which is at the back of the church, waiting to be wheeled to its place of honor up front. The lid is open, and Gran, looking incredibly small and frail—and completely unlike her normal self—is inside. I stare in horror.

"See?" Mom says in comforting tones, pulling me toward it. "It's all right. They did an incredible job. She looks like she's just sleeping."

Gran does not look like she's sleeping. She looks like a wax dummy. For one thing, whoever did her face put way too much rouge on her. And for another, they've put her in a blue dress with a collar that's too high and lacy—something she'd never have worn in life—and clasped her hands across her chest over a rosary.

A can of Bud would have been entirely more appropriate.

"You can kiss her good-bye if you want," Mom says to me soothingly.

I don't want to insult anyone, but the truth is, I'd sooner kiss DJ Tippycat.

"No," I say. "That's okay."

"*Maggie* kissed her," Mom says, looking a little affronted.

I look around for my niece, expecting to find her huddled in a corner of the church, rocking gently and telling herself everything's going to be all right. But she's over by the doors trying to fill a Snapple bottle with holy water and telling her cousins it's okay, she drinks it all the time.

"Uh," I say to Mom. "I'm good. Really."

I don't care if my six-year-old niece did it before me, and I don't care if it *is* Gran: No way am I kissing a dead body.

"Well," Mom says as the funeral attendant, obviously fuming about having been kept waiting this long, takes this as his cue to lower the lid to the coffin. "I guess it's too late now."

But in a way, I realize, it isn't. Also that Mom's right. And that the half hour Chaz spent driving crazily around town, insisting we not get to the church until he was certain the casket would be closed, had been for nothing.

Because seeing Gran like this—this empty shell of a body, this statue of her former self—has given me a form of closure. It's proven to me that the essence of Gran, what made her . . . well, Gran, is really and truly gone.

And when the funeral attendant snaps the casket closed, I suddenly don't feel sad anymore. At least, not as sad. Because that isn't my grandmother he's shutting up inside that box. I don't know where my grandmother is.

But she isn't there.

And that's a huge relief. Wherever Gran is now, I know she's finally free.

I wish I could say the same for me.

"Let's go," Mom says, taking Dad's arm and pulling him away from the wall of church bulletins, which he's been assiduously studying this whole time (Dad's always been powerless in the face of flyers). "Girls." She snaps her fingers at Rose and Sarah, who are trying to gather their progeny. "It's time."

And like magic, Father Jim appears with a few altar boys holding candles, and then we all fall into our places behind the coffin, which is wheeled to its place of honor before the congregation, almost none of whom I recognize . . . except Shari, whose gaze locks with mine as Chaz leads me down the aisle. She's standing with her parents, and at the sight of her I realize, guiltily, that I really ought to have checked my cell phone, which has been vibrating angrily all day, no doubt with messages from Shari, telling me she's arrived.

Well, I know it now. And she knows I know. And she knows something else too, judging from the expression on her face . . . she knows I've got beard burn from making out—and more—with her ex-boyfriend.

Honestly, I can't think about that right now. I look away from her, my cheeks on fire—and not from beard burn—and slip with Chaz into the front pew with the rest of my family as Father Jim goes up before the altar and the mass begins.

It soon becomes obvious that exactly what I feared was going to happen has happened: This isn't a funeral for my grandmother. It's a funeral for some woman with the same name as my grandmother.

But it could be any woman with that name. Because Father Jim didn't know my grandmother. He didn't know she hated tomatoes and mustard. He didn't know she liked television dramas and AC/DC. He doesn't know anything about Gran. She didn't care about any of the things Father Jim is talking about. She certainly never went to church (except on Christmas Eve, to see her grandchildren and great-grandchildren perform in the nativity, and even then she kept a flask in her purse until Mom found it and confiscated it. And then she begged everyone to buy her beer afterward).

It's not that the service isn't nice. It is. The flowers are beautiful, and the sun slanting through the stained-glass windows in the sanctuary is lovely. Father Jim gives off an air of good-humored sincerity.

It's just that none of this is about Gran. That reading Sarah just stood up and gave from the Gospel according to Luke? Nothing to do with Gran. At all. That nice song the choir just sang? So not something Gran would have liked.

But it won't embarrass Rose. And I guess that should make her happy.

But it doesn't say anything about the person whose life we're allegedly gathered here to celebrate. It's like the wax figure inside the coffin. It's not Gran. Gran, like Elvis, obviously left the building a long time ago.

Which is good for Gran. But it's not the way to memorialize her. It's just not.

But as I look at the faces of my family around me, I can see that they're all pleased with the way things are going. And why shouldn't they be? This is probably the first family event we've ever had that Gran hasn't ruined somehow. She wasn't exactly the easiest person to live with . . . as I know only too well. As fun as she could be—how many times did she show up at my school, saying I was wanted urgently at home, only to take me to the movies in the middle of the day because some big blockbuster was opening that she wanted to see before everyone else did and spoiled the ending for her?—she could also be a huge pain in the butt. I should know . . . I'm the one who cleaned up after her enough.

And I'd already heard Mom and Dad talking about how they were going to turn Gran's bedroom into a playroom for the grandkids. Which I can completely understand them wanting to do.

Still. It just seems like *somebody* could say *something* personal . . .

A hand settles over both of mine, which I'm clasping tightly together in my lap, and I look up to see Chaz smiling sympathetically at me, as if he's reading my thoughts. He's wearing a suit—the same one he'd been wearing that day outside his apartment building, when my heart had reacted so violently to seeing him. He left the baseball cap back in the hotel room. He'll never be as handsome as Luke—at least, not in the conventional way that the rest of society thinks of as handsome. He doesn't have Luke's long eyelashes, and his eyes aren't dark and sleepy-looking.

But my heart does another loop-de-loop as I look at him.

I'm gone. I know it now. I am in such deep, deep trouble.

And the worst part of it is, except for the trouble I know this is going to cause the people I care about—Shari, and of course, Luke—I don't even mind.

Suddenly Rose is elbowing me, saying, "Your turn," and I realize it's time for me to take my place behind the lectern beside the altar. I slip my hands out from beneath Chaz's and stand up, conscious of his whispered "Go, champ."

Then I'm walking to the lectern, the sheet of paper with the words Father Jim and Mom have picked out for me to read—the Gospel according to John—printed on it crumpled in my slightly sweaty hands. I climb the steps to the lectern and mess around with the microphone until it's the correct level, and then I look out at the sea of faces before me.

Wow. I had no idea Gran had so many friends.

Then I realize that she didn't. These are Mom's and Dad's friends. I see Dr. and Mrs. Dennis, Shari and her parents, and even, way in the back, the Pennebakers, Kathy's parents. I see my childhood dentist and, more embarrassingly, my gynecologist. Nice.

The one face I notice I don't see is my fiancé's.

But that's okay. Because we're on a break.

And I'm sleeping with his best friend, anyway.

"Um," I say. My voice reverberates throughout the church, sounding amazingly loud. I unfold the piece of paper Mom gave me. "A reading from the holy Gospel according to John." What's my *gynecologist* doing here? I mean, it's true she's Mom's gynecologist too. And maybe Rose's and Sarah's also, for all I know. But did she know Gran? Was she Gran's gynecologist? Did Gran go to a gynecologist? That is totally weird. I never thought about my grandmother's vagina before. I don't want to be thinking about my grandmother's vagina. Not here, at her funeral. In a church. While I'm doing a reading from the Bible.

"Jesus said to his disciples . . ."

Wow, my voice sounds loud. Why am I reading about Jesus? Gran couldn't have cared less about Jesus. I mean, if there's any justice in the world, she's with Jesus now, but chances are, she's with Elvis, like Chaz said, in hell. I mean, if there is a hell. And if Elvis went there, which I'm not saying he did. Hell probably is a lot more interesting than heaven. Less boring. I bet Gran would *rather* be in hell.

"'Do not let your hearts be troubled.'"

I'd rather be in hell. I mean, if Elvis is there. And Shakespeare. And Einstein. And Gran. And Chaz.

"You know what?"

Oh God. Everyone is looking at me. Mom looks like she's about to have a coronary. Oh well. She shouldn't have asked me to do a reading. She had to have known this was going to happen.

"My heart *is* troubled," I say, laying down the sheet of paper with the Gospel of John written on it. "It's troubled because I don't think any of this is what my grandmother would really have wanted to hear at her funeral. Don't get me wrong, I think it's very nice," I assure Father Jim, who is looking alarmed (although I can't help noticing that the altar boys seem delighted by this unorthodox turn of events—beneath their crisp white robes, their sneakers are filthy). "I just don't think anything that's been said so far actually has anything to do with my grandmother. Which is why I took the liberty of preparing an alternative reading earlier this morning." From the pocket of the black vintage jacket I'm wearing, I pull another slip of paper, on which I've penned a set of lyrics. "This is from a song I know my grandmother actually did enjoy. Don't worry—I'm not going to sing it." I see my sisters visibly relax. "But I think it's important that we honor the memory of those we've lost by actually mentioning a few things they really did enjoy . . . and this is something I know Gran really did like. So, Gran . . . this is for you. Wherever you are."

And then, unfolding the slip of paper, I read: "'Season ticket, on a one-way ride . . .'"

I risk a brief glance up. I notice that the assembled congregation are staring at me, most with open mouths. My mother, in particular, looks stunned. Dad, however, has a slight smile on his face. It grows larger as I read this next part:

"'Nobody's gonna slow me down . . . I'm on the highway to hell.'"

Now a few more smiles have joined Dad's. Angelo is smiling too. So is Chuck. Even Sarah has cracked a small one.

But that's pretty much it.

Except for Chaz. Chaz is grinning broadly. And giving me a thumbs-up.

I grin back at him.

"Thank you," I say demurely to the parishioners. And then I step down from the lectern.

• • •

"That was quite an interesting reading you gave," my former gynecologist, Dr. Lee, says an hour later, once we've all returned to my parents' house for refreshments after the funeral.

"Thanks," I say. I'm holding a plastic plate, on which I've piled as many different kinds of cookies as I could find. Thanks to the number of concerned friends and neighbors who've dropped off baked goods in the past couple of days, this turns out to be quite a lot of cookies.

I am not sharing these cookies with others. I am eating them all myself.

"Was that the Kinks?" Dr. Lee wants to know.

"AC/DC," I say.

"Oh, of course," Dr. Lee says. "How silly of me."

She drifts away, and Chaz ambles over to take her place. He's holding a plastic plate containing two different kinds of samosas, Korean barbecue, chicken satay, and cold sesame noodles. I can tell he's been visiting the table where my dad's grad students have plopped down their offerings.

"How's it going?" he wants to know.

"Great," I say. "My gynecologist liked it."

"That's two," he says.

"Two?"

"I liked it," he says, gnawing on chicken satay.

"Oh," I say. "Right. Dad liked it too. And Chuck and Angelo. And Sarah, I think."

"So five," Chaz says. "Out of two hundred. Not bad."

"So when do you think we can get out of here?"

"I was going to ask you the exact same question."

"Give it another fifteen minutes," I say. "Mom hasn't had a chance to really ream me out yet."

"Okay. And we're sticking around for that why?"

"To make her feel better?"

"You're a really good daughter," Chaz says. "Have I told you that you look hot in that skirt?"

"About twenty times."

"You look hot in that skirt."

"Twenty-one."

"You'd look hotter with it off. You know what you'd look hottest in? One of those really tiny Knight's Inn bath towels."

"Make that ten minutes," I say to him.

"I'll go make sure no one's blocked in the rental car," he says and abandons his plastic plate.

Not ten seconds after he's gone, Sarah and Rose corner me by the piano that all three of us loathed being forced to learn to play (and none of us succeeded in learning to play well).

"All right, spill," Rose says. "What's the deal with Shari's ex? And don't try to deny there's something going on. You reek of cheap motel shampoo."

"He can't take his eyes off you" is Sarah's more charitable contribution to the conversation.

"I don't know," I say to them. "Look, I don't have time for this. I have to go get reamed out by Mom."

"Mom's got a migraine," Rose says. "She's in her room with a wet washcloth over her face. You already killed her. So just give it up. What are you going to do about that Luke guy? Isn't he, like, Chaz's best friend?"

"Are they going to *fight* over you?" Sarah wants to know. It's been her dream since seeing *West Side Story* that two guys might one day fight over her.

"I really don't want to talk about it," I say, stuffing a whole chocolate chip cookie into my mouth so that, no matter what they say next, I won't be *able* to talk about it.

"Does this mean you're not getting married in France?" Sarah wants to know. "Because I was going to take some French lessons over at the Y. But if I don't have to, let me know. Because there are way cuter guys in the Italian class."

"If you think Mom's dead now," Rose says, "wait until she finds out you're not marrying this Luke guy. She's already told everybody in her scrapbooking class that you're engaged to a prince. This will totally finish her off. What AC/DC lyrics are you going to read out loud at *her* funeral, I wonder?"

I cannot speak, due to all the cookie in my mouth. This, I think, can only be a good thing.

"Lizzie?" I turn my head and see Shari standing there. My heart sinks. Not that I'm not happy to see her. I'm just not looking forward to what I know is about to follow.

I swallow. "Hi, Share," I say. "How are you?"

"Oh, fine," Shari says, eyeing my sisters with distaste. "I was wondering if I could have a word with you—alone—for a moment."

"No problem," I say. But of course it's a problem. I can tell from the expression on Shari's face that I'm not going to like whatever she's got to say.

I follow her up the stairs to my old room—which has been turned into a guest room—nonetheless, and sink down onto my old bed, trying to avoid the accusing stares of the Madame Alexander dolls my mom's parents sent me over the years. Jo March looks particularly disappointed in me as she glares down at me from my childhood bookshelf.

"Lizzie," Shari says, closing the door behind her. "What are you doing?"

"I don't know what you mean," I say, keeping my gaze on my feet.

"Yes, you do," Shari says. "Are you on those drugs my dad prescribed you? Because if you are, I want you to stop taking them. I thought they'd help, not send you into a complete break with reality. I mean, sleeping with Chaz? Have you lost your mind? What about Luke?"

Tears fill my eyes. I look up, only to find that Jo's mom, Marmee, is staring down at me with an even more accusing look than her daughter. Why, oh, why, had Grandma and Grandpa insisted on sending me a Madame Alexander doll for every birthday and Christmas until I turned sixteen? There are just so many of them, all looking down at us.

"It's . . . it's not like that," I say, my voice catching. "I never even took any of those pills."

"Then what the hell is going on, Lizzie?" Shari demands. She crosses the room in a single step and sinks down on the bed beside me. "Because this isn't like you. And don't try to deny it's going on, because it's written all over both your faces—beard burn not withstanding. I mean, don't get me wrong, I've always thought you and Chaz would make a great couple. I'll admit the whole Mae Lin thing was to make you jealous. I knew you'd never realize how great Chaz was until you saw him with another girl—a real girl, not a fembot like Valencia. I knew how he felt about you—it was totally obvious. He couldn't talk about anything but you. It's true you were the one thing he and I still had in common, but no guy talks about a girl that much unless he's crazy about her. Which he all but admitted to me. *You* were the one I wasn't too sure about."

I shake my head. "What do you mean, Mae Lin was to make me jealous? What are you talking about?"

"Well, it worked, didn't it? You were jealous, right? I couldn't believe how you stomped over there and picked a fight with the poor guy the minute Mae Lin and Valencia went downstairs. He had *no* idea what was going on. Oh my God, I nearly wet my pants I was laughing so hard."

Now I'm a little mad. Also a little stunned by Shari's underhandedness. She's been my best friend since forever. But I had no idea she was capable of this kind of duplicity.

"Shari," I say. "That's so mean. You were plotting all along to fix me up with your ex, when you knew perfectly well I'm *engaged*? To his best friend? And you used some poor girl from your office to do it?"

"Oh, whatever," Shari says, making a pooh-poohing gesture. "Mae Lin's dating a hot paramedic. She was willing to play along. But I never thought you'd actually fall into bed with the guy before *breaking up with your fiancé. At your grandmother's funeral.* What are you doing? Have you completely lost it?"

I glare at her. I'm pretty sure I look every bit as accusing—and disapproving—as the Madame Alexander dolls above our heads.

"For your information," I say, "I was *not* jealous of Mae Lin. And who I sleep with behind my fiancé's back at my grandmother's funeral is my business."

"Well, excuse me," Shari says, looking taken aback. "I just don't want to see you get hurt. You or Chaz."

"Oh," I say, unable to keep from letting out a bitter laugh. "*Now* you're worried about Chaz's feelings?"

"Hey." Shari narrows her eyes at me. "That's not fair. You know I loved him."

"Well," I say. "So do I."

"Do you?" Shari wants to know. "Well, then why are you still wearing Luke's ring on your finger?"

"I have some things I still need to figure out," I admit, uncomfortably pressing my left hand into the mattress so neither of us can see my ring finger. "I'm not saying I have all the answers just yet, Shari. I feel like I'm barely hanging on, as a matter of fact. But I know I love him, and I think I always have."

"What about Luke?" Shari demands.

"I'm doing the best I can, okay? Luke's in France," I say. "I'll wait until he gets back to figure out what's going on—or not—between the two of us. In the meantime . . . well, engaged isn't married, you know," I add. "Or dead." I'm a little startled to find myself parroting Gran's words. But what more appropriate place to do it, I realize, than after her funeral.

Shari looks at me as if she were seeing me for the first time. Maybe in a way she is. She shakes her head and asks, "Did you ever look up what solipsistic means?"

"Yes," I say indignantly. "And it's not true. I'm *not* extremely preoccupied with indulging my own feelings and desires. If I were, I'd never have moved out of Luke's Fifth Avenue apartment, much less looked twice at Chaz. He's a poor graduate student, whereas Luke's a rich prince, remember?"

Shari, to my relief, lets out a laugh. The Madame Alexander dolls look startled.

"That's true," she says. And she reaches over and takes my hand, the one with the engagement ring still on it. "Oh, Lizzie. Be *careful*. You're playing with fire here."

"*Me?*" I raise my eyebrows. "You're the one who just admitted you hired a girl from your office on purpose to flirt with Chaz to try to make me jealous!"

"But I thought you'd do the right thing and break up with Luke first," Shari cries. "Not start sleeping with Chaz during your grandmother's funeral. Not that it isn't a fitting tribute to her, one she'd have gotten a huge kick out of. Still. I'm just worried someone's going to get hurt. And I'm afraid it's going to be you."

I squeeze her hand. "I'm a big girl now, Share," I say. "I can take care of myself."

But as we make our way back downstairs, I wonder if that's really true. Can I? It's true I'm living on my own for the first time ever. I'm supporting myself, running my own business (well, practically), and at any given time spinning a dozen plates in the air at once. If I dropped just one, the whole thing would come tumbling down in a mess like no one would believe . . .

So what am I doing, having this torrid affair with my fiancé's best friend?

And it *is* torrid, I realize when I walk into the living room and notice him standing there waiting for me, and my heart slams into my ribs as it always seems to whenever I see him. I'm not going to escape from this unscathed. None of us are, I know.

But when Chaz lifts his head and I feel that electric shock that always seems to go through me lately when I look in his direction and his gaze meets mine, I realize I don't care. I don't care what's going to happen. As long as we can be together . . .

For now.

For however long now lasts.

A HISTORY *of* WEDDINGS

Flowers have always played an important role in weddings, since the very first recorded marriage ceremonies in ancient Greece, where they were used to make a crown for the bride to wear as a gift of nature. Floral wreaths and garlands were often used in ancient ceremonies to bind couples together in lieu of rings.

Different herbs and flowers—such as garlic flowers as well as bulbs—were often carried to ward off evil spirits. Evil spirits, of course, are not the only ones who'd be warded off if brides today started carrying garlic bulbs.

Tip to Avoid a Wedding Day Disaster

It's traditional to give your wedding guests a favor by which to remember the day. This is a centuries-old practice that stems from the French habit of giving bonbonnieres, or sugared almonds, to departing guests. Today's couples tend to choose candles or, if you really want to bring on the bling, rhinestone sunglasses.

LIZZIE NICHOLS DESIGNS™

Chapter 17

In all of the wedding cake, hope is the sweetest of plums.

Douglas Jerrold (1803–1857), English dramatist

I am standing with my forehead resting against the wide glass window overlooking the planes landing and taking off on the tarmac in front of me. Chaz and I have flown commercially out of Ann Arbor and are waiting for our connecting flight to LaGuardia from Detroit.

What I hadn't prepared myself for is Luke's unexpected phone call midway through the screwdrivers Chaz and I were downing at the Fox Sports Bar while waiting for boarding.

"How *are* you?" Luke had wanted to know. "I'm so sorry I couldn't be there for you, Lizzie. I know it must have been really, really hard. But you know I couldn't get away from the office. Uncle Gerald really needs me here."

I'd had to leave the bar and wander the concourse. I couldn't talk to Luke in front of Chaz.

"Of course," I'd said. "I know. And I'm good, I'm fine."

There are thunderheads gathering along the horizon. They're what's causing our flight to be delayed. Just a half hour so far. But who knows? We could be stuck in Detroit overnight.

And yet somehow the thought of being stuck in Detroit—or anywhere—with Chaz doesn't bother me. At all.

It's wrong that I'm talking to my fiancé on the phone and thinking about how much I don't mind being stuck in an airport with his best friend. Whom I can't seem to stop touching. Every time I'm away from him I feel something akin to a physical pain until I can get back to his side and lay my hand on his arm or touch his shoulder or slip my fingers into his . . . It's totally bizarre, and something I've never experienced before. Not even with Luke, the man to whom I'm engaged.

Rose is right. I *am* a slut.

"But I've been doing a lot of thinking," Luke is saying.

"You have?" I've completely lost track of the conversation. Behind me, one of those people movers is going *beep-beep-beep* as it tries to shuttle some elderly passengers to their gate, and no one will move out of its way.

"I have," Luke says. "How would you feel about coming to Paris for a week?"

I shake my head as if there were a bee inside it.

"Me?" I ask. "You mean . . . ?"

"Right. I want a break from our break," he says.

"Um," I say. "You want me to come visit you? In Paris?"

My God! He can tell! He can tell about me and Chaz! I hadn't mentioned that Chaz had shown up to the funeral. And Chaz obviously hadn't spoken to Luke since he'd arrived.

This is horrible. Luke's going to break up with me now, over the phone. Oh well. I deserve it. I'm a horrible person. I'm on the highway to hell.

I close my eyes, in preparation for being broken up with.

But all Luke says is "It's just, I've really been enjoying my time here. I know I shouldn't say that, considering what you've just been through. But it's true. I forgot how much I love Paris. And working with Uncle Gerald has been great. I'm really having a blast."

I open my eyes. Wait. This isn't breaking up with me. This doesn't sound like breaking up with me at all.

"I forgot how much I love working in the business world," Luke goes on. "It's really been fantastic. And I think you'd love it too. You know what a great time you had here last summer. It's such a shame you didn't come with me."

"Well," I say. "I really couldn't afford the time away from work." Each word sounds foreign as it falls from my lips. Except that I'm speaking in English.

"Sure," Luke says. "I know. Your job is important to you. I know that now. This break has taught me that. Really, Lizzie. It has."

I sneak a peek over at Chaz. He's watching the television over the bar. It's broadcasting a golf game. Based on his television viewing habits back in the hotel room—the few times we actually turned it on—I'm starting to realize there really isn't any sport Chaz won't watch.

"That doesn't freak you out, does it?" Luke asks. "I mean, that I'm enjoying it here so much?"

"Why should that freak me out?" I ask. What's freaking me out is that I'm sleeping with my fiancé's best friend, a guy who *also* happens to be my best friend's ex-boyfriend. Yeah, my best friend who's a lesbian now. *That*'s what's freaking me out.

Not that I'm going to mention this to him.

"Well, that's a relief," Luke says. "I mean, I haven't given up on the medical school thing yet. Not completely. I'm just . . . I'm not totally sure it's for me, and Paris . . . well, Paris is so incredibly great. I just think you'd really love it—"

Okay. Now I've officially freaked myself out. I have to get off the phone. I have to get off the phone *now*.

"Uh-oh, they're calling my flight," I lie. "I have to go. I'll talk to you later, Luke."

"Oh, right," Luke says. "Love you!"

"Love you too," I say and hang up.

What just happened? *What just happened there?* I don't even know if I can deal with it. I hurry across the crowded concourse to slide back onto my bar stool at the Fox Sports Bar, pick up my screwdriver, and drain it.

"Slow down, there, slugger," Chaz says, observing me with some alarm. "They have more vodka back there than just what's in that glass, you know."

I set down my empty glass and lay my head down upon the bar. "He wants me to come to Paris to see him," I say to the beer nuts that have fallen to the airport floor.

"The bastard," Chaz says. "Next thing you know, he's going to want to set a date for the wedding."

I lift my head and look at him. He's wearing a Wolverines baseball cap and is looking adorably—and sexily—rumpled, as if he's just rolled out of bed.

Which, in fact, he has. With me.

The guilt over what we've done slams me—as it does a hundred times a day—yet again.

I drop my head back onto the bar. I want to start sobbing. I really do.

Chaz lays a large hand on the back of my neck. "Cheer up, sport," he says. "It could be worse."

"How?" I demand of the bar top.

"Well," he says after stopping a moment to think about it. "At least you're not pregnant."

This doesn't have the comedic effect Chaz apparently intended it to.

"Chaz," I say miserably. "Everything you said that morning after Jill's wedding is true. I know it. Luke really did ask me to marry him only because he was scared of being alone. I realize that now. He doesn't care about me. I mean, he does, but not . . . not the way you care about me. If he did, he'd have shown up for Gran's funeral. *You* did. But even so. Now look at the mess I'm in. I've got a fiancé I don't love who wants to marry me. And a lover I do love who doesn't. Why *don't* you want to get married, Chaz? *Why?*"

"I've told you why," Chaz says. "And if you won't accept me as I am, warts and all, then maybe you're better off with Luke. He's the one offering you the ring, the investment banker's bonus, and the place on Fifth Avenue. You'd be crazy not to go with him. All I've got is a walk-up in the East Village and a low-paying teaching assistant's salary. Oh, and no ring. I don't know what you're doing sharing this bowl of beer nuts with me in the first place."

I stare blearily down into the nut bowl. He's not, I know, referring to beer nuts. At least entirely. I can't help remembering that cold night when we'd sparred so unpleasantly at O'Riordan's, and I'd asked myself afterward what, if you didn't end up getting married, the point was.

The crazy thing is, with Chaz, I'm sort of starting to see. I mean, the point is just to be together. Who cares about a stupid piece of paper?

Wait—did *I* just think that? What is happening to me? Who am I even turning into? Can I actually be turning into that kind of girl? The kind of girl who doesn't care about marriage?

I guess so. I mean, I'm already the kind of girl who cheats on her fiancé—with his *best friend*.

I groan aloud suddenly. "How can I do this to him? How can *we* do this to him?" I cover my face with my hands. "I'm going to throw up. I swear."

"Please do it in that trash can over there," Chaz says. "And stop beating yourself up. He hasn't exactly been a Boy Scout himself while you two have been together."

I blink at him from between my fingers. "What are you talking about?"

"Nothing. Do you want another drink? They just delayed our flight by another hour. I think you need another drink." He signals the bartender. "This young lady would like another screwdriver. Ketel One."

The bartender nods and takes away my old glass to make a new drink.

"I'd rather have a Diet Coke," I say to the bartender. I've lowered my hands and am gripping the bar in an effort to stay upright. The vodka I've just downed so quickly has made me light-headed. "What do you mean, Luke hasn't exactly been a Boy Scout while we've been together?" I ask Chaz.

"I told you, nothing. Look, I've always wanted to ask you. What's with the garter?"

"*What?*" I stare at him in an alcohol-befuddled daze.

"The thing with the garter," Chaz says. "At weddings. You know, when the groom peels the garter off the bride and throws it to the guys."

"Oh," I say. The bartender has delivered my Diet Coke, and I take a grateful swig. "That's from olden times, when people in the court were required to follow the newly wedded couple to their bedroom after the ceremony to make sure they consummated the marriage. They'd demand the royal bride's garter or stocking as proof that the defloration had occurred. Since peasants like to imitate the behavior of nobility, it became standard practice to demand that *all* brides give up their stockings or garters after the ceremony—sometimes the wedding guests would take the garter by force, so it became traditional for the groom to take it off during the reception so people wouldn't follow the bride and groom back to their bedroom, and also so that the wedding guests wouldn't rip it off her."

Chaz makes a face. "Now, see," he says. "That right there is reason enough why the institution of marriage ought to be abolished."

I stare at him, comprehension dawning. "It's not *marriage* you're against," I say. "It's *weddings*."

"True," Chaz says. "But you can't have one without the other."

"Yes, of course you can," I say matter-of-factly. But it doesn't, I realize, matter. Not really. Not considering the grave we've already dug ourselves. "Do you really not feel guilty about what we're doing?"

Chaz finishes off his screwdriver. "Not in the least," he says. "I've done a lot of terrible things in my day, Lizzie. But loving you is not one of them. I don't know what's going to happen when Luke gets back in the fall. But I intend to enjoy the weeks I have left with you to the fullest. Because as I know from my study of the philosophy of time, whatever is going to happen in the future is already unavoidable."

I blink at him. And say the only thing I can think of to say. Which is, "So?"

"So . . . what?" he asks me.

"So . . . what next?" I am really hoping he has the answer. Because I feel completely lost. And sort of scared. In a heart-pounding, excited way. The way I felt when Shari and I got off the plane from Michigan and were standing in the line for taxis at LaGuardia Airport, not knowing what we were going to find when we got into Manhattan. I didn't have the slightest idea where I was or what I was doing.

But that didn't mean I was in the wrong place, exactly.

"Next," Chaz says, signaling the bartender, "I'm going to have another drink. And I suggest you do the same. Because there's a lady I know who deserves to have her memory toasted, and *not* with Diet Coke."

I give him a somewhat watery smile. "I'm not good at not knowing what's going to happen," I say when our screwdrivers arrive, and we lift them to clink.

"Are you kidding?" Chaz says. "That's what you're best at. You take the road less traveled and turn it into gold every single time. Why do you think Luke's still hanging on so tight when he's half a world away? You've got the magic touch. And everyone knows it."

"I don't know," I say uncertainly.

"Lizzie." Chaz looks me dead in the eye. "Why do you think it was you, out of all the people in your family, your grandmother connected with so well? You, and no one else? You were the only other person in your family who, like her, would never take no for an answer, and just did whatever the hell you wanted. Now raise your glass."

I do, chewing my lower lip a little.

"To Gran," Chaz says, clinking the rim of his glass to mine. "A fine old drunk with some damn good taste."

"To Gran," I say, blinking back sudden tears. But they're happy tears. Because finally someone is saying what I've been wanting to say about Gran all along.

Gran, I know, would approve of what Chaz and I are doing. Whatever that is, exactly.

I lift my glass. And I drink.

To Gran.

A HISTORY *of* WEDDINGS

The first toasts were performed back in the sixth century B.C., when the ancient Greeks would pour wine for their dinner guests from a communal pitcher. The host would drink first to assure his guests that the wine wasn't poisoned (a common practice at the time for getting rid of pesky in-laws or neighbors). Later, the clinking of vessels at weddings became a popular method of keeping demons away from the newly wedded couple.

At a traditional modern reception, the first toast is always to the bride, usually by the best man. The last toast is generally from the father of the bride. After he has made a weepy spectacle of himself, the reception can officially begin. Only at a nontraditional modern reception does the bride get to give her own toast, thanking her wedding party and guests (who, after sitting through so many toasts, truly deserve thanking).

Tip to Avoid a Wedding Day Disaster

Keep your toasts short. Please, no crib sheets. The point of the toast is to wish the happy couple well and invite all the other guests to join you in doing so, not to embarrass the couple or show how witty you are. You should also thank the parents for hosting the wedding and the couple for bestowing the honor of allowing you to be their best whatever-you-are. Lift your glass, ask others to do so as well, congratulate them, then get your butt back in the seat, for the love of God, so the rest of us can eat our cold rubbery chicken.

LIZZIE NICHOLS DESIGNS™

Chapter 18

To love someone deeply gives you strength. Being loved by someone deeply gives you courage.

Lao Tzu, fourth century B.C., Taoist philosopher

I'm late for work Monday morning.

There is only one explanation for how I can be late to work in a place that is precisely two floors below where I live: Chaz.

It turns out there *is* a disadvantage to living two floors up from where you work . . . if you don't want the people you're working with to know you're sleeping around behind your fiancé's back, anyway.

I told Chaz that if he wanted to spend the night at my place he had to get out *before* anyone else showed up at the shop in the morning. I couldn't have Tiffany and the other ladies seeing him leaving. Which meant he had to be out of there before nine . . . preferably before eight thirty.

He would have made it too, if it hadn't been for my own insufferable weakness when it comes to men who bring girls breakfast in bed. It isn't a weakness I ever knew I had before. Because no guy has ever brought me breakfast in bed before.

And it wasn't just that he brought me breakfast in bed, either, but that he got up way before I did and must have crept around super-quietly so as not to wake me, and gone to the store—since there was seriously nothing in my refrigerator—and then made scrambled eggs and bacon and toast and brought it all in on a tray with a single red rose in a bud vase next to an icy cold Diet Coke still in the can . . . just the way I like it.

What girl wouldn't have melted? And then jumped his bones (as soon as she was done with her eggs . . . I didn't want them to get cold, after all)?

So I'm a little bit . . . frazzled . . . when I finally get downstairs to work. Frazzled in a good way. A highly relaxed, but still slightly disoriented and dazed way. It's how I've been feeling since I first kissed Chaz . . . good, but almost as if I had gone ahead and started taking those pills Shari's dad had given me, instead of flushing them down the toilet back at the Knight's Inn, like I actually did. The world seems . . . different. Not better, not worse, just . . . different. Suddenly, things that used to bother me—men who wear baseball caps indoors, for instance—don't bother me at all anymore. Fears that used to consume me—that I might end up shopping for vast amounts of cold medicine at my hometown grocery store on weekends like Kathy Pennebaker—no longer seem likely . . . in fact, they seem improbable. Instead of obsessively eating in one sitting the entire bag of cheese popcorn that I bought at the airport, I ate only a handful.

And I didn't even *think* about buying a Cinnabon.

Something is happening to me. I've even stopped wearing Spanx. I just don't care if my bulges show. Maybe because Chaz actually *likes* my bulges?

I never have to worry about being on top with him, or making sure I walk backward out of the room when I'm naked so my butt doesn't show. In fact, I'm pretty sure if I did this, Chaz would ask me what the hell I was doing, something Luke never seemed to notice. Or wonder about.

Maybe this is what comes from being a loose woman. When you give up your morals, they *all* just go, inhibitions too.

Anyway, I'm not the first person into the shop. Sylvia and Marisol are already there, working on the lace-and-tulle I. Magnin & Co. 1950s cocktail-style number we'd gotten from a punky bride whose mother had worn it and who wanted to squeeze into it as well . . . only she was a size 12 and her mother had been a size 8. We'd assured her we could handle it.

But from the way Sylvia and Marisol start staring, their mouths hanging open, when I walk in, I'm not sure we can handle much of anything, let alone retrofitting a size 12 I. Magnin cocktail dress to an 8.

"What?" I demand, staring right back at them.

They know. I don't know how they know, but it's obvious they do. I might as well be wearing a big scarlet letter *A* on my chest.

Great. The boss is a slut. In an hour, when Tiffany gets here, everyone in Manhattan (and parts of North Dakota, where Tiffany is from) will know it.

How do I handle this? There was never an article about this in *Fortune Small Business*. What to do when all your employees know that you're sleeping with your fiancé's best friend. At least I don't think so. Damn, I knew I should have paid more attention to that magazine and less to *Us Weekly*.

"This is looking good," I say about the dress the two women are working on. They've ripped all the stitching from the waist and bodice and will be inserting stretchy lace panels—the big girl's friend—in discreet locations. Yeah, that's it. Maybe I can distract them by complimenting their work!

The two women exchange glances.

"I was sorry to hear about your grandmother, Lizzie," Marisol says.

"Yes," Sylvia says. "I'm very sorry too."

I blink at them for a moment, then realize . . . they don't think I'm a slut at all! They weren't being weird before. They just didn't know what to say because I've just come back from my grandmother's funeral.

God! I'm such an idiot!

"Oh," I say, smiling. "Thank you so much. She . . . she had a good, long life."

I'm feeling much better about things—less disoriented, and actually caught up on the things I've missed, including phone messages, of which there weren't too many, due to the holiday weekend—an hour later when Tiffany walks through the front door, takes one look at me, and goes, "Oh my God. You had sex this morning."

I nearly choke on the Diet Coke—my second of the day—I'm sipping.

"Wh-what?" I cry, trying not to spill all over the appointment book I have open in front of me. "What are you talking about? No, I didn't."

"Oh, don't even try," Tiffany says in disgust as she sashays into the shop in her four-inch lace-up stilettos. "You think I can't tell by now when you've had morning sex? And whoever it was, he did you *good*. Who was it? It couldn't have been Luke. I've never seen you *glowing* like that before. It's kind of revolting." She halts midway across the shop and stares at me owl-eyed. "Oh my God, Lizzie. Did you and Chaz—"

"NO!" I leap up from the reception desk and begin to wave my arms at her like a madwoman. "No, of course not!"

"Holy shit." A slow smile begins to spread across her face. "You screwed your fiancé's best friend. You slut."

"I *didn't*," I cry. "I swear I didn't!"

"And now you're *lying* about it." Still smiling, Tiffany reaches into her Marc Jacobs bag and pulls out her Sidekick. "Monique needs to hear about this. So does Raoul. In fact, I can't think of one person I know who doesn't need to hear about this. This is sick. Little Miss Prudy Pants got her rocks off this weekend with her fiancé's best friend. Oh shit, her best friend's ex!" Tiffany laughs to herself as she types into her Sidekick. "Even better! Man, you are going to burn in hell for true!"

I reach up and lay a hand over her keyboard. "Tiffany," I say earnestly. "Please. Look at me."

Tiffany looks down from her towering six feet two inches (with the heels) and blinks her heavily mascaraed eyes. "What?" she asks. She's still grinning like the Cheshire cat.

"It's not what you think," I say. There's a knot in my stomach. All the yummy eggs and toast and things I put into it an hour ago feel as if they're about to come back up. "The thing is . . ."

"Oh, what?" Tiffany demands sarcastically. "You *looooooove* him?"

"Yes," I say tightly. I am so close to vomiting I don't know what to do. I don't want to throw up all over Tiffany's pretty Laundry sundress, but I'm not sure how much longer I can hold it in. "As a matter of fact, I do."

Tiffany lowers her Sidekick, leans down until her face is level with mine, and says, enunciating very clearly, "*Duh*."

Then she straightens back up, yanks her keypad out of my grasp, and, prattling on as she keeps her gaze on what her fingers are doing, says, "Jesus, Lizzie, do you think we don't know that? Frankly I think the only person in all of the tristate area who *didn't* know you were in love with Charles Pendergast the Third is you. It was so fucking obvious you like him and he likes you that it was just a matter of time until you guys did something about it. And you know what? I'm glad, because I am so fucking over Luke. He was getting on my last nerve. What is this spending the summer in France thing? Good riddance, as far as I'm concerned. I don't care if he *is* a prince. There're more important things than being royal, you know. Like, did he go to your grandmother's funeral? No? But Chaz did, right? Did he? Is that how this all happened?"

When I nod, dumbly, still stunned by her outburst, Tiffany goes on, turning her attention right back to her Sidekick. "See? I knew it. Monique owes me fifty bucks. Anyway. I can tell by your face you've been completely guilt tripping yourself about all this. Get over it, Lizzie. Yeah, Luke's a nice guy, and all, and he gave you a big rock . . . but when it's counted, has he ever been there for you? No, he hasn't. You're better off with Chaz, who really does love you—anyone can tell that just by the way he was looking at you at that Fourth of July party . . . though I'll admit most of the time it seemed like he wanted to kill you. The thing is, he's the real deal." She snaps her Sidekick closed, her message apparently delivered to all of the East Side, the West Side, Brooklyn, and most of Queens as well. "And that's the kind of guy you need. I'm glad he finally banged you."

I stare up at her. My urge to vomit has passed. I'm seized by a new urge . . . to hug her.

I know better than to act on this urge, however. Instead, I hug myself, and say in a soft voice, "Thanks, Tiffany. I . . . it's been kind of . . . weird."

"I can imagine," Tiffany says, sauntering the rest of the way across the room to her chair and collapsing into it. "I mean, for *you*. You're not used to being a bad girl. But the thing is"—she reaches into her enormous bag and pulls out a chocolate croissant, then gestures for me to make her a cappuccino, which I do—"you're not really even being that bad. You know? I mean, it's not like you and Luke are married. You're engaged. And, like, barely. You haven't even set a date. On the Bad Girl Scale, ten being really bad, and zero being barely bad, you're like a one."

I hand her the cappuccino I've whipped up, having already turned on the machine when I got in. "What are you?"

"Me?" Tiffany bites into her croissant and chews thoughtfully. "Well, let's see. Raoul's married, but his wife left him for her personal trainer. The only reason they aren't divorced is because he doesn't have his green card yet. As soon as he gets it—which should be any day now—he's going to divorce her and marry me. But we *are* living together. So, on the Bad Girl Scale, I'm like a four."

I've never heard of the Bad Girl Scale—never having done anything before to put me on it. I'm genuinely interested.

"What's Ava?" I want to know.

"Ava? Oh, let's see. She's sleeping with this DJ Tippycat guy, and *he*'s married. But, according to the tabloids, his wife came after him in an Outback Steakhouse parking lot with a chain saw, so he's got a restraining order out on her. That only puts her at about a five on the Bad Girl Scale."

"That's higher than you," I say, impressed.

"True," Tiffany says. "Tip's got a rap sheet. He tried to take an ounce of marijuana on a plane once. It was in one of his kid's stuffed animals. But still. Oh my God. I have to remember to tell Ava about you and Chaz. She's gonna be stoked. She had a fifty riding on it too. Little Joey's got a hundred on it!"

"Please," I say, raising a hand. Ava's a bit of a sensitive subject, since she still hasn't spoken to me since that morning we woke up to find the paparazzi swarming outside the shop. "Can we just keep it on the D.L. for now? There are people who don't know that I'm trying to figure out how—or if—I'm going to tell. Like Luke."

Tiffany blinks at me. "What do you mean, if? Of course you're gonna tell Luke."

I look down at the ring I'm still wearing on my left hand and don't say anything.

"You *are* going to break up with Luke, right, Lizzie?" Tiffany demands. "*Right,* Lizzie? Because, oh my God, if you don't, do you know what number you go to on the Bad Girl Scale? Like, directly to ten. You cannot string along both those guys at the same time. Who do you think you are, anyway? Anne Heche?"

"I know," I say with a groan. "But it's just going to hurt Luke so much. Not the part about me, but the part about Chaz. I mean, he's his *best friend . . .*"

"That's Chaz's problem," Tiffany says. "Not yours. Come on, Lizzie. You can't have them *both*. Well, I mean, *I* could. But *you* can't. You wouldn't be able to handle it. Just look at you. You're falling apart as it is, and one of them isn't even on the same continent, and there's no chance of you getting caught. You're going to have to decide. And, yes, one of them is going to get hurt. But you should have thought of that before you decided to become a Bad Girl."

"I didn't *decide* to become a Bad Girl," I insist. "It just happened. I couldn't help it."

Tiffany shakes her head. "That's what they all say."

At that moment the bells over the front door tinkle, and Monsieur Henri comes in, followed by his wife, looking tight-faced, and another woman I've never seen before. The woman is dressed in a summer-weight business jacket and skirt and is carrying a briefcase. She looks a little too young to be a mother of the bride, but a little too old to be the kind of bride who wears the type of gowns in which we generally specialize. Not to be ageist or anything. But it's true.

"Ah, Elizabeth," Monsieur Henri says when he sees me. "You've returned, I see. We were very sorry to hear of your loss."

"Um," I say. I haven't seen Monsieur Henri since his first—and last—venture to the city after his heart surgery. According to his wife, with whom I've spoken on the phone several times since then, he's been back at their home in New Jersey, brushing up on his *pétanque* skills and watching *Judge Judy*. "Thank you. I'm sorry I was away for so long."

I was actually gone for four days, only two of which were actual workdays. But I can't think of any other reason why Monsieur Henri should be back so suddenly, and with what appear to be reinforcements.

"Not to worry, not to worry," Monsieur Henri says, waving my concerns off as if they were nothing. "Now, Miss Lowenstein. This is the shop, as you can see. Let me take you into the back room."

"Thank you," Miss Lowenstein says, giving me the briefest of smiles as she passes by, following closely behind Monsieur Henri.

I turn my bewildered gaze on Madame Henri, who can barely look me in the eye. "Oh, Elizabeth," she says to the carpet. "I hardly know what to say."

"Oh, yeah," Tiffany says, breaking off while taking a slurp of her cappuccino. "I totally forgot to tell you . . ."

A HISTORY *of* WEDDINGS

For many years it's been assumed that the wedding veil, which was traditionally worn over the face, was used to disguise the bride, and thus protect her from evil spirits. But more recent historians argue that perhaps the veil served a more practical purpose . . . the veil may actually have been to keep her betrothed, in case of an arranged marriage, from seeing the face of his intended until after he was already committed. A less than charitable interpretation, but have you *seen* some of those twelfth-century portraits?

Tip to Avoid a Wedding Day Disaster

Make sure the color of your veil matches that of your dress! Not all whites are the same. Never choose an ivory veil to go with a cream-colored dress. You might think the difference is slight, but believe me, it will show up in the photos, and you'll notice, and slowly, over the years, looking at the photos will drive you insane. Make sure you match the color of your dress to your veil. These are two items you won't *want to mix and match.*

LIZZIE NICHOLS DESIGNS™

Chapter 19

Marriage—a book of which the first chapter is written in poetry and the remaining chapters written in prose.

Beverley Nichols (1898–1983), English writer and playwright

I should have told you," Madame Henri says miserably as she dumps another sugar packet into her latte. We're sitting at a table in the window booth at the corner Starbucks, and she keeps glancing nervously toward the doors of the Goldmark Realty Offices, through which her husband has disappeared with Miss Lowenstein, Goldmark's self-proclaimed top sales agent. "But it was all decided so suddenly, and you'd already had the bad news about your grandmother . . . I just didn't have the heart to pile on this bad news as well."

"I understand," I say.

I don't, actually. I really don't see how, after everything I've done for them—all my hard work these past six months—they can do this to me. I mean, I *can*—it's their business, after all, and they have the right to sell it if they want to. But it seems awfully cold. On the Bad Girl Scale, I'd give what they're doing about a five hundred.

"So . . . he really just wants out?"

"He wants to go back to France," Madame Henri says glumly. "It's so strange. All these years, before the heart attack, I was begging him to take more time off, to spend more time with me at our house in Provence, and he wouldn't hear of it. For him, it was always work, work, work. Then he has the heart attack, and suddenly . . . he doesn't want to work anymore. At. All. All he wants to do is play *pétanque*. That's all I hear about.

Pétanque this and *pétanque* that. He wants to retire to our house in Avignon and just play *pétanque* until he dies. He's already contacted his old friends there—his schoolmates—and formed a team. They have a league. A *pétanque* league. It's insane. I suppose I should be glad he's found something that interests him. After the operation, I thought nothing would, ever again. But this . . . it's obsessive."

I look down at the Diet Coke I've bought but haven't even opened yet. I can hardly believe this is happening. How could my day, which had started out so incredibly well, be going downhill so fast?

"But . . . what about your boys?" I ask. "I mean, doesn't he want them to come with you?"

I can't imagine Provence would hold any appeal whatsoever for the two club-hopping Henri boys.

"Oh, no, of course not," Madame Henri says. "No, and they don't want to come with us. They have to stay and finish school. But that's why we need to sell the building. We'll need something to pay for that. New York University is so expensive." She sighs. Her eyeliner, usually so carefully and expertly put on, is smudged, a clear sign of the stress she's under. "And then we'll need something to live on. If he's doing nothing but playing *pétanque* all day . . . I suppose I could look for work, but there isn't much a middle-aged woman who used to manage a bridal gown refurbishment shop can do in the south of France." She sighs again, and I can see the pain the admission has caused her.

"Of course," I say. The urge to vomit that I'd felt while speaking to Tiffany earlier returns. "And you don't think you can get by just from the sale of your house in New Jersey?"

"Well, we hope to get a nice amount for it, of course," Madame Henri says. "But nowhere near what we can get for the building. Miss Lowenstein is going to send over an inspector and then get an appraisal, but she says comparable buildings in this area are selling for four to five million dollars."

I nearly choke on my own saliva.

Four to five million dollars? Four to five *million*?

So I don't have a hope of being able to buy the shop myself. I'm pretty sure you can't get a mortgage for that amount. Not if you're me, and you're making thirty grand a year, and you have exactly two thousand dollars in your savings account.

So I'm homeless *and* jobless. Great. Just great.

"It's just," I say, clearing my throat. "The shop is doing really well. *Really* well." Nowhere near four to five million well. But I don't mention that. "And since you already own your home in Provence, and you'll have the money from the sale of your house in New Jersey, it just seems like—"

"Oh," Madame Henri says. She's looking across the street. Her husband is coming out of Goldmark Realty and glancing around impatiently for her. "Here he is. Elizabeth, listen . . . I know. I feel terrible. And I am doing what I can for you. I . . . will speak to Maurice, if you wish." I stare at her in horror. Maurice? The rival wedding gown rehabilitator who was trying to run the Henris out of business when they first hired me . . . but didn't, thanks only to my efforts?

"Um . . . that's all right," I say in a strangled voice.

"I will speak to you soon. Yes? I will telephone. Good-bye for now." She kisses me on both cheeks and is gone.

I sit there, trying to figure out what just happened. Did my boss's wife really just tell me that they're selling out and moving overseas? That I am out of both a job and a place to live? Worse, that I'm going to have to fire my staff? Where are Sylvia and Marisol going to go? I'm not so worried about Tiffany and Monique. They'll find some poor sap to hire them to answer phones somewhere. But what about my seamstresses? How am I going to break this news to Shari? I promised her I'd take care of them.

Oh my God, could my day suck more?

This can't be happening. It really can't. What am I going to do?

Sighing, I pull out my cell phone and look at my contacts. Who am I going to call? In times of crisis in the past, I've always called one number . . . home. And okay, generally I've wanted to talk to my mom. But Gran is always the one who answered. And whether I liked it or not, Gran is the one who generally gave me the single piece of advice that almost always ended up helping me the most.

But Gran's not here anymore.

I think about calling Chaz. But this isn't Chaz's problem. It's mine. If I'm ever going to stand on my own two feet, I can't go running off to the man in my life every time something goes wrong. I have to work this through on my own.

Besides, I know what Chaz is going to say: "Oh, you can move in with me."

No! I can't let that happen! I have to solve this myself, without a guy helping me. Besides, that's how I ended up in this mess with Luke, when I moved in with him out of necessity when Shari and I couldn't find a place together, as opposed to because the two of us were actually ready for cohabitation.

Suddenly, my cell phone chirps . . . and when I see who is at the other end of the call, I almost sag with relief.

"Hi," I say, picking up.

"Hey," Shari says in the gentle tone that I've begun to notice people use with the newly bereaved. "How *are* you? I've been meaning to call."

"Not good," I say. "I really need to talk. And not on the phone. There's—" I clear my throat. I am so phlegmy lately. Well, when you've been crying as much as I have, I guess it's only natural. "Something I need to tell you. Can you take a break and meet me somewhere?"

"Sure," Shari says, sounding concerned. "How about the bubble tea place down here near my office?"

Where Shari told me all but the real reason why she was leaving Chaz. How appropriate.

"I'll see you there in half an hour," I say and hang up, then start hurrying toward the subway. At this time of day, a taxi down the FDR would be quicker. But I'm about to be unemployed. I need to save every penny I've got.

• • •

Shari calls to say she'll be late, of course. A crisis at the office arises, and she's the only one, as usual, who can handle it.

Fortunately she calls just as I'm exiting the subway, so I'm able to use my sudden windfall of spare time to window-shop. Her office is so far downtown that it's actually on the fringes of Chinatown, and as I wander around, blindly going from window to window, I find myself walking past shops displaying wedding gowns. Some of them have Mandarin collars and toggles down the front, and yet the mannequins are wearing veils.

Despite the fact that they are being sold in shops that are right next to fish markets or restaurant supply stores, the gown's prices are right up there with those at Kleinfeld's. I overhear two women in front of one window speaking in rapid Chinese while pointing at a particularly gorgeous gown, and while I can't understand exactly what they're saying, the meaning behind the words is clear: eight hundred dollars for the pretty white sheath with lace overlay is too much . . . especially for something any talented seamstress could make at home for a fraction of the price.

I agree with them. Bridal gown shopping is a bitch.

I find a table at the bubble tea place and end up waiting only five minutes before Shari comes bursting in, effusing apologies and sliding into the chair opposite mine before saying kindly, "Now, I've told everyone at the office that I'm not to be disturbed. I've turned off my phone *and* beeper, and I have all the time in the world. So tell me. How are you? What's going on?"

I surprise both of us by bursting into tears. I try to hide my face in a napkin, but the few students and other scruffy-looking, writer-looking types working on their fancy laptops at nearby tables still glance over at us in annoyance. The waitress, who was approaching to take our order, decides to give us a wide berth instead and goes off in the opposite direction.

Shari is so shocked she can't help laughing a little.

"Lizzie," she says. "What is it? Is it your grandmother? I'm so sorry. I know you miss her, but she died happy, Lizzie, in her sleep, with a beer in her hand. She's probably in heaven right now, watching *Dr. Quinn* all the time. And every single episode has Sully in it!"

I shake my head so violently that my hair falls out of the sloppy ponytail into which I've pulled it. Strands of it stick to my now-wet cheeks.

"I-it's not that," I hiccup.

"What is it, then?" Shari wants to know. "Is it Chaz? Did he do something to upset you? I'll kill him. Just say the word and I'll go cut his wiener off—"

"No." I shake my head some more. "It's not Chaz. It's not Gran, either—"

"Oh." Shari nods knowingly. "I get it. You told him. Luke. Oh, Lizzie. I'm sorry. But, you know, it's for the best. I mean, the truth is, you're better off without him. I never could stand him. He was just so . . . *perfect.* Do you know what I'm talking about?"

I sit there staring at her in horror. I don't think I could have spoken if I'd tried.

"I mean, with the château and the good looks and the doctor thing and the apartment on Fifth Avenue," Shari goes on. "There was something almost creepy about it. Like . . . what lucky star was *he* born under? Then when he was so mean to you last Christmas . . . Seriously, I couldn't believe it when you said yes when he asked you to marry him. I pretended like I was happy for you because that's what best friends do, but now . . . When are you going to dump him? Because I so want to buy a Carvel cake." When she notices that I'm staring at her without having said a word, she explains, "To celebrate."

"Shari," I say when I can finally summon the ability to speak. "I didn't break up with Luke."

It's Shari's turn to stare at me for a while. Finally she says, "Oh. You didn't?"

I shake my head.

"So . . ." She chews on her lower lip. "So I just really put my foot in my mouth, didn't I?"

I take a deep breath. Then I release it. Because suddenly the tears are back.

Only this time I'm not going to let them win.

Then I say, "Shari. The Henris are selling the building I live and work in and moving to France. I'm losing my job, my apartment, and, basically, my life. Plus, even though you apparently think Luke is too perfect, I wouldn't exactly jump to that conclusion, because unlike Chaz, at least he actually wanted to marry me. Chaz most emphatically doesn't. Still, I'm really happy that you're so glad for me that I'm getting rid of him. But excuse me if I don't feel like I have too much to celebrate right now. Especially with a Carvel cake."

"Lizzie." It's Shari's turn to look horrified. "I—"

But I realize I can't sit there a second longer. I have to get out. I just have to. I push back my chair and stand up as the waitress is heading over. She gives me an annoyed look, but I keep heading toward the door.

"Lizzie," Shari calls after me. "Lizzie, come on! I didn't know. You can't just walk out of here like that! Come back here and talk to me. Lizzie!"

But I keep going. I have to. Even though my tears are blinding me and I can't see where I'm going.

A HISTORY *of* WEDDINGS

The reason brides have traditionally stood to the left of the groom is so that he'll have his sword (right) arm free to fend off any last-minute would-be gentleman callers who might still want to press their suit.

It's also for this reason that originally best men were not attendants on the groom's side, but the bride's. They were supposed to defend the bride from any unwanted male attention that was not the groom's.

Unfortunately, the incidence of brides running off with best men tended to be rather high, so the position of best man was switched to the groom's side, and a maid of honor was appointed to the bride to keep her chaste. Weddings (and wedding parties) sure used to be a lot more interesting!

Tip to Avoid a Wedding Day Disaster

*Don't be a bridezilla! Yes, everyone is going to have an opinion on who you ought to hire and what you ought to choose for your flowers, your cake, your wedding photos. Take the advice you like, and politely ignore or laugh off the rest. Don't take it all so personally! So what if your wedding isn't as grand/expensive/beautiful/bohemian as cousin Jacqueline's? It's not a contest! It's about your joining your life—*forever*—to someone else's. GET. OVER. IT.*

LIZZIE NICHOLS DESIGNS™

Chapter 20

Hail, wedded love, mysterious law; true source of human happiness.

John Milton (1608–1674), English poet

My cell phone won't stop ringing. I know who it is. But I won't pick up.

I am standing on Madison Avenue between Seventy-seventh and Seventy-sixth Streets. I am staring into the windows of a shop. I've stopped crying and can now see clearly. I can make out every inch of the yards and yards of creamy white silk and petal soft lace draped on the mannequin in front of me. I can see every minute detail on the stitching, so fine it's almost invisible, the delicacy of the beading, the luxuriousness of the stiff tulle crinoline that holds the skirt in place. The gown is perfection personified.

It must cost thousands of dollars. Tens of thousands, maybe.

And yet.

And yet I think I could come up with something fairly close that—though it wouldn't be quite as sumptuous—would make the girl wearing it feel just as special.

For a fraction of the cost.

I'm just saying. What I do is cheap—yeah, okay? I'll admit it. But it's still pretty good. People like it. Ava Geck liked it. Jill Higgins liked it. Hundreds—well, okay, dozens—of other brides have liked it. It was good enough for them.

Okay, maybe it wasn't Vera Wang.

But it was good enough for their wedding day. It made them feel special. It made them look beautiful.

And that ability—that talent for taking something not so great and making it into something pretty, for not a lot of money—it's all I have.

I realize this as I stand there on the busy sidewalk, as the summer heat beats down on me and busy New Yorkers rush by.

The reality is, that's all I've got to contribute to the universe.

It's true. Shari helps women who've been abused. Chaz is going to teach philosophy, probably to students as snotty about it as he is. (But hey. That's important. Probably.) Luke is going to save the children—or help already rich people get richer, depending on what he decides. Tiffany models and answers phones, and Ava Geck . . . well, Ava does whatever she does, while Little Joey protects her.

And I make old wedding dresses pretty again. Sometimes I create new ones. For a fraction of what a designer gown at the shops around the corner on Madison Avenue would charge to do it.

It's an okay thing to do.

It has to be. Because it's all I've got.

And there's nothing wrong with that. Right?

My phone rings again. This time, when I glance at the display screen, I see that it's not Chaz, but Luke. Unable to imagine why he could be calling, I pick up.

"I heard," he says in a grim voice after I say hello.

My heart seems to stop. For a second, all the sounds of the busy street behind me—the honking, the sirens, the squealing of brakes—seem to fade away. All I can hear is my own breathing. And that seems shallow and irregular.

"You . . . heard?" I manage to wheeze.

"About the shop closing? Yeah," he says. "I called there first. Tiffany told me. Lizzie, I'm so sorry."

And my heart begins to beat again. And all the sounds of the city come floating slowly back.

"Oh," I say.

God. I am so stupid. Also, I am the worst Bad Girl ever to grace the Bad Girl Scale in the history of Bad Girls.

"Right. Yes. It's awful. I don't know what I'm going to do."

"I do," Luke says. "You're going to move to Paris with me."

I am trying not to be run over by all the people who are hurrying along the sidewalk. For the most part, they are stepping around me. But every once in a while, a harried Upper East Side mom on her way to some important lunch appointment uptown doesn't see me and almost barrels her Bugaboo baby carriage into me, and I have to move. This happens now, and in the confusion, I think I've misheard Luke.

"I beg your pardon?" I say to him.

"I know what you're going to say, Lizzie." He is thousands of miles away, but he sounds as if he were standing right beside me. Except for the car horns and occasional police siren down Madison Avenue, which makes him slightly difficult to hear. I put my finger in my nonphone ear, just to be sure.

"But just listen for a minute," he goes on. "I tried the medical school thing. I did. You can't say I didn't give it a fair shot. But . . . I just don't think I'm cut out for it. I can't hack another five or six—or more—years of school. I can't do it. I think it will kill me. I really do."

I watch as another young mother, this one pushing a newborn, walks by, a seven- or eight-year-old skipping by her side, an ice cream cone dripping all over his hand, down his arm, and onto the front of his shirt. Neither he nor his mom seems to care.

"Oh," I say.

"But since coming to work for Uncle Gerald—Lizzie. It's been great. I love it. I really do. I know when you first met me I was doing the same thing, and I said I didn't like it, and I seemed burned out . . . but this is different. Gerald's offered me my own department. I'll have people working under me." I've never heard Luke sound so enthusiastic. About anything. He sounds like his father sounds when he talks about wine. He sounds young. He sounds . . . *happy.* "There's just one catch."

"What's that?" I ask.

"It's here," Luke says. "In Paris. I'd have to move to Paris. Permanently."

"Oh," I say.

"But that's why when I heard what happened today at the shop," he goes on excitedly, "I thought, it's a perfect opportunity. You're out of a job, and I just got offered a great one. Lizzie, you can come here, to Paris. You can start over, like I'm doing. You can open a new shop here. A bridal shop. I walked by one the other day, and your dresses are a thousand times nicer. And much more affordable. Everything here is so expensive. There's a real demand for affordable fashion. That's where your niche is, I think, Lizzie. That's what you need to do. Open your own shop here in Paris. A shop that offers beautiful couture for the ordinary girl, at prices she can afford. For brides."

"I already have a bridal shop," I say, sniffling. "In New York."

"I know," Luke says. "But that shop belongs to someone else. And they're selling it. I'm talking about a shop of your own."

"But . . ." I say, looking at the display window in front of me. "In *France*?"

"Look," Luke says. "You speak French. My family can loan you the start-up income. Lizzie . . . don't you see? This is a perfect opportunity for it."

"But." I look around at the people hurrying by in all their different shapes and colors, at the buildings all around me, at the taxis and buses and delivery vans and trucks whizzing by, the sun slanting through the leaves of a nearby tree, growing, against all odds, through the pavement, in the shadow of the skyscrapers all around us.

Because that's what New York City is all about. Trees growing up out of the pavement, in the shade, where no tree should ever grow.

And I say, "I love New York."

"You'll love Paris too," Luke says. "You've been there, remember? It's just like New York. Only better. Cleaner. Nicer."

"It's so far away," I say as a kid walking by with a dog fails to clean up after it, and a woman with a Chanel purse yells at him for it.

"From what, Lizzie?" Luke asks. "Your grandmother? She's dead. Remember?" But Gran isn't who I'm thinking about.

"I can't decide right now," I say. "I . . . I'll have to think about it."

"You do that," Luke says. "You think about it. You take all the time you need. But I think you should probably know . . . I've accepted the job my uncle offered me."

"*What?*" I think I must have misheard him again.

"We'll figure something out," Luke says hurriedly. "If you decide to stay in New York, we'll just do the long-distance thing for a while. People do, Lizzie. We'll make it work. Don't worry."

Don't worry? My fiancé—on whom, it is true, I am cheating—informs me that he is going to move permanently to another country, but that I shouldn't *worry*?

"And if you need a place to stay, you know you can always move back into my mother's place on Fifth. She already said it was all right. She'll just need to use the place one weekend a month, for her—you know . . ."

He means her monthly Botox injections. But I don't say that out loud, since Luke doesn't need me to remind him about that.

I am standing there, openmouthed in astonishment, when a voice behind me says, "Hey."

I spin around, startled, and see a flash of khaki and the brim of a baseball cap.

"Luke," I say into the phone. "I have to go. I . . . I'll call you later, all right?"

"Okay," he says. "Honestly, Lizzie . . . I don't want you to worry. About any of this. I'm going to take care of it. Of you. I love you."

"I . . . y-you too," I stammer. And hang up. Then I demand, "What are *you* doing here?"

"Standing in front of Vera Wang's flagship store?" Chaz quips. "Oh, I come here most days, actually. I like to try on a few of the mother-of-the-bride gowns. They feel so smooth and slinky against my skin." He blinks down at me. "Shari called me. What do you think? And then I called the shop when you wouldn't pick up any of my calls on your cell. Tiffany told me I might find you here. She says you like to come here to clear your head." He looks at the display window. "I can see why. It's so . . . *shiny*."

I stare at the shop window too. But what I'm actually looking at is our reflection, him so tall and lanky, with his University of Michigan baseball cap perched on top of his head, and his strong, muscular legs, so tanned, unlike the tourists who occasionally walk past. And me, slightly wilted in my sundress from having run all over town in the heat of high summer, my hair hanging in a bedraggled mess from my barrette, wanting, basically, to die. We make the strangest-looking couple.

If that's what we are. Which I'm not even sure of.

And of course behind our reflection is the beautiful, perfect Vera Wang wedding gown of the week. In a size two.

"They're closing the shop," I say to his reflection. "The Henris. They're closing it. And moving to Provence."

"I know. Tiffany told me that too." He shrugs, looking infuriatingly unconcerned. "So. What are you going to do?"

"I don't know," I yell at him. "What do you think I'm standing here trying to figure out?"

God! How can I be in love with him? How can he be so different from Luke, whom I thought I loved for so long? *I don't want you to worry. About any of this. I'm going to take care of it. Of you.* That's what Luke had to say.

Whereas all Chaz has to say is: *So. What are you going to do?*

Then again, I'm the one who was so keen on wanting to stand on my own two feet.

"Well, you'll figure it out," Chaz says now, with another shrug. "I'm starving. Have you had lunch?"

Have I had lunch? *That*'s all he has to say?

"*How?*" I demand. "*How* will I figure it out?"

He looks a bit startled by my outburst. So does the Chinese-food deliveryman hurrying by.

"I don't know," Chaz says. "You'll open a new shop."

"*Where? How? With what money?*" I demand, my voice breaking. Because that's what I'm pretty sure my heart is doing.

"Jesus, I don't know, Lizzie. You'll figure it out. You always do. That's what's so amazing about you."

I turn my head and look up at him. Him, and not his reflection.

And I realize—as I've been realizing over and over all summer . . . all year, actually—how hard I've fallen for him.

This is really it, I realize. There's no turning back. I think I've just gone up a notch on the Bad Girl Scale.

"Luke is dropping out of medical school," I say. "He's taking a job with his uncle's company in Paris. He's *moving* to Paris."

"Gee," Chaz says tonelessly. "I'm so surprised to hear that."

I stare at him, appalled. "You *knew*? He *told* you already?"

He shrugs yet again. "He's my best friend. He tells me everything. What do you expect?"

"You told me," I say, shaking my head in disbelief. "You told me he's never been able to stick to anything in his life. And I thought you were nuts. But you were right. You were a hundred percent right."

"Luke's not a bad guy," Chaz says mildly. "He's just . . . confused."

"Well," I say, slipping my cell phone back into my purse. "Are you going to ask me?"

"Ask you what?"

"If I'm going to move to Paris with him? He wants me to, you know. He says his family will loan me the money to set up a shop there."

"I'm sure they will," Chaz says. "And no, I'm not going to ask you."

I set my jaw. For someone I'm so crazy about, Chaz happens to be the most infuriating person I've ever met.

"Why not?" I demand. "Don't you *want* me to stay here in New York?"

"Of course I do," Chaz says. "But, like I said, what happens in the future is already unavoidable. So I'm just going to enjoy what time I have left with you."

"That," I say disgustedly, "is such crap."

"Well," he says in the same unruffled tone, "that's probably true too. What do you feel like? I feel like Thai food. Do you feel like Thai food? Isn't there a good Thai place around the corner from here?"

"How can you think about food at a time like this?" I yell at him. "Do you know—do you have any earthly idea—that every time I think about marrying Luke, I break out in hives?"

Chaz raises his eyebrows. "That," he says, "is not a good sign. I mean, for him. And, I'm guessing, for Paris."

"It's a *horrible* sign," I say. "What did you mean back in Detroit when you said Luke hasn't exactly been a Boy Scout the whole time he and I have been going out?"

Chaz rolls his eyes. "Look," he says. "I don't really want to talk about this in front of the Vera Wang flagship store, okay? Let's go home. We can change out of these hot sticky clothes and I can run you a cool bath and order some Thai food and fix us both a couple of gin and tonics and we can sip them while we discuss the vagaries of life and I give you a full body massage—"

"No," I say, resisting the arm he's put around me. "Chaz! I'm serious. *This* is serious. I don't want to—"

But I never get the chance to tell Chaz what it is I don't want to do, because at that moment, two women who were passing by stop in front of the window and gaze at the gown I was admiring.

"See, Mom," the younger woman says. "That's the kind of dress I want."

"Well, dream on," her mother says. "Because a dress like that costs twenty grand. Do you have an extra twenty grand lying around?"

"It's not fair," the girl insists, stamping her Steve Madden–clad foot. "Why can't I have what I want? Just this once?"

"You can," the older woman says, "if you want to be paying for it for the next thirty years. Is that how you want to start your married life?"

"No," the bride says, sounding as if she's pouting a little.

"I didn't think so. So get over it. We're going to Kleinfeld's."

"God," the bride says as her mother drags her away. "You're so cheap. If you had your way, we'd get my wedding gown at *Geck's*."

The mother and daughter drift away, and I find myself staring after them in astonishment. Every single nerve ending in my body is tingling. I feel as if I've just caught fire.

A shop that offers beautiful couture for the ordinary girl, at prices she can afford. For brides.

"Oh my God, Chaz," I say. "Did you hear that?"

"Hear what?" He still has his arm around me. "The part about the full body massage I'm going to give you?"

"Them." I open my purse and start digging around in it for my cell phone. "Did you hear what they said?"

"About going to Kleinfeld's? Yeah. Hey, maybe that's where you should get a job. That's where everybody goes to get their wedding dresses. That's where my sister went. Not that it helped. She still looked like me. In a wedding dress. Poor kid. She tried waxing and everything."

"No," I say, stabbing at the numbers on the keypad of my phone. "Not that part."

Be there, I pray. *Pick up. Pick up.*

A second later, a voice chirps, "Hello?"

"It's me," I say. "Please don't hang up. I know you hate me. But I've got a business proposition I've got to talk to you about. It's important. And you won't regret it. I promise. Where are you?"

"Me?" She sounds slightly confused. "I'm at the dog run. Why?"

"Stay there," I say. "*Do not move.* I'll be right over."

A HISTORY *of* WEDDINGS

Carrying the bride over the threshold is a tradition that harkens back to the ancient practice of capturing brides from rival tribes or villages. It was also thought to—say it all together now—trick any evil spirits that might be lurking in the new home.

Today's modern bride may find the practice sexist or—often more alarming, considering the state of many HMOs—may fear her groom will throw his back out in attempting to lift her.

It is, for these reasons, a tradition that is losing popularity and may safely be skipped in lieu of a kitchen witch.

Tip to Avoid a Wedding Day Disaster

There is a rumor flying around that the cost of the gift you give at a wedding as a guest should roughly equal the amount of the cost of the food and wine you are served at the reception. This is ridiculous. Your gift should be tasteful—and does not even have to come from the bridal registry—but does not in any way have to be proportionate to the cost of what you are being served. Any bride who suggests otherwise deserves the wooden spoon you give her applied to her backside.

LIZZIE NICHOLS DESIGNS™

Chapter 21

Love is composed of a single soul inhabiting two bodies.

Aristotle (384 B.C.–322 B.C.), Greek philosopher

"Wedding gowns?" Ava echoes, her carefully plucked eyebrows raised. "At Geck's?"

"Why not at Geck's?" I'm perched beside her on a park bench next to the small dog run at Carl Schurz Park. The small dog run is actually a raised, fenced-in stage along the boardwalk by the East River, where pedestrians can stop and watch the tiny dogs as they skitter after tennis balls thrown by their owners. This seems a source of particular delight to toddlers, whose parents lift them to stand along the edge of the stage, and who shriek in delight every time a Pomeranian or miniature pinscher comes dancing in their general direction.

Ava, however, is holding an exhausted Snow White in her lap. The Chihuahua has apparently run after so many tennis balls that she is virtually unconscious on her mistress's smooth, tanned thighs, a fact of which the reality television crew, filming Ava for the pilot she hopes gets picked up, *Slaves of Ava,* is taking pointed note. I can't help staring at the cameras looming over me, even though Ava has told me not to pay any attention to them.

"You don't even see them after a while," she says, with a yawn that, I can't help noticing, is made all the more elfin and charming by the fact that her bee-stung lips are perfectly glossed.

"Ava." It's even harder than usual to get her full attention due to the fact that DJ Tippycat is still inside the dog run with his French bulldog puppy, and Ava's gaze keeps straying toward him every five seconds. "Listen to me. You said you wanted to do something with your life. Remember? After you broke things off with Prince Aleksandros. You have to have meant something more than just another tired old reality show. Well, this is your chance. Not only to prove to the world that you're more than just an bubbleheaded heiress, but to help out millions of brides who want to have a beautiful gown but can't afford it."

Ava doesn't look remotely interested. She's gazing through the enormous black lenses of her sunglasses at a tugboat chugging down the river in front of us. I glance over my shoulder at Chaz, who is waiting for me out of camera range. He refused to sign the waivers the film crew demanded in order for me to speak to Ava while she was on camera, so he has to wait out of the shot until I'm done. He doesn't look too unhappy. He's found a hot dog vendor and is munching away, enjoying one with everything, along with a cold soda, in the shade.

"I don't know," Ava says. "What do I know about clothing design?"

"You don't have to design the gowns," I say through gritted teeth. "*I'll* take care of that part. You just have to market the clothes. And Geck Industries have to provide the labor and materials. I'm not talking sweatshop labor or cheap materials, either. I'm talking quality craftsmanship, sewn here, in America. The gowns have to look gorgeous and feel nice against the skin. But nothing can retail for more than four hundred dollars. It all just has to be designed by me and marketed by you . . . the Lizzie Nichols–Ava Geck bridal line."

She perks up at this. "Hey. I kind of like the sound of that."

"I thought you might," I say, eyeing the camera uncomfortably as they swoop around us.

"Lizzie and Ava," she says. "Or Ava and Lizzie?"

"Whichever," I say. I can't quite believe she's actually going for it. I'd been shocked she'd even taken my call, let alone agreed to meet with me. I hadn't planned much beyond my initial pitch, not thinking I'd get further than that. "Either works, I think."

"That's *so cute,*" Ava gushes with so much enthusiasm that Snow White nearly tumbles from her lap. "Can we, like, do bridesmaid dresses too?"

"I don't see why not," I say. One of the cameras comes in for a close-up. I am acutely conscious of the fact I haven't powdered my nose all day, and that I am sweating copiously. I pray to God this show won't ever get picked up by a major network. Or Bravo.

On the other hand, if Ava accepts this deal, who even cares?

"And flower girls?" she asks.

"Sure," I say.

"What about clothes for dogs," Ava says. "When DJ Tippycat's divorce from that ho wife of his comes through, we want Snow White and Delilah to be in our wedding."

I look down at Snow White, struggling to find purchase on Ava's vinyl mini. One of the cameras zooms in on Ava's crotch. I switch my prayer to a different one . . . that she's wearing panties.

"Um," I say. "Sure. We can do a line of wedding wear for dogs."

"Okay," Ava says. "That sounds like fun." She eyes me a little uneasily. "But if we're going to work together, Lizzie, I need to know we're not gonna have that same . . . *problem* we had before . . . are we?"

I shake my head. "Ava, I swear on my grandmother's grave, I will never blab something I'm not supposed to ever again." And I know, as I say it, that this time I really mean it.

Really.

"Okay," Ava says cheerfully. "Lemme call Daddy." And she gets out her cell phone.

"Wait." I stare at her. "You're going to do it *now*?"

"Yeah," she says, dialing. "Why not?"

"Um." I glance over at Chaz. He beams at me and gives me a thumbs-up. "Nothing. Go ahead."

A second later, Ava's removed the gum from her mouth with a murmured *Sorry* in my direction, and is saying, "Daddy? It's me. Yeah, hi. So, I want to start my own line of bridal wear at the store. What? The reality show? Oh, whatever, that's so two thousand and seven. Anyway, I'm working with Lizzie, the girl who did my dress for my wedding to Alek? Uh-huh. Yeah, the one who outed me to the paps. But that, like, wasn't her fault, really. Her sister did it, and she's, like, a fat-armed cow. I know. Anyway, she wants to—well, here, I'll let her tell you." To my horror, Ava holds her pink Swarovski-encrusted phone out to me. "Tell him the thing about the beautiful gowns for girls at prices they can afford."

I fumble for the phone, my mouth going instantly dry. "Um, h-hello? Mr. Geck?"

"Yes?" A voice, gravelly from too many years of cigar smoke, demands impatiently.

I repeat Luke's line about beautiful gowns that brides can actually afford, and somehow the same spiel I'd given Ava just seconds ago about how Geck's would be in charge of labor and materials—but they couldn't be cheap!—and I'd be in charge of design while Ava would be in charge of marketing comes spilling from between my lips.

And in that moment, sitting in the sunshine by the river, with the *Slaves of Ava* camera crew on me, and Henry Geck on the phone, and Chaz a few dozen yards away, watching over me like a shaggy sheepdog, I'm pretty sure I have an actual out-of-body experience. It's as if all the times I have ever blabbed a secret involuntarily or said something I didn't mean to or revealed an intimacy probably best left unsaid, and was called upon to exercise my powers of charm in order to make amends come back to me with laserlike intensity and focus on a single point—the man on the other end of the phone. I am no longer Lizzie Nichols, almost-certified professional vintage wedding gown refurbisher, fiancé of Luke de Villiers, on whom (by the way) she is cheating with his best friend, currently probably a two on the Bad Girl Scale, about to lose her home, her business, and her life.

I am Elizabeth Nichols, cool and collected designer of wedding attire, with a single desire: to make beautiful bridal gowns—and bridesmaid and flower girl and dog clothes—available to the masses, at a reasonable price.

Suddenly I am on fire. I am invincible. The cameras swing entirely from Ava and onto me. Even though, as she gazes at me, her thighs swing apart, and it becomes apparent she's going commando today. And she's gone and gotten herself a Brazilian.

"Well," Mr. Geck says when I'm through and have paused to take a breath. "Miss Nichols, I must say. That sounds like an interesting idea. I'd certainly like to hear more. Why don't you and Ava come over for dinner tonight and we'll talk about it some more? Put her back on the horn."

I hand the phone back to Ava, feeling dazed.

"He wants to talk to you," I say.

"Oh, goody," Ava says. "Hi, Daddy. You like Lizzie's idea? Yeah, I know, me too. Okay. Eight? Yeah, we'll be there. Okay, buh-bye." She hangs up and looks at me. "He wants you to bring some sketches. Do you have any?"

I look at her, feeling slightly nauseous.

But it's a good nauseous. It's a *great* nauseous, actually.

"By eight tonight," I say a little hazily, "I will have."

• • •

"You're going to design a line of bridal gowns for Geck's?" Chaz asks as we hurry down Seventy-eighth Street, back toward Chez Henri. "And Ava Geck is going to do . . . what, exactly?"

"Be my spokesmodel slash corporate representative," I say.

"Does Geck's even sell nice clothes?" Chaz wants to know.

"They will after they start selling mine," I say. "Ava will make sure of that. They're going to have her name on them too."

"And you trust her?" Chaz sounds dubious. "Ava, I mean. No offense, Lizzie, but—"

"If the next words that come out of your mouth are 'skanky crack whore,' you're never setting foot in my apartment again. For however little time left I have it."

"I'm just saying, like another person whose name I won't mention, Ava doesn't exactly have a reputation for stick-to-it-tiveness. Except where pudding wrestling is concerned."

"Maybe because no one has really given her a chance to prove herself," I say defensively. "I mean, she's an heiress. When has she ever *had* to stick to anything? But she seems really serious about this. The dog clothes were her idea."

"Oh yeah," Chaz says, with a chuckle, putting his arm around my shoulders. "She's serious about this all right."

"Chaz," I say, leaning into him. I don't care that I'm hot and sweaty (and so is he). Even when I'm annoyed with him, like now, I can't stop myself from touching him. It just feels . . . *right*. "People love their pets. They really want them to be a part of their special day."

"But doesn't the idea of your enabling them to do so by designing mini doggie tuxedos for them make you the slightest bit queasy?"

"No," I say firmly. "Not if it's going to save the jobs of everyone at the shop."

"And how is your designing doggie tuxedos for Geck's going to do that?" Chaz wants to know.

"I haven't figured that part out yet," I say as we hurry along. "I'm just taking this one step at a time. First I've got to get these sketches done. Then get the deal in place. Then I'll get to that part."

"You're incredible," Chaz says. And there's no hint of sarcasm in his tone now.

Still, I pull him to a stop and narrow my eyes as I peer up at him. "Are you mocking me?" I demand suspiciously.

"Absolutely not," Chaz says, looking down at me with a perfectly serious expression on his face. He's dropped his arm from my shoulders, but now he puts both his hands there instead. "I told you before—you're a star, Lizzie Nichols. And I am humbled to be allowed to hitch my wagon to your star. Just tell me what you need me to do to help, and I'll do it."

I blink up at him and my eyes fill with sudden tears. It's still astonishing to me how blindly stupid I'd been, refusing to see what was right there in front of my face for so long. That I could have been this happy six months ago, if I'd just been willing to admit to myself what I'd clearly known all along . . . that it wasn't Luke I was in love with anymore after all.

But I don't say any of this to Chaz. There's no reason to. Not now. Because I've said it already.

Instead, I say, "Diet Coke."

He tightens his grip on my shoulders. "You need Diet Coke? To get the drawings done?"

I nod.

"Done," he says. "I'll get you every six-pack in the city. I—"

Then his voice trails off, and I notice his gaze has as well. We've reached Chez Henri, where I'm startled to find, when I turn to look in the direction he's gazing, Shari sitting on the front stoop.

She climbs to her feet when she sees me looking at her, her hemp tote bag dangling from limp fingers as she stares.

"Well," Chaz says, dropping his hands from my shoulders. "*This* is awkward."

"Hi, Shari," I say unsmilingly, aware that Shari is close enough to have overheard every word we've just said to each other.

"Hi, Lizzie," she says. Shading her eyes from the sun with one hand, she squints down at us from the stoop and says, "Hi, Chaz. I need to talk to Lizzie for a minute."

"This is a really bad time," I say. "I'm in kind of a time crunch. Can we talk later?"

"No," Shari says and comes down from the stoop. "Look. I'm really sorry about what I said earlier. I was out of line."

"You were really trying to fix us up the whole time?" Chaz wants to know.

"Please stay out of this," Shari says to him. To me, she says, "Lizzie, you're my best friend in the whole world. I would never do anything to hurt you. I should never have said that about the Carvel cake. That was in poor taste, and I owe you an apology."

"What Carvel cake?" Chaz wants to know.

"I know you didn't mean it," I say to Shari, feeling suddenly remorseful over how I've treated her. "And I shouldn't have run out of the café like that. I'm a dork. I'm sorry too. Do you forgive me?"

"Of course I do," Shari says, and pulls me in for a hug. I inhale her Shari-like scent—grapefruit body lotion and Labrador retriever—and then let go of her.

"And now I'm sorry, but I really do have to go," I say. "I have to design a line of bridal wear for Geck's."

"Geck's?" Shari looks confused. "They sell bridal wear?"

"They do now," Chaz explains. "Or they will after they see Lizzie's drawings. Lizzie and Ava Geck are going into business together."

"Is that really such a good idea?" Shari asks, looking dubious.

"Why does everyone keep asking me that?" I demand. "*Yes,* it's a good idea. Now, bye—I have to go get to work."

I give them both kisses—Shari on the cheek, Chaz on the mouth—

and hurry into the shop to find Monique reading the latest copy of *Vogue*.

"Lizzie," she says, looking up when I come in. "*There* you are. God. Finally. Everyone and their brother has been looking for you, it seems."

"Keep taking messages," I say. "I've got some work to do upstairs. I'll be gone for the rest of the day."

"But, Lizzie," Monique says, looking dismayed. "You *do* know that—"

"Yes, of course I know all about it," I say. "I'm doing the best I can to save our skins. So hold all my calls, will you?"

"All right," Monique says. "But—"

"Thanks!"

I pop out the side door and hurry upstairs to my apartment, crank up the A/C, peel off my sticky, sweaty sundress, grab the last Diet Coke in my fridge—Chaz better hurry with his delivery—and get to work.

A HISTORY *of* WEDDINGS

Ever wonder why it's called a "shower"? In the late nineteenth century, a bride would invite her closest friends and relatives over for a little stress relief right before the wedding. Everyone would bring small token gifts that would be placed in an upside-down umbrella or parasol. This would then be raised and turned over the bride, and the gifts would "shower" down on her for luck.

How this charming little tradition transformed into the monstrosities we know as showers today is a mystery for the ages.

Tip to Avoid a Wedding Day Disaster

Bathrooms. No one wants to think or talk about them . . . until there aren't enough of them, or they're overflowing . . . during your reception.

We know you've got a lot on your mind, but when choosing a place for your reception, make sure you take into account the little things . . . like where your guests are gonna go. Because they're gonna hafta.

Are you going to be the one to tell them to hold it?

LIZZIE NICHOLS DESIGNS™

Chapter 22

Marriage is the mother of the world and preserves kingdoms, and fills cities, and churches, and heaven itself.

Jeremy Taylor (1613–1667), English clergyman

I am in a state of such advanced shock when I emerge from the Geck's limo shortly before midnight that I don't notice at first that the hall lights are on in the Henris' building when I stumble through the door. I didn't leave them on when I left, because I was in so much panic about my drawings—some of which were still only half-finished—I completely forgot.

But they're on now. Who could have switched them on? Not a burglar, surely. Why would he want to announce his presence to the world?

Could it be Chaz? He has a key, of course.

But Chaz would *never* let himself in knowing I'm not there. Especially when I'd made it very clear I'd call him when I was ready to see him. He just isn't the let-himself-in-unannounced type.

And while Sylvia and Marisol have been known to work late, they've never worked *this* late—and they don't answer when I call out toward the workroom.

Great. This is the one disadvantage of living alone. The part where I could at any time be murdered, and no one in the building can hear my screams. Because I'm the only one in my building.

Gripping my keys so that each one protrudes from between a knuckle, my hand now resembling Wolverine's from *X-Men*, I start up the stairs, my body tense as I strain to hear any heavy breathing or scraping of

Freddy Krueger–like claws that will give away whoever is waiting to strangle me on the top floor.

But I hear nothing. The hallway is silent. Maybe I'm imagining things. Maybe, in the excitement of the evening, I *did* flick on the lights before I left.

I've almost convinced myself of this as I unlock the front door to my apartment, throw it open, and find a strange man standing beside my living room couch.

I let out a scream loud enough to wake the dead.

"Jesus," Luke cries, laughing. "Lizzie! It's me!"

It is. It's Luke. Luke—my fiancé. Who is supposed to be in Paris, France.

Only he's not in Paris, France. He is standing in my living room.

"Surprise!" he cries.

Oh, I'm surprised, all right. I'm very, very surprised.

Just not as surprised as Luke might have been, had I not come home alone. And it's mere luck that I didn't.

"What are you doing here?" I can't help bursting out.

"I felt so awful about everything you were going through," Luke says, coming toward me. "I heard Uncle Gerald had booked a private charter to the city for a meeting, so I grabbed a seat on it."

He looks so handsome in his cream-colored linen suit, with his pale blue tie, and his dark tan and flashing white teeth. It's almost as if he were another species from Chaz.

But not a species I care to know. Anymore.

I can't help taking a quick step backward as Luke approaches me.

"Wow," I say. "A private charter! How . . . luxurious!"

"Yeah," Luke says, taking another step toward me. "I got here in six hours. Total travel time. From France! Can you believe it?"

"That's amazing." I take another step backward. If this keeps up, soon I'll be in the hallway again.

"I know," Luke says with another of his dazzling smiles. "Isn't it?"

Luke takes another step forward, and I'm trapped with my back against the door. He twines an arm around my waist and leans down to kiss me. I have to use every ounce of self-restraint in my power to keep from jerking my face away from his.

And then his lips are on mine—those lips I used to love so much—and he's kissing me hello.

And I feel . . . nothing.

Nothing! How can I feel nothing? I used to adore this man! I made love on a wine cask to this man! I wanted nothing on earth but to marry this man and have his babies and be with him for the rest of my life.

But I guess there's more to a relationship than making love on wine casks. Like making the other person laugh until milk comes out of her nose.

And being there for her when she really, really needs you.

I guess that's how, after not having seen him for nearly a month, when Luke kisses me, I'm capable of feeling nothing.

Luke lifts his head and looks down at me through half-lidded eyes—those eyes I've always found so dreamy, with those impossibly long, dark lashes.

"Is everything all right?" he wants to know.

"Sure!" I cry. "Everything's fine. Why wouldn't it be?"

"I don't know," Luke says. "You just seem . . . nervous about something."

"Oh," I say, laughing like a hyena. I'm aware that his hands are on my hips. My hips that are unadorned by Spanx. I think this is the first time ever. Since last summer, anyway. I mean, that he's touched my un-Spanxed hips and I haven't been naked in bed. Lying down in a prone position. "I am. I just came from a meeting with the Gecks."

"The who?" Luke looks confused.

"The Gecks. You know, *Get it at Geck's*?"

"Oh," Luke says. But I can tell he has no idea what I'm talking about. "And how did that go?"

"It went *great*," I say. I can still hardly believe it. Suddenly my nervousness is forgotten in my excitement over recounting my incredible evening. "Luke, you don't even know . . . your idea—offering brides beautiful dresses at prices they can afford—it was brilliant. A brilliant idea. Ava Geck and I—her whole family and I, as a matter of fact—we're going into business together. My designs, their business savvy. We're going to give brides across America beautiful, *nice* dresses that they can afford. Not just brides, either. Bridesmaids, mothers of the bride, flower girls, dogs—it's going to be *huge*."

Luke laughs—mostly at my enthusiasm, I think. It's pretty clear he has no idea what I'm talking about. I don't think he's ever even heard of Geck's. Well, his family probably never shopped there in their lives. Maybe his mom sent their housekeeper there to buy cleaning supplies.

But, ever the loyal fiancé, he *acts* like he knows what I'm talking about.

"Lizzie," he says. "That's *great!* I'm so proud of you!"

"Thanks," I say. "This all just happened. Just now. I . . . I'm still a little shell-shocked, I guess. It's exactly what I've always wanted, Luke. It's going to solve everything. Mr. Geck made me an offer—you can't even believe how much."

"Well, that's even better," Luke says, grinning more broadly. "We can both fly back to Paris in style, then!"

I stare at him. And realize I need to sit down. Fast.

Oh God. How can I do this? I can't—I can't do this. I'm *not* a Bad Girl. I'm not!

And yet, for the past week, that's exactly what I've been acting like. Maybe—deep down—I *am* a Bad Girl.

Either way, it's time to pay the price for my actions.

"Yeah," I say, heading for the couch, where I sink down before my knees can buckle beneath me. "Listen. About that."

"Uh-oh," Luke says. The grin has vanished. "I don't think I like the tone of your voice right now, Lizzie. Should I be scared? Because suddenly I'm scared."

I look up at him—his gorgeous, perfect face. I can't help shaking my head.

"Luke," I say, in a *Who are we kidding with this?* voice. "Come *on*."

He spreads out both his hands in a *What, me?* gesture. "What?"

"Seriously," I say. "Get real with me. For once. I know you're Mr. Nice Guy and everything. But was that not the worst kiss ever?"

He drops his hands.

And suddenly he drops the pretense as well.

And I realize I may not have to pay anything at all.

"Okay," he says in an entirely different tone, coming over to the couch and collapsing onto it beside me. It's as if all the bones have gone from his body. I can see the jet lag has finally kicked in. "Yeah. I'm glad you said something. God . . . Lizzie . . . I thought it was me."

The relief that surges through me is like an electric pulse. It leaves me slumped beside him like a rag doll. I think I must feel almost as exhausted as he is—and I haven't just traveled thousands of miles to get here.

"It's not you," I say. It's horrible to be falling back on a tired cliché like this. But in this particular case, it really is true. "It's me."

"No, Lizzie," Luke says. "It's not you."

"No," I assure him. "It really is."

But I'm not going to tell him about Chaz. If I have my way, he's *never* going to know about Chaz. At least, not until a suitable mourning period for our failed relationship has passed, during which Luke's had time to find a fabulous new girlfriend—maybe someone like Valencia, a size 2 who'll fit into that Vera Wang wedding gown I saw in that display window today—and who will cause him to forget all about me.

"I think I just . . . I pushed you too hard for a commitment you weren't ready to make," I say.

"No," he says valiantly. "That's not true. It's just . . . we're just at such different places in our lives right now. Jesus, Lizzie, we even ended up on different *continents*. How could we ever have hoped to make this work?"

I can actually think of a lot of ways we could have made it work. But considering it's clear neither of us *wants* to make it work anymore, it seems better to leave them unsaid.

So instead I say, "Well, we can still be friends, right?"

"Always," Luke says, trying to look sad. But I can see such relief in his sleepy brown eyes, it's almost comical. It's the same relief I'd felt out on my stoop that night before he'd left for France, when I'd told him we were taking a break.

I know exactly how he feels. How is this even possible? How could we have disentangled ourselves from this without so much as an angry word or even a tear? Is it possible that we're just . . . well, *adults*?

"Here," I say. "I want to make sure you get this back."

And I pull off the diamond that's been weighing down my left ring finger for so many months. It slips off so easily, it's almost scary.

"No," Luke says, looking slightly panicky, putting out a hand to stop me. "Lizzie—no. I want you to keep it."

"Luke, I can't keep it," I say.

"Really," Luke says, looking completely panic-stricken. I'm not imagining it. "I don't want it. What am *I* going to do with it?"

"I don't know," I say. I don't understand this. Why won't he take it? "Sell it. Luke, I'm breaking off our engagement. I can't keep it."

"No, *I'm* the one breaking off our engagement," Luke insists. "*I* can't keep it. *You* sell it."

The relief is gone from his eyes. Now I see genuine terror growing there. He *really* doesn't want the ring.

Something, I can tell, is wrong. Very wrong.

And our breakup had been going so nicely up until now.

"Okay," I say gently, slipping the ring under some magazines on the coffee table, since the sight of it seems to upset him so much. "I'll keep it."

The relief creeps back into his face.

"Good," he says, visibly relaxing again. "Good. I want you to have it. I do."

Um . . . okay. What kind of guy wants his ex to keep the ring? Especially a ring that cost as much as mine had to have. (Okay. Twenty-two thousand. Tiffany looked it up one day on the Cartier Web site. She was bored.)

I'll tell you what kind of guy: a guy with a guilty conscience. That's what kind.

But surely not. Not Luke. Not my sweet, handsome, loving Luke, whom I so cruelly wronged by boinking his best friend in a Knight's Inn when I went home for my grandmother's funeral. (Which, by the way, Luke did not fly home for. But he did fly home when I lost my job and apartment. Except that I was more upset about losing Gran. Let's face it, you can always get another job and find another place to live. You can never replace your grandmother.)

Luke would never do anything for him to have a guilty conscience about. He's exactly what Shari accused him of being—too perfect. Sure, I *thought* he might be cheating on me all those nights he spent studying at his place and those afternoons he was at the library, when he said he didn't want to see me.

But that was just my overactive imagination. *I'm* the only one with a guilty conscience in this relationship.

Luke yawns—then *does* look guilty. But only about his rudeness.

"Oh my God," he says. "I'm so sorry . . ."

"You must be exhausted," I say. "You should go. I'd offer to let you crash here, but—"

But we just broke up.

I don't have to elaborate. Luke gets the message.

"No," Luke says, getting up. "Sorry. I'll go to my mom's. God, this feels so weird. It's weird, isn't it? Is it weird?"

"It's weird," I assure him, standing as well. It's just not as weird as he knows. "But I think it's good. It's a good thing."

"I hope so," Luke says.

And, as we hug good-bye at my doorway, and he gazes down at me, I see that there are actual tears gathered in those deep brown eyes of his. No, really. They're hovering, like the tiny Swarovski crystals that dot Ava Geck's phone (only not pink) on the edges of his tremendously long eyelashes.

As if I didn't feel guilty enough. Now I've made him cry.

"You know I'll always love you, right, Lizzie?" Luke asks.

"Of course," I say. Though I'm thinking, Oh my God. This is so . . . Are those really tears? *Actual* tears? Why aren't I crying? Should I cry? I guess so, I'm the girl. Oh God, I should be crying. But I don't feel like crying. Is that because I'm not in love with him anymore, because I'm in love with Chaz? Shouldn't I cry for what might have been, for the children Luke and I will never have now? Is this because of the hives? It's hard to cry for a guy who gave me so many hives, I guess. And because he gave up medical school to be an investment banker. If he'd gone through with the doctor thing, I'd be crying, for sure.

I think.

Then Luke gives me one last affectionate hug, kisses the top of my head, and leaves.

As soon as I hear the front door close, and I see him walking slowly down my street through my front window, I'm on my cell phone.

"Get over here right now," I say into it.

"Is this a booty call?" Chaz replies, sounding delighted.

"You are never going to guess who was just here," I say.

"Seeing as how you were at the Gecks this evening," he says, "I am going to take a wild guess and say . . . Neil Diamond?"

"Luke," I say, clutching my phone so tightly my fingers hurt. "He shared a private charter over from Paris with his uncle. We just broke up."

"I'm on my way," Chaz says, not even a hint of humor in his voice.

A HISTORY *of* WEDDINGS

The first known bachelor party took place in Sparta in the fifth century B.C. Military comrades about to conduct a raiding party to fetch themselves some new brides toasted and feted one another. Since then, men have gathered on the eve before one of them is about to tie the knot to become inebriated, mourn the passing of their friend's singlehood, and ogle dancing girls.

Brides are encouraged to ignore this long-standing rite of manhood. It's been around way longer than you have, honey. Let him have his fun. You'll get your revenge . . . on your wedding night.

Tip to Avoid a Wedding Day Disaster

Mother of the bride (or groom), don't think we've forgotten you. You'll want to look your best on the big day as well. How? It's easy. Start shopping for your dress early, so you'll have plenty of time to find the perfect look for you. Neutrals are always elegant (leave red to your husband's trashy new wife and white is, of course, for the bride only), as is black if it's not a morning ceremony. Nothing too glitzy unless it's an evening reception.

And remember, you can never go wrong with a good support undergarment, such as Spanx.

LIZZIE NICHOLS DESIGNS™

Chapter 23

Let us celebrate the occasion with wine and sweet words.

Titus Maccius Plautus (254–184 B.C.), Roman playwright

He is at my apartment in fifteen minutes. It's amazing how fast a taxi can travel seventy blocks uptown along First Avenue after midnight.

"I want to know everything," he says, slinging his backpack—we have not progressed to the point where either of us has a drawer at the other's apartment yet—onto my couch. "But first . . . how did it go at Ava's parents' place?"

"Oh, Chaz . . ."

And the next thing I know, I'm in his arms, and it's— I don't know how to describe it. It's completely different from being in my former fiancé's arms. Instead of feeling self-conscious and strange and awkward, the way I had when Luke and I hugged a little while ago, I feel safe and comforted and, most important of all, loved—completely and wholeheartedly loved—when Chaz's arms are around me. I close my eyes, letting his warmth envelope me, and suddenly the tears that hadn't been there with Luke show up.

"Whoa," Chaz says with a gentle laugh, kissing my cheeks. "It was that bad? They didn't like your drawings? How could they not have liked them? I've always loved your little stick women. Did you put top hats on them? I love it when you put top hats on them."

"N-no," I stammer, shaking my head as he grips my waist. "Th-they l-loved the top hats! Well, I mean, I didn't put top hats on any of them. But they loved the drawings."

"They did? Then what's the problem?"

"I—I'm just so happy!"

It's true. I feel so happy, standing there in my living room slash dining room slash kitchen, with Chaz's arms around me, and—now that I'm no longer engaged—my status on the Bad Girl Scale back to negative, I think my heart might burst.

"So the Gecks are buying your designs," Chaz says.

I nod. "I'm in charge of design and quality control. Ava's doing marketing. Her dad's taking care of everything else. Chaz . . . I think this could be really great. It's not going to be crappy. It's really not. Because Ava's super-invested in it. Because her name's going to be on it. She's actually taking it seriously. I've never seen her take anything this seriously. It helps that she's so into this DJ Tippycat guy, and he turns out to have a business degree from Syracuse. His real name is Joshua Rubenstein. He was there tonight too."

Chaz looks impressed. "And what about the shop? Tiffany and Monique, and Sylvia and Marisol?"

I chew my lip. "I have a plan for them too," I say. "But . . . it's going to involve some driving."

"Driving?" he echoes. "Driving where?"

"To New Jersey," I say, taking his hand and pulling him down onto the couch. "But first . . . Chaz, seriously . . . and no joking around. Just tell me. I *need* to know. What did you mean when you said that stuff about Luke not being a Boy Scout while were dating? Because when we broke up just now . . . he insisted on my keeping this." I lean over and pick up the ring from where I've hidden it beneath a copy of *People*. "Chaz, this is an expensive ring. Why would he insist on my keeping it unless he felt *super*-guilty about something? Huh? It doesn't make any sense."

Chaz looks down at the ring and shakes his head.

"God," he says. "I can't believe he didn't take it back. Did he cry?"

"When we broke up?" I look at him in surprise. "Yeah, he did, a little. How did you know?"

Chaz takes a deep breath. Then he lets it out in a whoosh.

"Luke wasn't exactly Mr. Innocence himself the whole time you two were going out, all right?" Chaz lifts his gaze from the ring and locks it onto mine. "Did you really think he was studying all those nights he said he was at the library? Because that's not what he was doing."

I blink. "I *knew* it," I say. "Shari was right! He really *was* too perfect. There *was* something creepy about it." Then I add, "Wait. You'd better not be making this up to make me feel better about what *we've* been doing . . ."

"Better?" Chaz echoes. "Hell, all this time, I've been afraid to tell you. I thought you'd have a nervous breakdown if you found out."

"If this is a joke," I threaten, still not sure whether or not I believe him, "to make me feel less like a two on the Bad Girl Scale, it really isn't very funny . . ."

"I'm not joking," Chaz says gravely. "And I don't know what a Bad Girl Scale is. It was that girl Sophie, from his class, all right? The one who knew the guy who got us a table at the Spotted Pig that night. He was doing her behind your back all last semester. You should have seen her. You'd have flipped out. She wore that Juicy Couture stuff you hate. And those giant sunglasses with Dolce & Gabbana written on the side?"

I shake my head.

"No," I say. "Nice try. But you'd never have kept something like that a secret this long. You'd have told me."

"Actually," Chaz says, sounding dead serious for a change, "I couldn't tell you, Liz. How could I have told you about Luke sleeping with another woman behind your back when you were still so in love with him—or at least when I thought you were still so in love with him? How would that have looked? Consider my position, being in love with you, and wanting you for myself. Had I come to you before I'd actually, ahem, managed to win you over, as I apparently have now, and suggested to you that your fiancé was sleeping around behind your back, what, exactly, would I have accomplished? Yeah, you might have broken up with Luke, and yeah, you might have slept with me. But how would I know that I wouldn't have been just some revenge screw—some way for you to get back at Luke for what he'd done to you?"

I blink at him.

The thing is, I believe him. Mostly because of the details—he couldn't make up that Dolce & Gabbana thing. Chaz doesn't know anything about designers—look at his shorts. But also because of the incredibly coarse way he was putting it.

What he was actually saying is incredible.

But, given his bluntness, it might just be true.

"That's not what I wanted," Chaz goes on. There isn't a hint of sarcasm or laughter in his tone now. His blue eyes look almost pained. "That's the *last* thing I wanted. For the longest time—since way before New Year's, since the day I helped you move into this place—I wanted you any way I could get you. And that's the truth. But I wanted you for keeps, Lizzie. And you weren't going to stick around if that's all I was to you, a revenge screw, a way to hurt Luke. So . . . yeah, I didn't tell you. Until now. So sue me."

Then, his shoulders still hunched, he whips out his cell phone. "Besides. I can prove it to you."

The next thing I know, he's pressed a button on his keypad. A second later, he's saying, "Luke?"

"Chaz," I cry. "No—"

But it's too late.

"Oh, hey, man," Chaz says conversationally, into the phone. "Oh, sorry, did I wake you? Oh no? You're in town? What are you doing in town?"

I cannot believe this is happening. I flop back against the couch, slapping my hands over my eyes. I can't watch.

"Oh, you did? Really? Oh yeah? Oh, she did? Oh, really. Oh, that's too bad." Chaz leans over and pokes me, but I don't take my hands from my eyes. Finally, after a few more "really"s, I hear Chaz say, "Yeah, so, if you and Lizzie are splitting up, I guess that means things are really going to heat up with Sophie."

Chaz must have put the phone close to my ear, because I hear Luke's voice saying, "Well, you know, I'm going to be moving to France, so I guess I won't be seeing as much of Sophie. But you know there's this fantastic woman I've been seeing in my new office, that one I was telling you about, Marie . . ."

I take my hands away from my eyes and just look at him. Chaz's expression is a beguiling mixture of anxiety—that my feelings are hurt—and laughter. It is kind of hard not to see the humor in the situation. It's not as if I *care* who Luke's been doing behind my back.

I just hope he, like me, has been using a condom.

When he sees that I'm smiling too, Chaz puts the phone back to his ear and says, "Uh, Luke? So, listen, since you and Lizzie aren't seeing each other anymore, I was wondering . . . how would you feel if I asked her out? Because, you know, I think she's a great girl, and I've always sort of—"

Even from where I'm sitting, three feet away, I can hear Luke's voice curtly cutting Chaz off.

Chaz's grin grows more broad.

"Oh," he says, his blue eyes twinkling at me. "You don't think that would be a very good idea? Why? You think you're such a sex god you should just have *all* the great girls for yourself, even after you're done with them, is that it?"

Laughing, I gasp, "Chaz, don't!" and reach out to wrestle the phone away from him.

"No?" Chaz is saying into the phone, even as he wraps an arm around my waist and wrestles me noisily to the floor. "Oh, because she's in a very fragile state right now? I don't think she's in quite as fragile a state as you might think. What was that noise? Oh, I think that was just . . . my upstairs neighbor. Yeah, he just brought home another trannie from that bar down the street. Hey, Johnny"—Chaz takes the phone away from his face and yells at the walls as he tickles me mercilessly, while I try not to blow our cover by laughing—"it's called abstinence! You should give it try! Oops, Luke, I gotta go, he's puking in the hallway. Yeah, he's sliding around in his puke. I'll call you later."

Chaz hangs up, throws his cell phone over his shoulder, then dives on top of me, burying his face in my neck. I can barely breathe I'm laughing so hard.

And I realize something: I've never had such a good time in my entire life.

Which is a lot to say, considering the day I've had.

A HISTORY *of* WEDDINGS

Anyone familiar with her historical romances knows that any young bride worth her salt went to Scotland to elope in nineteenth-century Europe (even back then girls under eighteen weren't allowed to wed without their parents' permission). Even Elizabeth Bennet in Jane Austen's *Pride and Prejudice* despairs when she learns her flighty sister Lydia has not gone to Gretna Green with her lover, Wickham, for it meant he had no intention of marrying her.

Scotland is still a popular wedding destination for Americans, and many travel packages for that purpose can be purchased. Although care should be taken to fill out the necessary paperwork stateside before going, or the unwary bride could find herself in the same situation as poor, unhappy Lydia.

Tip to Avoid a Wedding Day Disaster

Eloping doesn't necessarily mean a couple has to miss out on the fun of wedding gifts! The couple's parents or other relatives or friends can still choose to host a reception for them upon their return. They can even still register for gifts and be within the confines of good taste and etiquette. With weddings growing to be so costly these days, some parents are finding it less expensive to pay their daughters to elope.

We should all be so lucky.

LIZZIE NICHOLS DESIGNS™

Chapter 24

There is nothing nobler or more admirable than when two people who see eye to eye keep House as man and wife, confounding their enemies and delighting their friends.

Homer (eighth century B.C.), Greek poet

I find Monsieur Henri in his back garden the next morning, precisely where his wife said he'd be: practicing on his homemade *pétanque* lane.

He seems surprised to see me.

Well, I don't suppose it's often he receives visitors from Manhattan to his suburban Cranbury, New Jersey, home.

Especially while he's still in his terrycloth bathrobe.

"Elizabeth!" he cries, dropping the *pétanque* ball in the dust and hurrying to close his robe. He casts an indignant look at his wife, coming up behind us with a tray of iced tea.

"I'm sorry, Jean," she says. But if you ask me, she doesn't look the least bit sorry. "Elizabeth phoned earlier this morning to say she was coming with something important to discuss with us. I did call out to you. But I suppose you didn't hear me."

Monsieur Henri watches, dumbfounded, as his wife sets the tray down on the small metal table beneath the rose-covered arbor at the end of his *pétanque* lane, then takes a seat on the bench beside it. Always a large man, her husband has lost a lot of weight since his surgery. But he is still sweating in the summer heat, even in the shade of the arbor. He looks down at the three glasses of iced tea before him.

"Well," he says. "I suppose I can take a break. For a moment."

"That would be nice," I say. I flick a glance toward the house. Chaz is driving around the neighborhood, having assured me he'd be back in half an hour to pick me up in the car we rented from Avis that morning. "I'll just cruise the strip malls," he'd said. "Pick you up a thong from Victoria's Secret. I've never seen you in a thong. Or anything from Victoria's Secret, for that matter."

There's a reason for that, I'd assured him.

I take a seat on the bench beside Madame Henri, after carefully tucking my vintage Lilly Pulitzer wraparound skirt beneath me, waiting until Monsieur Henri has lowered himself carefully into the teak Adirondack chair opposite us before I speak.

"I'm so sorry to bother you here at your home, Monsieur Henri," I say. "But it's about the building—"

"Now, Elizabeth," Monsieur Henri says with hearty kindness as he reaches for one of the glasses of iced tea and swirls around the twig of mint his wife has plopped into it. "I really don't think there's anything more we can say about that. We're listing it with Goldmark, and that's that. I'm very sorry about your having to find another job and an apartment, but like we said, we'll put in a good word for you with Maurice—you'll have the best references there are . . . you'll have no trouble at all finding a job—and you will just have to be satisfied with that. Really, this begging . . . it's not attractive. I'm rather surprised at you, I must say."

"Actually," I say, reaching for my own glass of iced tea, pleased to see that my hand isn't shaking at all as I hold it. Way to go, Lizzie! "I'm not here to beg for my job, Monsieur Henri. I've found another job. I'm here to make an offer on your building."

Monsieur Henri nearly drops the glass he's holding. Madame Henri chokes a little on the mouthful of iced tea she's just taken.

"I . . . I beg your pardon, Elizabeth?" She coughs.

"I know I ought to have gone through your Realtor," I say quickly. "But the thing is, I don't have *all* the money. Yet. But I will. Soon. And the rest I can pay as we go along, but it will have to be over a period of a few years. Which I know isn't exactly what you were hoping for, but"—I lean forward, speaking to both of them in a low, urgent voice, while somewhere off in the distance, a lawn mower roars to life and a bird begins a plaintive but still melodious song—"the advantage of selling to me, as opposed to some stranger, is that you won't be paying any Realtor fees. We can cut out the middleman completely, and you'll be saving yourself hundreds of thousands of dollars. I'm willing to make you an offer right now, here, today, no inspection, no nothing, of four point five million dollars. And before you say you think the building is worth more," I say, cutting off both of them, since I hear them inhale, "allow me to point out that I live and work there. I don't need an inspection because I know how much work the place needs. I've seen the cracks, plugged up the leaks, called the exterminator myself for the rats down in the basement more times than I can count. And I'm making my offer to you now, today, with my guarantee that you will have the whole amount five years from today. I'll sign anything you want guaranteeing it. All I ask is that you remember where the two of you were when I first walked through your door a year ago. And where you both are now."

I lean back against the bench and take a long swig from my iced tea. Even for a talker, I am spent after having given such a long speech. I eye the two of them as they stare uneasily back at me.

Then Madame Henri looks at her husband.

"The Realtor fees *are* a lot," she says in French. Even though they both know perfectly well by now that I speak their native language more or less fluently, they still slip back into it when they don't want me to overhear what they're saying, out of force of habit. "We could save a lot of money."

"But we'd have to wait for the money," her husband says petulantly. "You heard her."

"So?" his wife demands. "What are you planning on buying? A yacht?"

"Maybe," Monsieur Henri says with a snort.

"You heard what the inspector said," Madame Henri says. "About the asbestos in the basement."

"He also said if we left it alone, it wouldn't be a problem. *All* pipes in Manhattan are lined with asbestos."

I listen to this without blinking. I already know about the asbestos. The plumber told me months ago. I'd planned on using it as leverage if they balked at my offer.

"It's going to cost thousands to get it removed," Madame Henri goes on. "Maybe tens of thousands. Do you want that hassle?"

"No," Monsieur Henri pouts.

"This way," his wife says, "we can be done with it in an afternoon. We don't even have to pay to have our things moved out! She'll keep them!"

Monsieur Henri brightens at this. "Eh! I didn't think of this! But where's she getting all this money? She's not even thirty."

"Who knows?" his wife asks with a Gallic shrug. "The dead grandmother, perhaps?"

"Ask her," Monsieur Henri says.

Then they both turn to me. And Madame Henri asks in English, "Did you hear all that?"

"Of course," I say testily. "I'm not deaf. And I speak French. Remember?"

"I know." Madame Henri shakes her head. "The money is from your grandmother?"

"No," I say. "It's from a deal I made last night with Geck Industries. I'm going to be designing a line of wedding wear for their discount department stores."

Monsieur Henri looks confused. "But if you are going to work for Geck, then why do you still want the shop?"

"Because I'm still going to be doing gowns for my own customers," I said. "Independent of Geck. Besides, your shop . . . *my* shop, if you'll agree to sell it to me . . . it's *home*."

I feel ridiculous, but as I say the word, tears fill my eyes. And yet . . . it's true. That pokey little apartment—which I fully intend to renovate if it ever becomes mine—is the place where I've known some of the highest highs, and lowest lows, of my life. I can't let it slip away from me. I won't. Not without a fight.

Madame Henri blinks a few times. Then she looks at her husband. He arches his eyebrows.

"Well," Monsieur Henri says. "In that case . . . I think we have to sell the building to Elizabeth. Do you not agree, *chérie*?"

Madame Henri's face breaks into an enormous smile.

"I agree," she says.

Which is how, a half hour later, I end up drinking champagne in the noonday sun with Madame Henri in her back garden, while the birds chirp all around us, and her husband shows Chaz, who's returned from his odyssey at the mall, how to play *pétanque*—a sport at which, it soon becomes apparent, he excels . . .

Almost as much as he excels in coaching me in how to get my former bosses to sell me their place of business.

A HISTORY *of* WEDDINGS

It's important to remember that many of the most sumptuous and expensive weddings in history didn't always lead to romantic bliss. Look at Henry VIII and his many wives; Prince Charles and Princess Diana; and of course the always optimistic but unlucky in love Miss Elizabeth Taylor.

No matter how large or small your wedding, what's crucial is that you're marrying the right person, someone who loves you for who you are, not whether or not you can provide him with a male heir, how much money you have, or whether or not you look good in a bathing suit. Love is a many-splendored thing, it's true. But there is nothing more important than making sure your life partner is someone who can make you laugh when you are feeling down, will bring you cinnamon toast when you're feeling sick, and is willing to share the remote.

Tip to Avoid a Wedding Day Disaster

When the guests are gone, the gifts all unwrapped and put away, and the last thank-you note finally written, you might feel the tiniest bit depressed. This is normal! After all, you've just been through the most joyous time of your life—your (hopefully) only wedding! It's natural that you feel a little sad it's all over. But keep in mind you're about to embark upon the most wonderful and joyous journey ever . . . married life!

Still, it's okay to put your wedding gown on every now and then . . . even just to watch TV. Everybody does it.

Really.

LIZZIE NICHOLS DESIGNS™

Chapter 25

He is the half part of a blessed man,
Left to be finished by such a she;
And she a fair divided excellence,
Whose fulness of perfection lies in him.

William Shakespeare (1564–1616), English poet and playwright

Six months later

Oh, you make the most beautiful bride ever!"

"No, I don't," Tiffany assures me. "I look fat."

"Tiffany," I say severely. "You're four months' pregnant. You're *supposed* to look fat."

"Is it odd that that still frightens me?" Monique asks no one in particular. "The fact that Tiffany is going to be a mum, I mean? Does it frighten anyone else?"

Shari raises her hand, along with Sylvia and Marisol.

Tiffany glares at them. "I hate all of you," she says.

"What's nice about the fact that Tiffany is going to be a mum," Monique goes on, "is that it's turned her into such a sweet, caring person."

"This gown is what's making me look fat," Tiffany says to her reflection in the gilt-framed full-length mirror in front of her.

"No, it isn't," I say indignantly, offended. "You're pregnant. That's what's making you fat."

"This is a fat dress," Tiffany says, pouting. "You designed a fucking fat dress for my fucking wedding."

"You know what's awesome," Shari says, slipping a Milk Dud into her mouth from the box she's brought into the shop for the show she's been anticipating for days. "When brides swear. Especially pregnant brides."

Sylvia and Marisol making tsk-tsking noises and fuss over Tiffany, foofing out the train of the exquisite—and completely nonfat—original gown I've designed for her.

"I did not design a fat dress for you, Tiffany," I say, restraining myself with an effort from strangling her. "And that's not a very nice thing to say to the person who is responsible for paying you enough so you can work part-time for me and finally quit that job you hated at Pendergast, Loughlin, and Flynn."

Tiffany just glares at my reflection. "So? I'm just going to quit working for you in five months so I can stay home with Raoul Junior."

"It's a boy?" Marisol asks excitedly.

"Who knows?" Tiffany glares at her reflection. "Whatever."

"Seriously," Shari says, dropping another Milk Dud into her mouth. "This is better than *American Gladiator*."

"You can afford a nanny, Tiffany," I say to her, giving her sash a tug that is perhaps a little harder than necessary. "You aren't going to have to quit. And I picked out a health care plan that gives all you ladies a full four months' paid maternity leave, remember? Now, I designed this gown for you *personally*, with a gorgeous empire waist and a sweetheart neckline and a chapel train—which, by the way, is entirely inappropriate for the quickie wedding you and Raoul are about to have in the office of the city clerk . . . even if we *are* partying afterward at Tavern on the Green—so that your bump is completely disguised. No one can see it. How dare you call it a fat dress?"

Tiffany eyes Shari's box of Milk Duds. "Are you going to give me one of those?" she asks. "Or what?"

"No, she's not," I snap. "You are not getting chocolate on this dress I've slaved over for weeks."

"*We've* slaved over," Marisol corrects me. "I stayed up until two last night doing that crystal beading on the train."

"Right," I say. "That *we've* slaved over."

"Whatever," Tiffany says again, rolling her gorgeously made-up eyes. "Like there's not going to be a knockoff available off the rack at Geck's next week for two hundred bucks."

"There's not!" I cry. "I told you! It's a Lizzie Nichols Designs original!

There'll never be anything like it at Geck's. I mean . . . there'll be something similar. But it will retail for three ninety-nine."

Tiffany tosses her head until her newly coiled ringlets bounce. "I knew it," she says with another eye roll.

"The cars are here," Monique says in a bored voice.

"All right, let's go," I say quickly. "Or we're going to be late."

And we all troop out into the crisp winter air, past the new hot-pink awning with the words "Lizzie Nichols Designs™" emblazoned on it in white curlicue writing, and splitting up into the two waiting black Town Cars that Raoul ordered for us, me carefully folding Tiffany's train in after her, then climbing into the car behind hers with Shari.

"Thanks for coming," I say to her gratefully.

"Are you kidding me?" Shari says, pouring more Milk Duds into her mouth. "I wouldn't miss this for the world. So what happened? The guy finally got his green card?"

"And just in time. Five more months, and he'd be a dad before he was a legal."

"That has to be the quickest divorce in the history of mankind."

"Well, the former Mrs. Raoul got a pretty hefty settlement for being so accommodating with INS," I explain. "You know, not mentioning the part about how they hadn't lived together as man and wife in years."

"That's so *romantic,*" Shari says with a sigh, snuggling down into the leather seats.

When we reach One Centre Street, I jump from the car and hurry to make sure Tiffany emerges from her own without damaging the gown we've all worked so hard on. She manages to do so, though she isn't exactly gracious about it. Thanks to a united effort, we get her up to the hallway where the men—and Pat, who's rushed over on her lunch break—are waiting.

All of my anxiety turns out to have been worth it, though, when I see the look on Raoul's face as he gazes upon his bride for the first time in her wedding finery. Tears fill his eyes, and I'm so touched when he takes Tiffany's hand and whispers, "Baby, you look beautiful," that I have to look away.

"I know," Tiffany whispers smugly back. I guess she doesn't think she looks so fat after all.

An arm slides around my waist, and a second later, a man in a charcoal gray suit is kissing my neck.

"Hey," Chaz says. "You did good."

"Thanks." I giggle. Yes, really. I giggle. That is what Chaz does to me. "Do you like the ribbon work around the neckline? I thought that was a nice touch. I'm going to do that to the new line of flower girl dresses we're introducing for next year's resort line."

"It'll sell like hotcakes," he says.

He's wearing the yellow tie I love, in honor of the occasion. My knees are melting. The sight of Chaz in a suit and particularly that yellow tie still has the power to turn me into butter on a hot stove. I wonder if that will ever change.

I have a feeling it won't.

A bored clerk has just called Tiffany's and Raoul's names, and we're getting ready to crowd into a tiny chapel with them when there's a commotion in the hallway as a familiar voice shrieks, "Wait! Wait for me!"

"Oh God," Shari groans. "Who invited *her*?"

I bite my lower lip. "Um . . . I might have mentioned that Tiffany was getting married downtown today . . . right about now."

"Oh my God, Lizzie," Tiffany snaps. "Aren't you *ever* going to learn to keep your mouth shut?"

Before I have a chance to answer, however, Ava bursts in, wearing a demure business suit (complete with pillbox hat) and clutching the arm of her husband, Joshua Rubenstein, aka DJ Tippycat, followed, as always, by Little Joey.

"I'm so sorry I'm late," Ava says, with all the regality her recently acquired position as president in charge of marketing of Geck Industries has given her. "We got stuck in traffic on the way from the helicopter landing pad."

Tiffany glares at her, but Raoul says amiably, "So glad you could make it."

Then the clerk calls their name again, and we all file forward for the mercifully brief—but meaningful—ceremony.

It isn't until Latrell has uncorked the champagne, and congratulations have been exchanged all around, and we've been told to file out again to make room for the next couple, and Raoul's instructed us to get back into the Town Cars he's provided to take us back uptown to Tavern on the

Green that Chaz snags me by the elbow and pulls me into a corner by a water fountain and a bulletin board listing clerk's office personnel. There he shows me something he has hidden in an inside pocket of his suit.

"Do you know what this is?" he asks, a suspiciously bright twinkle in his sapphire eyes.

I look at the plain white envelope.

"It's the deed to my building?" I ask eagerly. "You paid it off with your secret inheritance, and I don't owe any money on it anymore?"

Chaz looks disappointed. "No. Is that what you want me to do? I thought you wanted to do it all by yourself, stand on your own two feet, and all of that stuff you said last summer?"

"Um, yeah," I say, trying to hide my disappointment. "I do. Totally. So what is it?"

Chaz opens the envelope and pulls out the folded paper inside. It's a pamphlet with *Office of the City Clerk of the City of New York* written on the top. Under it, it says, *What You Need to Know to Apply for a Marriage License.*

"Yeah," Chaz says when I turn my stunned gaze toward him. "I took one. And before you throw up, you can say no. I won't be mad or offended or anything. I don't care if we ever get married. It's not important to me at all. I love you and only you, and I always will. No piece of paper is going to change that. I just know it used to be important to you, and if it still is, well . . . we can do it. And this might be a way we can do it that won't cause you to break out in hives, or me to york. We could just fill out the application now, come back tomorrow—there's a twenty-four-hour waiting period—and do it. We don't have to tell anyone. I just figured, you know, since we're here anyway, we could go in there real fast—I wrote my name down on the list when I got here, the application office is downstairs. It's okay, we've got time, we're like number ninety on the list or something—while everyone else is getting into the Town Cars, and then join them up at Tavern on the Green. And no one will be the wiser. We'll be exactly the same. Only we'll be getting married. Tomorrow. Or whenever. They're good for sixty days. The licenses, I mean."

I am still staring at the pamphlet he's holding.

"You're asking me to marry you?" is all I can manage to choke out.

"If you want to," Chaz says. "You don't have to. And I'm not talking about one of those big monstrosity things your clients have, with a chocolate fondue fountain and the chicken dance. I don't want that. I will never want that, do you understand? My sister had that, and it was—" He shudders. It is clear he is beginning to lose it. I lay a steadying hand on his arm as he goes on, "Your parents will probably want to have that for you, and I am telling you right now . . . I will run. I will run as far and as fast as I can away from that. I will come back to you at night, when it's safe. But I'll hide during the day, where they can't find me. Even if I have to take to the swamps. I know there aren't any swamps in Michigan, but . . ."

I give him a gentle shake.

"Chaz," I say. "It's all right. I don't want that either, okay? I like your idea. Doing it this way, just you and me here tomorrow. No one else. Because that's what getting married is really about, right? Just us. No one else."

"No one else," Chaz says. "Because we're the only ones who matter. I mean, I guess we can tell people . . . someday."

"Someday," I agree. "When we feel like it. We can just mention it. Like, by the way . . . we got married. Although they'll probably be mad we didn't invite them."

"I don't care," Chaz says. "Do you care?"

"I don't care," I say. "We don't even have to tell them if we don't want to."

"I should probably mention to Luke that we're going out first," Chaz says. "To sort of cushion the blow. I can tell him we're married in a few years. Although he's juggling approximately four steady girlfriends in Paris right now. I don't know why he still thinks my seeing you is such a bad idea."

"Aw," I say. I still can't seem to summon up any animosity toward Luke. I'm still holding on to his engagement ring to give to my own daughter, if I ever have one. Or to my niece Maggie, from whom I'm expecting great things. "That's so cute."

"Cute, my ass," Chaz says. "Let me see your arm."

Obediently I roll up the sleeve to the vintage Lilli Ann pink wool suit that I'm wearing. We both stare at the inside of my elbow.

"No hives," Chaz says.

"That's a good sign. Do you feel like throwing up?"

Chaz shakes his head. "No."

I'm feeling optimistic about this, and about the number we are on the list. Ninety. That was Gran's age when she died. They both seem like gifts from above. Like maybe . . . maybe someone is watching out for us . . . someone who wants to make sure we aren't on the highway to hell after all.

Or that maybe we are, actually. Because maybe that's a good place to be.

Chaz and I both look down at the pamphlet in his hand. It is divided into frequently asked questions, which include, *Is a premarital physical exam or blood test prior to the ceremony required?* (Answer: No) and *Can two first cousins legally marry in the state of New York?* (Answer: Yes) and *Can I use the marriage license in another state?* (Answer: No).

It all seems so . . . *legal.*

"You really want to do this?" Chaz asks.

"I think so," I say. "But . . . you once said I'd make a terrible wife."

"I've sort of amended my opinion on that," Chaz says. "I think you'd make sort of a spiffy one now."

"Spiffy?" I grin up at him. "Did you really just say that?"

He grins back. "I think I did."

I grin even harder. "Do you promise to cherish and obey me?"

"I already do," Chaz points out. "Especially the obey part. In bed, when you get saucy with the whips and chains."

"Then," I say gravely, "Charles Pendergast the Third, I will gladly marry you."

"You guys," Tiffany shrieks from the doorway through which everyone is filing. "Are you coming or *what*?"

"We're coming," Chaz calls after them. He nudges me. "Hey, I don't think they heard me. You've got the big mouth. Tell them not to wait for us."

"Not me," I say happily. "I think I've finally learned how to keep this big mouth shut."